"The war of ideas is as dangerous as those waged
with weapons and magic as many, if not more,
lives are at stake. We must be diligent in our
stance against lies and superstition."

Praise for

THIEF'S MAGIC:

"The darling of the fantasy fiction scene returns with a magical new
trilogy to delight loyal readers and newcomers alike....Canavan
cleverly keeps you guessing...definitely an inviting introduction to
the series." —*SciFi Now*

"Canavan creates worlds in her book that are unlike any other.
Pulling many contrasting pieces together, Canavan forms two
unique and intriguing worlds where her characters, because of
the unique challenges of their world, develop distinctive qualities that make them compelling and dynamic. The plot of *Thief's
Magic* progresses rapidly as the characters are faced with choices
that will have life-changing results either way. The high stakes
and fast-paced, twisting plot will hook readers immediately and
they won't be able to put this thrill-ride of a book down until
the end." —*RT Book Reviews*

"Canavan brings the two very different worlds to vivid life."
—*Guardian*

"Rielle's story entrances...leaving readers eager for the next two
volumes." —*Publishers Weekly*

"Effortless reading...Delightful world building...Vivid and
enjoyable." —*SFX*

BY TRUDI CANAVAN

The Magician's Apprentice

The Black Magician trilogy
The Magicians' Guild
The Novice
The High Lord

Age of the Five
Priestess of the White
Last of the Wilds
Voice of the Gods

The Traitor Spy trilogy
The Ambassador's Mission
The Rogue
The Traitor Queen

Millennium's Rule
Thief's Magic

TRUDI CANAVAN

THIEF'S MAGIC

BOOK ONE OF
MILLENNIUM'S RULE

www.orbitbooks.net

Orbit
Hachette Book Group
1290 Avenue of the Americas
New York, NY 10104
www.orbitbooks.net

Printed in the United States of America

LSC-C

First U.S. Edition (hardcover): May 2014
First trade paperback edition: May 2015

10 9 8 7 6 5 4

Orbit is an imprint of Hachette Book Group, Inc. The Orbit name and logo are trademarks of Little, Brown Book Group Limited.

The Hachette Speakers Bureau provides a wide range of authors for speaking events. To find out more, go to www.hachettespeakersbureau.com or call (866) 376-6591.

The publisher is not responsible for websites (or their content) that are not owned by the publisher.

Library of Congress Control Number: 2013952801 (hardcover)
ISBN: 978-0-316-20925-0 (trade paperback)

PART ONE

TYEN

CHAPTER 1

The corpse's shrivelled, unbending fingers surrendered the bundle reluctantly. Wrestling the object out of the dead man's grip seemed disrespectful so Tyen worked slowly, gently lifting a hand when a blackened fingernail snagged on the covering. He'd touched the ancient dead so often they didn't sicken or frighten him now. Their desiccated flesh had long ago stopped being a source of transferable sickness, and he did not believe in ghosts.

When the mysterious bundle came free Tyen straightened and smiled in triumph. He wasn't as ruthless at collecting ancient artefacts as his fellow students and his teacher, but bringing home nothing from these research trips would see him fail to graduate as a sorcerer-archaeologist. He willed his tiny magic-fuelled flame closer.

The object's covering, like the tomb's occupant, was dry and stiff having, by his estimate, lain undisturbed for six hundred years. Thick leather darkened with age, it had no markings – no adornment, no precious stones or metals. As he tried to open it the wrapping snapped apart and something inside began to slide out. His pulse quickened as he caught the object . . .

. . . and his heart sank a little. No treasure lay in his hands. Just a book. Not even a jewel-encrusted, gold-embellished book.

Not that a book didn't have potential historical value, but compared to the glittering treasures Professor Kilraker's other two students had unearthed for the Academy it was a disappointing find. After all the months of travel, research, digging and watching he had little to show for his own work. He had finally unearthed a tomb that hadn't already been ransacked by grave robbers and what did it contain? A plain stone coffin, an unadorned corpse and an old book.

Still, the old fossils at the Academy wouldn't regret sponsoring his journey if the book turned out to be significant. He examined it closely. Unlike the wrapping, the leather cover felt supple. The binding was in good condition. If he hadn't just broken apart the covering to get it out, he'd have guessed the book's age at no more than a hundred or so years. It had no title or text on the spine. Perhaps it had worn off. He opened it. No word marked the first page, so he turned it. The next was also blank and as he fanned through the rest of the pages he saw that they were as well.

He stared at it in disbelief. Why would anyone bury a blank book in a tomb, carefully wrapped and placed in the hands of the occupant? He looked at the corpse, but it offered no answer. Then something drew his eye back to the book, still open to one of the last pages. He looked closer.

A mark had appeared.

Next to it a dark patch formed, then dozens more. They spread and joined up.

Hello, they said. *My name is Vella.*

Tyen uttered a word his mother would have been shocked to hear if she had still been alive. Relief and wonder replaced disappointment. The book was magical. Though most sorcerous books used magic in minor and frivolous ways, they were so rare that the Academy would always take them for its collection. His trip hadn't been a waste.

So what did this book do? Why did text only appear when it was opened? Why did it have a name? More words formed on the page.

I've always had a name. I used to be a person. A living, breathing woman.

Tyen stared at the words. A chill ran down his spine, yet at the same time he felt a familiar thrill. Magic could sometimes be disturbing. It was often inexplicable. He liked that not everything about it was understood. It left room for new discoveries. Which was why he had chosen to study sorcery alongside history. In both fields there was an opportunity to make a name for himself.

He'd never heard of a person turning into a book before. *How is that possible?* he wondered.

I was made by a powerful sorcerer, replied the text. *He took my knowledge and flesh and transformed me.*

His skin tingled. The book had responded to the question he'd shaped in his mind. *Do you mean these pages are made of your flesh?* he asked.

Yes. My cover and pages are my skin. My binding is my hair, twisted together and sewn with needles fashioned from my bones and glue from tendons.

He shuddered. *And you're conscious?*

Yes.

You can hear my thoughts?

Yes, but only when you touch me. When not in contact with a living human, I am blind and deaf, trapped in the darkness with no sense of time passing. Not even sleeping. Not quite dead. The years of my life slipping past — wasted.

Tyen stared down at the book. The words remained, nearly filling a page now, dark against the creamy vellum. Which was her skin . . .

It was grotesque and yet . . . all vellum was made of skin. While these pages were human skin, they felt no different to that made of animals. They were soft and pleasant to touch.

The book was not repulsive in the way an ancient, desiccated corpse was.

And it was so much more interesting. Conversing with it was akin to talking with the dead. If the book was as old as the tomb it knew about the time before it was laid there. Tyen smiled. He may not have found gold and jewels to help pay his way on this expedition, but the book could make up for that with historical information.

More text formed.

Contrary to appearances, I am not an "it".

Perhaps it was the effect of the light on the page, but the new words seemed a little larger and darker than the previous text. Tyen felt his face warm a little.

I'm sorry, Vella. It was bad mannered of me. I assure you, I meant no offence. It is not every day that a man addresses a talking book, and I am not entirely sure of the protocol.

She was a woman, he reminded himself. He ought to follow the etiquette he'd been raised to follow. Though talking to women could be fiendishly tricky, even when following all the rules about manners. It would be rude to begin their association by interrogating her about the past. Rules of conversation decreed he should ask after her wellbeing.

So . . . is it nice being a book?

When I am being held and read by someone nice, it is, she replied.

And when you are not, it is not? I can see that might be a disadvantage in your state, though one you must have anticipated before you became a book.

I would have, if I'd had foreknowledge of my fate.

So you did not choose to become a book. Why did your maker do that to you? Was it a punishment?

No, though perhaps it was natural justice for being too ambitious and vain. I sought his attention, and received more of it than I intended.

Why did you seek his attention?

6

He was famous. I wanted to impress him. I thought my friends would be envious.

And for that he turned you into a book. What manner of man could be so cruel?

He was the most powerful sorcerer of his time, Roporien the Clever.

Tyen caught his breath and a chill ran down his back. *Roporien! But he died over a thousand years ago!*

Indeed.

Then you are . . .

At least as old as that. Though in my time it wasn't polite to comment on a woman's age.

He smiled. *It still isn't — and I don't think it ever will be. I apologise again.*

You are a polite young man. I will enjoy being owned by you.

You want me to own you? Tyen suddenly felt uncomfortable. He realised he now thought of the book as a person, and owning a person was slavery — an immoral and uncivilised practice that had been illegal for over a hundred years.

Better that than spend my existence in oblivion. Books don't last for ever, not even magical ones. Keep me. Make use of me. I can give you a wealth of knowledge. All I ask is that you hold me as often as possible so that I can spend my lifespan awake and aware.

I don't know . . . The man who created you did many terrible things — as you experienced yourself. I don't want to follow in his shadow. Then something occurred to him that made his skin creep. *Forgive me for being blunt about it, but his book, or any of his tools, could be designed for evil purposes. Are you one such tool?*

I was not designed so, but that does not mean I could not be used so. A tool is only as evil as the hand that uses it.

The familiarity of the saying was startling and unexpectedly reassuring. It was one that Professor Weldan liked. The old historian had always been suspicious of magical things.

How do I know you're not lying about not being evil?
I cannot lie.
Really? But what if you're lying about not being able to lie?
You'll have to work that one out for yourself.

Tyen frowned as he considered how he might devise a test for her, then realised something was buzzing right beside his ear. He shied away from the sensation, then breathed a sigh of relief as he saw it was Beetle, his little mechanical creation. More than a toy, yet not quite what he'd describe as a pet, it had proven to be a useful companion on the expedition.

The palm-sized insectoid swooped down to land on his shoulder, folded its iridescent blue wings, then whistled three times. Which was a warning that . . .

"Tyen!"

. . . Miko, his friend and fellow archaeology student was approaching.

The voice echoed in the short passage leading from the outside world to the tomb. Tyen muttered a curse. He glanced down at the page. *Sorry, Vella. Have to go.* Footsteps neared the door of the tomb. With no time to slip her into his bag, he stuffed her down his shirt, where she settled against the waistband of his trousers. She was warm – which was a bit disturbing now that he knew she was a conscious thing created from human flesh – but he didn't have time to dwell on it. He turned to the door in time to see Miko stumble into view.

"Didn't think to bring a lamp?" he asked.

"No time," the other student gasped. "Kilraker sent me to get you. The others have gone back to the camp to pack up. We're leaving Mailand."

"Now?"

"Yes. *Now*," Miko replied.

Tyen looked back at the small tomb. Though Professor Kilraker liked to refer to these foreign trips as treasure hunts, his peers expected the students to bring back evidence that the journeys were also educational. Copying the faint decorations on the tomb walls would have given them something to mark. He thought wistfully of the new instant etchers that some of the richer professors and self-funded adventurers used to record their work. They were far beyond his meagre allowance. Even if they weren't, Kilraker wouldn't take them on expeditions because they were heavy and fragile.

Picking up his satchel, Tyen opened the flap. "Beetle. Inside." The insectoid scuttled down his arm into the bag. Tyen slung the strap over his head and shoulder and sent his flame into the passage.

"We have to hurry," Miko said, leading the way. "The locals heard about where you're digging. Must've been one of the boys Kilraker hired to deliver food who told them. A bunch are coming up the valley and they're sounding those battle horns they carry."

"They didn't want us digging here? Nobody told me that!"

"Kilraker said not to. He said you were bound to find something impressive, after all the research you did."

He reached the hole where Tyen had broken through into the passage and squeezed out. Tyen followed, letting the flame die as he climbed out into the bright afternoon sunlight. Dry heat enveloped him. Miko scrambled up the sides of the ditch. Following, Tyen looked back and surveyed his work. Nothing remained in the tomb that robbers would want, but he couldn't stand to leave it exposed to vermin and he felt guilty about unearthing a tomb the locals didn't wanted disturbed. Reaching out with his mind, he pulled magic to himself then moved the rocks and earth on either side back into the ditch.

"What are you *doing?*" Miko sounded exasperated.

"Filling it in."

"We don't have time!" Miko grabbed his arm and yanked

him around so that they both looked down into the valley. He pointed. "See?"

The valley sides were near-vertical cliffs, and where the faces had crumbled over time piles of rubble had built up against the sides to form steep slopes. Tyen and Miko were standing atop of one of these.

At the bottom of the valley a long line of people was moving, faces tilted to search the scree above. One arm rose, pointing at Tyen and Miko. The rest stopped, then fists were raised.

A shiver went through Tyen, part fear, part guilt. Though the people inhabiting the remote valleys of Mailand were unrelated to the ancient race that had buried its dead in the tombs, they felt that such places of death should not be disturbed lest ghosts be awakened. They'd made this clear when Kilraker had arrived, and to previous archaeologists, but their protests had never been more than verbal and they'd indicated that some areas were less important than others. They must really be upset, if Kilraker had cut the expedition short.

Tyen opened his mouth to ask, when the ground beside him exploded. They both threw up their arms to shield their faces from the dust and stones.

"Can you protect us?" Miko asked.

"Yes. Give me a moment . . ." Tyen gathered more magic. This time he stilled the air around them. Most of what a sorcerer did was either moving or stilling. Heating and cooling was another form of moving or stilling, only more intense and focused. As the dust settled beyond his shield he saw the locals had gathered together behind a brightly dressed woman who served as priestess and sorcerer to the locals. He took a step towards them.

"Are you mad?" Miko asked.

"What else can we do? We're trapped up here. We should just go talk to them. Explain that I didn't—"

The ground exploded again, this time much closer.

"They don't seem in the mood for talking."

"They won't hurt two sons of the Leratian Empire," Tyen reasoned. "Mailand gains a lot of profit from being one of the safer colonies."

Miko snorted. "Do you think the villagers care? They don't get any of the profit."

"Well . . . the Governors will punish them."

"They don't look too worried about that right now." Miko turned to stare up at the face of the cliff behind them. "I'm not waiting to see if they're bluffing." He set off along the edge of the slope where it met the cliff.

Tyen followed, keeping as close as possible to Miko so that he didn't have to stretch his shield far to cover them both. Stealing glances at the people below, he saw that they were hurrying up the slope, but the loose scree was slowing them down. The sorceress walked along the bottom, following them. He hoped this meant that, after using magic, she needed to move from the area she had depleted to access more. That would mean her reach wasn't as good as his.

She stopped and the air rippled before her, a pulse that rushed towards him. Realising that Miko had drawn ahead, Tyen drew more magic and spread the shield out to protect him.

The scree exploded a short distance below their feet. Tyen ignored the stones and dust bounding off his shield and hurried to catch up with Miko. His friend reached a crack in the cliff face. Setting his feet in the rough sides of the narrow opening and grasping the edges, he began to climb. Tyen tilted his head back. Though the crack continued a long way up the cliff face it didn't reach the top. Instead, at a point about three times his height, it widened to form a narrow cave.

"This looks like a bad idea," he muttered. Even if they didn't slip and break a limb, or worse, once in the cave they'd be trapped.

"It's our only option. They'll catch us if we head downhill," Miko said in a tight voice, without taking his attention from climbing. "Don't look up. Don't look down either. Just climb."

Though the crack was almost vertical, the edges were pitted and uneven, providing plenty of hand- and footholds. Swallowing hard, Tyen swung his satchel around to his back so he wouldn't crush Beetle between himself and the wall. He set his fingers and toes in the rough surface and hoisted himself upward.

At first it was easier than he'd expected, but soon his fingers, arms and legs were tiring and hurting from the strain. *I should have exercised more before coming here. I should have joined a sports club.* Then he shook his head. *No, there's no exercise I could have done that would have boosted* these *muscles except climbing cliff walls, and I've not heard of any clubs that consider* that *a recreational activity.*

The shield behind him shuddered at a sudden impact. He fed more magic to it, trying not to picture himself squashed like a bug on the cliff wall. Was Miko right about the locals? Would they dare to kill him? Or was the priestess simply gambling that he was a good enough sorcerer to ward off her attacks?

"Nearly there," Miko called.

Ignoring the fire in his fingers and calves, Tyen glanced up and saw Miko disappear into the cave. *Not far now*, he told himself. He forced his aching limbs to push and pull, carrying him upward towards the dark shadow of safety. Glancing up again and again, he saw he was a body's length away, then close enough that an outstretched arm would reach it. A vibration went through the stone beneath his hand and chips flew off the wall nearby. He found another foothold, pushed up, grabbed a handhold, pulled, felt the cool shadow of the cave on his face . . .

. . . then hands grabbed his armpits and hauled him up.

Miko didn't stop pulling until Tyen's legs were inside the cave. It was so narrow that Tyen's shoulders scraped along the walls. Looking downward, he saw that there was no floor to the fissure. The walls on either side simply drew closer together to form a crack that continued beneath him. Miko was bracing his boots on the walls on either side.

That "floor" was not level either. It sloped downward as the cave deepened, so Tyen's head was now lower than his legs. He felt the book slide up the inside of his shirt and tried to grab it, but Miko's arms got in the way. The book dropped down into the crack. He cursed and quickly created a flame. The book had come to rest far beyond his reach even if his arms had been skinny enough to fit into the gap.

Miko let go and gingerly turned around to examine the cave. Ignoring him, Tyen pushed himself up into a crouch. He drew his bag around to the front and opened it. "Beetle," he hissed. The little machine stirred, then scurried out and up onto his arm. Tyen pointed at the crack. "Fetch book."

Beetle's wings buzzed an affirmative, then its body whirred as it scurried down Tyen's arm and into the crack. It had to spread its legs wide to fit in the narrow space where the book had lodged. Tyen breathed a sigh of relief as its tiny pincers seized the spine. As it emerged Tyen grabbed Vella and Beetle together and slipped them both inside his satchel.

"Hurry up! The professor's here!"

Tyen stood up. Miko looked upwards and pressed a finger to his lips. A faint, rhythmic sound echoed in the space.

"In the aircart?" Tyen shook his head. "I hope he knows the priestess is throwing rocks at us or it's going to be a very long journey home."

"I'm sure he's prepared for a fight." Miko turned away and continued along the crack. "I think we can climb up here. Come over and bring your light."

Standing up, Tyen made his way over. Past Miko the crack narrowed again, but rubble had filled the space, providing an uneven, steep, natural staircase. Above them was a slash of blue sky. Miko started to climb, but the rubble began to dislodge under his weight.

"So close," he said, looking up. "Can you lift me up there?"

"Maybe . . ." Tyen concentrated on the magical atmosphere. Nobody had used magic in the cave for a long time. It was as smoothly dispersed and still as a pool of water on a windless day. And it was plentiful. He'd still not grown used to how much stronger and *available* magic was outside towns and cities. Unlike in the metropolis, where magic was constantly surging towards a more important use, here power pooled and lapped around him like a gentle fog. He'd only encountered Soot, the residue of magic that lingered everywhere in the city, in small, quickly dissipating smudges. "Looks possible," Tyen said. "Ready?"

Miko nodded.

Tyen drew a deep breath. He gathered magic and used it to still the air before Miko in a small, flat square.

"Step forward," he instructed.

Miko obeyed. Strengthening the square to hold the young man's weight, Tyen moved it slowly upwards. Throwing his arms out to keep his balance, Miko laughed nervously.

"Let me check there's nobody waiting up there before you lift me out," he called down to Tyen. After peering out of the opening, he grinned. "All clear."

As Miko stepped off the square a shout came from the cave entrance. Tyen twisted around to see one of the locals climbing inside. He drew magic to push the man out again, then hesitated. The drop outside could kill him. Instead he created another shield inside the entrance.

Looking around, he sensed the scarring of the magical atmosphere where it had been depleted, but more magic was already beginning to flow in to replace it. He took a little more to form another square then, hoping the locals would do nothing to spoil his concentration, stepped onto it and moved it upwards.

He'd never liked lifting himself, or anyone else, like this. If he lost focus or ran out of magic he'd never have time to recreate the square. Though it was possible to move a person rather than still the air below them, a lack of concentration or moving parts of them at different rates could cause injury or even death.

Reaching the top of the crack, Tyen emerged into sunlight. Past the edge of the cliff a large, lozenge-shaped hot-air-filled capsule hovered – the aircart. He stepped off the square onto the ground and hurried over to join Miko at the cliff edge.

The aircart was descending into the valley, the bulk of the capsule blocking the chassis hanging below it and its occupants from Tyen's view. Villagers were gathered at the base of the crack, some clinging to the cliff wall. The priestess was part way up the scree slope but her attention was now on the aircart.

"Professor!" he shouted, though he knew he was unlikely to be heard over the noise of the propellers. "Over here!"

The craft floated further from the cliff. Below, the priestess made a dramatic gesture, entirely for show since magic didn't require fancy physical movements. Tyen held his breath as a ripple of air rushed upward, then let it go as the force abruptly dispelled below the aircart with a dull thud that echoed through the valley.

The aircart began to rise. Soon Tyen could see below the capsule. The long, narrow chassis came into view, shaped rather like a canoe, with propeller arms extending to either side and a fan-like rudder at the rear. Professor Kilraker was in the driver's seat up front; his middle-aged servant, Drem, and the other student, Neel, stood clutching the rope railing and the struts that attached chassis to capsule. The trio would see him and Miko, if only they would turn around and look his way. He shouted and waved his arms, but they continued peering downward.

"Make a light or something," Miko said.

"They won't see it," Tyen said, but he took yet more magic and formed a new flame anyway, making it larger and brighter than the earlier ones in the hope it would be more visible in the bright sunlight. To his surprise, the professor looked over and saw them.

"Yes! Over here!" Miko shouted.

Kilraker turned the aircart to face the cliff edge, its propellers swivelling and buzzing. Bags and boxes had been strapped to either end of the chassis, suggesting there had not been time to pack their luggage in the hollow inside. At last the cart moved over the cliff top in a gust of familiar smells. Tyen breathed in the scent of resin-coated cloth, polished wood and pipe smoke and smiled. Miko grabbed the rope railing strung around the chassis, ducked under it and stepped on board.

"Sorry, boys," Kilraker said. "Expedition's over. No point sticking around when the locals get like this. Brace yourselves for some ear popping. We're going up."

As Tyen swung his satchel around to his back, ready to climb aboard, he thought of what lay inside. He didn't have any treasure to show off, but at least he had found something interesting. Ducking under the railing rope, he settled onto the narrow deck, legs dangling over the side. Miko sat down beside him. The aircart began to ascend rapidly, its nose slowly turning towards home.

CHAPTER 2

It was impossible to be gloomy when flying with a steady tail wind on a clear, beautiful night. The bright reds and oranges of the setting sun had ended the banter between Miko and Neel, and an appreciative silence had fallen. Leratia's capital and home of the Academy, Belton, could put on some grand sunsets, but they were always tainted by smoke and steam.

To Tyen's senses, the aircart appeared to have a bow wave. Unlike a boat in water, the ripple in the atmosphere was caused by the removal, not displacement, of something: magic. In its place the dark shadow of Soot remained, and trailed behind them like smoke. Soot was hard to describe to anyone who couldn't sense it. It was merely the absence of magic, but when fresh it had texture, as if a residue had been left in magic's place. It moved, too – shrinking as magic slowly flowed in to fill the void.

As Tyen drew in more magic to power the propellers and heat the air in the capsule he relished the opportunity to use magic without restraint. It felt good to use it, he reflected, but it wasn't a physical pleasure. *More like the buzz you feel when something you're making is all coming together exactly as you planned*, he thought. Like the satisfaction he'd felt when making Beetle, and the other little mechanical novelties he sold to help finance his education.

While it was not difficult driving the aircart, it did demand concentration. Tyen knew that his skill with sorcery had guaranteed him a place on the expedition, as it meant Professor Kilraker didn't have to do all the driving.

"Getting chilly," Drem said to nobody in particular. Kilraker's manservant had dug around in the luggage earlier, careful to avoid losing any of it overboard, and found their airmen's jackets, hoods, scarves and gloves. Tyen had been relieved to know his bag must be in the pile somewhere, not left behind in the rush to leave Mailand.

A hand touched his shoulder and he looked up to see the professor nod at him.

"Rest, Tyen. I'll take us from here to Palga."

Letting his pull on magic go, Tyen rose and, holding the tensioned rope railing for balance, stepped around Kilraker so the man could take the driver's seat. He paused, considering asking why Kilraker had let him dig where the Mailanders hadn't wanted them to, but said nothing. He knew the answer. Kilraker did not care about the Mailanders' feelings or traditions. The Academy expected him and his students to bring back treasures, and that was more important to him. In every other way, Tyen admired the man and wanted to be more like him, but he'd come to see on this journey that the professor had flaws. He supposed everyone had. He probably had a few as well. Miko was always telling him he was well behaved to the point of being boring. That didn't mean he, or Kilraker, weren't likeable. Or so he hoped.

Miko and Neel were sitting with their legs dangling over one side at the central, widest, point of the chassis, while Drem sat cross-legged on the opposite side for balance, surprisingly flexible for a man of his age. Settling on the same side as the servant, but a small distance away, Tyen took off his gloves, tucked them in his jacket pocket and drew the book out of his satchel. It was still warm. Perhaps he had imagined it earlier and now it only gave off the body heat it had gained from Tyen himself through the satchel pressed to his side. In the hours since then he'd almost convinced himself he'd imagined the conversation he'd had with it, though he hoped not.

He ought to hand her over to Kilraker now, but the man was busy and Tyen wanted to establish exactly what he'd found first.

"So, Tyen," Neel said. "Miko says you found a sarcophagus in that tomb. Was there any treasure in it?"

Tyen looked down at the book. "No treasure," he found himself saying.

"No jewellery? None of those baubles we found in the other caves?"

"Nothing like that. The occupant must have been poor when he died. The coffin lid wasn't even carved."

"Nobody buries poor men in stone coffins. Robbers must've got in there. That's gotta be annoying, after you wasted all that time working out where a tomb might be."

"Then they were very considerate robbers," Tyen retorted, letting a little of his annoyance enter his voice. "They put the lid back on the coffin."

Miko laughed. "More likely they had a sense of humour. Or feared the corpse would come after them if they didn't."

Tyen shook his head. "There were some interesting paintings on the walls. If we ever go back . . ."

"I don't know if anyone will be going back there for a while. The Mailanders tried to kill us."

Tyen shook his head. "The Academy will sort it out. Besides, if I'm only drawing the pictures on the walls, not taking anything away, the villagers might not object."

"Not take anything? Maybe when you're rich and can pay

for your own expeditions." From Neel's tone, he didn't expect rich was something Tyen would ever be.

It's all right for him. Dumb as a brick, but family so wealthy and important he'll pass no matter what his marks are or how little work he puts in. Still, Neel was genuinely interested in history and did study hard. He idolised the famous explorers and was determined that he'd be able to hold a conversation with one if the opportunity came.

Sighing, Tyen opened the book. It was too dark to see the page now, so he created a tiny flame and set it hovering above his hands. Making a flame involved moving a tiny bit of air so quickly it grew hot and began to burn the air around it. Refining it to such a small light took concentration but, like a repetitive dance step, once he got it going he could focus on something else. When he fanned through the pages he was disappointed to see that the text that had appeared before was gone. He shook his head and was about to close the book again when a line appeared, lengthening and curling across a page. He opened the book at the new text.

You lied about finding me.

He blinked, but the words remained.

You're not what they'd consider "treasure". Wait . . . how do you know that? I hadn't opened you yet.

I only need someone to touch me. When they do I can form a connection to their mind.

You can read my mind?

Yes. How else could I form words in your language?

Can you alter anything there?

No.

I hope you're not lying about being unable to lie.

I am not. I am also as open to you as you are to me. Whatever information you ask for, I must give. But, of course, you must first know that information exists, and that I contain it.

Tyen frowned. *I suppose there had to be a price to using you, as with all magical objects.*

This is how I gather knowledge quickly and truthfully.

I have the better side of the deal, then. You can hold a lot more knowledge than I do, though it will depend on what was known by the people who have held you. So what can you tell me?

You study history and magic. Obviously I can't tell you about the last six hundred years because I was in the tomb, but I existed for many centuries before then. I have been held by great sorcerers, historians, as well as philosophers, astronomers, scientists, healers and strategists.

Tyen felt his heartbeat quicken. How much easier would it be to learn and impress his tutors with a book like this at his disposal? No more searching the library and studying late into the night.

Well, not as much of it, anyway. Her knowledge was at least six hundred years old, and much had changed in that time. A great revolution in reason and scientific practice had occurred. She could be full of errors. After all, she had collected knowledge from people, and even famous, brilliant people made mistakes and had been proven wrong.

On the other hand, if the Academy was wrong about something he couldn't use her to convince them. For a start, they'd never accept one source, no matter how remarkable. They would not accept her as proof of anything until they'd established how accurate she was. And then they'd decide she had more important uses than allowing a student to satisfy his curiosity, or take short cuts with his education.

Your friends and teacher keep some discoveries for themselves. Why shouldn't you keep me?

Tyen looked over at the professor. Tall and lean, with short-cropped hair and moustache curled as was the current fashion, Kilraker was admired by students and peers alike. His adventures had brought him academic respect and furnished him

21

with many stories with which to charm and impress. Women admired him and men envied him. He was the perfect advertisement to attract students to the Academy.

Yet Tyen knew that Kilraker didn't quite live up to the legend. He was cynical about his profession and its benefits to the wider world, as if he had lost the curiosity and wonder that attracted him to archaeology in the first place. Now he only seemed to care about finding things he could sell or that would impress others.

I don't want to be like him, he told Vella. *And to keep you could mean I was depriving the Academy of a unique and possibly important discovery.*

You must do what you feel is right.

Tyen looked away from the page. The sky had darkened completely now. Stars freckled the sky, so much more brilliant and numerous away from a big city's glow and smog. Ahead and below the aircart lay lines and clusters of lights more earthly than celestial: the town of Palga. He estimated they'd arrive in an hour or so.

The book – Vella – had already connected with his mind twice. Did she already know everything about him? If so, anybody who held the book could find out anything about him. They had only to ask her. She had admitted that she must give whatever information she contained to whoever asked for it.

But what did he have to hide? Nothing important enough to make him wary of using her. Nothing that wasn't worth the risk of others finding out embarrassing things and teasing him about them. Nothing he wouldn't exchange for the knowledge gleaned from centuries of great men handling the book.

Like the "great sorcerers" she had mentioned. And Roporien himself. He looked back down at the page. He wouldn't reach the Academy for several days. Perhaps he would be forgiven

22

for holding onto her until then. After all, Kilraker might not have time to examine her properly during the journey home. Tyen might as well learn as much from her as possible in the meantime.

Do you know everything that Roporien did?

Not everything. Roporien knew that for me to be an effective store of knowledge I must be able to access the minds of those who hold me, but he had secrets he wasn't willing to risk revealing. So he never touched me after my making. He had others ask questions of me, but he rarely needed to.

Because he already knew all that there was to know?

No. Since a stronger sorcerer can read the mind of a weaker one, and Roporien was stronger than all other sorcerers, he did not need me in order to spy on anyone's mind. Most of those he wanted information from did not attempt to withhold it. They gave it out of awe or fear.

Tyen's mind spun as he contemplated sorcerers with the ability to read minds. They must have been powerful indeed. *But why would Roporien create a book that he couldn't use?*

Ah, but he didn't have to touch me in order to use me. By having others touch me he could teach them and spread knowledge.

That is an unexpectedly noble act for a man like Roporien.

He did so for his own benefit. I was a tool for teaching his fighters the lessons of war, to show his servants how to provide the best in everything, and inspire the greatest makers and artists in all the worlds so that he could use the magic produced by their creating.

Magic produced by their creating? Wait. Are you saying . . . You're not saying . . . ?

That their creativity generated magic? Yes, I am.

Tyen stared at the page in dismay. *That's superstitious nonsense.*

It is not.

It certainly is. It is a myth rejected by the greatest minds of this age.

How did they disprove it?

He felt a flash of irritation as he realised he did not know. *I will have to find out. There will be records. Though . . . it could be simply that it has not been proven to be true, rather than disproved.*

So you would have to believe it, if someone proved it was true?

Of course. But I doubt anyone would succeed. Rejecting primitive beliefs and fears and embracing only what can be proven is what led us into a modern, enlightened time. Gathering and examining evidence, and applying reason led to many great discoveries and inventions that have improved the lot of men.

Like this aircart you travel in.

Yes! Aircarts and aircarriages. Railsleds and steamships. Machines that produce goods faster than ever before – like looms that make cloth quicker than twenty weavers working at once, and machines that can print copies of a book, all the same, by the thousands, in a few days.

Tyen smiled at the thought of all that had changed in the world since she had last "lived". What would she make of the progress men had made, especially in the last century? She would be impressed, he was certain. A feeling rather like pride swelled within him, and suddenly he had another reason to delay handing her over to Kilraker and the Academy.

She needed to know how the world had changed. She needed her store of knowledge updated. He would have to teach her before he handed her over. After all, if she still believed in superstitions then they might not just declare her an inaccurate source, but a dangerous one.

A familiar, unsettling feeling in his stomach told him that the aircart was beginning to descend and he looked up. Palga was much closer now. Closing the book, he slipped her into his satchel, which he'd kept slung across his chest since escaping the Mailanders, and let his flame die, but Vella was foremost in his thoughts as they slowly dropped towards the small town.

I suppose there is no way she could be an accurate source of knowledge, having missed the last six hundred years of progress and knowing nothing more than what the people who held her did. Yet that makes her a fascinating insight into the past. In return for what she teaches me it seems fair that I give her the knowledge she was designed to absorb. The Academy will only be interested in what they can take from her, so I must do it before I hand her over.

Palga's landing field was, as with most towns, on the outskirts in a field next to the main road. Two more aircarts lay on the grass, their cooling capsules carefully pegged down next to their chassis. As Kilraker's descended Tyen moved to the front to take the looped nose rope, while Drem ducked under the railing in preparation to leap to the ground. Neel had taken the tail rope and Miko was at the rear.

"That's Gowel's cart, isn't it?" Miko said as they floated past the landed carts.

"It certainly is." Kilraker chuckled. "Let's hope he's recently arrived, or there'll be no good dusky left at the Anchor Inn. Ready?"

Drem and Miko barked an affirmation.

"Jump!" the professor ordered.

As the pair leapt to the ground the aircart's descent slowed abruptly and, with less weight bearing it down, it began to rise again. Kilraker looked up at the capsule. Flaps lifted, allowing hot air to spill out. The ascent slowed, then the cart began to sink again.

"Ropes!"

Tyen tossed the nose rope down to Drem, who caught it and drew up the slack. They were a well-coordinated team now, having landed the cart several times on this expedition. As the chassis settled on the ground, Tyen tossed a ring peg down and used magic to ram it into the earth. Drem fed the rope through the ring while Tyen hurried to the back to repeat the process with Miko.

With the cart secured, Kilraker, Neel and Tyen could step off the chassis. The professor strode away to arrange transport to the Academy Hotel, while Drem set to untying their luggage.

"Put what's to be locked inside the chassis on the right and what you're taking to the hotel on the left," he told them as he lifted the first item.

"Left," Miko said. Then, as the servant sorted through the luggage: "Hurry up, Drem. Gowel's been away for a year. He'll have some tales to tell."

"I'm going as fast as I can, young Miko," Drem replied. "And there's plenty of hours left until the ridiculous time of the night Gowel will keep us all up to."

"I'm sure the professor will let you go to bed long before then," Tyen said. "One of us has to be lucid enough to get this thing off the ground tomorrow morning."

"Tomorrow afternoon, most likely," Drem grumbled.

By the time they had the deck clear, the capsule had cooled enough that it could be tied down beside the chassis. A hire cart had rolled up and Kilraker had haggled down the fee to a reasonable rate. Tyen helped Drem to pack luggage into the aircart chassis and the servant locked the hatch, then they all grabbed their bags and hastened to the hire cart.

Kilraker was smiling as they piled on board. *Looking forward to catching up with his friend and competitor*, Tyen thought. *I wonder . . .* perhaps he should slip Vella down his shirt again. She might learn something from the stories the two archaeologist adventurers would tell that night.

CHAPTER 3

The Academy maintained a hotel in every city and town in the Empire worth visiting. Though Palga was too small to be called a city, Tyen wasn't surprised that the town had one. Favourable winds made it a favourite stopover for air and sea travellers, of which many were Academy graduates of some sort.

He had been amazed at the size of the hotel, however. It seemed disproportionately large for the town, and most of the locals were employed in servicing or supplying it. Yet though everything was of exemplary quality, Kilraker assured them that it was to the Anchor Inn, the establishment on the other side of the road, that the younger graduates flocked to share a "bite" of dusky and boast of their journeys to the far reaches of the Empire and beyond. Adventurer men, and the occasional woman, of the non-academic and foreign kind also frequented the inn, and were often willing to share a tale or two.

As Tyen followed Kilraker and the other students into the inn's public room, noise and warmth surrounded him. At the same time he was conscious of the book tucked into his shirt, its shape hidden under his waistcoat. Drem had insisted they all change into their usual city clothes: shirt, waistcoat, trousers, jacket and cap – not worn since they'd passed through Palga on the way to Mailand, after which they'd donned practical dust-coloured mar-cloth trousers and shirts along with warm airmen's jackets, hoods, scarves and gloves.

As he entered the drinking room, Kilraker set his hat on one of a row of nails along the nearest wall. The students set their caps in a line below it and followed the professor towards a cluster of four men sitting at one of the inn's trestle tables. One of the four looked up, his teeth flashing in a well-tanned face as he saw them.

"Vals!" he bellowed. "I thought you weren't due back for another week or two."

"I wasn't," the professor replied, moving around the table so he could slap the other man's shoulders in greeting. "We had a bit of trouble with the natives. Nothing I couldn't have dealt with by myself, but I didn't want to risk harm coming to the boys." He turned to Tyen, Miko and Neel. "I think you have met Tyen Ironsmelter and Neel Long before, but not young Miko Greenbar. Boys, this is Tangor Gowel, the famous adventurer."

"Famous?" Gowel waved a hand dismissively. "Only among our kind, where fame has less value than friendship." He gestured to the other men. "Kargen Watchkeep, Mins Speer and Dayn Zo, my travel companions. Friends, this is Vals Kilraker, professor of history and archaeology at the Academy. Now sit and tell me where you've been." He waved at a passing server. "Four more glasses here!"

"Tell me where *you've* been first," Kilraker retorted. "I heard you'd crossed the Lower Latitudinal Mountains and reached the Far South."

Gowel grinned, his moustache broadening. "You heard right."

"In that little aircart we tied up next to in the landing field?"

"Indeed."

"Did the air get a little thin during the crossing?"

All four men nodded. "But we found a pass of sorts. A passage through the peaks."

"And what lay on the other side?"

The server arrived with the glasses, and Gowel poured a generous measure of rich, dark dusky into them and those of his friends. "The Far South is as Discoverer Lumber described," he answered, handing them each a glass. "Strange animals and stranger people. The atmosphere is strong in magic and what they do with it . . ." His eyes brightened with the memory. "We saw the legendary Tyeszal – which Lumber translated as Spirecastle. A city carved into a great pinnacle of rock as tall as a mountain. Suspended platforms haul people and produce up and down its hollow centre, and children fly around the outside carrying messages and small items."

Kilraker took a good swig of dusky, his eyes never leaving Gowel's face. "So not an exaggeration after all." It seemed to Tyen that some muscle twitched or tightened in the professor's face, and gave a fleeting impression of envy. "What are the natives like?"

"Civilised. Their king is friendly to foreigners and open to trade. Their sorcerers are well learned and they have a small school. Though far behind us in technological invention they have developed some methods and applications I had not seen before." He shrugged. "Though I could be mistaken. Magic is not my area of expertise, as you know. My mission was not for the Academy but for Tor and Brown Associates, who directed me to find untapped resources and new trade, as well as an aircart route through the mountains."

Kilraker finished his drink. "Did you find any resources and new trade?"

Gowel nodded and drew a large, leather-bound book out of his jacket. He flicked through the pages, giving them glimpses of neat writing and sketches. The adventurer stopped at a page to describe the plants and animals, both domestic and wild, that he'd found. He opened the book at a map, where he pointed out the location of the different peoples he and his companions had encountered. Tyen noted a line threading through an arch of mountains bordering the top of the map. Was this the route the adventurers had taken?

When Gowel had finished, Kilraker looked from the book to his friend and smiled.

"Surely that's not *all* you brought back with you?"

"Oh, the usual samples of flora and fauna, minerals and textiles."

"No treasures to sell to the Academy?"

Gowel shook his head. "Nothing that would have weighed down the aircarts."

The professor grunted in reluctant agreement. "Gold and silver are cursedly heavy."

"Knowledge is of greater value than gold and silver," Gowel told him. "I make more money from my books and lectures than from treasure these days, even if the Academy calls me a liar. Perhaps because they do." His gaze shifted from Miko to Neel and then Tyen. "Don't let the venerable institution narrow your minds, boys. Get out there and decide for yourself what is folklore and what is truth."

"It's all very well for wealthy men like you, Gowel," Kilraker said. "But most of us can't afford to come home empty-handed. We need to justify the Academy financing our expeditions by adding to the venerable institution's wisdom or wealth. Preferably wealth."

"And we don't want to get ourselves thrown out of the Academy, as you were," Neel added, giving the older man the sort of challenging stare that only those from his class would dare. Kilraker chuckled.

Gowel stared back at the boy. "Contrary to what the gossip papers say, I wasn't thrown out: I resigned from my position."

Neel frowned. "Why would you do a thing like that?"

The adventurer's smile was grim. "I once found a marvel – an object of little monetary value but great magical potential that might have benefited thousands – and they locked it away where nobody but they could see and use it."

Tyen felt his heart skip a beat. *Is that what they will do to Vella? Lock her away where nobody would touch her? She would hate that.* But surely, once the Academy realised how useful she could be, she would be held and read all the time. By men with greater knowledge and intelligence than his. How could he deny her that when it was what she'd been made for?

"I should have kept it." Gowel scowled, and Tyen was surprised to see Kilraker nodding. "From what Vals tells me, it's sitting unused and forgotten in the vault. The Academy is greedy and selfish. Knowledge and the wonders of the world should be available to all, so that anybody can improve themselves if they wish to," Gowel continued. "My dream is to build a great library in Belton that people may come to free of charge, to learn of the world and its wonders."

It was an admirable dream, and Tyen felt a stab of guilt at his wish to keep Vella. To do so would be selfish. Others should benefit from her, too. But if the Academy treated her the same as the object Gowel had found, would anyone benefit from her? And while Kilraker's words about justifying their expeditions had reminded him of the other reason he should hand her over to the Academy, wouldn't doing so simply to gain higher grading be just as selfish?

Whatever he did, he ought to update the information she contained first. And work out if she did always tell the truth. It would increase the likelihood of the Academy seeing her as a valuable object worth using, and it was what she would want, since her purpose was to gather knowledge. It would also give him time to decide what to do.

The longer he kept her the worse it would look when he finally did, so he'd have to work quickly, taking every opportunity to teach her. It was clear telling her that she was wrong about something wasn't enough to change the information she held. She had resisted when he'd tried to correct her on the relationship between creativity and magic. He needed proof to convince her of her error. And by the time he handed her over to the Academy he must be able to demonstrate that her knowledge could be corrected.

He looked around, wishing he could start now. It would draw premature attention to Vella if he took her out and started reading in the inn, but if he went back to the hotel it would be hours before the others returned. Miko and Neel would be amazed he was willing to miss out on Gowel's tales – not to mention free dusky – but it had been a long, exciting day and he'd spent a large part of it driving the cart, so they'd believe him if he said he was tired. He drained his glass, set it down and yawned.

"Forgive me," he said. "But I'm going to turn in for the night."

The other students were staring at him in surprise, but Kilraker nodded sympathetically. "It has been a long day. Perhaps you all should—"

"I'm fine," Neel declared. "Not tired at all." Miko straightened and nodded in agreement. The pair looked at him sidelong.

Tyen hesitated as if nearly persuaded by their mockery, then shook his head. "I'm bound to get the first driving shift tomorrow," he retorted quietly. He rose and nodded politely to Gowel and his companions, then Kilraker, then strode over to retrieve his cap before climbing the stairs to the main doors.

He slipped out and crossed the road. The Academy Hotel was quiet, two older men reading papers in the lounge and few staff about. Tyen hurried up the stairs to the dorm he shared with the other students. Though more simply furnished than Kilraker's suite, it was much finer than the room he shared with Miko back at the Academy itself.

He hauled his bags off the bed he'd claimed when they'd first arrived and took off his boots. Then he settled with his back against the headboard and fished Vella from inside his shirt. Opening to the first page, he waited for the letters to form.

Hello, Tyen.

I have a few hours before the others get back. Can I ask you some questions?

Of course. Answering questions is what I was made for.

Where to start? I have so many. Where are you from? What were you before you became a book? Why did Roporien choose you? How did he make you?

One question at a time is best. Each new question nullifies the previous one.

I beg your pardon. So . . . Where are you from?

I was born in the city of Ambarlin in the country of Amma in the world Ktayl.

The world Ktayl? Are you saying there are other worlds?

Yes.

How many other worlds are there?

Nobody knows. Not even the great Roporien knew.

A lot, then.

Yes.

Tyen felt a thrill of excitement. The theory that other worlds existed was often debated in the Academy. Many historical sources referred to worlds beyond this one, yet nobody had been able to physically prove it. Some well-respected academics believed it to be true. They had formed the Society of

Other-Worlders, a group that was mocked, but not as loudly or derisively as other, equally strange societies.

Can you prove that there are other worlds?

I can teach you how to travel between them, if you have the strength — or, as you call it, the reach.

His heart began to race. To explore other worlds . . . he'd become more famous than Gowel.

How much reach do I need?

That depends on the amount of magic this world contains. From what I have seen of it in your mind so far, I doubt it would be within the reach of any but the most powerful sorcerers.

Tyen's heart sank. He knew his reach was good, but there had to be plenty of other sorcerers with greater ability than him.

Could you still prove there are other worlds even if I didn't have enough reach to travel to them?

Judging by your disinclination to believe me when I tell you that creativity generates magic, I doubt it.

He laughed quietly at that.

Tell me more about yourself. How did you meet Roporien?

When I was not many years an adult I travelled to Uff, a great city that attracted artists and writers from all over Ktayl. I established myself as a sorcerer-bookbinder and my wares were soon so sought-after that I began to grow famous and wealthy.

From making books?

Yes. My books were not only beautiful, but they used magic in new ways to display, preserve and hide their contents. They might glow so you could read them in the dark. They might use magic to preserve themselves, so they lasted longer. They might contain a magical lock, or burst into flames if taken too far from their owner. My clients were wealthy and powerful: sorcerers, successful artists, intellectuals, the rich and powerful, and even royalty. That was how Roporien learned of me. He saw one of my books and realised that I knew something he did not, so he came to me to seek my secrets.

And you refused to give them to him?

34

Of course not! I knew of Roporien, as anyone who moved among the powerful did. Only a fool would deny him what he sought. Since he could read it all from my mind anyway there was no point in trying to hide anything. My mistake was pride. He approached me while I was drinking one night with my friends. They were all artists of one kind or other, and I could see they were impressed and afraid. I wanted to show off and prove I was not fearful, so I invited Roporien to my home. He accepted.

But you were afraid? Tyen guessed.

A little. But he was also very handsome, or so I thought at the time. I learned later that he could alter his appearance to enhance what a woman found attractive about him. It was said he had always valued artists, for that reason you consider superstitious nonsense.

Tyen went back to read the last two paragraphs again.

Are you saying . . . ?

That I took him as a lover? Yes.

He stared at the book to remind himself that it was a collection of pages and binding that he was conversing with, not a full-grown in-the-flesh woman. Did it make it easier, somehow, to accept what she had told him without thinking less of her? He wasn't sure. *She lived in a different time and a different place — a whole other world if that is true. Perhaps this was acceptable behaviour for a respected woman in that place and time.*

It wasn't the scandal it would be in this time and place. But it was a stupid thing to do.

Because it led to him making you into a book?

Not directly. But it is dangerous to put yourself in the presence of someone who has lived so long that the lives and feelings of others are of no concern.

He was . . . you invited an old man to your bed?

Yes, but not as you imagine. Roporien was many, many centuries old, but, like most of the unageing, he had the body of a man in his prime.

Unageing? But he is only mentioned in history over a fifty-year period.

He found this world in the last fifty years of his life. As I told you, there are many, many worlds. Even a man as old as Roporien could still discover new ones.

Tyen wanted to ask more questions about Roporien, but he also did not want to stray from Vella's story.

So what happened that led him to make you into a book?

I showed him the books I had made, including a new kind that I had recently succeeded in creating that allowed the person holding it to write on the page using mere thought. But in creating it I'd had another leap of insight, and saw a way to make that writing remain invisible until the reader willed it to appear. He was impressed. In the morning I rose to find him examining the book closely. He lifted me up and laid me on the table, but I realised too late that his purpose was not seduction. Instead he began to make his own book, using my body as the sole source of his materials.

Tyen shuddered. *He killed you.*

I am not dead.

But you're not walking and breathing either. Surely you aren't happy with what was done to you?

I am not happy, but neither am I unhappy.

You were rich and young and I imagine you were beautiful, too. He took all of that away. I'd be furious!

I do not feel in the way that I would if I had a whole body to express it with. I *know* that what was done was cruel and unjust. I am aware of the absence of a body somewhat like an amputee is conscious of the absence of a limb. But without it I cannot rage or grieve.

Can you feel pain?

No. Not since the transformation began.

Since it began. *So most of it did not hurt?*

Yes. His work was easier once he blocked the pain.

How did he . . . no, I don't want to know.

You do, but you fear I will be offended by your revulsion or distressed by the memory. I do not mind. Remember, I cannot feel such emotions.

Tyen looked at the book lying open in his hands, noticing for the first time the elegance of the script, and a sadness

36

welled up inside him. She hadn't asked to be made into a book. If she could not feel emotions then she had lost not only the ability to feel fear or revulsion, but also love and hope. She might have lived a thousand years, but not as a whole person.

He heard familiar laughter from somewhere beyond the door and sighed. Closing the book, he slipped her into his satchel.

The Academy had better take good care of you, Vella, he thought. *You've been through too much to end your life unconscious and slowly deteriorating in a lost corner of the vault.*

CHAPTER 4

Some time during their night in Palga the helpful breeze that had shooed them out of Mailand turned into a bossy gale. It shoved the aircart along with unnerving gusts that had them straddling the deck and holding on tightly as if it was some kind of untamed beast. They flew as low as possible in case they needed to make a hasty landing, but it meant they had to steer well clear of tall obstacles.

The wind was blowing in the right direction, at least. Several times Kilraker had considered landing and waiting out the weather, but the advantage of having such a strong wind in their favour was that it reduced their journey from several weeks to less than one. And these gales could last a number of days.

They dared not fly over the Northern Straights in such weather, however, so when they reached the city of Widport, the closest on the Western continent to the island of Leratia, they holed up until a steamship arrived. Once on board, Tyen, Miko and Neel took turns on guard duty watching over the aircart in the cargo hold for the three, gut-wrenching days it took to get to mainland Leratia.

From there they boarded the recently extended East-to-West Railsled for a much more civilised final leg of the journey home. Though not as thrilling as air travel, railsled was still the fastest and most comfortable form of transport to be developed in the last century. It was also the most reliable, since the storms that were so dangerous to aircarts and ships did not stop a railsled.

They pulled into the East-to-West Leratian station the next afternoon. As Kilraker supervised the removal of the aircart by crane from the freight sled to a waiting longcart, Tyen listened to the rain hammering on the glass-panelled roof high above and couldn't decide if he was relieved or disappointed to be back. He longed for the simple comforts of the boarding room in the Academy, but once he arrived he ought to hand Vella over.

Could he get away with delaying that moment? Since Palga he'd had few opportunities to talk to the book, and there was still so much he needed to teach her before he gave her up.

If he did at all.

He jumped as a hand slapped him on the shoulder.

"Not as convenient as landing the aircart on the Academy lawn, but at least we're all in one piece," Kilraker said, smiling. "Good work back there, young Tyen Ironsmelter. You certainly earned your place on this expedition. I'd have you as co-driver any day. You've got a real knack for flying."

Tyen felt his face warm at the compliment. "Thank you, Professor."

"Now, I'll ride back with the cart, but there's no room for you three. Catch a three-seater to the Academy. I'll have your bags sent to your rooms." His smile widened into a grin. "See you in class, my fellow adventurers."

He tapped his hat to them in farewell, strode to the longcart and swung up next to the driver. As the vehicle moved away, Miko turned to Tyen and Neel and put a hand on each of their shoulders.

"Can I owe you for the ride, my fellow adventurers? I'm broke."

Tyen shrugged and nodded. He could afford half the fare. Then his stomach sank as he saw that Neel was shaking his head.

"Mother always insists I visit her as soon as I arrive back from any trip. I'll see you at the Academy later." Neel tugged his cap brim and headed for the station entrance.

Miko sent Tyen a disbelieving look, but said nothing as they turned to follow. Neel could have easily lived at home and caught a one-seater to and from the Academy each day – in truth, he would have been driven there in the family's carriage – but he'd taken the opportunity to escape his parents by requesting a room in the students' house. *Or so he says*, Tyen thought. *Maybe his parents make him stay there, knowing that he'd never go to classes at all if he didn't live in sight of the professors.*

They emerged from the station to the usual roar of the city, made louder by the rain beating down and the splash and rush of water in the drains. The city's usual stink had been reduced by the downpour, thankfully. Dung collectors were rushing to pick up the droppings of morni, the thin-legged animal that hauled the city's carriages, before the rain washed them away.

Though most of the pay-by trips had been hired by the other railsled passengers, plenty of one-seaters were waiting, drivers perched atop the smaller breed of morni suited to the light vehicles. Neel hurried through the rain to one and was soon borne away. Tyen and Miko joined the queue for two-seaters under the station awning. Four two-seaters arrived before it was their turn. As their luck had it, the next one to arrive had a leaky canopy and was pulled by a bedraggled morni that looked about ready to expire – something Miko pointed out as he failed to haggle down the price. The driver flatly refused to give them a discount. Why would he when there were plenty of passengers waiting for a ride in this miserable weather?

The city was cluttered with traffic. Overflowing drains forced vehicles closer to the centre of the street, where they passed with barely a finger's width to spare. Tyen tucked his satchel inside his coat and winced as the wheels of other vehicles sent spray over his legs. Rain bounced off the sides of carriages and shop awnings into their laps with unerring accuracy. He could have used magic to protect them, but to do so would have risked a fine. Only in the Academy grounds was he allowed to use it for anything other than his own or his country's defence. Elsewhere it was needed to drive railsleds and the numerous other machines of industry. *And the last thing I want to do is cause an aircart or aircarriage to fall from the sky*, he thought.

All around he felt magic moving, pulled here and there to feed the city's needs. There was something thrilling about the way it constantly flowed through the city, billowing down from above then swirling off in all directions. In contrast, the magical atmosphere outside the city had barely stirred, like a calm lake rather than a fast-running river.

As a large carriage passed, a cascade of water spilled off its roof and over Miko. The student let out a yelp of surprise and annoyance. As he grabbed the collar of his coat and lifted it to stop the water going down the back of his neck, his pogbag slipped off his lap. Tyen leaned forward to catch it, but only managed to grab one strap. The bag landed on its side and sprang open.

It was called a pogbag because the top hinged open like the jaws of a giant swamp creature. Something round, polished and gleaming rolled out from the jaws, glittering like a wrapped sweet. Tyen grabbed it before it could roll out of the two-seater, then turned his hand over. In his glove lay a gold ball, etched with designs.

Miko snatched it away. He righted the pogbag, stuffed the ball deep inside and snapped the top closed.

"Was that a poible?" Tyen began.

"Yes," Miko said, hugging the bag to his chest. He scowled at Tyen. "It's all right for you. You have magic to help pay your way on these expeditions. I don't."

Tyen opened his mouth to retort that his ability did not make it as easy as Miko claimed, then paused. *If I support Miko's decision to keep something from the Academy now, perhaps if he finds out about Vella before I'm ready to hand her over he'll return the favour.* It would be out of character for him not to object a little, however.

"At least you found *something*."

Miko narrowed his eyes then, not seeing disapproval, he straightened and grinned. "Yeah, you had back luck with that tomb."

Tyen sighed and looked way. "I have nothing but all the calculations I made to find it."

"If it's any consolation, the professor'll probably take all the credit anyway. I expect he's already showing off everything to his Academy friends."

"He won't let them touch a thing until it's all properly labelled and recorded," Tyen assured his friend. "Which we'll probably have to do after class."

Miko groaned. "Well, so long as we still get Market Nights off to visit Nectar Ally."

Tyen narrowed his eyes. "I thought you were broke?"

"Won't be soon." Miko patted his bag and grinned.

"You'd better pay me back for this ride before then."

"Of course!"

The two-seater broke from a knot of traffic and put on some speed. They grabbed the handholds and whooped as the morni dashed between slower vehicles, making up the time lost in the clotted streets around the station. Soon she settled into a steadier pace, slowing for corners and the occasional obstruction, until the stone pillars and iron fence that surrounded the Academy appeared. The driver reined her back to a walk and directed her through the open gates into the courtyard.

A few students were huddled in the shelter of recessed windows and doors, but no one else was about. There was no sign of the longcart that Kilraker had hired. Tyen assumed it had entered by one of the delivery gates. He paid the driver and they climbed out. Miko moved close to Tyen's side, then looked up and grimaced as rain splattered over his face.

"Aren't you shielding?"

"No," Tyen replied. Though using magic was legal in the Academy, frivolous use was still frowned upon.

"Must you always be so well behaved?" Miko gave a little huff of annoyance, left Tyen's side and ran to the entrance. Tyen chuckled and followed at a fast walk, wet enough from the ride that it wasn't worth trying to avoid a little more rain. As they made their way through the building he was surprised to find himself relaxing.

Maybe I am more relieved than disappointed to be home. It was reassuring to be in familiar, safe surrounds. As they passed the library he inhaled deeply. How had he not noticed before how wonderful the smell of books was? They took a corridor past the lecture halls, imbued with the scent of wood polish and dust. Instead of crossing another rain-soaked courtyard they detoured past the laboratories, from which all kinds of odours and sounds emerged, both pleasant and disgusting in equal measure. Their senses hadn't recovered by the time they reached the Student House, so the smell of the evening meal cooking didn't tempt them to stop. They called out to and were greeted by other students as they climbed the stairs to their room. Tyen found himself automatically peering into the dining hall to note the time displayed on the big round clock. An hour until dinner. Enough time to change and unpack.

The upper floors were where the poorer students took residence, as the rich ones preferred to avoid the daily climb. Tyen and Miko's room was on the fourth floor, second from the top. When they finally reached their door they were both a little breathless. They tossed their bags on the floor, threw off their jackets and collapsed onto the beds.

"Home," Miko said.

"Yes," Tyen agreed.

"I'm hungry."

"Dinner isn't for an hour."

Miko tapped his fingers together. "Then I'll take my gear to the washhouse. Want me to take yours?"

"Thanks."

They set to unpacking, and soon Miko had gone off with a bundle of dirty clothing under one arm. Alone, Tyen looked at the rest of his travel gear, now strewn across his bed. He began putting everything away. Miko had emptied the contents of his luggage on his desk, but Tyen's was covered in tools and parts for making insectoids. A few partially made beetles, hoverflies and arachnids sat within rings of components needed to finish them. The cleaners had learned long ago not to disturb anything, so all was covered in a fine layer of finger-marked dust – thicker away from the central work area. Tyen did most of his studying and essay writing while sitting on the bed.

I wonder if Kilraker will make me help catalogue Neel and Miko's finds, he thought. *Perhaps he'll take pity on me, since I didn't find anything. Then I can finish these.* The insectoids always found eager buyers, especially the customised ones with special abilities like playing tunes, or imprinted with specific commands.

"Beetle," Tyen called. A whirr came from his satchel as the insectoid came to life. "Come." One side of the bag's flap lifted and the little machine emerged, scuttling to the edge of the bed, its auditory antennae waving. "Guard the room," Tyen ordered.

Iridescent wings sprang open then blurred, carrying the insectoid up and over to the door. It landed and scurried into the gap beneath. Tyen smiled. Miko's habit of barging in without knocking had been one of the reasons he'd created the insectoid in the first place.

With most of his gear stowed away, he sprawled on the bed and dragged the satchel closer. Taking Vella out, he considered where he should keep her.

Hide her? Knowing Tyen's luck, Miko would burst in just as he was slipping her in whatever hiding place he came up with. *Tell Miko about her?* He shook his head. It wasn't that he didn't trust Miko, but the young man lost the ability to keep secrets when he was drunk. Though he remained good at keeping his own secrets, so perhaps he would stay silent because Tyen knew about the poible he'd kept.

And that was another point. *If Miko can keep something, why shouldn't I?*

Because Vella is no mere bauble. He sighed as the same old arguments ran through his mind. Disobeying the Academy made him uneasy, but Gowel's story of the Academy letting discoveries go to waste worried him. He needed time to think about it, and in the meantime . . . around Miko he would simply behave as if Vella was an ordinary book. He might even be able to read her while Miko was around, though he'd still have to make sure he angled the book so his friend didn't see the text appearing on the paper. Perhaps he'd tell Miko she was a boring textbook. *No, he won't believe that if he sees me reading it all the time.* Perhaps a book about magic – something that sounded difficult and complicated. And if Miko still grew curious enough to investigate? *Perhaps Vella can make herself look like an ordinary, boring textbook.*

Opening the cover, Tyen looked down at the first, blank page.

I can't do that. It would be a lie, and I cannot lie.

Can you say nothing at all then?

No. Remember, I must reply to questions if I know the answer. People often think in questions. He has only to think "What is this?" or "Why is Tyen reading a book with no text in it?" and I will have to answer.

I see. Though Miko is more likely to ask "When's dinner?" or "Can I owe you for that?"

Both questions that he knows the answer to, therefore I know the answer to, and must reply.

Tyen chuckled as he pictured *that* conversation. Would Miko, like Tyen, find Vella's honesty refreshingly frank or be put off by it?

From what I see of him in your mind, his taste in women tends towards those who offer physical rather than intellectual interaction.

You are – I am – probably right. At least Miko knew how to relate to women in one way. *Unlike me . . . could Vella help with that?*

Probably. Mostly because you are wrong to think you don't understand women. You understand more than you believe. Men and women's minds are not as different as you have been taught.

The world was different when you were whole. Women were different.

People stay the same. Only culture changes: traditions, ideas about right and wrong, what civilisation is and what threatens it. Your society has rigid ideas about the roles of men and women, class, manners and ethical behaviour while at the same time it has opened its mind to technological innovation and understanding of nature and the universe.

Tyen nodded. Perhaps these rules of society provided a safe feeling of stability when everything else was changing. Which reminded him of his obligation to her. *I have so much to show you. But it will be some days before I am free to leave the Academy.*

Take me with you anyway. Show me the Academy.

But I can't get a book out and read in the middle of classes.

You don't have to. Keep me against your skin and I will see all that you see and hear all that you—

A high-pitched noise jolted him from the page and he looked down to see Beetle scurry out from under the door. His heart skipped as he realised Miko was returning, but he made himself stay as he was. The door opened and his friend caught hold of the frame with the other hand to halt his forward motion.

"Dinner – you're reading?"

Tyen closed the book and tossed it onto the bed. "Sorcery. Statistics. We'll be back in class tomorrow. May as well get my head into the right frame of mind."

Miko grimaced, then jerked his head in the direction of the stairs. "Come on. Neel's back and has an audience already. He's probably making up stories about us."

"Can't have that." Getting to his feet, Tyen put Vella into his satchel then held the bag open. "Beetle. In." The insectoid whirred into the air and dived inside. He slung the bag by its handle over the back of his chair, then followed Miko out of the room.

The sound of laughter drifted up the stairwell and when they reached the ground floor they found Neel sitting on a table, waving his arms around as he addressed a circle of students. Though they hadn't worn them for days, Neel had his aircart jacket on over ordinary clothes, scarf wrapped close under his chin and his goggles strapped around his forehead.

Tyen stopped. "What . . . why is he wearing that here?"

"Apparently it's the height of fashion to look as if you just landed an aircart. Women love it."

"He looks ridiculous."

"A right poser," Miko agreed.

Tyen chuckled. "Must we sit near him?"

"I'm afraid we must."

Shaking their heads, Tyen and Miko entered the dining room. *Maybe it isn't women I don't understand*, Tyen thought, *but why men make such fools of themselves over them.* Though it was more likely Neel wanted to impress his peers tonight, since no women were allowed here other than the serving staff. The few women students of the Academy were housed on the other side of the buildings, guarded by ever-watchful Matrons.

CHAPTER 5

With Vella safely tucked inside his shirt, Tyen strode out of the Academy gates. He hadn't left the grounds for five days, but it felt far longer and the expedition already seemed a distant memory from months before. As he'd predicted, Professor Kilraker had recruited him, Miko and Neel after classes to catalogue the artefacts they'd brought back from Mailand, keeping them working well into the evenings and giving Tyen no chance to educate Vella. Eventually Kilraker had given in to Miko's relentless appeals that they have their first Market Day free to attend to familial or other duties.

Tyen doubted Miko or Neel had anything resembling family or duty to attend to. Not wanting to waste his first opportunity to show Vella the great advances of the modern era, Tyen had slipped away early. He'd decided to start with a visit to a place she would find both familiar and greatly changed.

A distant voice called from behind him.

"Tyen! Wait!"

He checked his stride, then cursed himself for betraying that he'd heard Miko's call. As he heard two pairs of running footsteps behind him he knew that pretending not to would have been futile anyway. It was churlish to be annoyed that they wanted his company, too. He stopped and turned to wait.

"Where're you going?" Miko asked as he slowed to stop before Tyen. Neel grinned as he followed suit.

"To the printery."

Miko frowned. "Why?"

"I'm going to get a pamphlet made up denouncing the Academy as grave robbers."

Neel's smile vanished, but Miko laughed. "What are you *really* doing? Off to see some girl you haven't told us about?"

Tyen shrugged. "No, I really am going to the printery to see how it all works."

Miko's eyebrows rose. "You *know* how it works."

"In theory. I've not seen it for myself. Have you?"

To Tyen's surprise, Neel was nodding. "Like going to Mailand. You can read all about it, but you don't properly know about anything until you see it." Then to Tyen's dismay, he stepped up beside him. "I'm in. Let's go."

"Very well then," Miko said, then grinned. "So long as afterwards we go and see something *I* want to see."

"Sounds fair," Neel said, and looked at Tyen expectantly.

Suppressing a sigh, Tyen nodded. "And you after that, Neel?"

Neel shrugged. "If I think of something, and there's time."

The printeries of Leratia were within half an hour's walk of the Academy. Closer than most industries because the institution was a good customer, but not so close that the academics would be bothered by the noise and smells. Tyen picked a company name he recognised, Leadbeater & Sons, walked into the reception and enquired if he and his fellow students might see how it all worked.

Eager to please potential future customers, Mr Leadbeater himself took them on a tour of the premises, first showing them some paper samples.

"We use the best paper-makers in West Leratia," the man assured them.

"And vellum?" Tyen asked.

Leadbeater nodded. "We *can* get it. It is rarely asked for due to the expense, and we have very satisfactory alternatives." He moved to a chest of wide, shallow drawers and drew out a small, creamy sheet, then took what appeared to be a book from a case but which was, in fact, bound samples of paper. Placing both on a table, he opened the sample book to a page near the back. "Examine these, and see if you can tell the difference."

Tyen fingered the sheet and the page of the book, noting the surface texture and flex when he curled the page, then passed them to his friends. "I can't tell which is which."

Mr Leadbeater smiled and pointed at the sample book. "Paper can simulate vellum, but to do so involves extra processing therefore extra cost. For most purposes, ordinary paper will suffice – and I think people have come to expect the crispness of modern paper and its particular crinkle as the page turns. Would you like to see the printing machines?"

"Yes, please."

He ushered them to a heavy door. As it opened, their senses were assaulted by a cacophony of noise and a mixture of smells both unpleasant and familiar. They followed Leadbeater into a long room filled with men and machines. Tyen immediately noted the arms extending from each machine to a long, revolving shaft stretching across the roof to a hole in the far wall. Not all the machines were working, so not all the arms were attached, but those that were pumped steadily. The printery owner followed Tyen's gaze.

"We're connected to the same engine as four other printeries," Leadbeater told him, shouting to be heard above the noise. He waved at the far wall. "Behind there."

Tyen did not need to be told. The printery was dark with Soot. Even had he needed to use magic now, he would have had a difficult time finding any within his reach. *Though if I . . .* He stretched his senses beyond the high ceiling and felt magic flowing down to a point not far beyond the end wall.

Which meant a sorcerer must be there as well, directing the flow and keeping the engine working.

I could end up with a job like that one day.

As always, he had mixed feelings about the prospect. His father had been employed as a machine driver for most of his life. It was menial work, but it paid well. Enough that he'd been able to send Tyen to the Academy in the hopes his son would do something more interesting with his gift. *Trouble is, interesting uses of magic that pay well are few and far between.* Which was why he'd chosen to study history as well. If he didn't make it as an archaeologist and treasure hunter, or find something exciting to do with magic, at least he could stay at the Academy and teach.

Mr Leadbeater had stopped beside a two-tiered table. A man with blackened fingertips was plucking type from trays spread over the table and slotting it into a device rather like a short dustpan. As the printery owner explained the steps in setting the type, then led them over to printing machines to see the inking of type and sheets of paper being pressed to the plate, Tyen focused on the pressure of the book tucked into his shirt and wondered what Vella was making of all this. *Is the demonstration going too quickly? Does she understand all of what she is being shown? I wish I could take her out and see if she has any questions.*

They moved on to cutting and folding machines, slicing the printed sheets of paper to size and bundling them ready for binding. A row of men were sewing these together. Their guide took them aside to a corner of the printery that smelled strongly of glue. A grey-haired man wearing a leather apron peered at them through a single eye lens set within a bracket affixed to his hat brim.

"Mr Balmer is our cover-maker," Leadbeater explained. He turned to the employee. "Could you demonstrate to these young future academics the construction of a cover?"

The man's eyebrows rose, but he nodded then beckoned them over to a table. He moved aside stacks of stiff cloth rectangles piled on the table then turned to what looked like a bin of offcuts and drew out a scrap of dark green fabric.

"The cloth covering is more than decoration," he explained. "It forms the hinge. We use two thicknesses of card. These are for the covers . . ." – he took two rectangles of card from a shelf, cut into what Tyen guessed were standard measurements – ". . . and the spine is done with thinner, flexible strips of card." He now cut a strip from a large roll. "Glue it all into position." With practised efficiency, he took a brush from a large tin of glue and slathered the sticky substance over the front of the cards. Taking the thin strip, he laid it down the centre, then he picked up the two rectangles of thick card and placed them on either side.

"Now we cut." Taking a knife, he deftly sliced away fabric until there was an even overhang on all four sides of the card, and removed a wedge at each corner. Taking away the scraps of fabric, he smiled. "Glue and fold." He wetted the overhang then picked up a tool made of bone and began to coax the fabric over the back of the cards, first starting at the corners to tuck the excess in before concentrating on the edges.

"It must be dried in a press to avoid warping. Of course, this is very plain. We can create impressions by gluing thinner card with areas removed onto the front before applying the cloth, or add string to form ridges around the spine which, while only decorative now, emulates a form of binding from the past. Any questions?"

Tyen opened his mouth but Miko spoke before he had a chance. "How do you get the pages into it?"

The old man gestured to a long table in the centre of the bindery, where men were operating smaller machines. "You will see that in a moment, but essentially we glue them in, using a sheet of heavy paper at the front and back."

"Do you use leather for covers?" Tyen asked.

The binder nodded, and the skin crinkled around his eyes. "Yes, on more valuable books. It is a pleasure to work with."

"Do you prepare the leather yourself?"

"No." His nose wrinkled. "Tanning is an unpleasant process, best done well away from cities. The skin must be soaked in lime and the hairs scraped from it, then stretched and worked to make it supple. By the accounts I've heard, it makes quite a stink."

"Like that glue?" Miko asked.

The man laughed. "That makes a fragrant perfume compared to tanning."

Tyen grimaced. *I suppose he's used to the printery smells after all these years.*

"Any more questions?" Balmer asked.

Tyen hesitated as one came to mind. His friends would think he was crazy. But he couldn't ignore the opportunity. He steeled himself for ridicule.

"We're history students. I'm interested in strange old books. Ever heard of a book made of bones and skin and hair?"

The binder's eyebrows rose. "No." He looked thoughtful. "I suppose it could be done. Vellum is skin. Thread can be spun from hair. The bone . . . perhaps if you found a piece flat enough it could be used instead of the cover card. Though you'd need a flat bone, and I don't know enough about the bones of animals to say if there's one suitable." He shrugged. "You'd have to ask a meat man about that." Then he smiled. "Are you writing a book about that? A book about books?"

Tyen shrugged. "Maybe. I'll have to see if there's a story in it."

The man laughed. "Good luck to you, then."

Mr Leadbeater returned and took them past the machines that attached the covers to shelving where he stored books waiting to be delivered to their owners. Tyen thanked the man for sparing them the time to show them the process, and said he had gained a lot of useful information. The man ushered them out into a sunny late afternoon.

As they walked back towards the Academy, Tyen was conscious of Vella's form pressed against his skin. He itched to take her out and see what she had thought of the printery. It had been a good demonstration of industrial processes driven by magic. Did she have any questions? What would she like to learn about next?

Thinking back, he hoped she didn't mind him asking if the binder had heard of a book made of bones, skin and hair. *Was that a bit too personal a question? Would she rather I didn't know the details?*

A hand tucked into the crook of his arm.

"Well, that was more interesting than I expected," Miko said, steering Tyen in the direction of a side street. "But those fumes! I think we need to stop and have a drink to clear our heads."

Neel laughed. "Since when does drinking clear anyone's head?"

"And you promised we could go somewhere I picked next," Miko added.

The side street was more of an alley, and Tyen felt a chill as they moved into its cooler shadows. Men and women in work clothing hurried along it, hunched and frowning. "Where are we going?"

Miko let his arm go and took the lead. "A short cut. Don't worry. I know where we are. I've been here before."

The alley kinked and curved, never staying straight enough

for them to see its far end. They stepped into a doorway to allow a woman carrying a huge bundle to pass. Two children followed, tottering under equally large burdens. After a few hundred paces Miko turned into another alley, as busy as the previous, and a familiar smell tickled Tyen's nose – the mingled smells of overly sweet perfume, cheap drink and blocked drains. *It reminds me of . . .*

"Nectar Alley?" Neel asked.

"No," Miko said. He glanced over his shoulder and grinned. "Its more respectable cousin, Flower Court."

"More respectable?" Tyen muttered. "Not from what I've heard."

Neel sent him a curious look, but Miko grinned.

"I've said it before and I'll say it again, you're too well behaved, Tyen."

Tyen huffed. "How many times do I have to come with you to these places to convince you I'm not?"

Miko laughed. The sound sent a thrill of apprehension down Tyen's spine. It wasn't that he hadn't visited places like Flower Court before, thanks to his friends, but he'd never done so in the company of a woman – even if she was a book.

"It's still light," he said. "They won't be open."

Miko patted the pocket of his coat. "They won't mind a few early customers."

"How are you going to afford . . .?" Tyen stopped as he realised Miko must have sold the bauble. "Hey! You haven't paid me back for the ride from the station yet."

Miko had turned away. "I'll buy you a drink," he tossed over his shoulder.

The alley descended via crumbling steps. The damp smell became stronger and the perfume more powerful as if to compensate. Tyen could hear the sound of many voices, growing louder at every step. The final flight of stairs made a twist to

the right and they stepped out into the roar and hectic swirl
of a crowded, bustling courtyard.

Looking back once to make sure they were following, Miko
started wending his way through the crowd. At the edges of
the courtyard men and women stood talking and drinking,
some sitting on old half-barrels or boxes. In the centre, people
strode about their business, their paths criss-crossing. As far
as Tyen could tell, all of the buildings facing the yard were
drinking houses. Plant boxes below the windows of the higher
floors were filled with flowers, but, from the gaudy colours
and stiff shapes, Tyen guessed they weren't real.

He and Neel followed their friend into one of the drinking
establishments. The inside was furnished with sturdy chairs
and tables, and a high bar and stools. There were fewer
customers inside than out, but the sense of relaxed expectation
suggested the calm was due to the hour and it would be busy
soon. Miko hopped up onto a stool and waved at the server,
who was talking to a thin young woman with large, startlingly
blue eyes.

"A round of your best dusky," he declared.

Tyen sighed. He doubted he'd ever get his money back now.
He didn't particularly want a drink so early in the day, but
there was no point refusing. Miko would insist, then berate
and tease Tyen for being no fun to be around.

The server nodded and turned back to the woman as he
poured their drinks. She was staring at Miko appraisingly.
Miko was staring at her. He grinned. She smiled back. Tyen
groaned silently.

If this goes where I think it's going . . . He was all too conscious
of Vella resting against his skin. *If it weren't for Miko I'd have
never set foot in a place like this*, he told himself. But a part of
him didn't mind – no, was glad – that Miko had. He'd have
never had the courage to come alone. *Because Father had warned*

me against it. Yet it was almost expected that the spirited young students of the Academy would enjoy all the city had to offer. *Just . . . I wish Miko hadn't picked now*, he thought.

Miko turned to face the woman as she walked over.

"I'm Gija. You look like you're celebrating," she said as the server set down their drinks.

Miko took his and handed it to her. "Hi, Gija. We recently got back from a successful trip to Mailand."

"Oh? What took you over there?"

"Treasure hunting."

"Find any?"

"Nothing to compare with what stands before me now."

Gija smiled and lowered her eyes. Tyen let out a long sigh and reached for his glass. Whatever sweetener they'd added didn't quite mask the bitterness of cheap alcohol. Best dusky indeed. Neel took one sip then grimaced and tossed the rest down.

"What brings you here?" she asked, lifting the glass delicately to her lips and taking the smallest sip. She ran her tongue over her lips, leaned close to Miko's ear and whispered.

"Just you?" Miko asked.

Her eyes slid to Tyen and Neel. "I'm expecting some friends. They'll be here soon."

Tyen nudged Miko in the ribs. "Don't worry about me. I can't afford it."

His friend glanced back. "As you said, I owe you for the ride."

"Not *that* much."

Miko shrugged. "Let a man give a friend a gift, will you?"

More like favour he'd have to return, Tyen corrected. Still, as two much prettier women bounced down the stairs, saw Gija and sidled over, he had to acknowledge he wouldn't have resisted as much if he hadn't been carrying Vella. Perhaps if he put her in his coat pocket . . .

Introductions were made, Miko bought more drinks. Tyen found himself with two glasses, so he took Neel's example and tossed down the contents of one. It burned down his throat. A warmth filled his belly and began to seep into his limbs. The dusky might not be quality, but it wasn't weak.

Miko began a flippant conversation with one of the other women, a round-faced brunette. Gija turned her attention to Neel, who appeared to find her more fascinating than was justified. *He always was a fast drunk*, Tyen thought. He regarded the glass in his hand and considered whether he should drink it or not. Slender fingers plucked it out of his grip and he turned to see the smaller of the three women smiling up at him.

"I've got something better in my room," she told him.

They all began to move towards the stairs. Tyen's head spun a little. He couldn't remember why he hadn't wanted a part in this. They staggered up the stairs to the first floor, where the girls pulled them in different directions. Neel was giggling. Tyen looked back in time to see Miko wave and grin as the brunette ushered him through a door. He saw Neel and Gija walking away before he found himself gently shoved into a dark little sweet-smelling room. Hands grabbed his jacket and tugged it off. The movement unbalanced him and he stumbled and fell half onto the bed.

He heard a smothered laugh. Turning over, he pushed himself up so he was sitting on the bed, closing his eyes and holding his head until it stopped spinning. When he opened his eyes again, the girl was standing a step away, holding out a new glass and smiling.

"This is better than what they serve downstairs."

He reached out to take the glass. "Thanks. Um. Who . . .?"

"Mia."

She dropped to her knees, skirt rustling as she moved forward and pressed between his legs so she could reach his shirt. "You?"

"Oh. Tyen."

"Drink," she ordered gently as she began unbuttoning. "Don't waste it."

He brought the glass to his lips then froze as cold fingers slid down his chest and stopped where Vella lay against his side.

Vella. Heat rushed to his face as he remembered why he'd been so reluctant to accept Miko's generosity. A rush of alarm cleared his head as she drew out the book. She regarded it for a moment, then shrugged and set it aside on a low table mostly covered in clothing.

"Wait." Tyen reached over and picked up the book. Though he knew it was a strange thing to do in this situation, he opened it and stared at the pages, gathering his dusky-addled thoughts enough, he hoped, to communicate an apology of sorts.

The dusky contains a drug. The whores intend to rob you and your friends.

Tyen stared at the words, reading them over and over. Then he closed the book and slipped it back into his shirt. Putting the dusky down he pushed the girl away gently but firmly, stood up, located his jacket and the door and staggered out.

Once in the corridor, he paused only to fasten enough buttons to be sure Vella wouldn't slip out if he had to physically remove his friends from their rooms. Or his friend's possessions from the women. The next ten minutes involved a lot of swearing, and not all from the women. By the end he and his friends were walking, Neel supported between Tyen and Miko, down the alley that had brought them to Flower Court – or so Tyen hoped.

"How did you know they were going to rob us?" Miko asked for the third time.

"I pretended to be asleep and she started going through my coat," Tyen lied.

"But . . . how did you . . .? Why pretend you were asleep?"

"I . . . I had a feeling they were up to something."

"A feeling?" Miko's tone was disbelieving.

"A hunch."

"You never have hunches."

"Yes, I do."

"It's why you never found anything in Mailand. Wasting all that time measuring and looking for logical ways to predict where the caves were dug. Should have just got digging, like we did – eh, Neel?"

Neel shook his head. His face was blotchy and pallid as he looked up at Tyen, his eyes wide.

"Thanks for rescuing us," was all he said.

Then he stopped, bent double and vomited on Miko's shoes.

CHAPTER 6

*S*o . . . *what the binder said . . . was that how you were made?*
    More or less. The writing on the page was, as always, graceful and confident. Skin instead of cloth and paper. Hair instead of thread. Bone instead of card. Glue from sinew, rendered down.

So there is bone large and flat enough in a human body?

Bones can be moulded and reshaped with magic, just as a person's appearance can be changed — if the sorcerer has the knowledge, skill and enough flesh and bone to apply it to. Roporien could alter his appearance to be more appealing or more frightening to others, if the advantage was worth the effort.

I've never read of anyone capable of doing that, but I suppose he would not have needed to change often in this world since everybody was already so impressed by him. But shaping your bones, making glue, tanning skin . . . wouldn't that have taken a long time?

The process can be accelerated with magic.

Even so, you must have been . . . well . . .

Conscious. Yes and no. That part of me that became a book stayed so. The rest died with what remained of my body.

Which was most of it, surely?

Yes. And possibly most of my mind.

Possibly? You don't know for sure?

I cannot lie. I cannot stop myself storing information and answering questions. I feel no emotions. Therefore some things were taken away, along with the parts of the mind concerned with controlling parts of the body I no longer have.

Could those parts be replaced? Could you become a woman again?
I don't know the answer to that.
Hasn't anybody tried?
Once, a young sorcerer attempted it.
And failed, obviously. Do you wish to be a woman again?
I know that I am not whole but I do not miss what is gone. I am not in great anguish, as you fear.

Perhaps because you cannot feel it. I wonder if, now, in this age of discovery and invention, we could find a way to restore you. If you wished it, of course. It is likely you would then age and die, so I would not try such a thing if you did not want it. Though . . . forgive me for pointing this out, you've lived an awful lot longer than you would have if you hadn't been made into a book.

Yes, though if you only count the time I have been conscious I have not yet lived as long as I might have as a human.

Perhaps, if you exist for many hundreds of years more, you will surpass a normal lifetime. After all, you're in very good condition for a thousand-year-old book. I guess what I wish to ask is: if you could become a living human again, would you choose to?

I would, because in this form I am a servant at best, a slave at worst. I would like to feel again. To experience all that being human entails.

I would like to meet you, as your whole self.

And I would like to meet you. Would you teach me how to live in this new era, with its fabulous machines and strange rules?

Yes, I would be honoured. I—

The book jumped in his hands then began to buzz. Tyen looked up, his heart racing, and realised it wasn't Vella making the noise, but Beetle hovering behind her. The insectoid made a hoarse piping sound, as if something was wrong with the whistle it used to sound the alarm for—

The door burst open. Miko strode inside, kicking the door closed behind him. Startled, Tyen snapped the book shut.

"How were sorcery classes?" Miko asked, but didn't pause for a reply. "Neel didn't show today so I went by his room. Still sick he reckons. What?"

Tyen realised he had been staring at Miko, still frozen in surprise. He shook himself.

"Nothing. You startled me."

Beetle flew over to the desk and settled among the machinery, as it was meant to do when it needed repairs. Miko's gaze dropped to Vella, then rolled towards the ceiling. "Are you reading that book again? Honestly, you are such a bore." He moved closer and peered at it.

Tyen resisted the urge to put Vella somewhere out of Miko's reach, knowing it would convince the other student that he was hiding something. Miko reached out and snatched the book from Tyen's hand.

"I thought you said it was about statistics or sums or some such thing. There's nothing written on the cover."

Tyen shrugged, though his heart was now racing. "It's old. The title's worn off." He leaned forward to take it back, but Miko stepped away. His stomach sank as his friend ran his thumb over the edges of the pages, fanning them open. Miko frowned, then opened the book. Tyen's insides turned over.

"There's nothing written in here." Miko shook his head. "Why would you . . .? Oh."

Tyen bit back a curse. He watched Miko's eyes move from left to right and back again, then widen and rise to meet his own.

"A magical book!"

"I did say it was a book of sorcery."

"About sorcery. Not *of* sorcery."

"I wasn't that specific." He held out his hand. "Give it back."

Miko's gaze had moved to the page again. As Tyen rose and

64

reached for the book he sidestepped. "It says that you found it in the tomb. That you didn't give it to the Academy even though you knew they'd want it." He glanced up at Tyen and grinned. "Seems you *can* misbehave, when it suits you."

This time Tyen cursed aloud.

"But you do plan to eventually," Miko continued. "After you've filled in the last six hundred years of history and invention. What do you want to do that for? I wouldn't."

"Give her to the Academy or add to her knowledge?"

His lips pursed in thought, Miko held the book out to Tyen. "Both, I suppose. I'd find out everything it knows then sell it. I've never heard of a book like this before. It's probably very rare."

Tyen took Vella back and slipped her into his inner jacket pocket. "She is. That's why I have to give her to the Academy." As Tyen said the words his heart sank. "But not until she's ready."

"Well, better that than keep her. It."

Tyen frowned. "Why?"

"Magical objects can be dangerous. They should be handled by an expert."

"She's not dangerous." Tyen shook his head. He'd never taken Miko for a superstitious type. "All her magic is in storing knowledge. She's no more dangerous than any book in the Academy library."

"Knowledge can be dangerous." Miko's expression was serious. "If the wrong person gets the wrong information at the wrong time. And why do you call it a 'she'?"

Tyen smiled. "She was once human. A woman." *But I'd best not mention she was made into one by Roporien. That will convince him she's dangerous.*

Miko's eyebrows had risen. "Really? Has she shown you a picture of herself?"

65

"No."

"You haven't asked her to?"

"Well, no."

"Aren't you curious?"

"No. Well, I suppose I am now."

"She might be good-looking." Miko moved over to his desk and sat down. "It would have been the first thing I'd have asked."

Tyen snorted. "Of course. And the second thing would be to see her without clothes on." He retreated to his own desk.

"Aha! So that's the real reason you spend all your time staring at the book. Now it's all making sense." Miko grinned.

"It is not," Tyen replied. He sighed and picked up Beetle. *I ought to be studying, but it shouldn't take long to fix this.* Soon dinner would be served, then he and Miko would have to meet Professor Kilraker and continue labelling and cataloguing the Mailand finds.

"You won't tell anyone about Ve— the book, will you, Miko? Not yet, anyway."

"I don't know. What do I get if I don't?"

"I won't tell anyone about the gold poible you sold."

To Tyen's relief, Miko laughed. "Fair enough. Your secret's safe with me."

For the next hour they worked at their desks in companionable silence. All the Beetle needed was a few screws tightened and a bit of oil, so after that was done Tyen turned his attention to finishing one of the arachnids that were so popular with prank-playing students, and a musical hoverfly commission for a professor's daughter.

He was halfway through the latter when a faint chime signalled mealtime. With Beetle in his pocket and Vella tucked into his jacket, Tyen followed Miko downstairs to find Neel sipping some plain soup and nibbling at a piece of bread. The whore's drug had upset Neel's sensitive digestion. While he said he was feeling better, Tyen guessed he was not being entirely truthful.

"Well then," Miko said as he and Tyen finished their meals. "If you're well enough for dinner, you're well enough to do some labelling and cataloguing."

Neel winced. "I . . ."

"I think we can let him have another night off," Tyen said firmly, kicking his friend under the table. "One for recovery, one in lieu of an apology."

Miko looked as if he might argue, then sighed and got to his feet. "All right. Only one night, though," he told Neel, then jabbed a thumb in Tyen's direction and grinned. "After that you start owing me for leaving me stuck alone with him."

"Hey!" Tyen protested as he stood up.

Neel managed a smile, and made a shooing motion. "Off with you. The sooner you get there, the less work for me to come back to."

Grabbing Miko's elbow, Tyen guided him out of the dining room before he decided to drag Neel along anyway. They made their way through the Academy to the collections wing, where Professor Kilraker was waiting for them in the storeroom allocated to him on his return.

"Neel still sick?" Kilraker asked, his thin eyebrows lowering in concern.

"Reckons he is," Miko replied.

"Yes," Tyen added. "Not as ill as last night, but his digestion is still uneasy."

Kilraker shrugged and gestured to two boxes on a nearby table. "Well, there's not much left to record so the two of you should get through most of it tonight." He opened the first of the boxes and they began unwrapping the contents. All of the items were spherical and etched with ancient writing and pictures – versions of the same kind of artefact Miko had kept and sold. Some were wooden, some clay, some stone, and a few were made of precious metals.

"Strange," Kilraker said as he dug through the remaining packing material in the box. "I was sure there was another gold one."

"Not this one?" Miko said, picking up another, plainer, gold poible.

Kilraker shook his head. "I recall a fancier one. I hope it wasn't mislaid or fell out during our rushed exit."

"Didn't Drem drop a box at one point? Neel said something about it."

Kilraker narrowed his eyes at Miko. "No."

Miko ducked his head and lowered his eyes. "I didn't mean to suggest that Drem was clumsy. He is nothing less than the most competent servant."

The sharpness in the professor's gaze eased. "I will ask him if he recalls a gold poible. Possibly he—" A knock interrupted him. Looking up at the storeroom door, he waved at the poibles, boxes, labels, measuring devices, catalogue and pen on the table and stood up. "Make a start."

Tyen pulled the catalogue and pen over while Miko picked up the most humble of the poibles, made from crumbling unfired clay. The storeroom door clicked open. Hearing a familiar voice, Tyen glanced over his shoulder. Professor Delly, the head of the sorcery department, stepped into the room.

"Number two-oh-nine," Miko said. "Clay poible." Tyen added the details to the catalogue book.

Miko started to measure the diameter with a calliper and in the pause Tyen heard the professors speaking.

". . . could be proof of our theory," Kilraker was saying.

"Could be. Could be," Delly agreed.

"We should keep this to ourselves for now. Others might seek to destroy the evidence."

"You mean . . . the radicals?"

Kilraker's reply was lost behind Miko's reading of the poible's measurements. Tyen wrote them down, all the while straining his ears to hear more of the professors' conversation.

". . . what they believe."

Delly sounded puzzled. "But why would they—?" Miko dragged the scales closer, the noise drowning out more of the conversation.

Kilraker's voice grew louder. "If magic from these other worlds could be tapped, the rebels' hatred of the machines will be seen for what it is: fear of modernity and envy of the wealth earned by innovation."

"It weighs nine and three-quarter plats," Miko said. He held out the poible. "You should draw the designs. You're much better at it than me."

Tyen took the clay artefact and began copying a diagram of one side, taking care to record the words and pictures accurately. Miko leaned closer.

"That night at the Anchor Inn, Kilraker and Gowel had a fight over the ideas those two are talking about now," he murmured. "Gowel said we should turn a few machines off and see what happens to the magical atmosphere in the city and I swear steam came out of Kilraker's ears. I reckon Gowel's become a radical."

Tyen looked at his friend. Miko's expression was serious – an unusual enough occurrence that he looked strangely unfamiliar. From across the room they heard Kilraker make a sound of disgust.

"I'd rather destroy it myself than let it fall into their hands."

"Well, there will be no need for us to go to those extremes, I assure you," Delly said in reply.

Silence followed and as it began to lengthen Tyen could not help imagining the two professors watching him and Miko, wondering how much they could hear. He kept the pen moving over the page, completing the diagram of the poible's other side. He blew on the ink and turned the page.

"Number two-one-oh," Miko said, reaching for another poible.

The door closed softly behind them, then a single set of footsteps drew nearer. Tyen glanced back to see Kilraker walking towards them, his face creased by a scowl. The professor met Tyen's eyes and his expression softened.

"The war of ideas is as dangerous as those waged with weapons and magic," he told them as he sat down. "As many, if not more, lives are at stake. We must be diligent in our stance against lies and superstition." Drawing the other box closer, he began to unpack its contents.

CHAPTER 7

On the following Market Day, Tyen and Miko woke to find Belton blanketed in one of the impenetrable fogs that the city was famous for.

Apologies, Vella, Tyen thought as he picked up the book. *Even if I made myself go out in this there's nothing outdoors you could see and with the ferries not running most industries will be understaffed and not willing to indulge a student of the Academy with a tour of their premises.*

"What'll we do?" Miko wondered aloud, peering out of the small window of their room. He was leaning on Tyen's desk, his hand perilously close to a row of fragile varnished paper wings.

"I'm planning to make some more insectoids, if you don't break them first, then study."

Miko looked down and withdrew his hand. His eyes slid to Vella. "Study, eh? I know what you'll be studying. You hardly do anything else."

"That's not true."

"You don't study as much now — proper study, not reading that book." Miko frowned. "That's not like you."

Tyen raised an eyebrow at his friend. "It's not like you to worry about how much work I'm doing."

Miko's frown vanished. "No." Then he crossed his arms. "She's giving you an unfair advantage."

TRUDI CANAVAN

Tyen shook his head. "Not as much as you'd think. The information she has is old so I have to check everything before I submit an essay or do an experiment." Was Miko jealous? He smiled at his friend. "Is there anything I can ask about for you?"

But Miko didn't appear to have heard Tyen's reply. He was frowning again. "Can't believe I called it a 'she'," he said, shaking his head. "And you. It's like she's your girl. Like you're in love with her. With a book. Mad." He shook his head and turned to the door. "Well, I'm off to the library. The Bonnets finally got permission to use it whenever they want."

Tyen smiled. The more determined female students were known by the old-fashioned head covering they'd adopted to reassure the Matrons that their need to visit the library was based on scholarly interest, not access to the male students.

"Don't give the Academy reason to change their mind. The girls will never forgive you."

"I won't," Miko assured him.

The glint of mischief in his eyes did not inspire confidence. Tyen sighed as the door closed behind his friend. Knowing his luck, Miko would be back soon, evicted from the library for being a nuisance.

Perhaps I should talk to Vella first.

He moved to the bed and sat down, pushing the pillow up between his back and the headboard. Opening the cover, he held his breath and waited for words to appear.

Hello, Tyen. Don't be disappointed. The weather can't be helped, and you've taught me a great deal these last few weeks. Perhaps I can teach you something instead today.

You've taught me plenty already, and I've had enough of sorcery and history lessons this week. It's Market Day. We should talk about something else.

Is there anything else you would like to know about?

Tyen's mind immediately returned to the conversation he'd overheard between Professors Kilraker and Delly.

You've said before that there are other worlds. How many have you visited?

One thousand, six hundred and forty-nine.

You know exactly *how many?*

Yes. My purpose is to record information, so it is not hard for me to keep track.

Was Roporien the only one who took you between worlds?

No, he occasionally loaned me to a trusted sorcerer, and I was stolen once. After Roporien died I remained in this world, however. None of my owners were capable of travelling between them.

Did you spend much time in each world?

Sometimes weeks, sometimes mere moments. Unlike most other sorcerers, Roporien could move between worlds as easily as walking between rooms.

Are there any worlds that are more important than others?

That depends on what you consider important. Everyone's birth world or world of their childhood has an emotional importance for them, even if the reasons are unpleasant. The most important worlds for the sorcerers who moved between them were those that contained the strongest magic. They made those worlds their home, and ruled empires from them. Whether those worlds are important today depends on whether those sorcerers still live, or still want to live there.

Still live? Tyen's heart skipped. Vella was more than six hundred years old. *Do you mean there are more sorcerers like Roporien, who did not age?*

Yes.

How many?

I do not know. A few thousand, perhaps.

So many.

And yet very few, when you consider how many people there must be in all the worlds. Each world might contain many, many millions of people. Of them, perhaps one person each century might be able to preserve their body, but few survive long enough to learn the secret of agelessness. The life of a sorcerer is often a dangerous one, and the techniques of halting ageing are not always shared freely.

Surely if a sorcerer was that strong, nothing could harm them.

They may be ageless, but no one and nothing is invulnerable, and when someone is powerful they tend to mix with or become people who have dominance over others. The probability that someone wishes to harm them is very much higher.

Tyen shivered. He was fortunate, then, that he lived in this world and wasn't as strong as these sorcerers. The greatest danger he faced was to end up in a boring machine operator job. Perhaps that was why so few powerful sorcerers had ever come to his world. Other worlds might be more dangerous, but they'd also be more exciting.

So why might a sorcerer no longer want to live in the worlds they considered important?

Worlds can change. Empires fall eventually, no matter how powerful their rulers. Land can become infertile or turn to desert from over-harvesting or changes in weather. Some worlds have seasons that last centuries, so people may flourish then starve in turns. Some worlds grow slowly colder, warmer, drier, wetter. Plagues, creatures and plants may be introduced that make a world less liveable. Resources that made a world wealthy may run out. Wars may cast it into ruins or empty it of magic. I know of three worlds that were devastated by huge rocks that fell from the sky, and another that shook until the land split apart and bled molten stone. There are legends of worlds that disappeared, only an airless void or searing light at the end of the paths that led to them.

Path? Tyen's imagination painted a shining ribbon with travellers walking back and forth. Could such a route be wide enough for a carriage? *Do people make roads between the worlds?*

Not in the way you imagine. You don't physically *walk* the paths between worlds, but transit leaves an impression, like the tracks worn in turf from the traffic of many feet. When used frequently and recently, the paths stay clear. Unused, they slowly fade, like a road disappearing as vegetation on either side grows back over the surface.

Or magic flowing in to replace Soot?

Yes, tracks are very much like the absence of magic. Some believe it is the same effect.

There could be tracks leading to this world, or away from it, Tyen realised. But only if sorcerers travelled here often enough. Surely, if any had, it would have been so incredible that everyone would know of it. Or, at least, the Academy would.

It is more likely those sorcerers do not make their abilities known to others. Or they do only to those who agree to keep their presence a secret.

Why would they do that?

To be left in peace — to live in this world without everyone treating them differently. Fame can be very inconvenient, even dangerous.

He considered his earlier doubts that this world would be an appealing place for such sorcerers. *I suppose they might come here to hide from those who would harm them.*

Perhaps. But not the ageless ones. It requires plentiful magic. This is not a powerful world — even less so now than when I last saw it.

This world is growing weaker?

Yes.

Are you sure?

Yes.

What proof do you have of that?

Soot never used to linger as it does now.

Tyen shivered. *Could this world run out of magic? Is it possible for a world to exist without any magic in it?*

I don't know. I have never been in one that was devoid of magic. I expect I could not exist, as I need some magic to draw upon.

Tyen caught his breath. The prospect of no magic had already roused fears of a machineless future in Leratia, but he hadn't thought of what it would mean for Vella.

Would you revive once back in a magical world?

It depends on how long I remained in that state. I store a little magic in order to survive when the magic around me is depleted, or else I'd never survive if I passed through an area of Soot. But if this world ran out of magic I would perish, since there would be no magic available to transport me to another world.

Tyen stared at the page. *How long do you think it will take before this world is completely depleted of magic?*

I don't know enough to estimate a time. If all machines use magic at the rate of those I have seen so far, then it is diminishing at a far more rapid pace than in any other world I've encountered except those experiencing great magical conflict.

Tyen chewed on his lower lip. The words of Professor Kilraker repeated in his memory: "*If magic from these other worlds could be tapped . . .*" The professors would not have been discussing this if they didn't already know the magic in this world was running out. Was what Kilraker said possible?

I have a few records of this being attempted on other worlds, but without success.

He shook his head. Surely there was a way to replenish the magic of this world. His stomach sank as he remembered one she had suggested before. *I suppose you think the solution is for everyone to be creative, and generate more magic.*

Yes, but it would not be an easy or fast solution. Even if I could convince you that it would work, you would have a difficult task persuading others. People will not give up their wonderful machines willingly.

Tyen sighed. She was right in that, at least. He wasn't ready to give up, though. *We live in an age of invention and discovery. Surely we can find a way. Tell me about these attempts to bring magic in from other worlds. Perhaps we will succeed where others . . .*

A whistle interrupted him. He bit back a curse and looked up, expecting to see Miko entering the room. But when the door opened, the visitor was someone much older.

"Professor Kilraker!" Tyen closed the book and leapt to his feet. Then, as another man moved into the room, he stepped back to make space. "Professor Delly."

"Young Ironsmelter." Kilraker's tone was stern. His eyes dropped to Tyen's hands. "Is this the book you found in Mailand?" He extended his hand towards it.

Tyen's heart froze, then began to race. He looked down at Vella. What should he do? Lie? *No, there's no point. Nothing will dissuade the professors from looking at her, and as soon as they do they'll know what she is.* Tyen took a deep breath. *Sorry Vella. You're about to have a new owner. Thanks for all you have taught me, and I hope I've taught you enough in return.*

Stepping forward, Kilraker plucked Vella from Tyen's hand. "Is it?" he repeated.

"Yes," Tyen admitted. "Did Miko tell you about it?"

The professor examined the cover, his eyebrows lowered. "He did. He was worried that you had been trapped by it somehow. Why didn't you tell me about it?"

Tyen shrugged. "As you can see, it's not a very impressive object. I didn't think I could convince anyone it was valuable."

"A magic book?" Professor Delly did not sound convinced. "Of course it's valuable! Why would—?"

"That depends," Kilraker interrupted. "What does it do?" He looked up at Tyen, his fingers moving on the cover as if he itched to open it, but wasn't sure if was safe to do so.

Tyen spread his hands. "It takes in knowledge from its owner and stores it, and answers questions according to the information it has accumulated from previous owners."

Delly peered down at the book eagerly. "A knowledge store!"

"But that information is centuries out of date," Tyen added. "Its accuracy is only as reliable as its former owners'." He shrugged. "I've been checking what I learn against Academy records, naturally."

"If it is such an unreliable source, why have you continued to read it?" Kilraker asked.

"It is interesting for other reasons." Tyen paused, trying to think of a way to explain. "It – she – was once a person. Talking to her is like travelling back through time and meeting someone from the past." He shook his head. "I always meant to give her to the Academy. I just wanted to understand who and what she is."

As Tyen had spoken, Kilraker's eyebrows had slowly risen. Now he rubbed his moustache with a thumb and gave Delly a thoughtful look. "I think we had best leave this book closed until an examination can be arranged," he said, placing a hand over the cover. Kilraker turned back to Tyen. "Your attendance will be required."

Tyen nodded. "Of course."

Professor Delly made a small noise of protest. Kilraker turned to face him. "We will need to question him about his use of the book before anyone else risks reading it."

Delly's lips curled downward at the edges in defeat. "Yes, I suppose we will. I will make the arrangements." He nodded at Tyen. "I will inform you of the meeting time and place."

"Thank you, Professor Delly," Tyen replied.

Kilraker stepped back out of the doorway, pushing the door closed behind them. Tyen stared at the back of it, then down at his hands. As his heart slowed from the panic of discovery he was left with a feeling of loss. *Of a possession*, he told himself. *Just a book. That I was going to give to the Academy anyway.*

But Vella was more than just a book. She was a person. A woman who had never asked to be made into a tool, treated like a useful object and nothing more. She might not be a whole, normal woman but he had enjoyed her conversations and her company. *This is more like losing a friend*, he realised. *Like if Miko suddenly . . .*

Miko. Tyen scowled. Where was the turncoat? How long before he came slinking back to the room, all "I-was-concerned-for-you-this-is-for-the-best"? Or would he be full of self-righteousness and tell Tyen to get over it. Miko wasn't one for apologies.

But he must have truly believed Vella was a danger to risk Tyen revealing his theft of the gold poible.

Either that, or he was jealous. He did say she gave me an unfair advantage. Tyen found himself facing the window, fists clenched. He'd been pacing, and oblivious to it. Staring outside, he realised he could see details now. The fog was lifting. *I don't want to be here when Miko returns. I might strangle him.*

He turned on his heel, strode to his cupboard and grabbed his coat, scarf and cap.

"Beetle," he said. "Pocket."

A soft whirring filled the room as the insectoid obeyed, landing on Tyen's shoulder. He didn't wait until it had scuttled inside his coat before opening the door and striding outside.

He paused briefly at the Academy gates. He'd only intended to walk that far, but it wasn't enough. As he hunched into his coat's warmth and set out into the city, he reminded himself that he knew enough sorcery to fend off most attackers. He almost wished someone would try so he had a legal excuse to use magic. Beetle ran on magic of course, but barely a trickle, and so long as it stayed hidden it would take a particularly alert sorcerer to notice any was being used.

After several hundred paces or so Tyen began to feel a little better. *Perhaps all I needed was to get out of the Academy. Sometimes it's too easy to get caught up in its little dramas.* Except that Vella wasn't a little drama, to him.

They'll realise she's more than a book once they talk to her, he told himself. Once they knew she was a person, what would they do? It was wrong for a person to be owned. That was slavery. He stopped as he realised what that meant. *Then it's wrong, perhaps even illegal, for the Academy to own Vella!*

He doubted they'd see it that way, or that such an argument would hold up in a court of law. She did not believe herself to be a whole person. Even if the law agreed that she was enough of a person that owning her was slavery, that would mean Tyen couldn't own her either. Nobody could. She would be stored away somewhere, unconscious and forgotten.

Tyen sighed and began walking again. *Perhaps it's better that the Academy has her. She'll get to meet many people. Smarter, more knowledgeable people than me. She'll be safe. After all, if that whore had managed to drug and rob me, Vella could have ended up sold to someone who didn't value her, or even dumped in the rubbish or thrown on a fire.*

In the pale gloom, Tyen heard a laugh and looked up to see he was passing one of the many "delooms" – short for "deliberation rooms" in the area around the Academy. The little shops catered for intellectuals seeking social discourse outside of the stuffy Academy atmosphere, and were probably to blame for cultivating a taste for stimulating drinks and smoking among students and professors alike.

At the thought of a hot drink, Tyen was suddenly more conscious of the cold, damp air. He didn't much like the smoke in these places, but it would hardly be much worse on his lungs than the fog. Probably there would be nobody in the deloom that he knew, but he didn't mind sitting alone for the time it took to enjoy a drink. By then he might be ready to head back to the Academy.

Pushing through the door, he was amused to see the inside was only a little less shrouded with smoke as the street was with fog. Most appeared to be coming from a large group of men sitting at the back of the shop, taking up the attention of two servers. He looked around, hoping to see an isolated chair in a less smoky corner. A man was sitting in an alcove nearby, and Tyen realised he knew him. At the same moment the man looked up and blinked in surprised recognition.

"Gowel," Tyen said, touching the brim of his hat in greeting. *Is this man really a radical?* he wondered, remembering Miko's story of the adventurer and Kilraker arguing.

The adventurer gazed at Tyen steadily. "One of Kilraker's boys, right?"

"Yes. Tyen Ironsmelter. We met in Palga a few weeks back, at the Anchor Inn."

Gowel was nodding before Tyen finished. "The student who turned in early. Vals praised your aircart driving, said you might be his best student. What brings you out on such a sorry day?"

Tyen shrugged and decided that would have to do for an answer.

The adventurer chuckled. "You have the look of someone who needs a bit of fresh air."

"Yes. Well. Picked a bad day for it."

Gowel laughed. "You certainly did. Ah, I know that feeling well. I had it plenty of times before I left the Academy." One of the servers appeared at Tyen's side. "Why don't you join me?" Gowel invited, gesturing to one of the three empty chairs at his table.

"Thank you." Tyen chose a seat that allowed him to look out of the shop window, then decided to treat himself to a pot of lall – a drink made from the ground, bitter seeds of a tree that grew on the other side of the world. It arrived quickly and steaming hot, with a dish of solidified syrup beside it. It took several lumps of the sweetener before the drink's bitterness was softened enough for Tyen's taste buds.

All the while, Gowel gazed out at the fog in silence. The lines on the adventurer's tanned face seemed deeper, and this time he looked more sad than travel-wizened. Tyen realised that the man was looking in the direction of the Academy.

"Do you miss it?" he asked.

Gowel looked away from the window and smiled faintly. "Sometimes."

"Will you be dropping in to see Professor Kilraker?"

The man's mouth tightened and he looked away. "No. These days he and I have different eyes."

It was an old saying often favoured by northerners. From what Tyen recalled, it came from a tale in which two strangers, gazing at a landscape, noticed entirely different features and concluded that their eyes must be at fault.

Was this different viewpoint a radical one, as Miko suspected? *Should I be talking to him? What if Kilraker finds out?* He couldn't leave now without being rude to a man who, if not a radical, could be a useful peer in the future. If he stayed he might find out how radical Gowel's views were, and know to avoid him in future.

Tyen put down his cup. "Aren't different viewpoints meant to be good for the Academy? Different ideas lead to investigation which leads to truth?"

Gowel smiled. "Yes. But this current lot . . . they're too frightened of a few possible truths to investigate the evidence that is right in front of them."

"What could be so frightening?"

The adventurer's eyebrows rose. "If I tell you, you'll mark me for a radical."

Tyen looked away. Such a direct admission left him unable to think of what to say next. Some excuse to leave, at least . . .

Gowel sighed. "By your expression I am well marked already. Tell me, young Ironsmelter, where do you think magic comes from?"

Tyen looked up. "The atmosphere."

"How did it get there?"

"From the sun, or generated by lightning."

"Theories that have never been proven." Gowel leaned forward. "On your visit to Mailand you must have noticed that there is more magic in the atmosphere the further away you are from cities – particularly Belton. Or perhaps it is better to put it this way: the closer to the cities you are, the less magic there is. Whatever the source of magic is, cities are using it too fast for it to replenish itself. Do you agree with that?"

Tyen shrugged. "I suppose."

"So what should we do about it?"

"Use less?"

Gowel nodded. "And make more."

As Tyen tried to hide his dismay, the adventurer chuckled again.

"Ah, I see your fear. I am not saying what you think I'm saying. The idea that creativity generates magic is too foolish to be true. Then your grandmother darning your socks could be creating it. However, just because an idea is old doesn't mean it doesn't contain a grain of truth. Magic was once more abundant in our cities than outside of them. History tells us that. It is still more abundant in cities where there are no machines. So the first question you should ask is: why is there more magic in these cities?"

Tyen shook his head to indicate he had no answer.

"Because there are more *people*." Gowel thumped his fist softly on the table at the last word, startling Tyen enough that he met the adventurer's gaze, despite his efforts to the contrary.

"It is easy to see how the impression could come about that magic is generated by making things," Gowel continued. "People are always making things, so why not claim they make magic, too? It's good for business. It attracts commissions from the wealthy and powerful." He waved a hand dismissively.

"Most likely magic is a more earthly emission. A by-product of human existence, like sweat or excrement or body heat."

"But Belton contains more than a million people," Tyen pointed out. "Surely that would generate a lot of . . . by-product."

Gowel nodded. "What makes Belton so different? Machines! All gobbling up magic faster than even this great city can replace it."

Tyen tore his gaze away from the adventurer's intense stare. Comparing magic to sweat or excrement did not lend his explanation much appeal, yet the idea that magic was a by-product – an emanation – from the presence of humanity had a pleasing simplicity. *And there has to be a reason why people believed that creators made magic, I suppose, even if they were wrong.*

"So . . . we need to get rid of the machines?" he prompted.

Gowel let out a short laugh. "Of course not. But we should be judicious in their use. Stop wasting magic on indulgences. Make the machines more efficient."

Tyen nodded. Gowel's theory made sense. It was based on evidence and logic. The radicals weren't as foolish as he'd been led to believe. At least, this one wasn't.

"Can you prove this?" he asked.

Gowel sighed. "Not easily. Only by taking others far outside the draining caused by the great cities, to the lands I have visited where the cities are rich in magic, could I convince them of what I've found."

"So why don't you? Do they refuse to go?"

"Either that, or they point out that when they return they will be accused of being radicals, too."

"You have to find another way to prove it, then. Or convince enough people to make opinion sway in your direction."

Gowel looked at Tyen appraisingly. Tyen felt his face warming as he realised he was agreeing with a radical view-point. *Of course, Gowel could be lying. I'm not sure why he would, though. I wish I had Vella with me. I could get him to touch her, then ask her if he was telling the truth . . . oh!*

He sat up straight. Once the Academy understood how Vella worked, they could use her to confirm the truth of Gowel's words. If Gowel would consent to hold her, that was. That, he suspected, would be the easy part. If the Academy was as frightened of the truth as Gowel claimed, what chance had Tyen to persuade them to try? He sighed as his excitement faded.

"See?" Gowel said, grimacing. "I told you I'd frighten you with my radical ideas."

Tyen shook his head. "You didn't. I already knew we were running out of magic. I thought I had a way to prove what you're saying, but I'm not sure it would work."

"It's always worth trying," Gowel said.

Tyen considered the man. Perhaps he was right. "You'd have to agree to have your mind read . . . by a book."

As the lines on the adventurer's face converged in an expression of bewilderment, Tyen smiled. Then he began to explain.

CHAPTER 8

To Tyen's relief, Professor Kilraker sent for him that evening, after dinner. Tyen was eager to explain his idea, and had hoped he wouldn't have to wait days, even weeks, to get the chance. His relief evaporated, however, when the servant sent to fetch him led him to the Academy Director's office.

Sudden anxiety closed Tyen's throat and he croaked out a thank you as the man held open the door for him. Though the room was large the scrutiny of the five men watching him enter, the warmth from a roaring fire and the smoke from their pipes made it feel close and airless. Kilraker gave him a nod and smile of reassurance as he approached. Another history professor, Cutter, stood beside him, along with Delly and a professor of sorcery, Hapen, who taught final-year students. Those two regarded Tyen with disapproving frowns.

"Tyen Ironsmelter," Director Ophen boomed from behind his desk. "Come here." His hand did not stop beckoning until Tyen stood a few inches from the desk's edge, then it dropped and picked up a small, familiar object. "Is this the book you found in the tomb in Mailand?"

"I believe so." Tyen reached out to take the book, but the Director lowered it to the desk again, his fingertips resting on the cover.

"Tell us how you came by it."

"It was in the tomb I found. In the sarcophagus, in the corpse's hands and wrapped in a covering."

"The tomb you went to great lengths to ascertain the location of, I hear. Did you go to such effort because you were looking for anything in particular?"

"No. I had no clue that the tomb would be any different from the others. I only wished to save myself some digging."

The Director smiled. "Applying scholarly thought to make a task more efficient is a commendable approach. When did you discover the book's magical nature?"

"After I removed the covering. I was surprised to find the pages unmarked, but then words appeared."

"What did they say?"

"From what I recall . . . 'Hello, my name is Vella'."

"In what language were these words?"

"Leratian."

One of Ophen's eyebrows rose and his mouth twisted to one side. "How is that possible, if this book has been entombed for six hundred years? Even if the words were Leratian, they would be an early, almost indecipherable form. Can you read early Leratian?"

"No. But Vella – the book – is able to adopt the language known by the man who holds her."

The Director frowned. "How does she – it – do that?"

"She links to their mind. That is how she collects information."

Ophen quickly withdrew his hand from Vella. He stared at her, then looked up at Kilraker.

"You didn't tell me that."

"I did not know. I did warn you against—"

"Yes, yes. I haven't opened it," the Director said, scowling.

Tyen opened his mouth to tell them that Vella did not need to be opened to read their minds, then thought better of it. They seemed too suspicious of her, and at any rate the damage

– if any – was already done. Kilraker, Delly and Ophen had already touched her.

The Director looked up at Tyen. "You have examined it several times since you found it. What did you learn?"

"She is over a thousand years old and from another world. She was created from a person – a woman – and is only conscious when touched by a living human. Her purpose was to collect and spread information. Ask her a question and she will answer it to the best of her knowledge – and she can only tell the truth."

"Ingenious," Kilraker breathed, then he turned to look at Tyen with narrowed eyes. "And you didn't think she was valuable enough to hand over to the Academy?"

Tyen winced. "Not at first."

"At what point did you realise she *was* valuable?"

"When I . . . Though actually . . ." Tyen sighed. "At the same time that I realised she wasn't ready for the Academy."

The Director leaned back and crossed his arms. "What do you mean?"

Tyen met the man's gaze. "She had been locked away in that tomb for six hundred years, so her store of information was out of date. Some of the ideas she had needed disproving."

"Such as?"

Taking a deep breath, Tyen forced himself to tell them what they would discover soon anyway. "Such as the belief that creativity generates magic."

Professor Delly chuckled. "Hard to disprove, when nobody has yet proven where magic comes from."

Hapen's expression was serious. "If she – if *it* contains such superstitions and is so out of date, why would you trust the rest of the information contained within?" he asked.

"I didn't. Not until I had checked it against other sources," Tyen explained. "Not all of her knowledge is incorrect. Just as a great deal of our knowledge is built on the wisdom of the past, so is hers. Just as we are constantly reassessing our knowledge, so is she. Like the Academy library, she is only as useful as the information stored inside her, but because she is more portable it is easier to expand that store and . . . and perhaps educate people beyond the Academy walls."

"Because sharing our secrets with the rest of the world would be of great benefit to all," Ophen said, his scowl and tone suggesting otherwise.

"We need only take care that we do not fill it with *our* secrets," Kilraker said in a low voice.

This time Tyen did wince. He should tell them that Vella had already read their minds, but still he hesitated. *They will find out as soon as anyone reads her. Though if they don't know she can then perhaps nobody has tried yet. Perhaps they all have secrets they fear will be revealed. Perhaps if I offer to do it for them — yes!* That way he could continue to talk to her, and the Academy would have the benefit of using her for her true purpose.

"You don't have to read her yourself to use her," he told them. "Roporien used to have someone else do it for him."

Five heads turned to stare at him and he cursed silently as he realised his mistake.

"Roporien," Delly gasped, his eyes wide.

"You didn't say—" Kilraker began.

"Well, who else could have made such a thing," Hapen said. He gave a low laugh. "Out of a poor, innocent woman, too."

Director Ophen's hands were now braced against the desk, as if to push himself as far back in his chair and away from Vella as possible. But his gaze was avid, as if he was both attracted and repelled.

"How do you know that she must tell the truth?" he asked. His gaze lifted to Tyen. "Have you tested her?"

"No. I haven't had time to think of a method to do so, but

so far I have not found an instance where she has lied to me. Even when doing so would have been in her best interests."

The Director slowly turned his head from side to side in a shudder of denial. "No," he said. "No, no and no. It is too dangerous. If this got into the hands of the radicals . . ." He rose, picked Vella up and handed her to Delly. "Lock it away."

Tyen's stomach swooped down to his knees. "But she's only conscious when—"

"But Director—" Kilraker said at the same time.

"No," Ophen said firmly, fixing first the professor then Tyen with a direct stare. "Nobody is to read it or even touch it without my permission." Then his attention returned to Kilraker. "Or discuss the uses to which it could be put."

Delly carefully slipped the book into a pocket. "I will take it to the Librarian."

The Director nodded and sat down again. "Tell him to come and see me, once it is in the vault." He looked up at Tyen. "As for you, I am satisfied that your intentions were good, but it is not up to you to judge when an artefact owned by the Academy is ready to be possessed by it. You should have delivered the book to us as soon as you arrived. No, in fact you should have given her to Kilraker as soon as you'd found her."

Tyen bowed his head. "You are right. I apologise."

The man exhaled, then waved a hand. "Kilraker can decide the appropriate punishment, since it was he who you should have deferred to. Now, with that sorted out, you may all go."

All four professors hesitated, as if they were not used to such a dismissal, then stepped away from the table and headed for the door. Tyen forced himself to follow. If Kilraker wasn't willing to argue with the Director, then Tyen certainly would gain nothing but the man's ire by lingering.

I didn't even get close to explaining Gowel's theory and how we could use Vella to prove it, he thought. *Maybe if I come back when he is in a better mood he'll listen. Especially if I point out a way Vella could be used for the good of the Academy. And if I can get Kilraker to support me . . .*

As if hearing his name in Tyen's thoughts, the professor turned around and smiled apologetically.

"I'm afraid I will have to make sure you are seen to be appropriately disciplined," he said.

Tyen nodded. "I know," he replied. But he doubted anything could be as awful as knowing he might have condemned Vella to oblivion for the rest of her existence.

CHAPTER 9

Three days later Tyen set out to find himself a job.
It was the kind of crisp, sunny weather that made up for the more common miserable grey days of winter, but the sunshine did not cheer him. Inside one of his coat pockets was the page of the *Reporter* that listed jobs a young Academy student might apply for. In the other was Beetle, in case the opportunity arose to attract another commission.

The entire employment section had been considerably smaller than he'd expected, but since he'd not had to seek a job in the city before he had no idea what size it ought to be. Professor Kilraker's punishment had been to suspend Tyen's lessons for the rest of the half-year. That meant Tyen would have to begin that half-year again to have any chancing of passing it.

The other professors had accepted nothing less, Kilraker had told Tyen. Especially since Tyen had managed, somehow, to avoid direct censure from the Director. Some, Tyen knew, thought he ought to have been expelled for "stealing" treasure rightly belonging to the Academy. Clearly they did not know how common it was. It had been tempting, so very tempting, to reveal Miko's theft of the poible. After all, Miko's crime had been worse – he'd actually stolen *and sold* a treasure.

But it wouldn't have gained Tyen anything but petty revenge, and it would have lost him a friendship. Though he had to admit he did not find Miko's company as comfortable as he had before. Every morning, Miko slipped out of their room early and looked alternately guilty or defiant whenever they were both there and awake. As much as Tyen told himself Miko had broken his promise because he was concerned about Vella's influence, he did not feel he could completely trust his friend now.

He wished he could discuss it with Vella, then cursed under his breath. None of the professors would even talk to him about her and the Director had ignored all requests for a meeting. *At least it doesn't matter if it takes me a few weeks or months – or even years – to get her out of the vault. She won't be aware of the time passing.*

Tyen could not yet see how he would free her, but he was determined to do it. As his father had always advised, he'd broken the task down into smaller ones. He needed to persuade the Academy to let him use Vella. To do that he'd need to convince the Director it was both safe and beneficial to do so. The chances of having the Director's ear would be better if Tyen had Kilraker's support. To do that Tyen would have to restore his standing with the professor by being a first-rate student.

Since that required remaining in the Academy, and his father had saved barely enough to send his only son there in the first place, the most pressing task for Tyen was to earn enough money to cover the extra half-year of rent, food and, since his Academy-sponsored trip to Mailand now wouldn't count towards his scores, another expedition.

And with his lessons suspended, it wasn't as if he'd have much else to do between now and the end of the half-year.

Turning a corner, Tyen found the street he was looking for. He took in the neat, evenly spaced buildings with their matching gold-painted signs and hesitated. Unfolding the job advertisement page, he located the address he sought. Grand & Pog Insurance Co. was at number 36. He was standing by number 2, belonging to Mill & Sons Finance and Investment Brokers. It became clear, as he walked along the street, that this was where Belton's main accountancy, insurance and law firms were based. He doubted any of these respectable businesses would wish to employ a history and sorcery student when there were plenty of more suitably trained young men in the city.

An hour later, proven right, he had almost reached the Academy when a man handing out pamphlets stepped forward and pressed one into Tyen's hands.

"On the back," the man told him.

Continuing on, Tyen looked down and felt a wave of nausea at the bold words shouting out from the page.

"MAGIC IS RUNNING OUT!"

His hand clenched, crumpling the paper, and he was about to throw it away when he remembered the pamphlet man's words. Smoothing it out, he turned it over.

"Meet me at the deloom."

Tyen's heart sank. It had to be Gowel. The adventurer had said Tyen should leave a message at the deloom once a meeting with the Academy had been agreed upon. Tyen hadn't had the heart to tell the man his chance of being heard had grown slimmer. Reaching the Academy gate, Tyen paused then kept walking. If it was Gowel waiting for him, he would give him the bad news. Tyen didn't want to waste his time. Perhaps Gowel would be able to suggest a way to persuade the Academy to use Vella, too.

When he reached the street where he'd found the deloom he realised he wasn't entirely sure which it was, since last time the front had been shrouded in fog. It was only by peering inside that he recognised the place. It was crowded and very smoky and, once inside, it took him a few minutes to realise that Gowel wasn't there.

"Are you Tyen?" a voice asked.

He turned to find one of the servers at his elbow.

"Yes."

The man bowed slightly then gestured to an alcove. "Take a seat. He will be here soon. Can I get you something?"

"Lall, please." Moving over to the alcove, Tyen sat down. After a few minutes noting the people in the room while trying not to be obvious about it, he settled for examining the page of job advertisements, mentally crossing out those he now realised he was never going to get and reconsidering a few he'd judged too menial or beneath his standing. He only had to work until the start of the next half-year, after all.

Before long he had read every word on the page, the lall had arrived and he had drunk it. He took Beetle out of his pocket but the insectoid attracted some alarmed looks from other patrons so he put it away again. Bored, he reluctantly brought out Gowel's message. Some arrangement must have been made with the pamphlet man. He'd recognised Tyen. Unless the message had been written on the back of all the pamphlets.

It was such a vague message it wouldn't matter if the man gave it to the wrong student. He wondered how many other students went to a deloom today to see if they could spot who had sent the mysterious message, or assumed it was from a friend. He turned over the sheet of paper.

"*Citizens of Leratia be warned,*" it read. "*MAGIC IS RUNNING OUT! We are fast speeding towards a FUTURE without sorcery. Without HEALERS. Without a DEFENCE AGAINST INVADERS. Without MACHINES. The Society of Magical Preservation invites you to learn of this IMPENDING PERIL, and how it might be AVOIDED.*" A date and place had been scrawled on the bottom of the sheet.

The message might be a ploy to get people to keep the

pamphlet, or leave it in a deloom when nobody turned up to meet them and perhaps lure other patrons to a meeting with the radicals. He sighed. And he had just fallen for . . .

"Tyen Ironsmelter."

Tyen jumped and looked up to find Gowel standing at the edge of the table. "Ah! Gowel!" He glanced at the door of the deloom, sure that he hadn't heard anybody enter, then turned the pamphlet over. "Did you send this?"

"Yes." The man removed his hat and sat down in the opposite seat. "Are you well?"

Tyen shrugged. "Well enough."

"For a student suspended from lessons?" Gowel asked, his eyebrows rising briefly before his face relaxed into a grim smile. "I heard about it from some old Academy friends. I guess your meeting with the professors didn't go as well as you hoped."

Tyen shook his head.

"I am sorry to hear it. Their choice of punishment seems a little extreme. In my day, attempting to keep treasures was almost a hobby among Academy students. But maybe they're trying to stamp that out by making an example of you. They kept the book?"

"Yes. The Director locked her — it — away in the library, with orders that nobody is to open it."

"Now, that is a pity."

"Yes. I still hope to persuade them to listen to you, but there isn't much point mentioning your idea until they trust Ve— the book."

"Is there anything I can do?"

Tyen shook his head. "Unless . . . unless you know of anyone who can give me a job."

The adventurer's eyebrows rose. "Thinking of leaving the Academy?"

"No. I need to pay the rent until I can start lessons again."

Gowel grimaced and shook his head. "There's not much work about even for an honest young man like you. Sorcery won't help you, since you're not allowed to use it. The restrictions are forcing companies to move their factories to other cities and other lands, so the city is full of men of all kinds of skills seeking new employment. Do you have family?"

"Only my father, in Tammen."

"Can you move in with him for a while?"

"If I move out of the Academy I'll lose my room and have to rent in the city when I start classes again."

"And pay double for the inconvenience." Gowel sighed.

Tyen nodded. "I need to stay here. Earning Kilraker's approval is my best chance of regaining everyone's respect and trust."

"And since he and I don't get along so well now, being seen with me won't help you," Gowel said. "As much as I try to keep my distance from the Society of Magical Preservation, I have friendships there that I am not willing to sever and so I am tainted by association."

The admission made Tyen's stomach sink. He'd not thought how meeting Gowel might spoil his chances of regaining Kilraker's trust, and the man's admission to links with radicals filled him with dismay.

Gowel shrugged. "I will understand if you don't want to meet me again. But . . . if you do, I may be able to enlist their help to retrieve the book."

Realising what Gowel was suggesting, Tyen stared at the man.

"I am not recklessly suggesting we do this unless you have run out of options and are willing to accept the consequences, of course," Gowel added.

Disbelief was replaced by temptation, but that was soon chased away by the thought of the punishment he'd face for such a crime. At best, theft from the Academy would have him expelled. At worse it would see him incarcerated.

Then he remembered something that made him realise Gowel was teasing – or testing – him. "It's in the library vault."

"That will be no obstacle." Gowel smiled.

Tyen raised his eyebrows, not bothering to hide his scepticism.

"You don't believe me." The adventurer chuckled. "I can't tell you how, of course, but be assured it can be arranged – on relatively short notice and at no risk to you. Of course, if my friends are going to be taking that risk they will want access to the book. Would you consent to that?"

Access or ownership? Tyen wondered. But then, perhaps it would be better if Vella was used by the radicals than locked away in the Academy library.

"I . . . guess so."

"Well, in my view, it would be better to find a solution that involved the co-operation of the Academy," Gowel said. "And you will be more likely to succeed if you are not seen to associate with me. I will see what I can do about finding you a job. When I do, I will have the employer contact you directly. In the meantime, keep hunting for one so nobody thinks it odd when they do."

Tyen made himself nod and smile with a gratitude he didn't quite feel. "Thank you."

"I can't guarantee that it will involve magic." Gowel sighed. He stood up. "I hope you weren't planning on making a career out of sorcery. If only it were true, what the radicals believe. All we'd have to do is take up painting or something, and we'd have all the magic we'd need. A pleasure talking to you, young Ironsmelter."

Tyen rose. "And you, Gowel."

Feeling uneasy, Tyen watched the adventurer retrieve his hat from the stand and exit through the main deloom door, then he headed back to his room.

All the way there and through the afternoon, Tyen could not shake the feeling of disquiet their conversation had generated. He tried to distract himself with work, finishing three insectoids and delivering them to their buyers. Having some extra money should have cheered him, but instead his thoughts kept returning to Gowel's words. As soon as he returned from dinner, before Miko joined him, Tyen cleared a space on his desk, took out a notebook and pen, and wrote a list.

1. *Gowel does not believe creativity generates magic*
2. *Gowel has friends in the Society of Magical Preservation, who do believe this*
3. *Gowel says the SoMP can steal from the library vault, which is supposed to be the most secure place in the Academy.*

Next he began to write a list of questions.

– *Why would the SoMP want to help me steal Vella?*

The obvious answer was that she currently agreed with their belief that creativity generated magic. But they didn't know she did. They didn't even know she existed. Unless Gowel had told them about her.

– *Why would Gowel want to help me steal Vella?*

To convince the Academy of his idea about the source of magic. But stealing her would not achieve that. For the Academy to accept the idea they needed to trust and use Vella, which couldn't happen if she was stolen.

Perhaps it wasn't the Academy Gowel hoped to convince. If enough people outside the institution were persuaded by his ideas, the Academy would have to investigate. Gowel would recruit people with power and influence, who could push for the implementation of laws to reduce the use of magic.

If Gowel was right, he needed the SoMP to steal Vella. They would hardly risk such a daring theft without a good incentive. Tyen looked at the previous question.

– Why would the SoMP want to help me steal Vella?

Gowel might hope that Vella would turn the SoMP to his way of thinking, but he wouldn't tell them that. He'd tell them she supported their beliefs. They wouldn't steal her to help Tyen, they'd do it for their own benefit. He doubted Gowel's motive was to help a young student either. When Gowel had assured Tyen that it would happen "at no risk to you" he meant he didn't need Tyen's involvement at all.

Looking back over his questions, Tyen crossed out "*help me*" in the last two questions. He sat back and regarded the result.

– If Gowel is right, and the SoMP can steal from the vault, then I may be about to lose Vella for good. The only thing stopping them stealing her was simply not knowing that they might want to.

Gowel knew that Vella read minds, but the society didn't. Would its members be willing to use her – to steal her – if they knew? Tyen grimaced as his mind took a leap sideways. He hadn't yet told anyone that it took a touch for her to read someone, afraid that the Director would decide she was too dangerous ever to be removed from the vault.

Perhaps she was. From the way the Director and professors had spoken, and the care they'd taken not to open Vella, it was clear they wanted to protect *something*. Something that

Gowel and the Society of Magical Preservation would discover if they stole Vella.

Tyen's heart lurched. What if the information Vella had gathered was so important it would endanger the Academy if it were discovered? What if it threatened Leratia? Or the whole Leratian Empire?

Though he resented the Academy for locking Vella away, he would never wish harm upon the institution. Not only because he was hoping it would be his future employer, but because he was, like many Leratians, proud of its achievements and its noble aims. He had worked hard to earn a place there. It had been his dream, and his father's, that he would become a graduate of the Academy one day.

At that moment he realised he had never seriously considered stealing Vella, just as he had never intended to keep her for himself. He was determined not to abandon her either. His fight to free her was as much about helping her as it was about supporting and improving the Academy, because they both had a lot to gain from each other.

That would never happen if someone took her away.

It wouldn't hurt his chances of regaining the professors' trust either, if he alerted them to the fact that the radicals believed they could steal from the vault – *how was it that Gowel had put it?* – "on relatively short notice".

A shiver ran down his spine. Looking back up at his first list, he considered the third point. Remembering what Gowel had said, he added *"on relatively short notice"* to the end. He stared at the words and his heart faltered.

How short could that notice be? *As short as tonight?*

He had to warn the Academy now. Standing up, he grabbed his coat, slid the notebook in his pocket and hurried out of the room.

CHAPTER 10

He walked – too late to stop – straight into Miko. They both grunted at the impact, then Miko let out an embarrassed laugh. "Steady on, Tyen. What are you in such a rush for?"

"I have to find Kilraker."

"Oh, I bumped into him before. Well, not as literally as we just did. He was heading for the library."

To the vault? Had he discovered the threat? "Right. Thanks." Tyen ducked around Miko to the stairs and descended them two at a time, then hurried through the Academy. He passed a few students and one professor. The former ignored him and the latter eyed him suspiciously. When he burst through the library doors at last, a few heads peered around bookcases to see what the noise was. Kilraker was nowhere in sight, but this was the lowest of five levels and only the wide central aisle with its reading tables was visible. Tyen started along the room, looking between the rows of shelving on either side.

Then he started to a halt as a voice spoke from directly above him. "Who might you be looking for, young Ironsmelter?"

Looking up, Tyen saw that the Librarian was leaning on the railing of the second level. Nobody had ever told Tyen the man's name, and it was hard to guess his age. His hair was silver-threaded, his back a little hunched and he wore lenses, but his face was not overly lined and his teeth were good.

"Good evening, Librarian. I'm after Professor Kilraker."

"He was here earlier. I'm afraid you have missed him. Is there anything I can help you with?"

Tyen opened his mouth to say "no", then hesitated. He could chase Kilraker around the Academy all night only to find Vella had been stolen in the meantime. The Librarian was in charge of the vault, so he ought to be warned of a possible theft attempt.

"Yes," Tyen said. He looked around, wondering how far his voice might carry. "Is there somewhere private we can talk?"

The Librarian's eyebrows rose. "My office. I'll come down."

As the man's footsteps on the floor above moved towards the stairs, Tyen wondered how he was going to convince him – or any of the professors – of his fears. And how much he would have to admit to. Warning the Academy might improve him in their eyes, but fraternising with Gowel might spoil any good regard he gained.

The Librarian descended the stairs and led Tyen between two bookshelves to a tiny office, furnished with a small desk and two chairs. Noting Tyen's expression, he smiled. "I need little private work space," he said, then gestured out of the door. "And if you consider the whole library as my work space then I have the largest office in the Academy." He gestured to a chair. "So, what is bothering you?"

"I have no solid proof," Tyen began as he sat down. "Only conclusions drawn from evidence that may be in part coincidental." He paused, then pushed on. "A man approached me today who is not a radical but associates with them, and offered to help me steal Ve— the book I found in Mailand."

The man's eyebrows rose again. "Did he really?"

"He said the Society of Magical Preservation could get into the vault – and at short notice, too."

"So you had told him the book was in the vault."

Tyen felt his face warming. "Ah . . . stupidly, yes."

The Librarian smiled again. "He seemed an ally? A sympathetic listener? Helpful, and made you wish to help him in return?" As Tyen nodded, he sighed. "The best beguilers always do, and smarter men than you and I have given away a little too much of far more important information for lesser reasons." He stood up. "Your discovery is safe."

"Are you sure?" Tyen bit his lip. "He seemed very certain."

The Librarian chuckled. "I can see I won't convince you unless I show you."

As the man stood up Tyen's heart skipped. Few students ever saw the vault, but not because it was forbidden. They were allowed inside in the company of a professor or the Librarian, usually for research purposes. Rising, Tyen followed the man out of the room and down the central aisle to the furthest wall. The Librarian opened one of five doors, all similarly sized and decorated. A flame of magic appeared in front of him and floated outward to reveal a small, round room with a domed ceiling – and no floor. Walls descended into darkness. The Librarian stepped past Tyen out into nothingness . . .

. . . but didn't fall. Instead he stood suspended, as if standing on an invisible floor. Looking closely, Tyen saw the ripple of air across the room and sensed the Soot forming around the Librarian in an aura of fine, radiating lines.

Seeing that aura, Tyen realised that the man was a sorcerer of some skill. Drawing magic in such a delicate pattern meant he would not deplete all the magic in one location at once. The finer the lines, the sooner the Soot would fade and be replaced by magic again, though it would be thinner overall in the room until the greater magical atmosphere evened out.

The Librarian beckoned. Ignoring a tingling anxiety, Tyen stepped onto the "floor". The resistance under his feet was slightly spongy, giving him the unwelcome impression he might sink through it at any moment. When they began to slowly descend he thought that they were – and gasped.

"Do not fear, Ironsmelter. We will not fall. You are a student of sorcery. Have you learned to elevate yourself yet?"

"Not officially."

"Unofficially?"

"It seemed prudent, since I was driving Kilraker's aircart on our recent expedition, to teach myself."

"A wise precaution." The Librarian chuckled. "Touch the wall, Ironsmelter."

Tyen obeyed. The surface was unmarked and slippery smooth.

"Hard to climb." The flame had followed them down, so that the ceiling above them was no longer visible and Tyen was unable to track how far they'd dropped. "Now we turn."

A floor of sorts rose to meet their feet. It was not flat, however, but curved. Like the inside of a tube, it curled to the right and upwards again.

"Someone might secure a rope in the doorway we passed through, but they would have nothing to attach one to, to get up the next section," the Librarian explained. He pointed up to the underside of the passage, where the wall briefly became the ceiling. A metal edge had been inserted into the stone, jagged and sharp. "If they used a very long rope and managed to throw the other end up over the next turn, the blade would cut it. Even if they managed to protect the rope or remove the blade, there's nothing at the other end for a grapple to catch onto, unless someone leaves the next door open." The Librarian's invisible platform carried them through the turn and up to another, that had them descending again. "The only way a non-sorcerer could enter the vault without magical help or incredible luck would be from a helper already at the vault. As for sorcerers . . ."

Another floor appeared below, but this time it was flat. As their feet touched the ground the Librarian turned to the outline of a doorway.

He brought a chain out from under his collar. On it was a tube with several lines of holes down its length. He inserted this into a hole in the door and twisted several times one way, then the other, then back again.

"The combination changes each time we open it," he told Tyen. "The formula is known by a select few."

With a soft sigh, the door swung outward. It was as thick as a man's thigh. They moved into a short passage, the Librarian closing the door behind him. Several small alcoves were set into the opposite wall, surrounding another door. Tyen was unable to see what the man did as he reached inside them.

"Again, a combination lock that just a few can work and only if the first door is closed," the Librarian told him.

At a clunk the man withdrew his hand. The door swung inward and the Librarian led Tyen into what looked like another library but one of more modest dimensions. It was a single, long room divided by thick, square columns and filled with cabinets rather than shelving, and enormous chests instead of reading tables. The chests were so large that Tyen could not see how they had ever been brought through the door.

So this is the vault. Normally Tyen would have been excited and full of curiosity. Few students ever saw the inside of the Academy's most secure room, and it was likely a few professors had never had good cause to venture down here either. Yet it seemed a cold and lonely place for Vella to end up. And while he should have been reassured by all the precautions that she was safe, he knew he wouldn't be until he laid eyes on her.

The cabinets were full of boxes of different sizes, each collection identical but for numbers on a small plate. The Librarian opened a door and lifted one out. He smiled at Tyen.

"No touching, of course."

The lid opened and Tyen felt his heart skip as he saw Vella lying within. She was separated from the inner walls of the box by a bed of cloth that made her look somehow cleaner and more like a treasured object. The hue of the Librarian's flame made her leather cover seem a little redder – or perhaps they had rubbed her with preserving oil.

"See? Still here," the Librarian added.

Tyen nodded. It was frustrating to be so close yet unable to give her some relief from the oblivion she was trapped in. Yet it was also a relief to see she was where she was supposed to be. *Ah, but I wish I could tell her she was safe, and that I am going to free her.* Perhaps she could sense his thoughts if he was close enough. He extended his senses, looking for that faint warmth that he remembered, or some stirring of her presence, but found nothing.

Sighing, he reluctantly forced himself to look at the Librarian and nod. The man closed the box and replaced it in the cabinet.

"So, do you find our protection adequate?" he asked, gesturing around the room.

Tyen smiled. "I do. I should not have doubted the Academy's vault would be secure. You will check on h— it, now and then, just to be sure?"

The Librarian's attention had moved away, however. He was staring at something past the nearest column and he frowned. "That's odd . . ." he said. "Stay here."

The man's sudden concern sent a thrill of anxiety through Tyen. The Librarian walked past the column to a chest. The lid was partly open and an object protruded from inside. As the man lifted it fully open, Tyen saw that the object was the corner of a piece of cloth. It slithered back inside and the Librarian sighed as he reached in and adjusted something within the chest. He closed the lid and returned to Tyen.

"Nothing to worry about. Some people are incapable of leaving things as they find them." He led Tyen back to the door. "What was I saying? Ah, yes. You were right to tell me. No vault can ever be inaccessible to thieves without being inaccessible to those who legitimately need to enter it. But I think that ours is secure enough, don't you agree?"

Tyen nodded. "Yes. I do."

They made the return journey in silence. Tyen could think of nothing to say now that his anxiety had proven unfounded, and the Librarian radiated a quiet satisfaction. Once in the library, he thanked the man then started back towards his room.

Passing a clock, he noted the time and felt a mild surprise. It was two hours past dinner, but it felt much later. It had been a long day, he decided. First the job search, then Gowel . . . What *had* Gowel been up to, by suggesting he could help Tyen steal Vella back? Was he testing Tyen, to see if he was willing to act against the Academy, and therefore be a potential recruit to the Society of Magical Preservation? Had his radical friends lied to him about their ability to steal from the Academy? The Librarian's words repeated in Tyen's mind: "*No vault can ever be inaccessible to thieves without being inaccessible to those who legitimately need to enter it.*"

Which meant that the thieves, if there were any, had to be those who already had access.

Tyen stopped. *Is the Librarian trying to tell me that one of the professors might try to steal her?*

He looked over his shoulder, even though the library was far behind. Surely the man had only been telling him that it was highly unlikely, even if it wasn't completely impossible.

Sighing, he turned away and continued walking. He would not sleep easily tonight. He'd now have fear to add to his loneliness, shame and worry over Vella. He wished he could talk to someone – someone who would tell him he was worrying about nothing. Miko? No, it was too soon. Neel? No, Neel had been avoiding him as if afraid the taint of disfavour would rub off on him.

Professor Kilraker? He should not disturb the man during his private hours. But Kilraker might want to know what his former friend had suggested. He would be a better judge of what Gowel was capable of, too. *Better to risk disturbing him than neglect to tell him. If he looks unconcerned I'll apologise and leave.* Changing direction, Tyen headed for the professor's quarters.

He was glad of his coat as he walked through the garden towards the building that provided on-grounds accommodation to professors. A clear night sky meant no insulating clouds blanketing the city, so the air was frosty. He'd heard that a heated underground tunnel allowed the professors to access the main buildings and return to their private quarters, but it was off-limits to students. Burying his hands in the pockets of his coat, he felt something smooth and metallic and wondered what it was before he remembered he'd taken Beetle on his job-seeking trip.

Kilraker's rooms were on the second level. The stairs and hall were empty, but he could hear muffled voices, laughter and even music from inside the rooms. He reached the professor's door and knocked. No response came for long enough that he was ready to assume the professor was out, but as he turned away he heard a noise from behind the door. He stopped and turned back in time as it opened. Kilraker regarded Tyen with an odd expression.

Tyen stepped back. "Is this a bad time, Professor . . .?"

"No." Kilraker shook his head. "I was just thinking about you, and here you are. What can I do for you at this time of night, Ironsmelter?"

Tyen resisted the urge to look around and make the secret nature of his visit obvious. "Can we talk privately?"

The professor hesitated, then opened the door wider. "Come in." He moved to a small table flanked by two reed-woven chairs and sat down. A flask and glasses sat on a tray – one with a finger's width of the dark liquor inside. "Dusky?"

He was already pouring a second glass, so Tyen answered with a nod and a shrug. Sitting down in the other chair, he looked around. The professors' suites were four times the size of the students' shared rooms, with separate bed- and bathrooms. Their servants lived, along with the general domestic staff, in a different area of the Academy. Kilraker's sitting room was filled with objects he had acquired on his various expeditions that were of no interest or value to the Academy. A few looked more precious, though. Tyen assumed those had been purchased by Kilraker from his own funds. It made for distracting surrounds, and each time Tyen dragged his eyes from one fascinating object he noticed another.

"What is this matter you wish to discuss?" Kilraker prompted.

Tyen tore his eyes away from a crudely made clay statue of a naked woman, her features highly exaggerated. "I ran into Gowel today. I thought you might want to know."

The professor's eyes narrowed. "I had heard he was in the city. What did he say?"

"He had heard that my lessons were suspended and was sympathetic."

Kilraker leaned back in his chair. "And?"

"He had also heard about the book," Tyen continued. "He said . . . and I don't know if he was testing me or was in earnest . . . that he could help me steal it back."

A faint smile curled the professor's lips. "He did, did he? That's Gowel for you. Did you accept?"

"I neither accepted nor refused. I was too shocked. Afterwards I was worried that he was not overstating his abilities."

"So you went to the library, and the Librarian took you to the vault to assure you how safe it was."

"Yes."

"Were you reassured?"

"Mostly. Something he said—"

A knock interrupted him. Kilraker's gaze snapped to the door and a worried frown creased his forehead before he adopted a calm expression and rose to answer it. As the door opened, Tyen heard Drem's voice.

"Are you ready, Professor?"

"Nearly. I have a visitor. Can you give us a few minutes?"

The servant's voice lowered. Kilraker glanced at Tyen. "A moment, Ironsmelter," he said, then slipped outside and closed the door.

Tyen took a sip of the dusky then set the glass down. Kilraker didn't seem overly concerned, and it was clear he was now interrupting the professor. Was there any other vital inform-ation to deliver? He considered. *No, I'd best leave him alone.* He stood up, but did not want to barge into a private conversation so he took the opportunity to have a closer look at Kilraker's collection. As he approached a cabinet he glanced at the open door to the bedroom and his gaze was arrested by several rectangular shapes.

Cases. The professor was leaving.

Another expedition, perhaps? It was odd that he had not informed his students, but then Tyen's lessons were suspended so why would he be told? Tyen turned away, not wanting to be caught staring at the personal contents of a man's luggage if that man returned, and set his gaze on the shelves. Some of the objects were strange, ugly things, and he could not see why anyone would want to collect them. Perhaps there was something magical about them? He sought the darkness of Soot, but there was the tiniest flicker of it coming from something stuffed under a black-etched tusk.

He leaned closer, then closer again. He could see the spine of a book. A book about the same size as . . . A chill went through him. His hand operated of its own accord. Even as he touched the book, he knew. It *felt* familiar.

"No," he whispered. "It's not possible."

As the pages fell open, words formed.

Tyen. Kilraker is setting you up to be blamed for stealing me.

He could not think, breathe or even move, so when the door opened he only had time to close the book.

"Ah," Kilraker said.

Tyen forced himself to look up at the man, hoping the hurt and fear didn't show in his face.

"Why?"

The professor spread his hands. "We knew Gowel was going to attempt to steal her, so we put a fake in the vault."

Liar, Tyen thought.

But then a more shocking thought came to him. What if Vella was lying? What if she had lied about being able to tell the truth? What if she would say anything, to avoid being locked away again?

Kilraker held his hand out for the book.

If I give it to him, and Vella is right, he'll shout out to draw witnesses, then claim I had stolen the book. It'll be his word against mine. But if he's telling the truth . . .

"No," Tyen found himself saying. "I'm keeping hold of it. We're going to the Director's office. I'll give it to him, and nobody else."

The professor stared at him wordlessly. Tyen wondered what

he was thinking. Was he annoyed and perplexed by Tyen's defiance? Or was he contemplating the fact that his larcenous plans had been discovered? Tyen hoped badly that it was the former, but then realised that it would mean Vella was the unreliable, dangerous object that the Academy feared. The disappointment would be preferable to Vella being right, however. Especially if the professor resorted to force to retrieve the book. Tyen didn't think he could stop him.

Kilraker smiled. "Well, you are wise to be cautious." He turned to the door. "Let's go and see him, then."

Relief and disappointment came at that. "Thank you," he said. "I want to trust you, but this last day has been . . ." He shook his head. "Very unsettling."

The professor opened the door and held it open for Tyen. Slipping Vella into his shirt, Tyen stepped past and out into the hall. Drem was waiting. The servant, who was wearing an aircart jacket, regarded him warily then, and at a murmur from Kilraker, moved into the suite. The professor looked relaxed as he led the way down the stairs, but as he reached the ground level he turned to continue down to the basement.

Tyen stopped. "Where are you going?"

Kilraker looked up and smiled. "You've not heard of our shortcut?"

The underground passage, Tyen recalled. Feeling foolish, he started after the professor again.

Instead of a basement, the stairs finished at a long corridor decorated as tastefully as any within the more refined Academy buildings. Paintings had been hung along the walls. Alcoves held statues. Lamps burned every twenty steps or so. Kilraker waited until Tyen caught up so they walked side by side.

"Where does the tunnel end?" Tyen asked.

"Near the hall."

Which would be convenient for events that required formal dress. The air was warm and not at all stale. Every hundred paces or so an opening led into a small stairwell, with a spiral staircase leading upwards.

"Where do they go?" Tyen could not resist asking.

"The gardens above. They are a precaution, in case of flood or fire."

Tyen could see the far end of the corridor in the distance. It was empty but for the two of them, and very quiet.

Kilraker sighed. "There is something I should tell you, Tyen, though I don't know how to since you are in no mood to believe me. The Academy intends to destroy Vella."

Tyen felt his heart drop to his stomach.

"Why would they? She is a rare and valuable object."

"Because she contains Academy secrets, thanks to you neglecting to tell us she could absorb our memories at a touch."

Tyen felt his face heat. "Oh. I meant to tell you but . . . well, by the time I had the chance it was too late."

Kilraker slowed to a stop and faced Tyen. "I don't agree with them," he said, his voice lowered. "That is why I swapped her for a facsimile."

A thrill of triumph went through Tyen at the admission of theft.

"Tyen, will you help me save her?" Kilraker asked.

Staring at the professor, Tyen felt hope war with suspicion.

"Vella says you were setting me up to take the blame." He blinked at a flash of insight. "That's why there was something out of place in the vault, wasn't it? To put me out of the Librarian's sight long enough that he couldn't say whether or not I had made the swap while his attention was elsewhere."

Kilraker's smile faded. "Ah. Well, I had to do something. If he swore he'd not taken his eyes off you everyone would believe him, and they'd consider who else had been in the vault recently. Of course, they'd never find her in your possession so they couldn't charge you."

"But I'd always be under suspicion. Nobody would trust me, or give me opportunities."

"A small price to free her. If you help me, I'll let you talk to her."

Tyen shook his head. "No. If she does contain dangerous secrets about the Academy we have to return her to the vault, then convince the Director she is too valuable to be destroyed."

"We won't get a chance to. They plan to destroy her tomorrow." Kilraker's expression was serious. "You have in Vella a source of learning greater than the Academy and a teacher better than all the professors combined. She is too valuable to risk that those fools won't see sense."

Tyen placed a hand against his chest where the book rested against his skin. *I can't let them kill her.* Vella had been right about Kilraker's intention to frame Tyen. What should he do? He undid a shirt button and drew her out. Opening the pages, he saw words starting to form.

Don't trust him.

Something invisible caught his wrists and tightened, almost jolting her out of his hands. Looking up, he saw Kilraker's gaze was fixed on Vella, his eyebrows low in concentration. Taking a step forward, he reached for her.

Tyen tightened his grip on the cover and tried to back away, but his hand was held in place. Kilraker's fingers snapped onto the pages and began to pull. Knowing he was about to lose his grasp on her, Tyen drew in magic and stilled the air around the professor's arm to cool it.

The air frosted. Tyen felt Kilraker's grip falter as his muscles chilled. The force holding his arm weakened as the man's concentration wavered and Tyen felt triumph as he managed to pull away, staggering backwards a few steps. Tyen looked up and his gaze locked with Kilraker's. The professor's face twisted in a scowl and he launched himself at Tyen.

The attack was both magical and physical; Tyen fended off both with a solid shield of stilled air. Cursing as his knuckles cracked against this, Kilraker stepped back again.

Then Soot filled the tunnel behind him and Tyen's shield began to shake and vibrate.

Standing frozen, Tyen widened his protective wall, so appalled that his teacher was actually striking hard enough to kill that he could not think what else to do. He'd never fought in a real magical battle before, though he'd read about plenty. Then a blackness formed around him, like a warning shot to his senses that jolted his mind out of its shock. The magic around him was diminishing and if he didn't move he would soon be unable to defend himself.

It was a typical battle situation, he recalled. If one did not defeat the other through skill or trickery, combatants eventually used up all the magic within their reach. They had to move to a fresh source before they used what they'd taken. The only direction Tyen could move in the tunnel was backwards.

The professor might also reach around Tyen's shield to take all the magic behind him. Tyen had two defences against that: take that magic first, or retreat faster. Or better still, do both.

He backed away, robbing the space he moved into as he did. Kilraker followed. To Tyen's relief, the professor had stopped attacking. Perhaps the man had run out of magic. Tyen briefly considered a return volley. *No*, he decided. *I can't risk that. I might kill him. I don't want to. I don't think I need to yet. And besides, it's up to the Academy to punish its own.*

"What's going on here?"

Not letting his shield fall, Tyen glanced over his shoulder. Three men were hurrying towards them. One was the professor of sorcery from the meeting with the Director, Hapen. The other two were from another department.

"He—" Tyen began.

"Stop him!" Kilraker shouted. "He has stolen the artefact from the vault!"

The three men looked down at Vella. The professor of sorcery scowled.

"The sooner we destroy that thing the better!"

"I didn't—" Tyen's words were choked off as a force wrapped around his chest. He saw the radiating lines around Professor Hapen. *I'm trapped*, he thought. *Can't even speak.* And the man's words had confirmed Kilraker's claim. The Academy did intend to kill Vella.

He couldn't let that happen. But what could he do? He was trapped. Then he remembered the stairway leading to the surface. A way out, if he could get loose.

And then what? Run away? Lose everything he'd worked for?

His stomach sank as he realised he'd lost it already. From the way the three newcomers regarded him, it was clear they believed he was a thief. What chance did he have to convince them otherwise when it would be Kilraker's word against his?

He should stay and fight to clear his name and prove that Kilraker was the real thief, but he would never manage it before Vella was destroyed. If he left he could find a safe place for her, then return to sort things out here.

If he could get away from Hapen.

He was surrounded by Soot, which meant he had only the magic he had taken but not yet used. Unless he could reach further.

Taking a deep breath, he stretched out. He reached beyond the tunnel walls. He reached past the four men closing in on him. He reached below the ground and up towards the sky from which he had so often sensed magic billowing down.

He was a little surprised to discover how far he could stretch, when he really tried.

Then he drew all the magic in. Some he channelled out to throw off the force restraining him. Some he shaped into a shield. Blows rained upon it as he dashed towards the nearest stairwell. Shouts filled the tunnel and their echoes chased him up the stairs, which were too short and fussy for what was supposed to be a quick escape. A circular groove in the ceiling suggested a hatch of some kind, but it did not budge as he pushed against it.

"Just as well there isn't a flood or fire," he muttered as he shaped more magic, smashing the hatch upward. Climbing out, he found himself in the middle of a flower bed, the hole through which he'd climbed an ugly wound in the arrangement. Hearing sounds of pursuit in the tunnel, he chose a direction and ran, stumbling over the garden edging onto a path and narrowly avoiding two servants hurrying past.

I'm in the gardens somewhere between the professors' apartments and the hall. Where now? Out of the Academy? Which way will they expect me to go? To the closest exit. So he should go a different way. The path he was on was taking him towards the professors' apartments. They wouldn't expect him to go there. But it was straight and as soon as his pursuers climbed out of the hatch they'd see him. He dashed down the next side path. It was a narrower one that wound around to the back of the building.

At one of the turns it gave him a glimpse of the area he was heading for. He skidded to a halt. Behind the professors' apartments was a flat and featureless pavement that offered no cover at all.

Then he saw what waited there, capsule inflated and ready to fly.

And he swallowed a laugh as he leapt into a run again.

PART TWO

RIELLE

CHAPTER 1

A s the doors of the temple opened, the bright sunlight turned all to white. Rielle followed her companions out, locating them mostly by the sound of their voices. Even when her eyes had adjusted, the paved courtyard seemed leached of colour and the heat set the mud-rendered houses shimmering.

"Uh. It's *horrible* outside," Bayla muttered. "I wish we could go straight home."

"It won't be so bad in the market," said her twin, Tareme. She turned to Rielle. "Would you like to come along?"

Rielle smiled in gratitude at the invitation. "I'd like to, but I can't. My aunt is expecting me."

"But Ako will be there. He said he'd like to see you again. He must have found you interesting."

Rielle kept her smile intact with an effort. She wasn't the slightest bit interested in the twins' brother. Any respect she'd had for him had died after she'd had to fend off his amorous advances during a silly hide and hunt garden game at their birthday celebration. The twins didn't know about that, however. Nobody else had been around to witness his behaviour, and he was bound to deny it if she complained. Unable to explain why she now despised him, she could only pretend simple disinterest. It was fine for the twins to talk about their

121

brother's flaws, but not polite for anyone outside a family to criticise their relatives. Especially for women to.

"I'm surprised to hear that," she replied. "Though he probably has me mixed up with someone else. He seemed to mistake me for someone hired as entertainment."

Tareme grinned. "His habit is to act before he thinks. It is a part of his charm. He has a great enthusiasm for life, don't you think?"

She shrugged. *Life? No, his enthusiasm is for something a little more specific. But, then, I suppose he's not specific when it comes to which women he is enthusiastic about.*

"Enjoy the market," she said. "See you next quarterday."

As the two girls strode down the stairs and off across the courtyard, Rielle felt a pang of regret. She was looking forward to a painting lesson with her aunt that afternoon, but an invitation to join the other girls after temple classes was rare and more than she had hoped for when she'd first started attending. In the beginning, most of the girls' first conversations with her had been about their surprise and relief that she didn't smell bad.

They were all from the most powerful and wealthy families in Fyre. Rielle's was also wealthy but not so well regarded, thanks to the reputation that clung to those who worked in the dyeing trade. Of course, Rielle had never actually done any of the dirtier work. Her parents hired other families to do it, providing them with housing and food along with income. Their generous donations to the temples guaranteed that no one would openly ostracise them for their unclean profession, but Fyre's great families had other, subtler ways to exclude people they didn't approve of.

The trouble was, the most memorable fact about dyeing was that the substances that produced the best colours were so often the most repulsive and odorous. Urine and faeces, extracts of sea creatures, rotting vegetation and crushed insect larvae were the worst of them. Even the mordants and fixers were harsh to the nose – and some of them poisonous. All good reasons why dyers must, by law, establish their premises on the outskirts of a town or city, downriver from the rest of the inhabitants.

That meant it was a long walk home from the temple, unfortunately. She tugged her scarf up over her head and tossed the corner tassels over her shoulders. It was too hot to tie it close to her throat, and most of the girls in the small city considered a tied scarf too matronly. Still, she'd have to fasten it properly before she got home, or her mother would lecture her on modesty.

Nobody is around to see anyway, she reasoned as she checked that her purse was tucked safely inside her skirt and under her tunic. She crossed the courtyard and started for home. Temple Road, one of the main streets of Fyre, would take her most of the way. It was one of the busiest routes, but at this time on a quarterday, between the morning lessons and worship and the afternoon market, even this thoroughfare was quiet. And as the fourth set of four days – the end of a halfseason – it was a day the more pious of the city's citizens spent at home fasting and praying.

Odd how this made her feel less safe, as if the threat from thieves was greater where fewer witnesses were around. From what she'd heard, robbery was more likely to occur in a crowd where everyone was distracted.

Ahead, a young priest stepped out into the road, and she relaxed. It was Sa-Gest, the reedy young priest she had seen about the temple. The other girls mocked him when he was not around. His grey robes, darker under the arms and around the neckline from sweat, marked him as a lower ranking member of the order. He hurried into the next side street.

Curious, she looked down the street as she passed and saw him striding away.

The streets were busier than the main road. Perhaps they offered more shade and therefore more relief from the heat. She had explored the maze of them many times in the company of her cousin Ari, before he left to join her brother in the importation side of the dyeing business. Many were shaded by awnings like the stalls at the market, but woven with intricate designs. There were courtyards and shops where streets intersected, and people sat on rustic furniture or bench seats built into the sides of the mud-rendered walls to eat, drink and gossip.

In this part of the city, known as the artisans' quarter, the awnings were patterned with black thread and woven by the occupants of the houses. The houses were painted in bold, bright hues. A new coat of mud and colour was applied once a year ready for the Festival of Angels. The next festival was a halfseason away, and most houses had faded dramatically in the last eight or so quarterdays as the stronger summer sun bleached them.

Despite the easy pace she'd set she was already sweating. She longed for a breeze, but when she passed another side street and felt an eddy surround her it was full of grit and warmth. She was tempted to walk faster just to get out of the heat and to a drink of fresh water sooner.

As she continued on, another, older priest emerged a few streets ahead, this time heading towards her. This one she didn't know, but his grey-blue robes told her he was a more senior priest – the closer to the Angels' colour the higher the rank. His grey-streaked hair was damp with sweat. If he noticed her at all she could not tell. From his distracted expression, she gathered his thoughts were on more pressing matters.

At last she reached Tanner Street, a thoroughfare that would shorten her journey home by cutting a straighter line across a loop of Temple Road. She knew her mother would prefer her to stay on the main road, but her cousin had told her that plenty of people used the short cut so she should be safe so long as she did not stray from it. More people were using it than Temple Road, she noted. Keeping to the narrow strip of shade to one side, she made sure she looked alert and confident. Behaving meek and afraid appealed only to those looking for an easy victim, Ari had taught her.

A few hundred paces along, a blackness billowed out of a side alley and blocked her path.

She froze as she recognised it, then quickly bent one knee and adjusted her shoe in the hope that anybody watching her would think this was the reason for her stopping.

Stain! She had rarely sensed it outside the temple, and then only after a temple procession. It had been after one such procession, when Rielle had tried to touch the lingering after-effect of the priest's magic, that her aunt had discovered her little niece could sense it.

"*You must always pretend you can't see it,*" Narmah had warned. "*And never tell anybody that you can, no matter how much you trust them. Don't write it down. Don't even say it aloud when you think nobody can hear. If the priests find out, they'll take you away.*" Rielle had asked if this would mean she would get to learn magic. "*Women don't become priests. Only men approved by the Angels can,*" her aunt had told her, so uncharacteristically severe that Rielle never dared to do anything her aunt had warned her against.

Everybody knew what caused Stain. A priest must have used magic – and a lot of it. He must be somewhere further down the side street since she could see no priest on Tanner Street.

So I can't stand here adjusting my shoe for ever or he'll notice me. I'm going to have to walk on. Which meant walking through the Stain. She knew it wouldn't harm her, but the thought repelled her. It was, after all, the taint that magic left behind. Priests undertook secret rituals of cleansing to counter the effects. She did not have that knowledge. Crossing to the other side of the street to avoid it would be too obvious, however. Taking a deep breath, she made herself walk towards it. She resisted looking down the side alley to see what the priest was up to, took a deep breath and held it.

Then gasped as she collided with something hard and invisible.

Something grabbed her arm and yanked her to one side. Her first thought was that Stain wasn't supposed to be solid. The second was that at least she hadn't betrayed herself when she had gasped, as the priest must expect anyone walking into a solid wall to notice. The third thought, as she stared at the man holding her arm, was that this was no priest.

Instead he was a shabby, dirt-grey creature with wild eyes. In one hand was a knife and she flinched as he thrust it at her face.

"Shut up. Say nothing. Do what I say," he snapped. "Understand."

She stared at the knife, mouth dry and heart pounding, and nodded.

He turned and dragged her down the alley after him. Her body responded by losing all strength and she nearly staggered to her knees, but he hauled her up and onward. So much for Ari's opinion about the safety of Tanner Street. So much for being alert and confident. What should she do now? What would he do, once he stopped? Rob her?

The alley was empty. If he was quick, he could have her purse before anyone came along. But he wasn't stopping. Her stomach swooped. He must want something more. She could not help imagining the worst. Cold fear made her knees weak again. She had always told herself that she would rather die than *that*. That she would fight. She'd imagined throwing off attackers, even dragging them to the priests for punishment. But his grip was like iron and he hauled her along as if she weighed nothing. Despite being thin and not much bigger than her, he was stronger.

You're weaker than him, but you might be smarter, she told herself. *So think!*

Somehow she made her mind stop spinning and consider what she knew of him. Remembering the Stain, her blood went cold. There had been no priest around and nobody else close by, so only this man could have used magic.

He was a tainted. It meant he had chosen to learn how to use magic. It meant he was willing to steal that magic from the Angels. It meant he did not care that they would see its taint on his soul when he died, and tear it apart. What could make someone choose such a fate? Having given up his soul, what other terrible things might he be willing to do? How much more terrible could they be, with magic at his command?

Fear rushed through her, but it was tempered by another thought. If the blotchiness of the Stain he'd left was any indication, he had no skill with magic. The Stain the priests made was different – a radiating halo.

In theory, she could use magic, too. Anyone who could see Stain could, but she had no idea how and even if she used it to save her life, she would see no afterlife.

She might face a choice between death and eternal death.

Before she could begin to contemplate that, he slowed to approach a cross street, peering around the corner before he pulled her after him. He was watching out for something. Or someone. She instantly thought of the priests she'd seen earlier. Out on a hot day when they would prefer to be in the cool temple. Her heart swelled with hope. Were they looking for the tainted? Were they close? Was rescue only a few street corners away?

Was this why he had abducted her? Was she a hostage, an innocent he would threaten to kill if they cornered him?

Approaching another intersection, the man peered down the cross street then recoiled. He stepped past her and hauled her back the way they'd come. Rielle drew a breath to yell at whoever he was running from, then let it out again. What if all he was doing was trying to avoid passing other people? She might lead someone into danger.

He dragged her on, his grip never loosening. Gritting her teeth, she silently drew up all the curses her cousin had taught her. The mildest had earned her a good slap from her mother once when she'd tried them out for herself, wrongly believing she was alone. Speaking them in her mind somehow made her feel steadier, the terror that had weakened her receding to a simmering fear.

To her surprise, he began to drag her along populated streets. The people they passed were either indifferent or showed an interest that reminded her of some of her parents' clients – all calculation and greed. The walls were painted, but the colour was cracked and coming off in flakes. Shutters hung crookedly from window frames. A smell almost as bad as the mingled odour of the dye pits permeated everything. Fragrant smoke from burners did not mask it.

I'm in the poor quarter, she realised, simultaneously amazed and dismayed that they had come so far. *Surely the priests are far away.*

Yet the man did not relax. He kept to the quieter streets, still checking before turning corners or emerging into cross-roads. This had begun to feel needlessly obsessive to her when he suddenly backed away from an intersection and, casting about, stepped into the alcove of a doorway. He yanked the scarf from her head and turned her so she faced outward, taking hold of the waistband of her skirt to prevent her from fleeing.

Something sharp pressed against her ribs and she froze.

"Stay still. Say nothing. Draw no attention to yourself."

She stood as still as she could. Glancing back down the street, she realised the women they'd passed, hovering in every third or fourth doorway, were not wearing scarves either. They were dressed in fabric so thin that the brown of their skin was visible through the undyed cloth. A man leaned against the wall further down the street, talking to one of them.

A figure stepped into the space where the roads crossed and her abductor's grip tightened. The priest looked out of place in his blue robes. She didn't know this one. He was taller and older than Sa-Gest and his robe colour indicated a higher rank. As he looked down the alley his gaze flickered over Rielle without pausing. She expected disgust, but his expression only conveyed amusement.

Looking back down the crossroad, he shook his head. A thrill of hope went through Rielle as his attention returned to the street she was in, and he started towards her.

Help me, she thought at him as he passed, but she was conscious of the blade pressed against her ribs and stayed silent. The priests looked her up and down and kept walking. The other women did not seem at all shamed by his gaze, and simpered at him. Disgusted, Rielle looked away. *As if a priest would be interested in their services.* She heard him stop and ask one if she had seen a lean, grubby man hiding nearby. The woman said that described a lot of people around there. He turned away and continued down the alley.

Looking back at the intersection, she considered how the priest had looked back down the cross street and shaken his head. Had the gesture been directed at someone further down the street? Another priest, perhaps?

A slim hope stirred. A plan formed. It was risky, but she decided it was worth it.

"Is he gone?" the abductor asked.

She glanced back. The priest had disappeared around a corner. "Yes."

The sharp edge was withdrawn from her ribs and he grabbed her arm again. Pushing past her, he moved to the intersection and started to peer around the corner.

"I think he's coming back," she lied. "Yes, he is." He glanced back but she turned to hurry after him and blocked his sight. "Hurry!" she whispered, pushing him gently forward.

He took a step out into the crossroads. She followed then pretended to trip and fall, crying out as she dropped to her knees. Looking down the side street in the direction the priest had nodded, she saw an older priest – the one she'd passed earlier – looking over his shoulder at her. Her abductor cursed her and began to haul her up.

Blackness blossomed around the priest.

It was the halo of Stain she had seen so many times before – the same radiating lines that surrounded the Angels painted on the temple walls, except in white, as if she had stared at the holy images for a while then closed her eyes to see them reversed behind her eyelids.

The hand slipped from her arm. A choked yell came from above her, echoing in the narrow space. The knife clattered to the pavement. She turned to see her abductor clutching at his throat. Held by invisible, holy magic.

Guessing it was dangerous to be between the priest and his prisoner, she crawled to the wall.

Stain billowed around her abductor like ink dropped in water.

"No," the priest said. "We'll have none of that."

The suspended man shrieked and writhed. Rielle's stomach plunged and she got to her feet and hauled herself into the alley again only to find herself facing the blue-robed priest.

His eyes narrowed in recognition, then he gestured behind

him with a jab of his thumb. "Get out of the way, but don't leave."

Rielle hurried past him, then slowed as she neared the women. The prostitutes were watching the man writhing at the end of their street with fascination. *He said not to leave. Where should I wait?* As the screaming behind her stopped she felt a wave of relief and dizziness.

Hands grabbed her shoulders and steadied her. Startled, she looked up to see that the man who had been talking to one of the prostitutes had caught her. He smiled. *What a nice smile*, she found herself thinking. He was young, but not as young as she was. She took in his dark, straight hair, well-balanced brows, cheekbones and jaw before she lowered her eyes. *He's very handsome.* Or did it only seem so because his was the first friendly face she'd seen in hours?

"That was very smart, what you did, Ais," he said.

She blinked in disbelief. "It was?"

"Yes." He turned to look back down the street. "Looks like he's giving up."

Rielle followed his gaze. Her abductor was now lying face down on the ground. The two priests stood on either side, surrounded by Stain. She resisted the urge to avert her eyes. It was as if all the light and colour around them had been burned away.

"Please! I didn't mean to learn anything," the man on the ground whined. "I was tricked!"

"There is always a choice," the older priest replied.

The man's head sank to the ground. "It was worth it," he said in a voice so quiet Rielle barely heard it. "If I die now, it is still worth it."

"Get up," the priest said.

"Get it over with. Kill me."

"That is not your decision to make." The older priest nodded at the younger, who stepped forward and hauled their prisoner to his feet. Then looked down the alley. Rielle flinched as he met her eyes. Leaving the younger priest, the older priest approached, his brow creasing into a frown.

"I am Sa-Elem. Are you harmed, Ais?"

She shook her head.

"What is your name?"

"Rielle Lazuli."

His eyebrows rose. "The daughter of Ens Lazuli. How did you come to be in the company of the tainted?"

"I was walking home from temple classes when he grabbed me. He forced me to go with him. He has a knife."

"Not any longer." The priest glanced around. "We cannot abandon you here, in unfamiliar streets, but we must deal with the tainted first. I'm afraid you will have to accompany us back to the temple."

All the way back to the temple? "I . . . I'm sure I can find my way. I just want to go home. My family will be worried."

The priest frowned. "But you must surely wish to be escorted, after what you have endured?"

"I . . ." Rielle paused, unsure what she wanted. The desire not to walk the streets alone was as strong as the need to go home.

"Might I escort Ais Lazuli, Sa-Elem?" the handsome man asked.

The priest frowned at him. "And you are?"

"Izare Saffre."

"The painter." The priest nodded, and looked at Rielle. "I suppose in this exceptional circumstance it would be acceptable, if the young woman is willing to have you as an escort."

Rielle nodded. "I am."

"Then be sure to take her home directly, Aos Saffre. We will need to question her."

"I promise to deliver her promptly and unharmed."

That appeared to satisfy the priest. "No need to leave the safety of your home again, Ais Lazuli," he assured her. "We'll visit once the tainted is secure."

Rielle nodded again. "I'll let father know you are coming."

He traced a blessing in the air, then joined the other priest, who was holding her abductor by the arm as firmly as the man had held her. The sound of cheers and approving whistles surrounded her and she looked around to see that people were leaning out of windows and peering from doors.

"Well, you heard what he said," Izare said, giving her a smile as dazzling as his earlier one. "I'm to take you straight home. Follow me."

CHAPTER 2

After they had been walking for several minutes, Izare turned to her. "Thanks to you the city is safe again."

Rielle looked away. "I had no idea a tainted was free in the city."

"Priests have been hunting him for weeks." He gestured to a side street. "This way."

Earlier he'd led her straight through the lingering Stain left by the priests. With no choice but to follow, Rielle had held her breath as she stepped into the darkness. Unlike in her earlier encounter, she'd felt no resistance. Relieved, she'd trailed behind Izare, feeling a little shy of this handsome stranger. The streets were only wide enough here for two people to pass anyway, and she didn't want to block the way for oncoming traffic. But as they reached wider streets Izare slowed until she walked beside him.

He is very good-looking, she mused. *And it's not just because he was a friendly face at the end of an ordeal.* His hair was straight and black, his flawless skin the same hue as the stormwood shavings the dyeworks used to make a rich gold-brown. As he glanced at her she noted that his eyes were a tawny yellow-green. He moved with an unconscious grace, arms swinging. When he turned away again she looked closer, wondering what it was about the shape of his face that made it so appealing. Was it the high cheekbones? The angle of his jaw?

He met her gaze again. "How are you feeling? You seem remarkably well recovered."

"Do I?" Rielle shrugged. "I'm alive. That's something to be happy about. Though . . ."

"Though . . .?"

She shook her head. "I'm also a little disappointed."

"Disappointed?" His eyebrows rose.

"In myself. I always imagined I'd do better, if something like that happened to me."

"You tricked him into stepping in sight of a priest. It was very brave of you."

"Yes, but before then I didn't even try to fight him. His grip was so strong."

"Men are usually stronger than women," Izare pointed out. "You could hardly expect to fight him. Instead you were smarter. You could have panicked, or not done anything to risk his anger, but you didn't."

She sighed. "I suppose you're right. I only . . . I wish I was stronger."

He grinned. "Then you would be all big arms and bulging muscles. I have to say, I'm glad you are not. You are . . ." He stopped abruptly, stepped back and examined her. "Not beautiful but pleasing. Well-proportioned. Tall enough to give your limbs grace yet not too thin. Your face . . ." – he moved closer, staring at her intently – ". . . is *interesting*. Not a classic shape but . . . unique. Rewarding to those who take the time to look again."

Nobody had ever dared to speak to her, the daughter of a wealthy family, so plainly before. Conflicting feelings rose: hurt and the beginnings of outrage at his directness and honesty, amusement that he was right that she was not beautiful. Her skin was too light a brown and her nose too straight. Yet as he'd described her face his voice had softened and his strange praise sent a shiver through her that was both discomforting and pleasant.

He straightened. "I'm sorry. I have made you self-conscious. It is a bad habit and a consequence of my profession. Let's continue."

"Your profession? Ah. You are a painter," she recalled as they started walking again.

"Yes."

"What do you paint?"

"Whatever people pay me to paint. Mostly spirituals. Occasionally portraits."

Spirituals were the backdrops to the small altars every household in Fyre maintained. Even foreigners who did not follow the same traditions purchased them so that their guests could perform the rituals. Aunt Narmah had painted the one in Rielle's home, choosing a night scene, which was the time when the Angels were at their quietest and most communicative. The sky was coloured an intense dark blue that could only be achieved using a rare, expensive pigment from distant Surlan that was more expensive than gold and told visitors of the family's wealth as well as its piety.

Cheaper spirituals painted in less pricey hues were sold in the market. Did Izare produce some of those? The priest, Sa-Elem, had recognised his name, however, which suggested better-quality work.

"Do you paint for pleasure, too?" she asked.

"When I have the time."

"What do you paint then?"

"My friends and . . . well, anybody I can persuade to sit for me. What about you?"

"My aunt, the workers," she told him. "Objects around the house. The view across the river. Only for pleasure, of course."

He blinked in surprise. "You paint?"

"Yes. My aunt teaches me. She's very good."

Izare nodded, but his attention had shifted away as they emerged from the poor quarter onto a wider road. Rielle recognised it as Temple Road, and stopped.

"Ah. I know where I am, now. I can continue on my own, if you need to return to your work."

"Oh, when I make a promise I keep it," he told her. But he did not move, and was looking at her thoughtfully. "I would very much like to paint your portrait, Ais Lazuli."

She stared at him in astonishment, but as he met her eyes and smiled she had to look away. Putting a hand up to lift her scarf over her head, she found no sign of the light material and felt a stab of alarm.

"Oh! My scarf! I must have lost it."

"You were wearing one when I first saw you." He looked back the way they came. "I will search for it after I see you home."

"No, I must go back. If mother sees me without it she'll be furious."

She took a step towards the poor quarter, but he stepped in front of her. "I think you have a very good excuse and, besides, Sa-Elem said you were to go straight home. It's only a scarf and I'm sure a girl like you has plenty more."

Her face warmed at his casual reference to her family's wealth. He was right, though. Drawing in a deep breath, she turned to face home. As they walked she considered what Sa-Elem might ask her when he eventually turned up. He would want to know how she had come to be abducted.

She couldn't tell him about the Stain she had seen, but she didn't think she'd need to. While seeing Stain was not forbidden – her aunt had been stretching the truth when she'd told Rielle that the priests would take her away – if the priests learned that she could they would always be checking to see if Rielle had learned to use magic. If it became publicly known, her family's trade might be affected. People avoided those who could see Stain. Some thought the ability was passed down through family lines and others thought it was a punishment for a sinful nature. Either way, it limited a person's marriage prospects.

Remembering how the tainted had screamed, she shuddered. Why anyone would learn magic, she couldn't imagine. Thanks to Stain, it was impossible to hide the use of magic. Eventually the priests would find you, and nobody truly knew what happened then. Tainted people were taken out of Fyre to a place across the desert.

Sa-Elem was only half of the source of her worries, though. Her mother was going to be horrified to hear how her daughter had been dragged through the poor quarter. She might forbid Rielle from walking home alone from temple classes again, sending one of the servants to accompany her. Probably one of the dyers, who would confirm everything the girls in temple lessons thought about dye workers smelling bad. *That's a little unfair. Everyone cleans up when they need to and they can't help it that some odours linger.* But Mother would probably remember at the last moment and whoever she sent wouldn't have time to wash. Everyone was busy preparing for the coming Festival, not least her parents.

"So," Izare said, breaking the silence. "Will you pose for me?"

Rielle looked at him sideways, amused that he had asked again. "Looking for a new client, are you?"

"I would paint you free of charge."

She regarded him with unconcealed disbelief. He smiled. *What is he playing at?* she wondered. *Does he truly want to paint my portrait, or is he hoping to gain something by flattering me?*

"I doubt my mother would approve," she replied.

"You *doubt* it. That's a start. Doubting does not erase the possibility."

"Perhaps it would be more accurate to say: 'Mother will *never* approve'," she corrected. "Therefore I cannot accept."

She expected him to be annoyed by the rebuttal, but he merely sighed and nodded. "Is there no situation in which she would allow you to sit for your portrait?"

"None comes to mind."

"Well, you must let me know as soon as it does. Is that your home ahead?"

Looking up, she saw the familiar walls of the dyeworks coming into view. A rush of longing went through her. "Yes."

"To think that I have passed it so many times not knowing that such an intriguing woman existed within."

She raised her eyebrows at the flattery. He grinned. "Too much?"

"Definitely."

He laughed. "You have brothers, haven't you? No woman is immune to praise that does not have a sibling to blame for it."

"A cousin. My brother is much older than I, so we didn't play together as children."

"I would like to meet this cousin."

"If you think he'd like a portrait done you'll be disappointed. He runs the ordering side of the business, finding dyes and fabric to import and making sure they get here."

"So you are all alone?"

"Of course not. I have my family."

"Nobody your own age at home, though."

His words brought an unexpected pang of sadness. She did miss Ari, and all the children of the dye workers her age now spent most of their time working in the pits or looking after their young families, or had left to live with their new husbands. *And I'll be doing the latter soon if Mother has her way.* Finding a husband was the main reason she was going to temple lessons.

By meeting girls her age and of the right class her parents hoped she might meet eligible men among their brothers and cousins.

And Izare is definitely not from the right class.

She shook her head at the thought. *Why did I even think that? I've only just met him. I don't even know if I like him. Is it because he's good-looking, or I am fool to flattery?* She frowned. *And wasn't he negotiating with a prostitute when I first saw him?*

They had reached the dyeworks now. As they walked towards the shop door, it flew open. Rielle flinched as her mother strode out.

"Rielle! Where have you been? Where is your scarf?" Mother's eyes moved to Izare. "Who are you?" she asked in a more restrained tone.

Izare bowed. "My name is Izare Saffre. I offered to escort your daughter home after she was rescued by the priests."

She stared at him, then her gaze shifted to Rielle. "Rescued?"

"I was . . . It was . . . It's a long story." Rielle sighed. "Sa-Elem will be visiting later to explain."

Her mother's eyebrows rose and she looked at Izare again. "Well, then. I suppose you'll be wanting—"

"—to leave now that I have seen your daughter safely home. Farewell, Ais Lazuli," Izare finished. He bowed to Rielle, then turned and walked away.

Her mother looked uneasy as she watched him go. "What was his name again?"

"Izare Saffre."

"I suppose we can find and reward him, if he did rescue you."

Which is why he left so abruptly. He doesn't want one. After all, he didn't rescue me, the priests did. Once again, her mother hadn't been paying attention. In fact, she looked as if she might run after him, so Rielle stepped around her. "I'd better clean up before the priests arrive."

Narmah stood in the shop doorway, her expression anxious. "Are you unharmed?" her aunt asked.

"Yes. Unless you consider embarrassment an injury."

"Did I hear right? Something happened to you and the priests are coming? And why aren't you wearing your scarf?"

Rielle smiled. "Yes, you heard right, but it's nothing to be alarmed about. I'll tell you all about it, once we're inside."

CHAPTER 3

The stones and dust that poured out of the jar onto the grinding bowl were a rich brown. Narmah seized the smooth round rock and began crushing.

"Get to work," she told Rielle.

Looking down at the thick slab of polished stone before her, Rielle sighed. "You said we were going to paint."

"No time for that now, but we may as well put what we have left to good use."

Taking down a jar from the shelves, Rielle measured out some of the chalk within and dumped it on the mixing slab. She added the tree sap, thankfully already pulverised, and mixed it in with a scraper. By the time it was well combined Narmah had swept the results of her grinding through a filter and into a smaller jar. Taking this, Rielle measured out the pigment and added it to the mound of powder, stirring it all together. Next she added water and a dash of nectar to preserve, working with the scraper until all the powder was wet. The mix was now a gritty blood-red paste. Picking up the refiner, she set the large head down, seized the handle in both hands and began to grind.

Though it was hard, boring work, today Rielle found the motions calming. She let her thoughts circle along with her movements. Memories of the day flashed through her mind all out of order: the wall of blotchy Stain that had spilled out across her path, Izare's smile, the priest pushing past her in the poor quarter, the tainted writhing and screaming.

She stopped. The paint had spread out over the slab in a thin, red smear. She pushed it to the centre with a scraper and began grinding again.

It had been horrible seeing the man suffer, but the priest had done it to stop him using magic, no more. He *had* learned something he knew to be forbidden. He had stolen from the Angels. He'd dragged her around the poor quarter . . . though why she could only guess. Had he hoped to use her as a hostage, if he was cornered? It was the most likely reason, she decided. Would the priests have let him go to avoid harm coming to her? Would he have taken her with him, to ensure they didn't follow?

She shuddered and paused to scrape the paint to the centre again.

Despite everything, she couldn't help feeling some sympathy for the man. He must have grown up, like her, knowing he could do something that was forbidden. But that was the only similarity between them. He had succumbed to the temptation. As a child she had wondered what she might be able to do with magic and wished she was free to find out, but whenever she had looked at the paintings of the Angels in the temple and on spirituals and heard stories of their kindness, she wanted so badly to meet one that she knew she would do nothing to anger them.

Looking down at the growing swirls of paint, she remembered the Stain created by the abductor. Had he observed her noticing it? Would he tell the priests? Would they believe him? With the scraper, she moved the paint into a puddle at the centre then pushed the refiner over it again. If he had and they did there was nothing she could do about it.

The priests had cleansing rituals to erase the taint of using magic from their souls. She had once longed to be a priest and thought it unfair that women were barred from the role, but that wish had faded. Life held other attractions. Love. Children. Painting. Izare's face rose in her memory and she nearly laughed aloud. He was interesting, but not as a prospective husband. She was mostly curious to see his work.

"What are you smiling at?" Narmah asked.

Rielle shook her head. "Nothing."

"Nothing, eh? It's never nothing when someone smiles like that." She was continuing to grind down the pigment, stopping to filter it into the jar. "It's that young man who walked you home, isn't it?"

"Yes and no. I was wondering how good he is at painting."

"Izare Saffre? Oh, he's very good."

Rielle stopped grinding and turned to stare at her aunt. "You've seen his work?"

Narmah smiled. "So have you. He did the paintings at our local temple."

"*He* did those?" Rielle felt a shiver run down her spine. The smaller local temple had been built a few years ago, a few streets away from the dyeworks. Since then Rielle's family attended the regular ceremonies and sacrifices there. Rielle would have preferred to have lessons there, too, but the girls from families her mother wanted her to associate with went to the main one.

The paintings had amazed Rielle when she first saw them. The Angels were so real she sometimes felt sure they were about to move and speak. The sun was coloured so cleverly that she wanted to shield her eyes, and the storm clouds loomed with a tangible sense of threat.

Her mother did not like them, saying they were too unconventional. Which only made Rielle love them more.

Turning back to her grinding, Rielle pushed the refiner in circles and found her feelings and opinion of Izare shifting. It was hard to reconcile the impression she'd formed of him with someone who could produce such glorious temple paintings. He was too forthright, too cheeky. A painter of spirituals should be dignified and pious. But perhaps it was the memory of him chatting to the prostitute that lowered her opinion of him.

Hmm, she thought. *What was he doing there?*

"He offered to paint my portrait," she told her aunt, to see what reaction she would get. "I told him Mother would never approve."

"No, she would not," Narmah said. She looked up. "You were right to turn him down."

Rielle shrugged. "But I've painted you, and Ari, and some of the dyeworkers."

"Family. People you know and trust, who live in your home. He is a young man and you an attractive young woman. People would assume he was doing a lot more than painting a portrait. And that may be his intent."

Rielle laughed. "You have a higher opinion of my looks than anyone else, Aunt." *Except for him.* She stopped to scrape the paint again, then paused. "What if he came here to do it?"

Narmah straightened and set her stained hands on her hips. "Don't even consider it. Besides, you're the artist here."

"Not the only one, or else why am I learning from you?" Rielle set to grinding again. "And if he's so good, maybe we would both learn something from watching him."

Her aunt frowned. "Why are you suddenly so interested in having your portrait done?"

"I'm not. But if he's so good, and willing to do it for free then why not let—?"

"Free?" Narmah's eyebrows rose. "Now that's suspicious." She opened her mouth, then closed it again and tilted her head to the side. "I think that's . . . yes. The priest is here. Did you get any paint on you? No. Give me your apron."

Rielle untied the apron and handed it to her aunt. "Are you coming?"

"Yes, but I'll finish up here first. Go on. Off you go. Don't talk too much. Don't be opinionated – it's vulgar in a woman. And don't forget your scarf."

Picking up her scarf from a nearby chair, Rielle left her aunt's room and started down the corridor. Muffled voices came from the receiving room at the end. Narmah had left the door partly open so she would hear when the priest arrived.

As she walked she considered what she would say to him. Or, rather, what she wouldn't. *Nothing about seeing Stain. Nothing about taking the short cut down Tanner Street.* But even as she thought of it, she realised she couldn't lie about her location. She would have to admit to taking the short cut. Nobody would believe the abductor had snatched her from Temple Road without anyone seeing it. The priest would look for Stain on Temple Road, or find it on Tanner Street, know she had lied and wonder why.

Her mother was going to be furious.

Yet Mother had forgotten about her missing scarf the moment she had heard Rielle's tale of being dragged away at knifepoint by the tainted. She had gone pale, then briefly embraced Rielle in an uncharacteristic show of emotion. "My daughter," she had whispered. "I could have lost you."

Narmah had then insisted Rielle must still have her painting lesson. As soon as they were alone together she had asked Rielle if she had *seen* anything she couldn't speak of.

Rielle had paused to consider her words. "Yes. I pretended to see nothing. I will not speak of it."

"Good girl."

Reaching the door, Rielle draped the scarf over her head,

tied the ends behind her neck, then drew in a deep breath before pushing through to the other room. Three people stood by the spiritual: her mother, father and Sa-Elem. Dark spots were slowly fading from the stone where the priest had sprinkled water. Not unlike Stain. She tore her eyes away and smiled as all turned to face her.

Sa-Elem smiled. "Rielle Lazuli. Have you recovered from your ordeal?"

"I think so." She shrugged. "I feel fine."

"Come and sit down," Mother invited, gesturing to carved stone benches the family had passed down for several generations.

The priest paused as he saw the cushions, which were blue with silvery grey stitching to match the spiritual background. "This is lovely work."

"Rielle and my sister made and embroidered them."

He smiled at Rielle. "You are very talented."

She inclined her head at the compliment. This room was where her parents entertained important clients, so they took care to fill it with belongings that showed their products in the best light. But she had hated the stitching, preferring paint to thread.

Sa-Elem sat down. "So, Rielle. Tell me how your encounter with the tainted began."

"I was coming home from temple lessons. It was hot, so I decided to cut my journey short by walking along Tanner Street. I hadn't gone far when I encountered something solid but invisible . . ." It was not often that etiquette allowed her free rein to talk to visitors. Her parents expected her to remain largely silent, to respond only when addressed and to keep her answers short and to the point. Fortunately, telling stories well was a skill highly valued and discussed in temple classes. She tried to follow those principles as she described the day. Orient the listener in the setting, describe action with clarity, maintain attention, lead to the point of the story, then establish the moral. "If I had stayed on Temple Road none of it would have happened," she finished, hanging her head.

"Oh, Tanner Street is no more dangerous than Temple Road," Sa-Elem told her. "We have as many incidents of crime on one as the other – not that we have many," he added as Mother drew in a breath. "And it saddens me to say, had you chosen to stay on Temple Road it would not have prevented the crimes of the tainted. Instead your actions enabled us to capture him, and for that we thank you."

She lowered her gaze and kept her expression demure, though she wanted to grin. She was not in trouble. The priest was pleased with her.

Her mother shrugged. "At least something good came of it all."

"This is the third tainted in the last year," Father said. Rielle looked up at him, surprised. He looked as if he would go on, but seeing her surprise he closed his mouth again.

Sa-Elem nodded. "You are not the only one who has noted this." He sighed. "I fear we may have a corrupter in Fyre."

"The tainted said he had been tricked," Rielle ventured, earning herself a frown from Mother.

The priest's expression hardened as he nodded. "He has refused to speak of it. But we will get the truth from him, I assure you."

Mother reached out and took Rielle's hand. "I will make sure Rielle does not walk home alone from lessons from now on. The corrupter will have no chance to tempt her."

The look Sa-Elem gave her made Rielle's blood go cold. She stared at her mother in horror, wondering if Narmah had changed her mind and told the woman of her ability. The priest's gaze shifted to Rielle, then he smiled.

"I'm sure Rielle would be of no interest to a corrupter."

Mother flushed as she realised what she had implied. "I didn't mean . . . Rielle isn't . . ."

"Of course not," he said. "As for anyone who *does* have reason to be tempted, they will soon be well dissuaded." He stood up, and manners dictated that they all got to their feet. "I will take no more of your time – and I must also thank Izare Saffre for bringing Rielle home safely."

"He is known to you?" Father asked, as he led the priest to the main door.

"Yes."

To Rielle's disappointment, Sa-Elem said nothing more, and she could discern nothing positive or negative from his tone. As the main door closed behind the two men she opened her mouth to tell her mother that Izare had done the temple paintings, then remembered how much she detested them and changed her mind.

The inner door opened and Narmah entered. She looked around and frowned. "Did I miss him?"

"Yes," Mother said, her lips thinning.

"Did it go well?" Narmah asked, looking at Rielle.

"Very well," Mother answered, turning away.

Rielle met her aunt's gaze and nodded. Only then did Narmah relax.

"Well, then, we still have a painting lesson to finish before dinner. Come along, Rielle. We must finish what we started."

Slipping her hand out of her mother's, Rielle obediently followed her aunt out of the room. As they walked down the corridor she considered the meeting. Her mother hadn't been too angry that she'd taken a short cut. Sa-Elem's assessment of the safety of the street had helped with that. Rielle didn't think she had said anything to suggest she could see Stain. Her mother's ill-considered comment might have raised his suspicions, though. At times like those she wished her mother wasn't so disinclined to obey the social rule that women should remain silent in company and business, though if she did then nothing would be said at all when visitors came. Her father was far too inclined to be silent.

Sa-Elem saw I was aghast at what Mother said, and when Mother realised what she'd implied she was mortified. He must know she isn't as clever as she thinks she is. In fact, if he did he'd realise she could never manage to hide a secret like that, as Aunt Narmah knew all along.

But if Rielle had been a priest she would have to consider the possibility it wasn't a mistake, and store that fact away in the back of her mind.

Along with a thousand other meaningless comments. The priests are surely trained to know the difference between a foolish remark and true hints at magical ability.

She had to believe that. And put it out of her mind. Following her aunt into her room, she resolved to think of nothing but paint preparation for the rest of the night.

CHAPTER 4

Four days later, Rielle sat among the daughters of the richest and oldest families of Fyre. She tugged her scarf back so she could let her eyes drift slowly across the vast painted half-dome that arced over the altar, as she always did when their affable old teacher, Sa-Baro, began to waffle.

Though bigger than the one at her family's local temple, the style was old-fashioned and static in comparison. The scene was divided into quarters. To the left, all was idyllic. Perfect trees laden with fruit overhung fields of crops and garden beds full of herbs and flowers. Rain was falling from improbable clouds that barely disturbed the pale blue sky. People tended the crops, harvested the fruit and herbs, and stood engrossed in conversation, as indicated by little curling lines emerging from their open mouths. This time was known as The Beginning.

But as the observer moved to the right, the scene grew darker in hue and subject. This was The Strife. Storm clouds covered the sky. Men were shown fighting in pairs and small groupings, then armies battling armies. Red magic spilled from sorcerers' hands, enveloping their victims in writhing flames. Women wept over dying children while priests watched, hands cupped and empty to indicate they had no magic with which to heal.

Then a scene of desolation followed. Blackened earth, dead trees and skeletons formed the landscape, with ruined or ramshackle houses occupied by thin, sickly people. It was the time of The Waste. But in the background a shining figure stood at the head of a glowing crowd – a priest surrounded by his followers. Storm clouds still filled the sky, but they broke apart and shrank in the fourth quarter, where The Restoration began.

In the final section the sky was blue again but the land was changed. Crops and herbs were growing, but in a desert land. Priests stood among the people, and in one place two with dark halos stood either side of a man kneeling in chains, surrounded by tiny red flames.

Above the sky and storm clouds the painting darkened into an expanse of deep luminous blue, with stars represented by tiny criss-crosses of silver. Ten Angels floated above the world, surrounded by white halos of fine silver lines. Their skin was the colour of milk, lighter than even the rare ruddy pink of the southerners who occasionally visited Fyre. Their hair was as blue as the night sky. *You would never mistake one for human*, Rielle thought.

The Angels furthest to the left smiled serenely upon the scene of bounty. Those above the scenes of human folly wept and scowled. Over the third panel they were stern and wise, but the last were joyous. To each Angel was attributed one of the great forces, both beneficial and destructive: birth, death, drought, storm, wild, tame, fire, snow, justice and love.

Below, the ghostly outlines of people rose towards the Angels, disappearing into their shining halos. But above the man surrounded by flames, the soul rising into the heavens had been torn asunder by the sweep of the Angel of Justice's hand.

Rielle shivered and thought of the tainted. She knew she ought to believe he deserved that fate, if not for learning to use magic, stealing from the Angels, then for abducting her and threatening her with a knife, but she couldn't help feeling sorry for him. And wondering if he'd been driven to do what he'd done, and why. *I suppose I want there to be good reasons, because to think he turned from the Angels deliberately and wanted to harm me is worse.*

Maybe that meant she was naïve. Maybe she could not bear to think that people could do evil for no reason.

The girls around her suddenly sighed as one, then began to turn to each other and speak. Jolted out of her thoughts, Rielle looked around and realised that the lesson had finished. She hoped Sa-Baro hadn't noticed that her attention had strayed. He had turned away and was walking towards the door to the inner temple where the priest, Sa-Gest, waited. The younger priest's gaze shifted to hers and his mouth widened into a smile. Remembering the other girls' whisperings about him, she managed a wan smile and quickly looked away.

As the others rose, she stood and followed Tareme and Bayla to the main aisle. They hurried to the temple doors. Once outside, the two girls and several others crowded around Rielle, their eyes wide and full of curiosity.

"So, what was it like?"

"Were you scared?"

"Did he do anything to you?"

"Did he use *magic*?"

Rielle never managed to finish answering the first question, or any after, before her reply was drowned out by the next enquiry. She gave up just as a voice boomed over them all.

"This nitternatter is disturbing the serenity of the temple." They turned to see Sa-Baro standing, arms crossed, in the doorway. "Off with you all, before the Angels come down to take away your voices."

As the girls scattered in all directions, Tareme grabbed

153

Rielle's arm and pulled her down the temple stairs, around the corner of the building and out of sight of the priest, her twin following.

"So? What happened?"

Rielle told them, keeping the story as short as possible. She looked for a familiar face among the few people in the courtyard, but saw no sign of a dyeworks servant waiting to escort her home.

Tareme and Bayla made appropriate noises of shock and relief.

"Sounds like you kept your blood cool," Bayla said. "I'd have never dared to try tricking him into walking into the priest."

"I think by then I was too tired to be scared," Rielle told them. "We'd gone all over the city, or that's what it felt like."

"Well, you shouldn't be . . ." Tareme frowned and looked over Rielle's shoulder, then adjusted her scarf and grinned at Rielle and Bayla. "You won't believe who is watching us." She grabbed Bayla's arm to stop her from turning to look behind. "No, don't look yet." Rielle froze mid-turn.

"Who?" Bayla demanded.

"Guess," Tareme said. "Dark. Handsome. Unmarried."

"Male?" Bayla asked.

"Yes, of course." Tareme giggled. "Who is it? More clues?"

"Yes," Bayla and Rielle said together.

"Talented. Famous. Has done some work in temples."

Rielle felt her stomach flip over. "Oh! Not Izare Saffre?"

"Yes!" Tareme's eyes were ablaze with excitement.

"But . . . why is he watching us?" Bayla asked.

"He was nearby when the priests caught the tainted," Rielle told her. "He offered to escort me home."

Tareme's hand flew to her mouth. "Oh, Angels! Did you accept?"

"The priest didn't advise against it so . . . yes."

The two girls smothered exclamations behind their palms.

Tareme looked behind Rielle again. "He's still there and looking at us. He must be waiting for you." She grabbed Rielle's shoulder and turned her around. "Call him over."

"No. But . . ." Looking up, Rielle saw that Izare was indeed standing twenty paces away. He smiled as their eyes met, then strode towards her.

"Ais Lazuli," he said. "Once again we happen to be in the same place at the same time."

Her face warmed. "We do, Aos Saffre," she replied.

His smile widened and he looked around her shoulder. "But I see you are already with friends. Would you introduce me?"

Rielle turned back to see Tareme and Bayla smiling broadly. She made the appropriate introductions, but she had barely finished when a voice called their names. Rielle's stomach sank as the twins stepped apart to welcome their brother into the circle. He grinned at Rielle as he joined them.

"Ais Lazuli, I hear you have become quite the heroine," Ako said. "You are gaining a reputation as a woman not to be trifled with."

"I'm glad you think so," she replied, trying not to emphasise the "you" overly, and failing.

His gaze shifted to Izare. Suppressing a sigh, she introduced the two men to each other.

"Aos Saffre escorted Rielle home after her ordeal," Bayla added. She hooked her arm around Ako's. "As you, brother, best do for your sisters now."

Tareme scowled at her sister as Ako nodded. "Of course," Ako agreed. "Farewell, Ais Lazuli and Aos Saffre." He offered his arm to Tareme, who took it reluctantly and sent her sister a dark look as she was led away.

Rielle watched them go, puzzled. Why had Bayla initiated such a quick exit? She had appeared as eager to meet Izare as Tareme had been. Maybe she didn't trust her brother not to offend or embarrass them in front of Izare. Or maybe she was less happy to have a male family member see her with a man of lower social standing.

"So, Ais Lazuli," Izare said. "You aren't walking home alone again, are you?"

Rielle turned to him. "No. Mother is sending a servant. Who I may miss if I linger here. Excuse me, Aos Saffre, I had best stand where they will find me." She started back towards the centre of the courtyard.

He followed her. "I see nobody waiting outside, or watching the door."

"They might have arrived after Tareme and Bayla took me around here, and thought me already gone, though they should have waited in case I lingered inside." Rielle winced at the irritation in her tone. More likely her parents had forgotten to send someone at all. Reaching the centre of the courtyard, she scanned the faces and shadows and saw nobody familiar. Nobody but Izare. They stood in silence for a while. Eventually she gave up.

"Well, I had better be heading home."

"Then I had better be escorting you."

She looked at him, then wished she hadn't. His expression had been serious, but as she met his gaze he gave her one of his dazzling smiles and her stomach did a little flip.

"I suppose," she said weakly. "I suppose I have no choice but to accept."

He laughed. "You make it sound so distasteful."

A flush of heat warmed her face and she looked down. "It's not that. It's . . . if I go with you Mother might think I deliberately avoided whoever she sent to meet me."

He laughed. "Now why might you want to do that?"

She narrowed her eyes at him. To her amusement, his face reddened.

"I suppose that might be taken as an invitation for a compliment," he admitted.

"So it wasn't?"

He opened his mouth to reply, then closed it, shook his head and gestured towards the beginning of Temple Road. "I promise I will leave your side when you are close enough home to be safe, but distant enough that nobody at home will see who escorted you."

Drawing in a deep breath and praying to the Angels for strength – though quite for what she wasn't sure – she let it out and nodded. "Thank you, Aos Saffre."

"Call me Izare," he said and fell into step beside her as she began to walk.

Temple Road was busier than last quarterday, thanks to it being a warm but not searingly hot day. Rielle searched the faces of those travelling towards the temple in case one was her servant escort. Izare was silent, maybe waiting for her to lead the conversation. Or was he bored already? Surely he had better things to do than this.

"I hope this will not take you far from home," she said

He shrugged. "Not at all. I live not far from your home, in the humbler side of the artisan quarter."

By humbler he meant poorer. She looked away, remembering that when she first saw him he was talking to a prostitute. Tareme and Bayla would be scandalised, if they knew.

"Why do you live there?"

"The rent is cheap, which is why most of my friends live there. An artist's income can be like a seasonal river – overflowing one hour and dry the next – only not as predictable."

"I am not keeping you from your work?" she asked.

"No. I am between commissions."

"What have you finished recently?"

"My last one was a spiritual. Quite a large one. I had to

talk the customer out of including the entire history of the Angels."

"That would have made for a very large spiritual. Though if you were paid by the hour it could be quite lucrative."

He was shaking his head. "Commissions are always for set sums."

"I see. What are you working on next?"

"I am waiting for confirmation on a portrait."

"Do you paint many portraits? Who have you painted? Anyone I know?"

He smiled. "Not as many as I'd like. Mostly friends, though a few wealthy customers have commissioned portraits in the past."

"And this next one?"

"Oh, you know her very well."

Rielle glanced at him, then, seeing his odd expression, looked again to see a glint of mischief in his gaze.

"Waiting for confirmation, is it?" She shook her head. "Haven't I already made it clear that my parents would never allow it?"

He grinned. "Yes, but would *you* allow it?"

She raised her eyebrows at him. "Disobey my parents?"

"It's only disobedience if they forbid it, and they won't forbid it if they don't know about it."

"You want me to *deceive* my parents?"

He spread his hands. "No, but surely you don't ask for permission to do every little thing you do in a day. Do you consult them on what you will wear, or what you will eat – or what you will paint?"

Rielle was so pleased that he had remembered that she, too, painted that she had to remind herself that he had asked a question.

"Parents are guides more than instructors," she told him. "They steer children away from bad decisions."

"Would sitting for a portrait truly be a bad decision?"

"Yes."

"Why?"

She looked away, unable to voice Narmah's concern that he might want more than a portrait. To raise such a subject was too bold, and might give the opposite impression to the one she intended.

"You must let me paint you," he said, a strange intensity in his voice. "Or do a quick sketch." He chuckled. "Besides, I never stop asking until a girl lets me paint her, so if you wish never to see me again all you have to say is 'yes'."

So if I want to see you again I should always say "no"? she wanted to ask, but she guessed he would take that as an invitation. "And what do you do then, after she has let you?" she asked instead, then felt her face warm as she realised there was as much, if not more, innuendo in the question she'd asked as the one she hadn't.

He hesitated, then looked down. "Ah . . . we usually become friends."

His sudden uncertainty made a laugh bubble up inside her, but she held it back. Maybe asking bold questions could have benefits. "You must have a lot of female friends, then."

"Yes. Well, no, but . . ." He frowned and slowed to look back over his shoulder. "Something is . . ."

The street had grown noisier and more crowded, Rielle saw. People around them were stopping to look back towards the temple, now hidden behind the curve of the road. More were emerging from side streets and the windows in houses on either side were filled with faces and torsos. A distant bell was ringing – a sound that she had been conscious of as she had talked.

She also noticed that she was nearly halfway home. She had hardly noticed the time passing.

Izare stopped. Reluctantly, Rielle came to a halt, too, and

returned to his side. The sound of the bell became louder as a shuffling figure appeared around the last turn. Rielle caught her breath as she saw that the man's walk was hampered by chains. More restraints held his hands locked behind his back, and a chain extended from a collar to the three men coming into sight.

Rielle recognised Sa-Elem and Sa-Gest, but the third priest, whose face was scarred, was unfamiliar. The sight of the trio sent a chill down her spine and she looked more closely at their prisoner.

It took her a moment to recognise her abductor. He was dressed in ragged, dirty trousers and sandals, and he was covered in muck.

She had barely had time to wonder where the latter had come from when the crowd now lining the streets began to pelt him with missiles. Most exploded wetly on impact, but she saw him flinch once as something hit harder. A shout came from one of the priests, but she could not make it out. The objects that flew towards the tainted did not seem to touch him then, bouncing away or exploding in front of him. After he had taken several shuffling steps they began to strike him again and the crowd cheered and renewed their attack.

"Are you all right?" a voice spoke softly, close to her ear.

She jumped, then turned to stare at Izare. The tension inside her eased at his concerned expression.

"Yes. I think so."

His eyebrows rose and he tilted his head to the side. "Would you like something to throw?"

Following the direction of the gesture, Rielle saw an enterprising foodseller walking along ahead of the tainted carrying a huge basket.

"Old fruit. Animal dung. A copee a bag," the woman called.

Rielle shook her head. People were now pouring out of side

streets, forming a disorganised crowd that parted as the tainted drew within twenty paces of them. Someone pushed past her, then another knocked her from behind and she heard Izare curse them.

"I would like to get out of this crowd," she said aloud, not knowing if he heard.

A hand grabbed her arm and pulled, and she froze as she remembered the grip of her abductor, a sensation that still woke her from nightmares. Izare looked at her, then the hand slipped down to her hand and fingers entwined with her own. She shivered again, but this time with the pleasant shock of such a personal contact, and let herself be guided out of the press of people.

The side streets were as full as the main road – if not even more tightly filled. Izare led her to a doorway, saying something to the two young men there that persuaded them to move, though reluctantly. Rielle realised why they'd valued their position when her shoes knocked up against steps. Climbing up beside Izare, she turned to find she could now see over the heads of the crowd.

And just in time to see the tainted pass. He trudged onward, head bowed against the rain of fruit and faeces. *Or in shame*, she thought. *It's hard to tell.* Once again she wondered why he had done what he had done.

The priests were solemn and watchful, their eyes on the crowd as much as their prisoner. Even Sa-Gest looked intimidating. Rielle could not help thinking they were searching for evidence of sympathy in the crowd. Or of guilt.

The tainted suddenly doubled up and something hard rattled over the ground. Sa-Elem called out and gestured at someone.

Wherever they're taking him, they want him alive and uninjured, Rielle thought.

"Why don't they protect him the whole time?" she asked.

"They must keep the crowd happy," Izare told her.

"Do they always take the tainted through the city like this?" she asked, remembering her father's observation that this was the third tainted found this year.

"Not always," Izare replied. "Sometimes they are never seen again. I assume they remove those ones from the city late at night, or in a covered cart."

"And nobody knows where they take them."

He shrugged. "A prison somewhere, I expect."

Rielle watched the chained man shuffle by. *Will he become a prisoner, or is he to be executed somewhere else?* Murderers were executed in public. What if a murderer was a tainted? What if they had used magic to kill someone? Maybe it was not such a safe or simple matter, killing a tainted. Maybe only a priest could do it. *And they'd rather we didn't think of our priests as killers.*

The priests and their prisoner had moved past now, and people were either returning from wherever they had emerged or falling in behind to follow the priests. Izare stared after them. He was still holding her hand, Rielle realised. She ought to extract it, but she was curiously reluctant to. Yet now the crowd had dispersed it was more obvious that she was letting him. Sighing, she pulled her hand away. Izare looked briefly surprised, as if he'd forgotten he was holding it.

He stepped down to the road. "Well, that was a spectacle. An ugly one, though."

Rielle followed. Gratitude filled her at his company. It would have been frightening to have been caught up in the crowd alone, and see the abductor again. *And Izare doesn't mind if I talk out of turn – or expect me to be silent*, she realised. *In fact, he seems to like it.*

"Makes you wonder why anyone would learn magic, doesn't it?" she ventured.

He grimaced and started walking, slowly so as not to catch up with the crowd. "Desperation can make a man do anything," he replied. "People are saying . . ." He paused to look at her. "People on the street, that is. People are saying he did it to heal his dying wife."

Rielle stared at him. "But he said he was tricked."

Izare shrugged. "Men will also say anything they think might save them." He nodded at the now-distant crowd.

"Well, *someone* must have taught him."

"Someone who knows how to avoid being caught," Izare agreed.

"Why do that? Why teach magic to someone, knowing it will condemn them?"

"Money." Izare's expression was grim. "Someone willing to steal from the Angels has no qualms about stealing from their fellow man. They don't care that they are ruining lives and tainting souls." He sighed. "And this city has many desperate and vulnerable people to prey upon. If the priests don't find him we'll be seeing more parades of shame."

CHAPTER 5

R ielle suppressed a yawn then, remembering why she was
  tired, felt her pulse quicken again. She had woken far too
early that morning, and once she'd remembered that she would
– might – meet Izare again, sleep wouldn't return. Even now,
despite the tranquil and sober surrounds of the temple, her
heart kept going all skittery.

Ridiculous, she thought. *He only wants to paint my portrait.*
Even if he wanted more . . . even if I wanted more . . . my parents
would never consider him an appropriate husband.

As old Sa-Baro began to speak she forced herself to pay
attention.

"You must all know by now that the tainted captured two
quarterdays ago, thanks to the bravery of one of our own . . ."
– Sa-Baro paused to nod at Rielle – ". . . was not the first
found in Fyre this last year. Sa-Elem has decided measures
must be taken to remind the population of the punishment
given to those who break the Angels' edicts."

He lifted a stack of paper-covered bundles.

"So today you will take a package each, then divide into
groups of four. You will be spending the morning walking the
streets, handing out these pamphlets to the citizens of Fyre.
Any questions?"

"Will priests be escorting us?" one girl asked.

"No. You will be safe enough if you stay together, though there are places you should avoid. I have had maps drawn up for each group, indicating where you should and shouldn't go. Now, stand and select your companions."

Rielle rose and followed Tareme and Bayla to the end of the row of seats. There were a few groans and protests, but none were too loud. It was a fine day outside, warm but with a breeze cooling the city streets. Handing out pamphlets was a welcome change from lectures, readings and the questions the priest asked to test how well they'd absorbed their lessons.

Once all had gathered into groups, Sa-Baro walked straight to Rielle and handed her a package. "I selected the area closest to home for you," he explained in a low voice. "So that you did not have far to walk alone when you are done."

Rielle nodded and felt a pang of affection and gratitude for the old man. Did he know that her mother had completely forgotten to send a servant to escort her last quarterday? The woman had looked guilty when Rielle asked what had happened, then pretended she hadn't forgotten, saying she needed everyone in the dyeworks occupied at this busy time and the city was safe now the tainted was gone.

Or had Sa-Baro seen her leaving the courtyard with Izare, and decided to ensure it didn't happen again?

As he moved away, Rielle looked down at the map and sighed. *Whether he did or not, it still means I won't be seeing Izare today.* She straightened to see Tareme and Bayla, and a girl named Famire who had joined their group, exchanging frowns. It would mean a longer walk home for them. And venturing near the poor quarter.

Izare lived near the poor quarter. Maybe they would cross paths.

"We're going to the artisan quarter," she told the others. "I've been there with my brother. It's quite safe and clean.

There are small public squares where people gather that would be ideal places to hand these out."

Tareme smiled. "We will follow your lead then."

Before long the girls were spilling out of the temple. Rielle led her friends down Temple Road. Famire was soon complaining that her feet hurt so Rielle slowed down. When they finally reached Tanner Street, Rielle confidently turned onto it, but she kept to the other side to the one she had taken last time, and avoided looking too closely at the place where the Stain had blocked her path. Even so, she was aware of a shadow still lingering there, smaller but as dark as before.

Opening the package, Rielle divided the pamphlets between them. The paper was coloured to conceal its low quality, and the warning on it had been printed in black ink, the grain of the wood block visible where the ink was fainter. They began handing them out, Rielle with the solemnity appropriate to their mission, Famire with a sullen reluctance and Tareme and her sister giggling and flirting.

Following the map, Rielle led them off Tanner Street to where she thought one of the squares must be. She was wrong, but they soon stumbled upon another, led by the sound of music. On all sides were shops selling food and drink, and two musicians were piping and strumming cheerful, rambling tunes. Under the plain awnings were tables and benches, many of them occupied by a mix of both local and foreign customers.

"This is nice," Tareme said. "Let's stop for a drink."

Not waiting for agreement from the others, she moved to an empty table. Bayla sat down beside her and Famire dropped onto a bench as if she were exhausted. Joining them, Rielle winced as the three girls tossed their pamphlets together in the middle of the table, on top of the leavings of spilled drinks.

Suddenly in a jovial spirit, Famire ordered juices from a

server clearly amused and pleased to have four well-off, unaccompanied young women as customers. When the drinks arrived Rielle was dismayed to find the juice was alcoholic. She sipped it slowly, knowing her mother would be angry if she came home tipsy.

"So Rielle," Tareme began. "What did Izare Saffre have to say to you, last quarterday?"

Noting how this made Famire look up sharply, Rielle shrugged. "He just wanted to ask if I had recovered from my encounter with the tainted."

"I doubt that's *all* he wanted," Bayla said, with a sly smile.

"He was very well behaved."

Tareme's eyebrows rose. "It was obvious he wanted more than to enquire after your health. Something about you interests him, I think, or he wouldn't have been waiting for you. So what is it?"

Rielle shook her head. "Nothing."

"You're a terrible liar, Rielle. Tell us, or we'll imagine the worst."

Rielle sighed. "It's not what you think. He asked me to sit for a portrait. Which, of course, I refused."

Their eyes went round. "Oh! Why would you do that?" Bayla asked. "He's very good, I've heard."

"Very good," Tareme agreed.

"My parents would never agree to it," Rielle pointed out.

"Why not?" Tareme asked. "What harm is there in sitting for a portrait?"

"None at all, so long as your clothes are on," Bayla said, then laughed.

The girls chuckled at the joke, but Rielle's attempt to join in sounded forced. Tareme patted her arm.

"We're being silly. Would you like him to paint you?"

Rielle felt her face warming, though there was truly no

reason to be embarrassed. "Well, yes," she admitted. "But only so—"

"Why is it that men can have their portraits done with no hint of scandal, but women can't?" Bayla interrupted.

"Because artists are men," Famire replied.

Rielle turned to look at her. "I paint. So does my aunt."

"But you don't paint professionally," Tareme pointed out.

"Which wouldn't be scandalous," Bayla added.

"Yes, it would," Tareme disagreed.

"A woman artist is unconventional," Bayla argued. "But a model is but one step from a prostitute. Both sell their bodies to men."

"Unless the artist is a woman?" Rielle asked.

They considered. "It doesn't seem as bad," Bayla replied. Tareme shook her head in disagreement.

"My aunt and I have painted each other," Rielle told them. "With our clothes *on*, of course. Is that like prostitution? Is it scandalous?"

"That's . . . family," Tareme said. "And you didn't pay each other, I'm guessing."

Rielle shook her head. "So how important is the money? If a woman poses for a male artist and he doesn't pay her is it still like prostitution? What if she pays *him* to pose for *her*?"

Bayla giggled. "Then he's the prostitute!"

They all laughed at the absurdity of that, then Tareme waved at the server.

"Another round of drinks!"

"Not for me." Rielle looked at the pamphlets. "We still have these to give out."

"Leave them there," Famire told her. "If people want them they'll take them. If they don't, Sa-Baro will never know."

"And if you're worried about going home drunk, just pretend you're tired after a long morning delivering pamphlets and go to your room," Tareme told her. "Don't get close enough to anyone for them to smell you and I'm sure they won't notice."

Bayla sniggered. Her sister gave her a fleeting, stern look and Bayla blushed, glanced at Rielle and covered her mouth with a hand.

It wasn't the snigger but the look that stiffened Rielle's back, confirming that Bayla's laugh had been at her expense. *Tareme has had to curtail her sister's rudeness before*, Rielle guessed. *Maybe she laughs along with Bayla in private.*

As the second round of alcoholic juices was served, suddenly Rielle did not want to linger any longer. Picking up a bundle of pamphlets, she rose. "Well, I'm not taking the chance that Sa-Baro isn't going to check on us. Anyone coming?"

The girls exchanged looks, then shook their heads. Anger flared through Rielle and she turned and walked away before she could say anything she would regret later.

Bayla's voice, too quiet to be directed at Rielle, reached her ears.

"We're supposed to stay together."

"Let her go. She said she knows her way around these parts," Tareme replied.

"I'm sure she does," Famire added.

Choosing a street at random, Rielle took a couple of steps but as quickly as it had risen her resolve vanished. Sa-Baro had said they should stay together. Returning to the corner, she saw that the girls were laughing again.

"Oh, everyone knows why she's there. She hasn't a chance," Famire said.

Tareme nodded. "I feel sorry for her. The only ones she's likely to catch are ones we don't want. The ugly, the stupid and the mean."

"Like Ako."

"No, there's no risk of that. He won't marry until he's forced to, and Father would never approve of him marrying a dyer's daughter. If we had a younger brother he might consider her, if links to her family were profitable enough."

Turning away, Rielle began walking again. *So. I suspected as much. I'm not good enough for the families, unless as a bride for the men nobody else wants. All these temple lessons and attempts to befriend my fellow students have been a waste of time.* She looked at the pamphlets and considered throwing them away, but her eyes caught the word "tainted" and reminded her that the priests, at least, were trying to do some good.

She began to offer them to everyone she passed. Few accepted them. Even so, her anger faded with each step.

But it was replaced by a creeping fear.

Memories returned of her abductor dragging her along streets like these. She remembered his knife pressed into her back. When people looked at her, their gaze dropping to the expensive cloth of her skirt and tunic, she began to feel out of place and vulnerable. While she never wore jewellery to temple classes, she couldn't be seen among the other girls wearing anything of low quality.

Then, like a cool breeze chasing away the summer heat, she remembered Izare. When escorting her home, after the tainted had passed, he had told her where he lived, describing how close it was to her home and how safe the area was. He had gone on to talk fondly of his neighbours, who were all either brilliant artisans and performers or drunks – or all three – and of the bold ways they had decorated their homes. His descriptions had made her want to see his neighbourhood. Which was all part of his attempt to persuade her to sit for him, of course.

And yet . . . she *did* want to see them.

So she kept walking, heading towards the area he lived in. Though this part of the city was more populated, fewer people accepted the pamphlets, but their refusals were polite and most people smiled at her. Her earlier anxiety faded a little. The brightly painted walls cheered her. She reached an area where they were not only coloured, but decorated with patterns around windows and doors. Looking down one alley, she glimpsed the edge of a much larger design and could not resist venturing down it to see. It was of an enormous tree painted on a wall, with all manner of objects hanging from the branches.

Ahead the alley ended at what looked like another small courtyard, with more decorated walls. She followed two women to the end and stepped out into a dizzying spectacle. All of the houses were covered in images of people, animals and plants. False doors and windows opened onto unfamiliar land-scapes, and even one of the Angels sleeping on a cloud. Rielle turned full circle, slowly taking it all in.

"Are you lost?" a voice asked.

She turned to see that one of the women she had followed, holding a pitcher up to the fountain at the centre of the court-yard, was looking at her. The fountain was as striking as the paintings, shaped to resemble a four-headed beast with water pouring from each mouth.

"No," Rielle replied. "But . . . I am looking for Izare Saffre."

The woman's gaze dropped to Rielle's clothes and she smiled. She nodded to the right. "He's in the third house down that street."

"Thank you." Rielle nodded then set off in the direction the woman had indicated.

This street was narrow and filled with groups of battered, mismatched old chairs. Some of them were occupied by a group of young men and women, laughing and drinking from cheap glazed cups. Children were dashing between the chairs – a shrieking swarm of varying heights. As Rielle neared the third house she saw that images of Angels in a striking, familiar style had been painted over the door along with the words: *Izare Saffre, Painter.*

Seeing his name, she stopped, frozen by a sudden doubt. Was this such a good idea? What if the other girls told Sa-Baro where she had gone? What if her aunt's warning about Izare's real motives were true? *What will I say to him?*

"Ais Lazuli?"

She started and turned to see one of the young drinkers walking towards her. Then she froze again as she realised this dishevelled man was familiar.

"Aos Saffre?" she said doubtfully.

He grimaced and looked down at himself. "Ah, yes. I apologise for my appearance. I have not yet been long out of bed."

"Not long!" another male voice exclaimed. A tall man rose and walked over to lean on Izare's shoulder. The artist immediately shook him off. "We dragged him out of there quite some time ago. But, to be fair, we haven't let him back in to wash. We were laying bets on how long it would take him, if he had to clean up quick in time to . . ." The man stopped, then stepped past Izare and peered at her. "Wait . . ." He scooped up one of Rielle's hands. "Who is this fine lady, Izare?"

"This," Izare said as she pulled her hand away, "is Rielle Lazuli."

"Ah." The man smiled. "Well, I can see why you were determined to be on time." His expression grew serious and intense as his attention roved over her face then shifted to her arms, down to her feet, then back again. She looked him up and down in return, noting how his skin was darker than the average Fyrian's, his chin bristled with stubble, and his clothing and hands bore colourful stains. Another artist? That would explain his oddly analytical scrutiny. *At least Izare responded to me like a person before he considered me a subject.*

"This is Dorr," Izare told her. "Setting maker and performer for the Sky Troupe, of which these other three are also a part." He looked over to the drinkers.

"*Artist* and performer," Dorr corrected, smiling. "Come and let me introduce you to the rest of us."

Rielle looked at Izare.

He shrugged. "There'll be no escaping him until you do."

Following them to the table, Rielle smiled and nodded as the two women and their other male companion were introduced. Greya, Jonare and Merem were all actors, and they had come to celebrate a profitable night's performance. Greya had pale hair and light skin, so was possibly a half-southerner. The other two looked like Fyrians. Jonare was holding a sleeping child. All three wore traces of face paint, and by the looks of it Merem had played the part of a woman. They were the sort of people she would normally watch perform, not get to talk to. She wasn't entirely sure her parents would approve of them as friends, but neither would they consider them dangerous.

"Sit," Dorr ordered. "Have some iquo." He offered her a cup but she politely declined.

"So you are Izare's desert girl," Greya said. "He's been talking about you for the last three quarterdays."

Rielle felt a little thrill of pleasure, but tried to keep it from her face by narrowing her eyes at Izare. "What stories has he been telling you?"

They laughed. "Nothing bad," Greya reassured her. "I haven't seen him this excited by a face since . . ." She frowned, then shrugged. "Well, it must be over a year now."

"You attend temple lessons at this time, don't you?" Jonare asked.

"I do, usually," Rielle replied. She lifted the bundle of pamphlets. "The priests decided we needed to remind the people of Fyre about the dangers of learning magic."

Dorr took one, read it and handed it back. "We hardly need

reminding," he muttered, "after all the harassment of the last—"

"They sent you out alone?" Izare asked her.

"No, in groups. But my friends were more interested in . . ." Rielle looked at the empty bottles and cups on the table. "They decided to throw away the pamphlets and do whatever they felt like."

Dorr smiled. "So you continued on your own. Well, you don't need to worry about finishing it. We can hardly have failed to notice the evils of magic users lately."

"I should still distribute them," she told him, "in case the priests check on us."

"How would they know if you handed them out or not?" Greya asked. "You'll never get anyone around here to take them."

"Well, I have to try." Rielle began to stand.

"Wait." Izare reached out and placed a hand over hers. "You're leaving? But I haven't started your portrait yet."

Rielle lifted the pamphlets. "I never said I came here for that."

"But will there ever be a better opportunity than now?"

As she opened her mouth to remind him of her parents' disapproval, Dorr took the pamphlets from her hands. "We'll take care of these. You have to let him sketch you at least."

"But—"

"There's no harm in a little sketch. All you have to do is sit here. You can even pretend that you didn't notice."

Izare leapt out of his chair. "I'll get some paper and charcoal."

As he dashed through the door of his house, Rielle sank back into her chair. The others were watching her, and she could not tell if their smiles were of amusement or sympathy at her dismay. Would they stop her if she tried to flee?

Should I?

She thought of Famire, Tareme and Bayla's opinion and felt an echo of her earlier anger. Narmah would disagree with them, she was sure. Posing for a portrait was *not* like prostitution! And to these friends of Izare, who painted their faces and performed in front of others, the temple girls' ideas must seem prudish and ridiculous.

The door to Izare's house opened again and he hurried out carrying a board onto which was pinned a sheaf of paper. His hair was combed flat and glistened with moisture, and he had put on a clean shirt. She had to resist a smile at that.

Izare began to circle the table, then made a shooing motion at Jonare. She immediately rose and let him take her seat, the child in her arms murmuring in his sleep.

"Well, we had better spread these all over the poor quarter," Dorr said, dividing the pamphlets between Merem and Greya. They rose and bid Rielle farewell, promising Izare they would return to see the drawing later, and walked away. Jonare followed, calling two of the other children away from the group.

The scrape and rub of chalk on paper brought Rielle's attention back to Izare. She watched him work, trying to stay still. She had never felt so self-conscious when Narmah had drawn her. Izare's gaze was intense but he was looking *at* her rather than meeting her gaze. He worked silently, his attention so focused on drawing that she almost felt as if she was alone.

Somehow she felt free to examine him closely in return. To paint his eyes she would begin with yellow earth, then almost completely cover it with flecks of copper-green. His skin would need a rich shade of brown and the shadows would require a little blue. The duller shade of beristone would be adequate. The expensive bluegem of her family spiritual was too expensive to be wasted on shadows.

Izare leaned back in his chair, then nodded. "It's a start."

Rielle blinked in surprise. "Are you done already?"

He looked up at Rielle, then turned the board around. She caught her breath. There she was, staring back at herself, like a reflection in a mirror. A mirror that reduced an image to the black of charcoal and the off-white of cheap paper, and yet every line was a simple and eloquent flourish that perfectly expressed the curve of a jaw, curl of an eyelash and fold of her scarf.

"You *are* good," she exclaimed.

She expected a grin, but he shook his head. "This is not my best. Would you . . . would you let me try again?"

A thrill ran over her skin. "That's not your best? Then I have to see your best."

He looked at her, then over at his house and smiled. "I have a few reasonable paintings inside. All that stands between you and them are stairs, a few walls and your distrust of me."

She looked from him to his house and back again. "You claim you are a man of honour. If you promise that all you will do is show me these paintings . . ."

He placed a hand on his heart. "I promise that I will escort you as safely into and out of my house as I have escorted you home the last two quarterdays."

Rielle considered his promise, then nodded and stood up. Putting the sketch under one arm, Izare led the way to his door. Despite his promise, her heart still raced, though not with a feeling as strong as fear. More like apprehension than true fear. Or not even that, since a part of her was enjoying the feeling.

He opened the door for her and she stepped into a short, narrow hallway with a single door to one side. Stairs at the end led upward. The air smelled strange, like wood polish but sharper. Remembering that he had mentioned stairs, she started up. At the top she emerged into a large room. Light spilled in through windows along one wall, swathed with thin cloth. The paint on the upper half of the walls was peeling and stained, but the lower part was hidden behind a multitude of objects, including shelving, clothing hanging from hooks, lengths of fabric, boards in various stages of preparation for painting, and paintings turned to face the wall.

The smell was stronger here. Her gaze was attracted by a small table covered in half-familiar things. The bottles of pigment and refiner for making paint were expected. Though she did not work with a standing easel they were known to her. But what were the odd little spade-like tools, tubes with twisted ends and oily yellow liquid for?

Izare moved to one of the walls and turned a painting to face Rielle. As it came into sight she caught her breath. Compared to this, the sketch he had done was like the crude scratches of a woodworm bird on tree bark. It was as though he was carrying a mirror over to the easel, but a mirror that had frozen with the image of the viewer intact.

"She didn't like it and wouldn't pay," he said, smiling. "Too accurate."

Coming closer, Rielle could see why. The woman was in her middle years and had a mean expression.

"How did you . . . her skin . . . I can't see any brush strokes."

"Blending," he said, then, as if that was explanation enough, he fetched another painting. "This one I did for my own pleasure. She has an interesting face."

The young woman did indeed have unusual eyes. But it was the look in her eyes that caught Rielle's attention. She could not decide if it was sadness or contentment.

"Here's another." The next one was of an old man he'd found sleeping on his doorstep one day. She had barely recovered from the stark reality of the painting when Izare brought another, then another.

Yet as she grew used to the startling quality of the faces she began to see flaws. A collar that did not sit right. A scarf that looked too stiff. Hair that did not fall or curl convincingly. Eyes that were too white. Her aunt loved to point out that the whites of eyes were not actually white, but a creamy colour that reflected colours, and deepened and cooled under the shadows of the brow.

Izare was not as good at painting clothing, hair and eyes as he was at painting skin. But what he could do with skin . . . it had stirred up an exciting mix of jealousy and desire.

She looked at the table again. A mixing board lay on top of the grinding glass, smears of colour on it spilling into and blending with each other. The paint glistened. She touched the red and it gave under her finger's pressure, still wet. A smudge remained on her skin so she rubbed it between her fingers. It was smooth and thick, spreading like a balm over her skin. The colour was vibrant even when thinned. It glistened. She sniffed and wasn't surprised to smell the same odour that permeated the room, but stronger. Izare watched her, moving to the other side of the table and smiling as she finally recognised it.

"Oil. You mix your paints with oil." Searching the table, she noted the missing ingredient. "Instead of sap, water and nectar."

He nodded. "It dries slowly, allowing me to blend the colours, and I don't have to mix up new paint constantly. It can be applied thick and opaque as well as thin and translucent."

"Will you show me how?"

He hesitated, his expression wary. Then he smiled. "If you promise never to show anyone else, not even your family. I have to be careful not to lose the advantages I have over my competitors. Though plenty of them are trying to paint with oil, they don't know which oils to use and how to mix and apply it."

"I am a painter, too," Rielle pointed out.

"You are not a competitor because you don't sell your paintings."

She could not argue with that, so she nodded.

"Also, I don't have time to show you now. You will have to come here for lessons. And there is a price."

Rielle nodded again. "That's fair. How much do you charge?"

"For you? Nothing. My price is that you sit for that portrait."

A laugh burst from her. "Of course. Why did I think it would be anything else?"

He moved around the table. "Well? Will you?"

She looked at the paintings, then at the colour glistening on the board. "How? My parents will never agree to it and even if I don't tell them . . . I doubt I'll be handing out pamphlets regularly."

"You walk home along Temple Road, which is not a direct route. I can show you a different way. A faster way. You would arrive home a little later than usual, but you can blame it on being held up by your friends after lessons, or how busy the roads are, or being tired." He paused and frowned. "But your family are sending an escort for you, aren't they?"

"No," Rielle told him. "Mother won't spare any of the servants, and she says the streets are safe enough now that the tainted is gone."

Izare frowned. "*I* don't like you walking alone. In fact, it might be safer for you if I meet you near the temple and ensure you get home safely after your sitting."

Rielle smiled at his concern, but then she remembered Narmah's warning. "But will I be safe here?"

His frown vanished. "Of course. What possible danger would I pose to you?"

"Well . . . my aunt says you won't be satisfied with a mere portrait. That you'll be after more."

His eyebrows rose. "Oh. Like what?"

Must he force her to be blunt? Well, she would not agree to anything unless he understood the limits of their arrangement.

"That you'll ask me to pose for a nude. Will you promise never to make any inappropriate requests?"

He laughed. "I would never dream of asking you to remove your clothing, Ais Lazuli."

"Do you swear it?"

"I promise I will not ask you to do anything you object to."

"Then I will pose for you in exchange for lessons in using oiled paint."

His smile made her heart skip several beats. "Wonderful! Now, we don't have time for a lesson today, but we do have enough for another quick sketch. Would you sit over there by the window?"

Sighing, but secretly pleased, Rielle walked over to the chair he had indicated and sat down.

CHAPTER 6

It did not surprise Rielle that her parents hadn't noticed she was arriving home a little later each quarterday, but it did surprise her that it had escaped Narmah's attention. As the festival days drew ever closer the entire family was involved in fulfilling orders, from the preparation of pigment and dye to delivering paints and cloth, so maybe that was distracting her aunt. Maybe Narmah *had* noticed, but assumed Rielle was dawdling to gain some time away from the work. Her aunt smiled sympathetically each morning when Rielle was sent to help with customers and tidy the shop, or help with the family's own festival preparations. In one form or other, the festival now consumed all Rielle's waking hours apart from the time she spent eating, attending temple ceremonies and classes, and posing for Izare. She might normally have grown bored with the latter if it wasn't such a relief to be still for a while, and it gave her an excuse to look at him as much as she wanted.

Seeing that Izare's eyes kept dropping to her hands, she looked down. Her mother had recruited Rielle to check the quality and hue of each load of freshly dyed cloth, which was often still wet. Despite her best efforts, her fingertips were constantly stained.

"I suppose I should have warned you not to include my hands," she said.

Izare shrugged. "Once I have the shape right I will get Jonare to sit for the skin colour."

Rielle sighed. "I tried to bleach it out."

"It doesn't bother me." He held up a paint-smeared hand. "I'm almost never completely clean."

"Paint is easier to remove than dye. And it's not just you I try to clean up for."

"No?" His eyebrows rose. "Who are you trying to impress?"

"Nobody. I'm trying to *avoid* making an impression."

"A bad impression?" He shook his head. "I doubt you could if you tried."

Rielle suppressed a smile. "Not everyone thinks so, Izare. Some look down on a stained girl from the stinking dyeworks."

"Then they are fools," he said firmly, eyes darting from her hands to the portrait.

Rielle thought of Tareme and Bayla and sighed again. Famire was always with them when Rielle arrived at the temple now. Snobbish, lazy and possessed of a cruel sense of humour, the girl always talked down to Rielle. It might have been tolerable if the others hadn't begun to follow suit. Rielle had found herself getting snappy with them that morning, then having to apologise.

Famire found particular amusement in suggesting suitable husbands for Rielle in the guise of being "helpful". She kindly informed Rielle which men were unlikely to consider her a prospective wife, then weighed up the good and bad traits of those left, asking which faults Rielle might be willing to put up with.

Most quarterdays, Rielle would have been eager to leave the temple as early as possible even if she hadn't had Izare's company to look forward to.

Izare's short cut took her through parts of the artisan quarter she hadn't seen before. Neither poor nor wealthy, most buildings were a combination of home, workplace and shop. It was an area where Rielle's family might have lived, if they were not obliged, as dyeworkers, to situate themselves on the edge of the city. Which meant they weren't *that* much more respectable than the artisans living around Izare's home.

A pounding downstairs drew Izare's attention away. He rolled his eyes.

"May the angels strike them. They're early."

Rielle felt her heart sink as he wiped his brush and dropped it in a jar of solvent. Though she found Izare's friends interesting and friendlier than the girls at temple lessons, he did not work on the portrait when they were around, and her time with him was so short. So far he'd spent little time teaching her, too – only showing her how to prepare paint and adjust the consistency. He walked over to the stairs.

"Come on up," he yelled.

The sound of a door opening followed, then footsteps and several voices – some familiar, some not. Izare's face lit up with a broad smile.

"Errek! You're back!"

A slim Fyrian climbed into view and embraced Izare. Greya and Jonare appeared next and kissed Izare on the cheek. As did Merem. The artists and actors who made up Izare's circle of friends were habitually affectionate in a way that Rielle found appealing, but it was more physical than she was used to. Narmah would consider it inappropriate and too familiar.

The newcomer was carrying a heavy, round-bodied iquo bottle. Rielle's heart sank. There would be no more painting, once they began drinking. As the newcomer turned to enter the studio he saw her and stopped, smiling.

"Who is this?"

"Izare's latest subject," Jonare said as she and the others

moved past him to the cluster of wooden seats they usually occupied when visiting Izare.

"This is Ais Lazuli," Izare said, gesturing towards her grandly.

Errek's eyes moved straight to the portrait and his smile faded a little before it returned, though looking a little forced.

Jealousy, Rielle noted. *He envies Izare's talent.*

"Rielle." Izare beckoned. "Come and meet Errek. He's back from Doem, where he's been painting the main temple's spiritual."

"Restoring," Errek corrected.

Rielle rose and walked over to stand beside Izare. Errek's expression shifted again. This time it was a change she was familiar with: the transition to the intense analytical observation of an artist.

"An honour to meet you," she said.

He reached out and took her hand. "Twofold in return." He shook his head. "Where does Izare find such beauties?"

Deftly flattering the both of us simultaneously, Rielle mused. "For once, not in Whore's Alley," she replied mildly. She'd learned the hard way that the disapproval her family felt towards prostitution annoyed Izare's friends, who considered some of the poor quarter's "working" women as friends, yet she did not want this newcomer thinking she was one such woman. Errek laughed and nodded, his expression telling her that he understood.

Izare uttered a weak sound of protest. "My models weren't *all* whores. And I can't keep painting the same five friends – especially when some insist on moving to Doem for two years. So, Errek, are you here to stay?"

Errek moved to stand before the painting. "For now." His examination of it was even more intense. Rielle looked closer, feeling awe again at the subtle blend of colours within the skin tones and the deft brushstrokes that, at a distance, suggested finer detail than was actually present. She was a little uncomfortable with the fact that Izare was painting her without a scarf, but she imagined that nobody but he and his friends would be seeing it.

Errek stepped back. "How close are you to finishing this?"

"It will be done when it's done," Izare replied.

"Not too soon, I hope," Rielle added. "He promised me lessons in return and we have barely started."

Errek straightened, and turned to regard her. "When he's done with you, may I paint you next?"

She stared at him in surprise, then turned to Izare for a clue as to how she ought to react. He looked unhappy, but at her look shrugged as if to say it was her choice. Was there any harm in it? She had let Izare paint her so why not Errek? But the more paintings of her there were, the greater the chance someone who knew her parents would see one and inform them. Yet she did not want to offend Izare's friend when there was still the unfinished matter of lessons. "Well . . . I should think *I* ought to get the chance to paint someone next," she said slowly.

Greya grinned. "Oh, definitely! I want to see her paint."

Jonare and Merem nodded.

"But who will you paint?" Errek asked.

Rielle began to turn towards Izare, then stopped. *No, not yet. He's already vain enough.* Instead she looked at the others. Jonare met her eyes and nodded, so Rielle pointed to her.

"Jonare."

She turned to Izare, then felt her stomach sink as she found him frowning. *Uh-oh. I hope I haven't hurt his vanity so much that he refuses to teach me. Or finish the portrait. Or see me again . . .*

"Though . . . maybe not in oils yet," she added, "lest my beginner's awkwardness reflect badly on my teacher."

Izare's eyes narrowed. "No, but there is no reason you cannot make preparatory sketches now. Here . . ." He moved away, collecting a board, paper and chalk then handing them to her.

Rielle looked down at the materials. Her heart was suddenly beating fast, for all that they were familiar and reassuring. She was conscious of the others watching her, conscious they would think of her only as Izare's latest subject until she proved herself to be more. *I can do it*, she told herself. Izare dragged a chair over and gestured to it wordlessly. Rielle sat, braced the drawing board on one knee, and began to sketch.

The light from the windows was muted, thanks to the overcast sky outside. Jonare remained still and relaxed – clearly used to the role of artist's model. Rielle began by marking out distances between the woman's features with faint marks, then made broad, soft strokes with the edge of the chalk to fill in the shadows. She added detail, varying the thickness and darkness of lines. Sweeping strokes for the hair. Some gentle hatching to describe Jonare's scarf, draped around her neck. A faint, soft line for the edge of the nose. A hard, quick curl of darkness for the nostril. Feathery dashes formed the eyebrows. Careful touches filled in the eyes, leaving a chink to suggest reflected light, then a gentle sweep over the whites to soften them.

After a few final touches to refine the drawing she drew in a deep breath and considered the overall result. Nodding, she looked up to find that Greya and Merem had left their seats but she had been concentrating too hard to notice.

"That's amazing," Greya said.

The voice came from near Rielle's shoulder. She turned to find Greya, Merem and Errek standing behind her, with Izare. Merem hummed in agreement. But from Izare and Errek there was only silence.

"Show me!" Jonare demanded. Turning the board, Rielle watched as Jonare's eyes widened. "You *are* an artist!" she exclaimed.

"Yes, she is," Izare said, crossing his arms. "But one with a lot to learn."

Rielle shrugged. "If I didn't think I had something to learn, I wouldn't be here," she reminded him. He met her eyes, and his expression softened.

Errek patted his shoulders. "I suspect *you* may have something to learn from *her*," he said.

Izare's eyes narrowed again, but he said nothing as a pounding came, once more, from downstairs. As he started for the stairwell, the sound of the door opening echoed below, followed by hurried footsteps. A head appeared behind the railing of the stairwell, turning to locate them. It was Dorr.

"The priests are doing an inspection," the man told them.

Curses came from all around. Rielle turned to see expressions of annoyance. Izare went straight to her portrait and unclamped it from the easel. Jonare stood and touched Rielle's arm.

"You had better leave."

Rielle's heart skipped. If the priests found her here they would tell Sa-Baro. Though she was sure he would believe her when she told him she was not up to anything scandalous, he'd be obliged to inform her parents. She sought Izare and found him slipping the portrait between several half-finished paintings leaning against a wall. He picked up a partially completed spiritual and placed it on the easel.

"Next quarterday, then." She handed the board and chalk to him. His expression was all concern now.

"Yes." He frowned. "I should escort you home, but if they see us together—"

"I'll go with her," Jonare offered. "No tainted will dare take on the two of us."

Rielle felt her stomach sink even further than before. "Is that why they're inspecting? Is there another tainted in Fyre already?"

Izare put the drawing aside and took one of her hands. "There is, but you'll be safe with Jonare." He stepped forward and, before she realised what he was doing, kissed her on the cheek. A thrill went through her entire body, and she suddenly could do nothing more than stare at the floor, conscious that her face had grown very warm and her heart was beating very fast.

"Come on," Jonare said, hooking a hand under Rielle's arm. "We had better hurry."

Submitting to the woman's guidance, Rielle all but stumbled to the stairs, looking back once before following Jonare down. Izare smiled at her, but could not conceal the worry in his eyes.

They stepped out into a street filled with gloom. Rielle pulled her scarf from around her neck and hastily covered her head. The clouds above were the dimpled grey that promised rain but never delivered. People hurried past, their shoulders hunched, casting backward looks. Rielle heard voices calling out and heard the warning in them, but not the words.

"The tainted will be well away by the time the priests arrive," she murmured.

"Oh, I doubt he or she is from the artisan quarter." Jonare shrugged. "Nobody wants to be the one to prove what's said about us is true."

"What's said about you?"

Jonare gave Rielle a disbelieving look. "That artisans are more likely to be tainted than anyone else."

Rielle stared at her. "Nobody ever said that to me."

The woman smiled sadly. "You've had a sheltered life then. Or maybe dyeworkers aren't regarded the same."

They walked quickly, Jonare guiding Rielle through

narrow streets, first familiar then not. They did not see any priests.

"I'm glad I left the children with my sister today," Jonare said. "They do love to play with Izare's neighbours, but the priests frighten them." Again, Rielle turned to regard the woman with surprise, but Jonare did not notice. "Izare enjoys their visits, too. He's good with children. He'll make a good father one day, don't you think?"

At the quick look Jonare gave her, Rielle suppressed a sigh. It was not the first time one of Izare's friends had sought her opinion on his suitability as a husband or father. She couldn't tell if they were warning her off or encouraging her. Unfortunately, it meant most of her conversations with them were about Izare, so Rielle settled for changing the subject.

"So does your sister look after your children when you are performing?"

"Yes, and I look after hers when she's working."

"What does she do?"

"Oh, a mix of things. Washing clothes. Cooking." She looked around and her pace slowed. Following suit, Rielle noted that the people they passed were no longer tense and harried.

"So, what did you think of Errek?" Jonare asked.

Rielle shrugged. "Hard to tell on a first short meeting, but he seems nice. He and Izare were . . . is there a conflict between them?"

Jonare laughed. "Just rivalry. Both are talented artists. Both are handsome young men, don't you think?"

"Errek? He's nowhere near as handsome as Izare."

The other woman's eyebrows rose, then she smiled. "Ah. Well. That's good to hear."

Rielle looked closer and understanding came. "You like Errek?"

"Yes." Jonare sighed. "But I suspect he does not like me as much as I like him."

"But what of your husband?"

Jonare's smile widened. "Husband?"

Rielle blushed as she realised her mistake. "Ah . . . the father of your children."

"Oh, their fathers don't know or care what their mother does. Which for one of them is a good thing, and the other . . ." She shrugged. "Even when he was alive he was as useless as fish traps in the desert."

"I'm sorry—"

"Don't be. I'm not. He's only bothering the Angels now." They turned a corner. "We are not far from Temple Road now."

The houses ahead were familiar. They turned into a street that led directly to Temple Road, though it emerged a little way from her home. She could slip down a side alley to emerge closer, however.

"I know where I am now." Rielle turned to Jonare. "I can find my way from here, if you want to return."

"I should get back in case the priests search my sister's house." Jonare sighed. "Angels curse them."

Rielle winced at the vehemence in the woman's voice. Being among people who did not respect the priests as her family did made her uneasy, perhaps mostly because she feared they had reason to.

"Thank you for coming with me."

Jonare smiled. "My pleasure. Can I have the sketch you did of me?"

Rielle nodded. "Of course!"

The other woman patted Rielle's arm. "I'm looking forward to seeing a painting of yours."

"So am I." Rielle grimaced. "Though I'm wondering if Izare is going to keep his side of our deal."

Jonare laughed and stepped away. "He will. He's making sure you have a reason to keep coming to visit, once his portrait

190

of you is done." She winked, then turned and strode back the way they had come.

Rielle watched her go, lifting a hand to touch her cheek where Izare had kissed her. Another thrill went through her at the memory. It had been no more than he did for other women in greeting or farewell. But what if Jonare was right, and he did want her to keep visiting?

She turned and began walking towards home. It did not matter if his interest in her was more than having a subject to paint or a student to teach. Her parents would never approve of him.

Or would they? Is there such a difference between an artist and a dyer? We all work with colour. In fact, Izare's skills could be useful in a dyeworks. Mother and Father respect Narmah's skill and they've encouraged me to paint. Maybe I can steer them towards the idea that another artist would be a useful addition to the family – especially as I'm having no luck finding a husband among the—

Sudden darkness surrounded her and she staggered to a halt. Looking around, she saw that she had stepped into a small convergence of streets, not quite big enough to be called a courtyard. All was dirtied by black streaks and blotches. She could sense the edge of it and staggered in that direction.

Coming out, her sight cleared and she found herself standing in front of a shrivelled old woman leaning on a stick.

Who was staring back at her.

"It's not dirty," the woman said. "It's just empty."

Rielle's heart, which had been racing, lurched. She cast about and felt relief flood through her as she saw that nobody else had been near to witness her reaction to the Stain. Nobody but this old woman.

The woman smiled. "Scares you, doesn't it? Don't want to see it but you do."

Which meant the woman could, too. *She won't say anything,*

191

because to reveal that I can see it would reveal that she can as well. Rielle stepped back – not too far lest she encounter the Stain again. The woman laughed and moved forward, her stick tapping on the ground.

"Run away then. Run from nothing. What did this is long gone. From what I heard, it was a good thing, too. Saved someone's life. Who's to say that's a bad thing, eh?"

What is she . . .? Who is she . . .? Could she be the corrupter? Rielle's blood went cold and she turned and fled.

The walls on either side rushed past, then disappeared and she had to pull up fast to avoid a well-laden cart. All around her was the traffic of Temple Road. Looking over her shoulder she saw an empty street behind her. The woman hadn't followed her.

How could she, as old as she is? But if she was tainted – and the corrupter no less – then only she and the Angels knew what she could achieve with magic. Rielle shrank away from the street and hurried away, crossing to the other side of the road though it meant fighting against the traffic.

I should report it. I should tell the priests. But she couldn't without revealing her own ability to see Stain. Taking deep, slow breaths to calm herself, she hurried on towards home.

CHAPTER 7

The sky had cleared by the time Rielle and her family arrived at the temple but the streets still smelled of rain. Though some of the parade participants looked a bit damp they were not going to let it keep them from enjoying the beginning of the Festival of Angels. Rielle's family was dry, having been protected by a large, brightly coloured waxcloth canopy that the dyeworks' servants had held over them as they walked into the city centre.

That canopy was now being dismantled and rolled into bundles. Rielle and her family would now join the crowd, much to her relief. As a child she had loved being part of the spectacle, but now, as a young woman, it embarrassed her. She looked down at herself and sighed. Her clothes were all new, made from fabric dyed a bright and expensive orange-red. The tunic was overstitched with temple scenes. She had to admit Narmah's work was beautiful, but it was overly gaudy for her tastes. At least she had been able to convince her aunt and mother that too much jewellery would unfairly distract the eye from Narmah's work.

She looked at her brother, as brightly attired in sky blue, and he smiled back at her. Every year Inot returned for the festival, and each time it shocked her to see how much more grown up he was. The seven-year difference in their ages seemed to grow wider. To her disappointment, he had not brought his wife and children with him, as Wadinee was heavily pregnant with their third.

As their parents started towards the temple, Rielle and Inot followed. They wove through the crowd, each of them holding a furled pennant dyed in their family colours. People let them through out of respect for her parents' status as the best and largest dyeworkers in Fyre, though Rielle could not help wondering if habitual avoidance also played a part. Her father would eventually stop when those in front did not step aside. *This is one way the residents of Fyre know where they stand in the hierarchy of status*, Rielle mused. *The closer the crowd lets you get to the temple, the higher your status.*

She was surprised, when they stopped, that her father had managed to penetrate quite so far into the crowd before people no longer moved aside. Nearby stood Bayla and Tareme's family, though the girls were not with them. Polite greetings were exchanged. Rielle's mother asked after Ako and the girls. Rielle caught the words "young ones" and "party".

"Are you not going to this party?" Rielle's mother asked her quietly, when their exchange was complete.

"I assumed you would want me here with you, as always," Rielle replied. Though she didn't care that she hadn't been invited, her mother would.

"Oh, you should have asked me. Hmm, maybe it is not too late to accept the invitation."

The crowd was quietening down. "Since I wasn't going, I didn't find out where it is."

"I'll just ask . . ."

"No!" Rielle grabbed her mother's hand and earned a frown. "Not now. I think the ceremony is about to begin."

She had seen no such sign, but fortunately it was not long before the temple door opened and priests emerged. The head priest, Sa-Koml, began to address them, beginning his usual summing up of the year's events.

Looking at the other priests, Rielle could not help smiling at Sa-Baro, who beamed down at the audience. *He so loves a celebration*, she thought, remembering the relish with which he read to them of the revels and feasting within the tales of the past. She also recognised Sa-Elem. The man stood with a straight back, looking down at the crowd soberly. His gaze moved slowly over all and she could not help imagining he was considering those who over the last year he had noted might have magical ability.

Then his gaze met hers, or at least seemed to. He was a little too far away for her to be certain. He paused, then his chin dropped slightly before he looked away. Rielle found herself staring at him, wondering if she had imagined his nod and resisting the temptation to look behind her to see if it might have been intended for someone else. Had he meant it for her? And, if so, why?

Someone else was looking in her direction, and Rielle's eyes shifted instinctively to the man beside Sa-Elem. Now it was the younger priest, Sa-Gest, who appeared to be looking at her. He was smiling but, perhaps because she already felt uncertain and self-conscious, it did not seem friendly. She tugged her scarf closer to her face and looked away, directing her gaze at her father in the hope that the priest – if he was watching her at all – would think she did so in response to being addressed.

Sa-Koml had finished his account of the year, and led them in a prayer of thanks. Rielle whispered an extra one of gratitude to the priests and Angels for her escape from the tainted. *And for introducing me to Izare*, she added silently. No mention had been made of the new tainted the priests were hunting for, or the corrupter who was teaching them. The festival was meant to celebrate the good things in life, not the bad.

As the prayer ended, hundreds of pennants rose above the crowd. Rielle broke the seal that held hers closed and felt it loosen and unfurl in her hands. She lifted it up, smiling as it and her parents' added a rainbow to the broad crop of family colours. All began to sing and circle around the temple. Once for thanks, several more times for good luck.

As they walked, they dropped coins into grates that were uncovered once a year for this ceremony. The coins fell through into the underground tunnels beneath the courtyard, where they would later be collected by priests and spent on improvements to the city. Not all citizens joined in this ritual – the entire city could certainly not fit into the courtyard these days and it freed the poorer Fyrians from the obligation to donate. At the edges of the courtyard people perched in doorways or crowded windows to watch. Parents held children high or let them ride on their shoulders.

A familiar face among these caught her attention and her heartbeat doubled. Izare smiled back at her and waved. She smiled back. He beckoned. She shook her head.

"Who is it?" her mother asked.

Rielle turned and was relieved to see her mother was searching the faces within the circling crowd. It would not occur to her that her daughter might know someone outside of it.

"A friend," Rielle told her.

"Oh, then you should go and join them."

"But what about—?"

"No, no. Narmah can find someone else to help with the feast. I'm sure your friends' party will be even grander than ours. Go and join them." She plucked the pennant from Rielle's hand. "Be home before dark."

Rielle yielded to the hand pushing her shoulder. She turned away, heart racing with both fear and excitement. If she joined Izare now she would have *hours* to spend with him. *Can I get away with this? Mother might ask Bayla's parents about the party later and learn I didn't appear. She'll wonder where I went instead.*

Those parties could be large, though. Rielle could claim she'd spent it in a quiet corner, talking to one or two people she'd just met, whose names she couldn't remember. If she said that one of them was handsome or nice her mother would be distracted by speculation about who it might be.

The edge of the crowd was moving faster than the middle so Rielle let herself be carried along until she reached the corner she had seen Izare standing in. Stepping out, she searched the faces. He was nowhere to be seen. Had he tried to follow the crowd and was now in a different part of the courtyard?

A hand suddenly curled under Rielle's arm and she jumped and turned. Greya smiled down at her.

"Don't you look impressive?" she said.

"Thank you," Rielle replied, though to her eyes Greya was the impressive one. Tall, pale and graceful, she stood out in the crowd.

"He's over here," Greya said, leading the way.

As they wove between the people, Rielle noted how the gazes of men were drawn to her guide more than to her own gaudy clothes. Their reactions were mixed. Some stared in appreciation, seeing the beauty in her graceful, long limbs, but others scowled, clearly only noticing the pale hair and skin that marked her out as having foreign blood. A feeling of danger awoke in Rielle.

"Bino," someone said as they wove through part of the crowd. Rielle gasped, appalled at the insult. It was slang for an albino, insinuating that her colouring was a deformation.

"How rude," Rielle said.

Greya shrugged. "It's just a word. That they mean it as an insult is more insulting to albinos than to me."

With a sudden flash of understanding, Rielle realised that Greya must endure such hostility all the time. How did she

197

gather the courage to step out on stage? Or, worse, to venture onto the streets of the city alone? Perhaps she remained close to her friends, relying on their protection.

"How long have you lived in Fyre?" Rielle asked.

"I was born here. My father was an actor in a troupe that travelled from city to city. He was seduced by a local singer. I saw him every time he returned to the city. When I was old enough to sing and perform I travelled with him until I was a young woman."

So she had Fyrian blood as well. Rielle looked up at the woman in admiration. Everyone Izare knew had such interesting, unusual pasts. The women were so confident and didn't hesitate to speak their mind.

"Why did you come back here to live?" Rielle asked.

"There was a man in the group who wanted to lie with me. I didn't like him. I told our leader that if the man didn't leave the troupe, I would." She shrugged. "Ah, here's Dorr."

The dashing actor joined them. In his reassuring presence, they continued on to meet Izare, Jonare and Errek. Izare grinned when he saw her, and his greeting was a kiss on the cheek that left her happily speechless for a few breaths. The others complimented her on her "costume".

"They'll be at this for another hour or so," Dorr said, glancing back at the circling crowd. "I'm hungry. And thirsty!"

"Back to the fountain?" Izare asked.

"Back to the fountain!" the rest agreed.

The six of them set off along a route now familiar to Rielle, ending in the little courtyard near Izare's home. The residents had brought out tables and chairs to fill the space and were laying out a feast, to which Izare contributed dishes of dried fruit and bottles of cheap iquo. It was a humble and rustic feast compared to what Rielle was used to, but she didn't care. The company was much more interesting.

Izare and his friends introduced her to so many of the residents that she doubted she'd remember anyone's names. A pair of women boldly introduced themselves as whores, though Rielle suspected they'd noticed her rich clothes and decided to shock her. A trio of acrobats arrived and treated the children to a display of tumbling and balancing. Someone began to sing, and soon instruments were brought out and people began to dance.

Hours passed. As the shadows lengthened, visitors started to leave and the residents settled into chairs to talk and to sip iquo.

"Monya, where is Dinni?" Dorr asked of one of the neighbours.

The woman grimaced. "She's still upset. She says 'why should she thank the Angels for ruining us?'."

"Is it that bad?" Jonare asked in a low, concerned voice.

"Not quite. Not if she starts working on a new sculpture straight away. She'll still get one finished by the customer's wedding if she starts soon and we borrow the money for the stone."

"Has she begun work?" Izare asked.

The woman looked at him and shook her head. "She gets so attached to them. It's like asking her to replace one child with another."

"Should I talk to her?"

She nodded. "That might help. But not today. Tomorrow. Or the day after." She looked up at one of the houses. "I'd better go and see how she is."

The group fell silent after the woman left. Rielle bit her lip, mystified by the conversation but uncertain if it would be nosy to ask about it. As Errek began talking with Merem, Greya leaned towards Rielle.

"Monya's wife is a sculptor," she said in a low voice. "She'd almost finished the largest commission she's ever had. It took her many halfseasons. It was . . . smashed."

Rielle sucked in a breath at the thought of all that work ruined. "By whom? Robbers?"

Greya shook her head. "The priests, during the last inspection."

"But . . . why? Was it offensive to them?"

"No."

"Then why?"

Greya shrugged.

"It could be she wasn't gracious enough," Dorr said. "Or didn't offer them a large enough donation."

Rielle frowned, guessing that he meant the donations were nothing of the sort. But why would the priests want bribes? Did the sculptors need them to turn a blind eye to something? *Like a tainted?*

"It's not the money," Jonare added, to nobody in particular. "It's her setting up with Monya."

So when Greya had referred to Dinni as Monya's wife, she hadn't made a mistake, Rielle mused. *That's a bit odd, but surely nothing worth punishing them so severely for.*

"Which priests were these?" Rielle asked.

None of the others replied, instead exchanging glances and shaking their heads. Izare smiled at her sadly and shook his head.

"It will do you no good to report them," he told her. "Nothing will change and you will only reveal that you've been talking to us."

"The priests will always harass artisans," Dorr added, shrugging. "We're used to it."

"Because people think we're more likely to be tainted?" Rielle shook her head. "I'd never heard that until Jonare told me. It's ridiculous."

"Is it?" Dorr asked. "Most of us will never be rich. Poverty can drive people to do desperate things. As the great poet Barhla said, 'artists are but a shade away from whores and slaves'."

"In Keya I knew whores who used magic to prevent conceiving," Greya said. She looked up and smiled at all the expressions of discomfort this revelation had produced. "It's forbidden to use it there as well, of course."

"How do they avoid detection?" Jonare asked.

Greya shrugged. "Stain sticks to a place, not a person. I gather they went somewhere to do it that the priests didn't go."

"Did you tell the priests about them?" Dorr asked.

"No. People there are more likely to ignore the occasional small transgression, especially if it was for a good purpose."

Rielle felt a chill spread through her body and a memory rose of an old woman. *From what I heard, it was a good thing, too. Saved someone's life. Who's to say that's a bad thing, eh?* She shivered.

"Well, no more talk of magic today," Izare said. "The festival is supposed to be a time of good cheer." He looked at Rielle and tilted his head to the side. "Perhaps I should take advantage of Rielle being here to work."

Rielle's heart skipped a beat. As he raised a questioning eyebrow she nodded. "It would be a shame not to, and once the festival is over my aunt may expect me home sooner."

"Go on then," Dorr said, then grinned, "and no need to worry. Your iquo won't go to waste."

Izare stood up. "Leave me at least one bottle."

"A bottle!" Jonare said. "You'll be lucky if we save you a cup."

Rising, Rielle smiled at them all. "If you're gone before we're done, a good year to you all."

To her surprise, they chuckled and exchanged knowing looks. Her face warmed as she realised how they had interpreted her words.

"Done *painting*," she told them firmly, then looked to the sky as their grins only widened. "Angels save my reputation." She turned to follow Izare to his door.

"Or at least ensure you have fun sullying it," Errek called after her. She glared over her shoulder at him, earning another laugh.

Izare did not seem at all bothered. He opened the door to his house and stepped aside to usher her through. She took a step towards the stairs, but a hand caught her and pulled her up short. Turning, she heard the door shut behind him and felt the warmth of his fingers curled around hers.

But these things were suddenly unimportant compared to what her eyes told her.

His gaze was intense, but not in the analytical way he stared when painting her. There was uncertainty and hesitation – which she had never seen. And then a strange, almost crazed light flared in his eyes and he pulled her towards him. Pulled harder than she expected, so that she lost her balance. But instead of falling against him she felt him catch her shoulders . . . and press his mouth to hers.

All of her froze except her heart, which did a crazy, impossible flip. Before she had time to recover he pulled away, searching her face.

"I'm sorry," she said, then giggled as she realised her voice hadn't suddenly deepened – he had spoken the same words at the same time. "You surprised me," she added.

"A nice surprise?" he asked.

Blood and heat were rushing around her body and it was not an unpleasant sensation. "Yes," she said slowly.

Being ready for it made the next kiss no less exciting but certainly more . . . interesting. What he did she mirrored, since he had clearly done this before. It continued for some time, and the barest of pauses separated one movement from the next. Rielle wondered how such a simple action could have so much nuance, and remain so deeply thrilling even as the time in its occupation lengthened. Her awareness gradually spread outward, to the brush of his cheek against hers, to the feel of his back beneath her hands, to the way his fingers moved up to tangle in her hair (where had her scarf gone?), trace the back of her ear, slide gently along her neck, cup her shoulders in his palms, encircle her arms . . .

. . . and then somehow move smoothly from there to her breasts.

She stilled, not drawing away but no longer kissing him. What was it about this that lit a spark of indignation? Why did this touch set off a warning? She knew she ought to pull away, that this was leading to things she ought not do, yet at the same time she wanted to know what those things felt like.

His thumbs ran over her nipples. The sensation was not unfamiliar – she could hardly have not noticed that this part of her body had become more sensitive in the last few years – but now it flowed inward and through her, amplified until her whole body was vibrating with it, awakening other feelings in other places that might also like attention.

At the same time, she had somehow wound up so much in contact with him that she could not help noticing a corresponding, and rather more obvious, physical change in his body.

Unbidden and unwelcome, words rose up from her memory. Words of her aunt. *"People would assume he was doing a lot more than painting a portrait."*

She gently took hold of his wrists and stepped away. He did not resist. She realised she was breathing quickly. He was, too. They regarded each other for a long moment, then he slowly smiled.

"Shall we go upstairs?"

She nodded. "To paint. You have a portrait to do."

"And I owe you some lessons."

"Yes. Lessons. In painting."

He did not move. "Do you think your family will notice, if you continue coming home a little late from temple?"

"Perhaps. We'll have to see. We'll have to make the best use of the time we have."

His smile broadened. "Indeed, we will."

CHAPTER 8

"So Mother is trying to marry you into one of Fyre's families."
Rielle looked up at Inot to see him smiling sympathetically. She sighed, nodded and looked back at the road ahead.

"Yes."

"No luck, then?"

"Of course not."

She heard him chuckle. "Don't be pessimistic," he told her. "Love is a great persuader."

"For me or for the unlucky man?"

He laughed. "Either." Then he fell silent, and she stole a glance at him. He was frowning.

"What is it?"

His eyes met hers. "Narmah told me about the tainted." He shook his head. "It would never have happened if you'd been with someone else."

Rielle felt a shiver of dismay. "It was bad luck, that's all. There aren't tainted roaming around the city all the time."

"Tainted aren't the only danger, for a young woman."

"Is this why you decided to escort me?"

"Yes. I have a friend to call on, too, but I will be sure to leave in time to meet you afterwards."

Her heart sank and she turned away to hide her disappointment. *But he's not staying in Fyre long. I'll see Izare again in a few quarterdays. We knew I might have to cut my visits shorter anyway, once festival preparations were over.* Still, she ached at the thought of not seeing him at all. Then she felt guilty for wishing her brother gone sooner.

"Was the desert crossing hard this time?" she asked, to change the subject.

He shrugged. "Just a dust storm. No bandits."

"Was the storm as bad as that one you told me about . . . it must have been three years ago?"

She had drilled Inot about his life outside the city every time he had visited, as she knew there was little chance she would ever leave Fyre herself. It gave him something to talk to her about, since their different ages meant they did not have a lot in common. *Thanks to him, I know how to cross the desert without getting lost, how to treat a tibba bite, find a well and tend the kapo.* Which was about as useful to her as it would be for him to learn how to make paint and prepare boards, but he always let her prattle on anyway.

She didn't want to talk about painting this time, however. She'd learned nothing new in the last year apart from how to make Izare's oily paint, and if Narmah heard of that she might guess who Rielle must have learned it from. Instead, Rielle kept Inot talking about travelling, the places he bought cloth and dyes from, and his family. When they arrived at the temple he repeated his promise to meet her, then strode away.

Inside, most of the other girls had already arrived. Famire was absent, to Rielle's relief. Tareme and Bayla were caught up in discussing something scandalous that had happened at the Festival Day party. They didn't stop, either oblivious or not caring that Rielle hadn't been invited.

Sa-Baro soon arrived and directed the girls to their seats. When they had settled he began to address them.

"The Festival of Angels is a time of thanks and marks the

end of one year and the beginning of another. As we begin the new year we priests offer the people of the city an opportunity to discuss matters that concern them, and that includes the teachers asking students how they feel about their learning and their future." The old priest smiled. "I hope that my fellow priests' claims that I have the easier task will prove true.

"I will speak to you all in turn. The rest of you will read the chapter on the Angel of Justice. Bayla, you will be first. Come with me."

Bayla rose and followed Sa-Baro into a side room for private worship. The other girls exchanged glances. All picked up the Book of Angels and opened it. Rielle followed suit, but from the whispering conversations that soon began she guessed few were actually reading.

Rielle had read the stories in the book many times, and though she had her favourites she found she could not keep her mind on reading. Each time Sa-Baro returned with one of the girls and selected another she felt a growing tension. What was there to be worried about? Of lessons there was not much to say. They were not difficult and Sa-Baro had never seemed displeased with her progress.

What she felt wasn't anxiety, she realised. It was more like excitement. This felt like a rare opportunity to fix something, but she wasn't sure what. Perhaps she could mention the rudeness of the other girls? Would it achieve anything? No priest could make them *want* to treat her as an equal.

If not her fellow students, who else would she like to settle something with? Her home life was as good as she could expect, and any complaints ought to be directed at her local priest, anyway.

Who else did she spend time with? The answer leapt into her mind.

Izare and his friends.

She couldn't tell the priest about them, yet there was a related matter she could discuss with the priest. She would have to be careful, however.

Time slowed, then. She used it to consider how she might approach the subject, and what she must avoid speaking of. When Sa-Baro finally called her name a thrill of apprehension went through her. She rose and followed him to the private worship room.

A large spiritual hung from the wall, and it looked quite old. The figures were all out of proportion and so unrealistic they seemed almost comical. The colours were vibrant, however. It had been painted with good-quality pigments, at least. Sa-Baro directed her to sit on one of the seats and settled on another.

"So Rielle. You've been attending my lessons for a year now. Are you satisfied with your education here?"

She nodded. "Yes."

"Are you happy coming here? It is a much longer journey for you than before."

"It is, but I do find the lessons more interesting."

He smiled, then grew serious again. "I have noticed lately that you sometimes appear relieved when classes finish."

Rielle looked down at her hands and sighed. "My parents sent me here in the hope I'd find a husband among the families of the other girls," she told him.

"That is probably true."

She looked up and met his eyes. "It *is* true. My mother made it clear to me. She is hardly a subtle woman." Rielle sighed and dropped her gaze again. "What is also true is it was a waste of time. I've overheard conversations, and the other girls have made it clear through hints and suggestions both polite and . . . less so . . . that none of the families would consider me a suitable match for their sons."

The priest nodded. "Ah. That is not entirely true. Everyone

wants their children to better the family status, and marriage is the best way available for young women – all young women. The women see you as a competitor. The men do not."

Rielle shook her head. "If any of them consider a wife below their family status an option they are strangely adept at pretending otherwise. If any do, their families are preventing them from meeting or associating with me."

Sa-Baro's shoulders lifted. "Perhaps they would prefer an older son who stands to inherit to marry a woman of equal status – or their priority is an alliance with another family."

Rielle paused, then lowered her voice. "The only available men that I've been introduced to have been either lecherous, gamblers or drunks, or had some physical or mental limitation. I might have considered some of the latter if they had not behaved as if they thought I was beneath them."

Sa-Baro regarded her, his eyes half closed in thought. That he did not argue gave her some confidence.

"It's my parents who are set on me marrying above their station, not me," she told him. "I would accept someone of equal, or even lower, standing if he was honest and kind."

He smiled. "Your humility and practicality do you credit."

She sighed. "Do they? To tell the truth, if the rudeness of these girls is what I'd be subjected to all the time, I'd rather not marry into the families at all."

He frowned and looked towards the main hall. "I will mention their behaviour to their parents. Don't worry – I will not name you as their target, only suggest that a general lack of manners has been noted." He turned back to her. Now, is there a man you have in mind as your possible future husband?"

Her face warmed at the question and she looked away. *I can't tell him that!* Lying to a priest was a terrible thing. But, then, her answer did not have to be specific.

"Perhaps someone in a trade," she told him. "Perhaps one

similar to my parents'. If my husband's interests benefited theirs, perhaps they wouldn't mind if he wasn't of higher status. A weaver or tailor, perhaps. Or someone with skills that could complement the dyeworks, such as those of an artist."

Sa-Baro nodded. "More likely the owner of a weaving house than the weaver himself. An artist? No need to aim that low." He frowned. "Why an artist?"

"They understand colour, as all good dyers must."

His frown had deepened. He regarded her silently, then lowered his voice. "Have you spoken to Izare Saffre since the day the tainted was captured?"

She blinked at him in surprise. Had even saying the word "artist" prompted him to suspect she was seeing Izare? *I can't lie*, she thought. *But I won't tell the truth unless I have to.*

"He escorted me home the quarterday after . . . that day, when Mother forgot to send a servant."

"And recently?"

She shook her head, deciding she was justified in assuming "recent" meant in the last few days.

He nodded and looked away. "That is a relief. I'm sure your parents would not approve of Izare."

She rolled her eyes. "Angels save me! That's the problem, don't you see?" His eyes briefly widened in alarm. "Not Izare. I mean the families my parents want me to marry into don't approve of me, but my parents won't approve of anyone who is not from those families. I'm beginning to think that this is all meant to keep me occupied until I'm too old to marry and the only future left for me is to be a doting aunt to future nieces and nephews and nurse to my mother, father and aunt when they get old."

He relaxed then. "I don't think that is their true purpose. But I will talk to them about it. If you wish."

She drew in a deep, slow breath and nodded. Perhaps he

would persuade them at least to *consider* the possibility of her marrying someone outside of the families. Perhaps, in time, their opinion would soften further. Perhaps even as far as considering Izare a suitable husband. *Not that Izare has said anything to indicate he wants to marry me. It's far too soon for that!* Another opportunity to have Sa-Baro talk her parents into less ambitious plans for her might not come again, though, which would still be good if her – whatever it was – with Izare never grew to be anything serious.

"Yes." She let the breath out and nodded. "Thank you." Then she smiled. "Though I do want to continue having lessons here, despite the other girls. I enjoy them." It would be much harder to find an excuse to see Izare if she no longer needed to walk home from the temple each quarterday.

He beamed at her. "Well, that's the best compliment a teacher could wish for! I will have to tackle a few other matters first, so will not be free for another quarterday or two, but after that I will see what I can do."

CHAPTER 9

"Don't overwork it," said the shadow at her shoulder. Rielle looked up from the painting she was working on. "Is it done, do you think?"

An odd half-smile pulled at Izare's lips. "I think so, but then I have other reasons to want you unoccupied."

She tried to adopt a lofty expression of suspicion, but it dissolved into a smile. He chuckled and leaned down to kiss her, plucking the brush out of her hand. She heard it clatter to the floor as he misjudged the distance to the table.

"So . . . is it done?" she repeated after some time.

He turned to consider the painting. It was a small one of a basket of fruit. "Is a painting ever done? I can always find something to fix. I usually stop when I've run out of time or money. Or it's starting to bore me. You have done very well. You only need practice and a little guiding hand." He took a step back and nodded. "I think if you continued now you would risk spoiling it. Which is a common beginner's mistake."

She sniffed. "I'm not a beginner."

"You are at this kind of painting. It is less detailed than what you are used to."

"And yet gives the illusion it is *more* realistic."

He sighed. "I love that you understand that. That you understand . . . me."

Rielle's heart leapt and drummed out several quick beats before slowing again. *Don't get too excited*, she told herself. *He didn't say he loved me.*

But it was impossible not to feel a thrill as the kissing resumed. Soon they had drifted to the cluster of old chairs. Each movement that necessitated the separation of their lips was resented, but the change of location brought new ways in which parts of their bodies might be pressed together. Rielle loved the feel of his skin under her fingers, warm and smooth. She had been the first one to explore under fabric, sliding hands beneath his shirt. She hadn't anticipated that he might do the same, but then it hardly seemed fair to object – and it proved to have very pleasant consequences.

She drew the line at removing clothing. He sighed wistfully at her modesty, or restraint.

"You do know I can't lie with you?" she'd said as she left, the day of the festival.

He'd smiled. "Can't or won't?"

"Won't." How she'd wanted to add "*yet*" to that.

"I know." His expression became serious. "I want you, but I would never want you hurt or diminished because of me, Rielle. I can't avoid that, if you have to choose between me and your family."

I think I fell in love with him at that moment, she thought. *At least, consciously.*

A door slammed below, and they both jumped. As the sound of hurried footsteps followed, she leapt away and quickly straightened her clothing. Izare rose from the chair gracefully and smoothed his shirt as he walked over to the stairwell and looked down.

"What is it, Errek?"

The footsteps stopped.

"Priests are about. Might be another inspection." Errek paused. "Is Rielle here?"

Izare sighed. "Yes. Thanks for the warning."

Rielle moved to the railing and smiled down at Izare's friend. "Thanks, Errek."

He shrugged. "Just looking out for our new friend." He turned and descended to the door, waving once before leaving.

"Well. I'd ask the Angels to curse them, except they'd hardly curse their own priests," Rielle muttered.

"Ask them to curse the tainted the priests are looking for," Izare replied darkly. "Or the one who's teaching them. He's the reason our homes are being searched so often." He turned and drew her into a close but quick kiss. "Go. And be careful. They might be chasing this new tainted."

Her stomach swooped. "Can you come with me?"

He considered, then nodded. "I'll hide a few things first."

She tied her scarf around her head, watching as he rearranged a few paintings. He slid his portrait of her into the hollow back of an unfinished spiritual. When he paused before her painting she shook her head.

"Don't worry. It's only a practice piece."

"They might guess that I'm giving lessons," he said.

"So? They won't know who you're teaching."

He turned away and waved her towards the stairs. "We shouldn't delay, anyway. Pull your scarf up and keep your head down. You should leave first, then I'll follow."

She would rather have walked with him, but his presence behind her was reassuring. He hummed as he walked, letting her know that he was still close by. When they were drawing close to Temple Road she felt a touch at her elbow. She looked back and stopped as she saw he'd caught up with her.

"I'd better go back now."

She nodded. He smiled and she hoped he would kiss her, but there were people nearby so he winked before turning and hurrying away. As she continued towards home disappointment ate at her. She had little enough time with him as it was, without the priests forcing her to leave early.

Early? I can't go home early. She stopped. *Narmah and my parents might notice and wonder why I don't make it home at this time every quarterday.*

But what if it *was* a hunt for a tainted that had brought the priests into this part of the city? She thought of the last time she had seen Stain, and her insides froze. It hadn't been that far from here. The memory of the crazy old woman sprung into her mind and she shuddered. She now avoided that convergence of streets. Each time she walked home she recalled the strange things the old woman had said. There had been too much of the lure about her words. All that talk of "good reasons".

The possibility that she had encountered the corrupter was frightening. But she also felt anger at the trouble the woman had caused and the lives she'd ruined. Yet it was followed by guilt. *I should have told Sa-Baro about her. I could have told him what she said. There was no need to tell him I'd seen Stain.* Yet the cryptic things the old woman had said did not prove beyond doubt that she was the corrupter. She could just be a mad old woman who could see Stain – who would tell the priests that Rielle could, too. And what if the priests thought it too much of a coincidence that Rielle had encountered both a tainted and the corrupter, and started to suspect she was more involved with both somehow?

Still, it might be worth the risk, if it led to the corrupter being found.

Rielle began walking again. *I need proof before I take that risk.*

I need to see her use magic. The woman was hardly likely to use it in plain sight, however. She'd have to be lured into it. Rielle slowed her steps. *What if I pretend to want to learn magic, then change my mind? Or pretended to fail?*

That would be dangerous. The corrupter was a magic user. Who knew what she would to do Rielle if she realised she was being tricked. Besides, if the old woman was the corrupter then surely she would never appear in the same place twice for fear of capture.

So if she is still there, that proves she isn't *the corrupter.*

Rielle slowed. Which meant there was no harm in checking. This, at least, she could have an answer to. If the woman was the corrupter, she wouldn't be there. If she wasn't, she was a crazy, harmless old woman. All Rielle needed to be careful of was not reacting to Stain, if it still lingered there, in case somebody else noticed.

As if making the decision for her, her feet took her in a different direction. Her heart was beating quickly by the time she arrived. Forcing her breathing to slow, she relaxed her shoulders and strolled into the small courtyard.

Her senses stirred. Stain did still linger, but it was shrunken and patchy. Another woman was striding across the space but she was only around ten years older than Rielle and didn't look up as she passed. A few steps from the other side of the convergence of streets, Rielle glanced back as if to look twice at the woman, letting her eyes move across the entrances of the other streets. Nobody stood there. She breathed a sigh of relief and turned back . . .

. . . to find her path blocked by a familiar, wizened creature.

"Looking for someone?" the woman hissed, ignoring Rielle's yelp of surprise.

"No!" Rielle replied and stepped around the woman.

The woman didn't move to block her, but she followed Rielle's every move with her unwavering gaze. Rielle turned to hurry away.

"She can help you," she said softly.

Rielle checked her stride in surprise. *"She?"* The old woman wasn't the corrupter. *But she knows the corrupter. She's here to find potential tainted and direct them to her*, she guessed.

She could tell Rielle how to find the corrupter. Slowly Rielle turned. She could not meet the old woman's eyes, but that would hardly be unusual among those who sought magical knowledge.

"How?" she whispered.

"Only she can tell you that."

The old woman moved closer, then extended a hand. Reluctantly, Rielle held out her own, palm upward. A curl of paper dropped into her grasp. The woman leaned even closer.

"Buy a yellow scarf and ask for the way to the baker. She will find you."

She backed away. Rielle stared down at the paper, then closed her fingers over it. The woman shuffled into a side street. The courtyard was still empty of people.

What should I do?

Unsure, she opened the curl of paper. A map had been drawn there, a tiny scrap of the city's plan. No words. No street names. No familiar landmarks. *How am I supposed to follow this?*

Then she saw the yellow dot. Was this where she must buy the scarf? Her eye snapped to a black mark where several streets converged. *Ah. Very clever. Only someone who could see Stain would know what that meant.*

The shop – if that's what it was – was not far away. *I don't have to go in. I don't have to do anything but find information that might help the priests.* Taking a deep breath, she set one foot in front of the other. The map contained no indication of a specific path to take, which left three different options. She chose the quieter, more shadowed streets that did not approach her destination directly.

What if this is a trap set by the priests to see who might succumb to the temptation? They might not believe that her intention was to help them. *Surely they will wait until the trap is sprung, and there is no question that the target had actually* learned *magic?*

As she reached the spot marked in yellow on the map she slowed. There was indeed a shop selling scarves. Coloured awnings shaded the front, and the owner's wares were tied up on rails across the wall, like a multi-coloured fringe. It was on the corner of a little courtyard of shops that sold jewellery, home furnishings and fabric. A few locals also lingered in the space: a musician, a shoe mender occupied with a customer and two children selling flowers. As Rielle moved forward to inspect the scarves a woman appeared in the doorway.

"Is there a colour you prefer?" she asked.

Avoiding the woman's gaze, Rielle touched a blue scarf, not quite but close to the rich shade associated with the Angels. It had silver bells instead of tassels at the corners.

"Midnight on the sea, the waves sing to me . . ." a voice crooned. Rielle turned to see that the musician was watching her, strumming a very round-bellied baamn as he sang the popular love ballad.

"Don't worry about him," the scarf seller said. "He always does that. It's a little strange at first, but there's no harm in it and some customers like it. So . . . the blue?"

"No." Rielle pretended to consider, allowing her hand to hover over one of the few yellow scarves. Her heart began to race. Would the woman guess her intention from her choice? "Blue is nice. But this . . . is for someone else."

"Yellow is a bright, happy colour. Even so, it does not suit many people. I think this is a safer gift."

As the woman untied a scarf the colour of dark leaves, the musician's song shifted into a lament about being lost in the forest. Rielle mused that she had never seen a forest. Or the sea. She shook her head and gestured at the yellow scarf.

"I know this person well," she explained. "She likes yellow."

The seller looked as if she might be prepared to argue, then to Rielle's relief she shrugged. "Well, if she changes her mind you can exchange it for another, if it is still in good condition."

Rielle nodded. Her skin itched as she haggled a little over the price because it would have been odd not to. As she counted out the coins, the musician's tune changed again and a chill ran down her spine.

"Your love is like sunshine . . ." he sang, clearly enjoying the game.

The seller rolled the scarf carefully and wrapped a piece of cheap cloth about it. Rielle watched, holding back her impatience and anxiety. Finally, she was free to go. She hurried away. Only when she had turned into the next street and saw she was in a narrow alley did she realise she hadn't asked where the baker was. She mouthed a curse and looked back.

A woman walking a few strides behind her looked up and smiled. Her clothes were the colour of the desert, and her face was well weathered. She was not quite Narmah's age yet she had deeper lines between her brows and around her mouth. At the woman's direct, appraising look Rielle felt her knees go weak.

"That's a lovely scarf you bought," she said, without taking her eyes off Rielle. "My favourite colour."

Her tone was full of expectation. Rielle stood frozen, her heart racing. *It is her! It must be her! What do I do now? Run?* She imagined herself caught by magic and lifted off the ground, writhing in pain, as had happed to her abductor. Taking a slow, shaking breath, Rielle held out the wrapped scarf.

The hand the woman extended was covered with rings. She took the package then gestured towards something behind Rielle. Turning, Rielle saw a longcart as weathered as the woman filling most of a nearby alley entrance. It was covered by a cloth canopy the same colour as the woman's clothes.

A hand hooked around Rielle's arm. "Come inside."

Heart pounding, Rielle let the woman guide her to the back of the cart. The corrupter pulled aside a flap. Peering in, Rielle saw a surprisingly comfortable interior filled with cushions and small travelling chests. She hesitated. If she entered first she would be trapped, with the woman between her and the exit.

The woman smiled faintly, then climbed the small ladder and crawled inside. She turned back to hold the flap open.

"See? Perfectly safe."

Rielle took a deep breath, let it out slowly, then forced herself to follow the woman inside. The corrupter settled herself onto the cushions, close enough to reach out and touch Rielle. They regarded each other in silence for a long moment.

"Did you enjoy the festival?" the woman asked.

Rielle nodded.

"Did you celebrate with family or friends?"

"Both," Rielle replied.

"You're a native Fyrian, right?"

Rielle nodded again.

"Have you ever travelled beyond the city?"

After Rielle shook her head, the woman regarded her in silence.

"Where are the directions you were given?"

Mutely, Rielle held out the slip of paper. The woman took it then tucked it under a pillow.

"You're not a chatty one," the woman observed. "That is good. So, tell me how I can help you."

Since deciding to follow the map, Rielle had considered and reconsidered what to say if she came to this point. She needed proof that the woman was teaching magic, but the woman was expecting that anyone who came to her badly needed her help. Whatever she asked for must be something about which it was reasonable for Rielle to change her mind. Or something she didn't need straight away. Remembering what Greya had said about the woman of her homeland using magic had given her an idea. She kept her eyes lowered.

"I . . . I don't need it right now. It's just . . . I've heard that there's a way to stop a woman . . . conceiving."

The woman smiled. "There are many. Have you tried any?"

Rielle shook her head. "I heard some make you sick, others don't work every time and some are permanent."

"And some are forbidden. But you must be willing to ignore that, if you have come to me."

Rielle bowed her head and nodded.

"Is avoiding a pregnancy worth that risk?" the woman observed.

Rielle grimaced and nodded again.

"Are you sure? The inconvenience or shame, for yourself or others, of you bearing a child is nothing compared to what they will do to you if they discover how you prevented it."

"I know," Rielle said. "But once I am married I won't need it. And . . . I might not need it at all."

The woman sighed, then reached forward. "You aren't already carrying, are you?" Rielle resisted the urge to shrink away from the hands that reached towards her.

"N-no. I don't think so," she mumbled as a warm palm pressed against her belly.

"Good," the woman said, her eyes fixed beyond her hand.

Twin knives cut into Rielle's flesh. She cried out, grabbed the woman's wrists and thrust her away. Looking down, she was sure she would see wounds leaking blood, but her clothes were undamaged and no red stain welled up from beneath them.

"What have you done?!" she demanded.

The woman's expression was hard and amused. "What you asked for."

"I thought you would teach me . . ."

"What? A trick to use each time you couple with a man? The worst places you can use magic are those you and others frequent, as they are more likely to detect the Stain. It is safer and more efficient to use magic once. You now need only use it when you are ready to undo the change I have made."

Rielle stared at the woman in horror. *She has made me infertile!* And the only way to reverse it was to use magic. The pain in her belly was an ache now, more like the pain she occasionally felt at the bleeding part of her cycle. *I should leave. Escape before she does any more damage.* But the thought of the childless women she'd known and their deep sadness, and of Jonare saying how much Izare loved children, kept her motionless.

I'd only need to use magic once. She wrapped her arms around her abdomen, closed her eyes and took several deep breaths. *Just once.*

Then she raised her eyes to meet the corrupter's.

"Tell me what I have to do."

CHAPTER 10

At first Rielle walked in a daze.

What have I done? When I die the Angels will know I have used magic. They will rip my soul apart.

But she had only used the tiniest bit of magic. Enough to demonstrate she had learned what the corrupter had taught her. Enough to make a tiny, fist-sized ball of Stain. Would the Angels forgive such a small act? Would they understand that she had sought the corrupter out with the intent of turning the woman over to the priests?

Or had the tiniest use of magic, no matter to what purpose, shut the door on any chance of her existence after death? *Have I made the ultimate sacrifice for the benefit of others? For people who would fear and reject me if they knew?*

It was incredible that it was still early afternoon, the sunshine warming her face. It ought to be night, the city shrouded in a darkness appropriate to forbidden, secretive deeds. People were everywhere. Those who looked at her frowned, as if seeing through her skin to the tainted soul beneath. Or perhaps her guilt was too easily read in her face.

They can't know, she told herself. *Only the Angels know. They are the only ones who ever will. Apart from the corrupter.* She couldn't even imagine telling the priests what she had done. They needed to know nothing more than that she had found the corrupter.

Who would tell them that Rielle had used magic, if she was caught.

They won't believe her, she told herself. But they would ask Rielle if it was true. If she denied it she would be lying. *If I tell the truth they'll send me away. Away from Izare and my family.* And then what was the point of her learning to undo what the woman had done to her?

A flash of anger briefly held back the fear. *She had no right to do that!* But she could see now how smart the corrupter had been. Her victims risked the discovery of their own crime if they betrayed her. Only someone truly willing to sacrifice everything could not be caught in such a trap.

Perhaps the Angels will forgive me, she thought. Priests used magic all the time, though they purified themselves afterwards. She wished she knew what those rituals entailed. Her skin itched for a bath. But it was unlikely to be a mere physical cleansing. More likely it involved offerings and prayers. Perhaps a robust version of what the priests suggested for those who sought forgiveness for other misdemeanours or mistakes. She could do both – more of both – though not so much that the priests might suspect her reasons.

At last she reached Temple Road. The short distance she had to walk to the dyeworks seemed to have grown. Finally, she pushed through the door. One of the servants was serving a customer. He gave her an odd, wary look. She ignored him, once again having to push aside the certainty that her stained soul was visible to all, and headed for the door to the family's private rooms. A bell rang, indicating that another server was required.

The door to the receiving room opened and her mother leaned out, but instead of looking around for the customer her gaze snapped straight to Rielle.

"You're here at last. Come in here *now*."

Rielle froze, staring at her mother, her stomach sinking as she read anger in her voice and face. *How does she know?*

"*Now*," Mother repeated.

She *can't* know, Rielle told herself. Forcing herself to move, she walked into the room. Her father stood there, arms crossed and face set in a scowl. Narmah sat behind him, head bowed and brow furrowed as always when Rielle had done something wrong or foolish.

"Why are you so late?" Mother demanded.

Rielle turned to her. "I heard of a shop that sold beautiful scarves," she said. "I thought I might buy one."

Her mother's eyes narrowed. "You are lying."

"I am not!" Rielle protested. "I . . . I'll take you there. The shopkeeper will remember me."

"It doesn't matter," Father said. "Sa-Baro said that he saw her leave. Where she went afterwards isn't the issue."

Rielle frowned and looked from one face to another. "Sa-Baro was here?"

"Yes," Mother answered. "He told us who you have been visiting, on your way home. That *artist*."

A shock of dismay went through Rielle, followed by a traitorous relief. They didn't know about the corrupter. How could they? But they knew about Izare. She frowned. How did they know about Izare?

"Rielle, dear." Narmah rose to her feet, walked over and took Rielle's hands. "I don't doubt that this young man is charming. You may not care that he is so much beneath this family in status, but the life of an artist is hard, even for those who succeed at it. Income is unreliable and big commissions rare. You would be poor most of the time. Would you really want to raise children in those conditions?"

Rielle opened her mouth but did not speak. She needed time to think, and behaving as if dumbstruck might buy her some time. What had they truly told her? That Sa-Baro had told them she was seeing Izare? Or had he? Nobody had said Izare's name yet. Perhaps Sa-Baro was jumping to conclusions after their meeting.

"You've got this all wrong." She turned to Mother. "I told Sa-Baro how you wanted me to marry into the families, but they were making sure I never met any but the worst of their eligible young men. He agreed that it was better I marry someone of equal status than someone higher who was a drunk, or a gambler, or who was cruel or lech—"

"Oh, don't exaggerate," Mother said. "They can't be that bad or their families wouldn't be rich. We all have to put up with a few faults in our husbands. It will hardly matter that he has a few indulgences if he can afford them."

Rielle felt her heart shrink inside. So this was all that her mother wanted for her? To put up with a horrible husband in order to be rich and increase their family's prestige, with no care at all for her happiness? Was there any use arguing? She turned to her father. "I suggested another trader might be more suitable. Perhaps even someone who could work here. And, I admit, I suggested someone like an artist but only as an examp—"

"You would have us *take in* this artist?" Father asked.

"I said it only as an example. It's become very clear I need to consider *all* options, considering where I come from."

That he didn't object to her reference to the family's status told her he wasn't listening. "So are you saying that this artist the priests followed you to – this *Izare* – is not someone you seek to marry?" he asked. "Why were you with him today?"

She hesitated. So they *didn't* know for certain her reason for visiting Izare. But Sa-Baro . . . Sa-Baro had followed her. The hurt of betrayal was followed quickly by anger. She gritted her teeth and held it back. She had known all along

226

it was far too soon for them to embrace the idea of her marrying Izare.

"Izare is teaching me to paint," she said firmly. "I asked him to give me a few lessons, that is all."

"Without our permission."

Rielle pulled out of Narmah's grip. "Yes. Izare offered to escort me home when you wouldn't even spare a servant mere days after I was attacked. Yet you place me among people who look down on us, and put me in the company of men who have used their influence to try to *ruin* me for marriage."

He frowned. "Have they—?"

Mother sniffed. "She's lying. They wouldn't dare."

The look he gave her was doubtful, but not doubtful enough. He straightened and turned to Rielle. "You are right that we should have sent a servant to escort you home. All I can say to that is you *seemed* recovered. I took you to be possessed of enough good sense and fortitude, and the town safe enough, for you to continue making your way home alone. But I see now that the incident with the fugitive has confused your judgement. You now see threats and prospects where there are none."

"I don't—" Rielle began.

"Yes, Rielle," Narmah agreed. She smiled sympathetically. "If the girls have been mean to you and Izare so kind it is no wonder you have come to doubt our plans for you. You must not judge everyone in Fyre's great families by their actions. Not everyone can be as bad as you say. There will be a nice man there for you. You will find him – and that won't happen if you ruin your reputation with this artist."

A tightness was growing around Rielle's throat. She threw up her hands. "I only wanted painting lessons!"

"Even if that were true, it's not how others will see it," Mother pointed out. "Sa-Baro promised not to speak of your association with Izare to anyone and he has not heard any rumours about you. You have a second chance."

Have I? More likely he'll spread the news about, considering how trustworthy he's proven to be so far. Rielle swallowed against the constriction. *And then what? The families will refuse to associate with us, or use the scandal as an opportunity to marry off a son nobody would willingly accept.*

"You will not leave here except with an escort. We will have you taken to and from temple classes from now on, to ensure that no further harm can be done by this Izare," Father added. "Even if we have to hire someone extra to manage it."

Rielle's heart began to race. *I'm never going to see Izare again. I won't even get the chance to say goodbye.*

Narmah patted Rielle on the arm. "I'm sorry, Rielle. You will forget him eventually."

Irritated, Rielle moved out of Narmah's reach. *No*, she thought, *he will forget me. He must have known this could happen. He will have hardened his heart to it.* She thought of his words on the day of the festival. It seemed like many halfseasons ago. *"I want you, but I would never want you hurt or diminished because of me, Rielle. I can't do both, if you have to choose between me and your family."*

If he hadn't cared about her he could have lured her into bed and had his pleasure, then cast her off, knowing that nobody would force him to marry her. But though he'd known something would eventually separate them, he'd held back, not wanting the inevitable end to cause her harm.

But it has. Or it will. Not only the selfish pain of the heart, but the doom of being passed off to the first man who consents to be burdened with me. Mother will never believe that any ill-character trait, no matter how ghastly, isn't worth enduring for money and status. And Father will clearly never believe anything is as bad as I say it is.

She could barely breathe now. She knew the sensation of

choking was panic. It was the fear of a creature thrust into a cage, facing captivity for the rest of its life. Struggling in the hope its captor's grip would slip and it would be free.

Free. She imagined herself running out of the door and into the city. To Izare. If not for ever, then at least to say goodbye.

Why not? Nobody was between her and the door. It might be the last chance she had.

They did not move as she dashed away. She caught a glimpse of them standing, wide-eyed with surprise, before she was dodging the two customers in the shop and pushing out of the main door.

The noise of Temple Road pressed in on her. It was busier than when she had arrived. She wound between carts and pedestrians. The gleefulness of her successful escape quickly dissolved into uncertainty. *What am I doing? I can't run away from my family!* she thought. But she did not stop. *I need time to think*, she told herself. *To know, if I go back, that it was my choice.*

As she reached the other side of the road she headed towards the nearest side street. From behind she heard a shout. Looking back, she caught a glimpse of three men standing outside the dyeworks door: her father and two servants. One of the servants saw her and pointed.

She dashed into the side street and kept running. The streets opposite the dyeworks were more open and regular. While she would not get lost here, neither would her pursuers. It would be easier to lose them once she got to the poorer areas.

At every step she expected someone to step out in front of her, or come up from behind, but all the people she saw were strangers, all regarding her with, at most, mild curiosity. Streets narrowed and became a tangle, but when they became unfamiliar it was not for long. Soon she would reach Izare's house, but at the thought she realised it was obvious she would run to him. Her father and the servants would look for her there.

She stopped. Would she reach Izare before they did? Father probably didn't know where Izare's house was. Sa-Baro might have told him, but for anyone unfamiliar with that part of Fyre it would still take time to locate it. She ought to get there first.

What then? She couldn't stay there. Father would arrive and have the servants drag her home. Where else could she go?

Would Izare's friends help her? They had no reason not to, as far as she knew. Rielle started towards the old house where Greya and Merem shared rooms. Izare had pointed it out to her once, when he'd escorted her through the city. She walked slowly, pulling her scarf forward to shade her face and checking the street ahead before turning each corner.

When she reached it, she paused to overcome doubt. Deep cracks indicated it had been years since the mud rendering had been applied. Dirty children wearing rags gathered in doorways, and older residents eyed her speculatively. Taking a deep breath, she forced herself to step through the entrance. Climbing the stairs, she stopped before the door she thought was the right one, listening to the muffled sound of voices within. Then she took a deep breath, and knocked.

Silence followed, then a murmur and the sound of scraping wood. Footsteps grew louder, then a voice spoke as the door swung inward.

"He's not here—" Merem stopped, his eyes widening as he saw her. "Rielle!" he exclaimed.

"Rielle?" a female voice repeated. Greya stepped into view, then grinned and beckoned. "Come in."

As Rielle stepped inside Merem closed the door, then both he and Greya looked up at the ceiling. It was covered in cracked and flaking plaster, and as she watched, a piece of it lowered, swivelling down to reveal a familiar face.

"Rielle." Izare said. He did not smile. His head vanished into the darkness above and a pair of shoe soles appeared. He dropped down, grabbing Merem for balance as he landed.

Rielle could not help smiling. His hair and clothing were covered in dust. But as he looked at her she felt all humour vanish and in its place came an unsettling feeling of mingled terror and happiness and doubt. He seemed . . . uncertain. Wary.

"The priests know you've been visiting," he guessed.

She nodded. "Sa-Baro had me followed. He told my parents. They said I couldn't see you any more."

He stared at her, then the corner of his lips quirked upwards. "Yet here you are."

"Yes."

His frown disappeared. He ran a hand through his hair, then, noticing the dust in it and on his clothes, began to brush it off.

Rielle looked up. "What were you hiding from?"

"Your family. The priests."

"So you already know."

He shrugged. "It wasn't an inspection. It was Sa-Gest come to tell me not to go near you again."

She realised she hadn't considered what might happen to Izare. "Did he break anything?"

He shook his head. "In too much of a hurry. Or he wanted to leave it to your family's servants."

"I don't think Father would do that." Or would he? She had barely begun to accept what the priests did to the artisans during their "inspections". It was suddenly not so hard to imagine her family taking revenge on Izare. Thinking of the paintings in his house, she winced and hoped he'd had time to hide some of them before he'd left. Especially his portrait of her.

She felt guilty then. She had brought him so much trouble, even if he had invited it. How could she ask him to suffer more, or worse? How could she ask his friends to?

"Will they come here?" she asked.

He looked at Greya, who nodded. "Probably."

"I should go." But where? She looked at each of them in turn. "Where can I go?"

"That depends on what you intend to do," Merem said.

"I don't know." Rielle shook her head. "I don't want to cause any more trouble. But . . . I don't want to go home. I think . . . I just need time to think."

The room fell silent, then Izare smiled.

"I know a place that might suit." He stepped forward and took her hand. "Even if all you want is a chance to say goodbye," he murmured.

She looked at him and felt her heart soften. "And if I want more?"

He smiled in that way he always did before kissing her. "Let's take things one step at a time."

Her face burned. "I didn't mean . . . At least not . . ."

"I know." He put a finger to her lips, then turned back to the others. "I'll see you tomorrow." Then he took her hand and pulled her out of the door, down the stairs and out into the sunshine. "We must hurry, but not attract attention," he told her. "The secret to that is to look more like people who need to get *to* somewhere than get *away* from somewhere."

He took a route that wove back and forth, sometimes going in a full loop. Time and parts of the city passed in a blur. At first she was terrified of running into priests or her father and the servants, but as hours passed and nobody apprehended them she began to hope that they might evade capture. By then she was far from familiar streets, but none as shabby or threatening as the worst of the poor quarter.

When he finally stopped they stood before a sturdy but unremarkable travellers' house. Everything looked colourless and quiet in the muted light of dusk.

"This should do," he said, then opened the door for her.

She stepped inside and stayed silent as he spoke to the owner. They inspected a room and Izare bartered down the price. He told the woman that Rielle was visiting Fyre and, because of a sick relative, could not risk staying with her family. She might leave in a few days or stay longer. Though the woman nodded and made the appropriate murmurs of sympathy, Rielle suspected she didn't believe a word of it. Which seemed to be confirmed when the woman made no comment or objection to Izare staying in the room after she left.

Rielle was too tired to worry about what the woman thought of her. The room was tiny – space enough for a bed, a small table and a chair. Rielle didn't have anything but the clothes she was wearing and her purse – which was considerably lighter than usual since she had bought that terrible yellow scarf the corrupter had kept as payment.

The corrupter. Magic. Rielle's knees felt weak and she sank down onto the bed.

"It has been an incredibly awful day," she gasped.

Izare drew the chair up to the bed and sat down.

"Not all of it. You didn't seem to mind the way it started."

The painting lesson. It seemed like days ago now. She looked up, and he gave her a lopsided smile. *Of course, he doesn't know what happened after I left his house. And he won't. Ever.* She forced her face into a happier expression.

"No. You are the one good thing." Then she looked away – down at the floor – before her eyes could betray what she had done.

He reached out and slipped two paint-stained fingers under her chin, lifting her head so she had to meet his eyes.

"If you try, you will find something good comes out of even the darkest times." Then he leaned down and kissed her.

Perhaps he was right, she thought, as the room seemed to brighten and the weight of gloom began to lift. As the kiss continued, and he drew her closer, a thought slipped into her mind.

At least there's no danger of me falling pregnant now.

It ought to have stirred horror. Instead, she felt a weary relief that she had one less thing to worry about. Yet if they did what she was contemplating, she would no longer be a virtuous bride for whoever she eventually married.

That was, if she dared . . .

But why not? If her parents dragged her home and made her marry into one of the great families, her husband would be some fool or monster nobody else would take anyway. He could hardly complain if she, too, had a flaw in her character.

And she was heartily sick of thinking of herself as carefully preserved stock, anyway. She wanted to be like Izare's female friends – bold and free of the obligations of her class.

Izare pulled back and frowned as she rose to her feet. She moved to the tiny window. The view outside was of a wall, so close she could have reached out to touch it. Even so, she drew the blind. He chuckled as she turned to look at him.

"Lock the door," she told him.

His eyebrows rose. As he turned away to do as she asked she pulled off her scarf and laid it on the table. Then she took off her tunic. The air on her bare skin was exhilarating.

He turned back and stilled.

"Well, well," he said in a low voice. "You've decided then."

She nodded. "Yes. If you . . .? I mean, I will understand if you don't want me to stay. It will bring you a lot of trouble."

His gaze rose to her face. He closed the distance between

them. Staring in her eyes, he nodded. "Of course I want you to stay. I love you."

Her breath caught in her throat. "I love you, too," she whispered.

His eyes were bright, but his expression serious. "Are you sure about this?"

"Yes."

He sighed and reached out to run his fingers down her bare arms. "I can think of nothing but you. I want nothing but you." Then he grinned. "And lots of commissions from wealthy clients so we can be rich and have a big happy family."

Rielle winced, then tried too late to hide it.

Izare frowned, then shook his head. "Sorry. I didn't mean . . . Why am I still talking?"

"Why indeed?" she asked.

Then he kissed her, drew her over to the bed, and they did not say much more for quite some time.

PART THREE

TYEN

CHAPTER 11

Looking upward, Tyen wondered if aircarts were circling above the fog. The only sign that dawn had arrived was that the fuzzy glow around the railsled station lamps was receding into a general paleness. The fog was a small stroke of luck, if a damp one, since the station was small with no waiting room to hide him from aerial searches.

Soon it wouldn't matter. He had decided, as the long flight cleared his head, that he must go back to the Academy and prove his innocence. But not until Vella was safe.

It was almost light enough now for him to read. He had been itching to talk to her since leaving the Academy. Driving Kilraker's aircart and keeping watch for pursuers had taken all his attention the night before. Being a clear night, there had been plenty of traffic to hide among. A few times he'd thought someone was following him, and breathed a sigh of relief when the other aircart descended or turned in another direction.

He opened Kilraker's pogbag. It was the smallest of the bags and cases Drem had strapped to the aircart chassis. With magic, it had been easy for Tyen to force the servant away from the vehicle without hurting him and to untether the craft. He'd had no time to untie the luggage, however. Though he'd been tempted to ditch it in flight he'd decided to search it all for evidence that Kilraker had set him up. He'd landed

239

in an aircart field on the outskirts of Belton and made a quick but thorough inspection, but found only clothing, items for personal grooming and correspondence, and a considerable amount of money.

He'd put everything he thought might be valuable in the pogbag, using some of the money to pay for the rest of the luggage to be taken to the closest Academy Hotel. He'd almost left it all behind in the field, vulnerable to thieves, but by then he knew he'd be going back to the Academy, and it would be better to appear considerate than spiteful when he came to face the professors.

When he did, he would need to be armed with as much knowledge of Kilraker's plans as he could be. Vella might have read something in the professor's mind that Tyen could use to prove his innocence. Hoping she wouldn't be affected by the damp air, he drew her out. He thought about his plans, then opened to the first page. His heart lifted as black marks began to form.

You will be taking a great risk, Tyen.

He shook his head. *I have to,* he told her. *I have to tell them the truth about Kilraker and clear my name. What other choice do I have? To keep running?*

It is a choice.

It seems like the wrong thing to do. If there is the tiniest chance I can convince them of my innocence I should try. But don't worry, I won't let them get hold of you. I'll find a place to hide you.

Thank you.

Before I do, I need to know everything you know about Kilraker's plan to steal you. Tell me what you read from his mind.

When he first took me from you he was thinking that, from what Miko had told him, I might be the opportunity for the wealth and fame he and Tangor Gowel were looking for. But since Professor Delly had seen me, Kilraker had limited time before he had to deliver me to the Director. He returned to his room and questioned me about many things. Mostly he sought clues as to where the great treasures of the past might be hidden, but also if there was any magical knowledge lost to history that might profit him. He decided then to steal me out of the vault and it occurred to him immediately that you were the obvious one to shift the blame onto. He then arranged to have as many other professors as possible hold me, so that later he might learn their secrets, before he handed me over to Director Ophen.

The next time I read his mind he had already taken me from the vault. He had recruited Gowel and his plan to shift the blame to you was already under way. He questioned me more, this time about the diminishing magic of the world, its causes and possible solutions. The idea that he might be the one to solve the problem appealed, as it would make him even more rich and famous. He wasn't in a great hurry, and he was interrupted, perhaps by you.

As the words stopped appearing, Tyen considered what he had learned. The news that Kilraker wanted to leave the Academy to seek his fortune was new. A tight knot of anger formed in his gut as he realised Kilraker had formulated his plan to frame him so quickly and easily.

Was there anything that he could use to prove his innocence and Kilraker's guilt? The fact that Kilraker and Gowel were friends but pretending otherwise might help establish that they were being deceitful, but it didn't prove anything. And something didn't make sense . . .

Kilraker and Gowel had been pretending to be enemies before they knew you existed. Miko said they'd argued that night in Palga, after I left. Why would they do that?

They weren't pretending to be enemies. Their disagreement was real but there was no rift. Gowel thought Kilraker should simply leave the Academy and join him, but Kilraker didn't want to lose his connection with it if he didn't have to. He wanted a guarantee that he would make his fortune before he left the Academy's support.

How long had he been waiting and planning to leave?

Five years.

Did he write down those plans anywhere?

241

He kept notes on possible sources of treasure in a notebook.

Which any archaeologist would. No, I need something more damning. Did he write down his plans to frame me?

No. He kept a diary, but took care never to mention anything that might incriminate him.

What about anything you told him that might prove he had you after you were stolen? Something he learned about other professors?

No, he didn't ask about them. He didn't have time to, before he was interrupted.

Tyen sighed and looked away. Kilraker could have written down something incriminating since then, but Tyen would have to convince the Academy to get hold of Kilraker's diary, without Kilraker finding out and destroying it first, and hope that the man's careful avoidance of recording information that could be used against him had slipped. He looked at the page.

Is there anything else that Kilraker has done that the Academy would disapprove of, that might convince them he is less than trustworthy?

He has kept some of the valuable items he and his students have found. Occasionally he has stolen ideas and research from his students, and from another student when he was one himself.

He wouldn't be the only one. He was breaking rules, but not ones that would make the rest of the professors suspicious of him. Tyen sighed. What he needed was evidence that Kilraker had entered the vault, or had planned the theft. The sort of evidence he'd find in the Academy and nowhere else. But first he must think of a safe place to hide Vella. His thoughts turned to his father. He'd have to travel through Belton to reach home, transferring to a different railsled line . . .

Professors will be waiting there for you, Vella told him. *Either they'll capture you there or wait until you leave to do it so they can find out what you told your father and whether you left anything with him. And if you post anything to him they'll intercept it.*

Tyen grimaced. She was right. Was there anyone else he could trust? Someone less obvious?

They'll visit all members of your family, all the friends you ever had. Anyone they know you might trust.

I could give you to the papers — or the police.

You don't want to reveal the Academy's secrets to the papers, and the police obey the Academy when it comes to matters of magic.

A rich collector? He shook his head. *No, I don't know anyone well enough. I wouldn't want you to end up in the hands of someone unscrupulous.*

And someone with scruples would give me back to the Academy when they realised I was stolen.

Tyen muttered a curse. Vella was telling him what he already knew but hadn't acknowledged. He considered the only other idea he'd had.

I could bury you somewhere.

If you thought that was a good idea, you would have done it already. But you know that the most likely consequence of you returning to the Academy is you'll be locked up as a thief.

And you'll be stuck wherever I buried you, Tyen finished. *For ever, if something happens to me. So what am I doing, Vella? What chance do I have of succeeding?*

Very little chance. You have no evidence that Kilraker stole me or even planned to, whereas he has witnesses who saw you take me from him in the tunnel. You stole his aircart and ran away, which makes you doubly a thief.

Tyen sighed again. *If only they trusted you to tell them the truth. But they won't even try to work out if you can be trusted. They think you are a danger to me, but now I am a danger to you. You would be safer with a new owner.*

I regret to say it, but you are right. But if you are to find one, you have little time to do it.

He rubbed his eyes, feeling the lack of sleep weigh down on his shoulders.

I need more time. I guess I have to delay returning to the Academy. Go somewhere the professors won't find me. I have to . . . I will have to—

A distant shriek cut through the fog. He looked up, recognising the sound of the railsled horn. It was early, and the sound was coming from the wrong direction.

Or is it? If I am to avoid capture, I will have to keep running. And that means heading away from Belton.

Another, louder wail set the air vibrating, then a great hulking shadow emerged from the mist. Heat radiated from it. Steam hissed from the engine. As it passed, Soot billowed above it as magic was drawn down to heat the water within the boiler. The great machine slowed to a stop.

Looking left and right, Tyen saw that a small crowd had formed, mostly shadows in the fog. He had deliberately chosen to sit at the end of the station, away from as many other travellers as possible. Those closest enough to see him were all looking towards the engine.

He stood up, crossed the line, walked around the end of the railsled and climbed aboard the end carriage. It was empty, since few people needed to travel away from the city this early in the morning. He sat down.

A whistle sounded, then the carriage jerked into motion. Slipping Vella into the pocket of his coat, he began to invent a story for the ticket checker about how, disoriented by the fog and not used to rising early, he'd bought a fare going the wrong way.

CHAPTER 12

Before long, Tyen had sunk into a misery of realisation as he thought of everything he was giving up and leaving behind. His father would be worried. Ashamed, too, if he believed the Academy's accusation of theft. *I will write him a letter, when I'm far enough away. Though I'll have to take care to ensure they can't trace where it was sent from.*

He thought of his friends, but the pang of regret was not as strong as he'd expected. Miko had betrayed him. Neel's loyalty was to himself and his family. Tyen hadn't seen his old friends from before he joined the Academy for a few years, and it bothered him to think that they might believe he'd become a thief.

What would happen to his belongings at the Academy? He supposed they would be sent to his father. As he began a mental inventory of his possessions he thought of his desk, covered in partly made insectoids, and his heart lurched.

The thought of leaving Beetle behind was unexpectedly painful. It was silly to be attached to a mechanical device. Silly to feel worse about abandoning it than anything or anyone else. He might see his father again one day, even if only as a visitor to his cell. Who knew what would happen to the little insectoid? He doubted anyone who took possession of it would appreciate the work that had gone into creating it. The Academy might even throw it away.

The Academy. Tyen's chest constricted. His dreams of becoming a professor had been all but stripped away. He'd completed a few years of classes out of the eight required to qualify as a sorcerer or historian. Not enough to broaden his employment choices beyond those of a mere machine operator. Though the chances of ending up bored and forgotten in a mundane job now weren't as great as ending up bored and forgotten in a prison.

The door between carriages opened and Tyen's heart skipped as he saw a uniformed man enter carrying a ticket punch and a satchel. The old man saw Tyen and strolled over with the practised ease of someone well used to the swaying of the carriage.

Tyen produced his ticket, then pretended surprise when it was the wrong one. The ticket checker's eyebrows lowered.

"Where'd you tell the seller you were going?"

Tyen searched for a believable reply. Was there a town on this line that sounded enough like Belton that the ticket seller would have mistaken it? The checker grunted at Tyen's hesitation.

"You told him you were goin' to the city, right?"

Tyen grimaced. "I think so. I can't remember."

"Well, either you don't travel much or you must've thought that tickets to Barral had got cheaper. A *lot* cheaper." The man opened a satchel and began searching inside. "It'll cost you another two-plat and four."

Tyen took his wallet out of his coat and paid the man. "When do we arrive?"

"If all goes well, fifteen past two. We make a longer stop at Millwend at around twelve for those who wish to stretch their legs." He handed Tyen a new ticket.

"Thanks," Tyen said. He stowed his wallet again and watched the man walk back to the door and disappear into the next carriage. Then he reached in his other pocket for Vella, thinking that when the man returned he would buy as many maps and timetables of the different rail networks as he could and read them while holding her. Something tickled the ends of his fingers, and he felt a vibration through the lining of his coat.

"Beetle! Come out!" A happy relief rushed over him as the insectoid crawled up his arm. He found himself blinking away the beginnings of tears. "Ridiculous," he muttered to himself. But to have something familiar – not to have not lost *everything* he valued – suddenly meant a great deal.

Well, not everything, he amended. Ordering Beetle back into his pocket in case the ticket checker returned, he reached in after it and brought out Vella.

So, he thought at her, *where should I go?*

Somewhere out of the Academy's reach.

He chuckled. *That means somewhere out of the reach of the Empire. There aren't many places outside of its control or not under a treaty to return criminals.*

But there are some.

Yes. Places that are far, far away and difficult to get to. Like the lands of the Far South, over the Lower Latitudinal Mountains, which Gowel explored recently. Or the deserts of the Grand Island to the west, though they're plagued by dangerous sand pirates. And the Peora Archipelago, otherwise known as the Cannibal Islands.

The Far South sounds safer. The people at Spirecastle were friendly towards foreigners, according to Gowel.

Tyen nodded. He wished he'd stuck around that night in Palga to hear more of the explorer's stories. Thinking back, Tyen recalled Gowel saying that magic was plentiful there, and describing a city carved out of a great spire of rock where people travelled up and down in cages, or flew. How much of that was true, Tyen couldn't guess. There had been plenty of dusky and adventurers were prone to boasting and exaggeration.

Have you been there?

Yes, but a very long time ago. It was far less developed than what Gowel described and I did not learn of this place called Tyeszal — Spirecastle. A land of many small kingdoms, all quarrelling. Still, that's better than pirates and cannibals.

I wish I had a copy of Gowel's map.

You were in contact with me when you saw it, Vella reminded him. Lines began to appear on the page, forming a map that Tyen could only half remember.

He smiled. *Now that is a handy skill. I'll need an aircart to get there. I can build one I guess, if I have time and the materials.*

Then my advice is: go to the Far South.

Tyen looked up, out of the railsled window. He'd travelled north-east last night. Judging by the time of day and direction of the shadows, they were currently heading east. He would have to change trains. And then? Perhaps board a ship sailing south to Wendland.

His Wendish was passable, but he had no grasp of any other languages. Fortunately, Leratian was understood in many lands within and outside the Empire. When he got to the Far South communication would become a problem, but he'd be no worse off than Gowel had been.

The train began to slow. Realising they were nearing another station, he quickly transferred some of Kilraker's money from the pogbag into his wallet, taking the opportunity to do so while nobody was around to see the large store of notes in there. A few passengers boarded when the train stopped, and when the ticket checker arrived Tyen asked for railsled maps. The man could only supply him with a map of the line they were on, however. Keeping hold of Vella in one hand, Tyen carefully examined everything, from the strip map of the line and all the stations to the timetable printed on the back.

He checked with Vella to see if she had stored the information, then pocketed her again. For now he could do nothing else, so he watched the outside world pass by. The houses and factories of the city outskirts had dwindled and been replaced by lone buildings and weedy, empty land. Soon fields replaced them in turn, broken by the occasional cluster of houses. The railsled horn blared less often to warn gatekeepers to stop traffic on the roads they crossed. Weary from a night spent driving the aircart, Tyen realised he had fallen asleep when the ticket checker shook him awake to tell him they had arrived at Millwend and he'd best hurry if he was going to "stretch his legs".

Fortunately, the men's room was close by and as he climbed back on board he encountered two of the local baker's boys selling pastries. They were well pleased when he bought their last two flaky triangles. He gave them a generous tip, enjoying a vengeful satisfaction at spending Kilraker's money.

The next two hours passed slowly. The railsled stopped less often and travelled faster between stations. The land became hillier, and the line twisted and turned. Looking back during turns, he could see the Soot trailing above them. They crossed a steep valley via an impressive steel bridge, then plunged into a tunnel and darkness for a while. On the other side they emerged among houses, which grew rapidly smaller and were built closer together until they suddenly gave way to larger buildings – factories and storehouses. Consulting his map, Tyen counted down the stations to Barral which, judging from the view outside his window of factories and machines stretching into the distance, was a city prospering mostly on industrial production. Soot clouds hung above everything, the tops appearing slowly to dissolve as magic flowed down from above.

The railsled line gradually curved towards two lozenge shapes hovering in the distance. He remembered from the map that an airpark lay near the main station of Barral. It made sense to connect the two forms of transport so that passengers could move from one to the other, though by being in close proximity they would be competing for the available magic. From the size of the distant capsules they were large aircarriages used to transport several people across greater distances than personal aircarts. As the railsled drew closer, one of them dropped out of sight below the rooftops.

As they stopped at more and more stations, the ticket checker returned more often. Tyen stopped him to ask if he would be able to take a railsled south to the coast from Barral. The man nodded.

"The Goldman line. Smaller than this one. Built by Mr Goldman for his private pleasure, then after he donated it to the Empire for public use it was extended north to Barral and south to Sacal Bay. That is, extended as far as Valley Road. To connect that line with this they'd have had to pull down some rich people's houses and cross Grand La' Gillweather's estate, and even the Emperor himself couldn't have convinced any of them to allow that." He chuckled. "You'll have to get a one-seater to Goldman Station."

Sacal Bay was a minor port, Tyen knew. He thanked the man, who didn't appear again before the railsled pulled under the arched glass roof of Barral's main station. Tyen followed signs pointing to where vehicles could be hired. Waiting in line, he saw that the man in front of him was reading a paper. Among the columns of text was a drawing of a face. Something about it was familiar, so he looked closer. Reading the headline below it, his blood went cold.

DANGEROUS SORCERER FLEES ACADEMY!
The Leratian Police Department informed the *Leratian Daily* today that they are seeking a former student of the Academy. Tyen Ironsmelter, pictured above, is considered a dangerous sorcerer and is not to be approached. If you see this man, report . . .

The text was replaced by an advertisement for ladies' hats as the man turned the page. Tyen cast about, looking for a paper seller, but none were about. He resisted the urge to dash away and seek one out so that he could find out what else the article had said about him. Better that he didn't lose his place in the queue.

The sooner I travel on from here the better, he told himself.

How far had the article spread? The *Leratian Daily* was printed overnight and sent out across the country early each morning. The fastest distribution was by rail. It might have travelled on the same train Tyen had and perhaps that man had just bought it, or it might have arrived earlier and Tyen's face and news of his crime had gone ahead of him.

His mind swelled to bursting with new and terrible possibilities. Trains heading directly from Belton to Sacal Bay would arrive hours before him. The Goldman line might not even run at night, forcing him to find a place to stay and delaying him by several more hours.

And when he arrived, more than the police would be waiting. The paper had called him a dangerous sorcerer. Requests would have gone out to sorcerers to help the police soon after Tyen had fled in Kilraker's aircart. They'd be watching for him at all the places he might attempt to leave Leratia. Like Sacal Bay.

His skin prickled. Someone might be waiting here already, to see who stepped off the trains from Leratia. Were they watching the station right now? He glanced around, expecting to see uniformed men marching towards him, but nobody was paying him any attention. That he'd made it to the line for one-seaters was . . . odd. Surely the Academy had found Kilraker's aircart by now and worked out that this was the line Tyen was most likely to have travelled on.

But nobody here could yet know that. Railsled was the fastest form of transport, and only one *following* the one Tyen had caught could deliver the news that this was the line he had taken. He had, at worst, an hour before it did.

If someone was watching the station, would they recognise him? He glanced down at his clothes. They were clean and fashionable but not expensive. He was dressed like any student of the Academy, but since the Academy was in Belton and not Barral he doubted many people looked like that here. He needed to change his appearance, and quickly.

He needed to appear ordinary and unremarkable. Common. The sort of clothes a factory worker might wear. He cast about in the vain hope there might be a suitable shop nearby, but wasn't surprised when he found none. He'd have to ask the one-seater driver.

"Can we help you?" spoke a voice behind him.

He turned to see a pair of women his father's age standing behind him. From their dress he guessed they were at the wealthier end of the middle class. He groaned inwardly as they gave him the indulgent smiles mothers bestowed on those who reminded them of their own sons. His own mother having died when he was a child, he was never completely sure how to deal with this kind of attention.

"You are new to town, I'm guessing," the taller woman said. "Perhaps a visitor. Where are you heading? These one-seater drivers aren't to be trusted, you know. They'll take you the long route and charge you five times as much."

Tyen felt a flash of inspiration. Perhaps a pair of overly helpful local women was exactly what he needed.

"Well, yes," he said. "I don't know my way around and I have a job interview in an hour. Could you advise me where I might buy a decent pair of hard-wearing shoes?"

The shorter woman shook her head. "The best shopping is over on the Parade, but the closest . . ." She paused to exchange a look with her companion, who pointed across the road.

"There are shops over at the airpark."

"We'll take you there. We have time."

They ignored his weak protestations and were soon guiding him across the road and into a grand new building that bordered one side of the airpark. He realised his mistake as soon as they entered. The clothing on offer was designed for aircarriage passengers who had an hour or two to fill before their flight continued on to Leratia. While pre-made rather than tailored, air travellers were wealthy and the prices and styles reflected that. Aircarriage tickets were out of the reach of factory workers. They were generally out of the reach of most Academy students, too.

That thought gave him an idea. An option that might solve all of his current problems.

A half-hour had barely passed before he had changed into a fine new woollen suit, new shoes and hat. His old clothes were stowed in the pogbag and while the clerk's attention had been elsewhere he'd quickly transferred Kilraker's money to a new leather satchel along with Vella and Beetle. After thanking the two helpful women by paying for their fare home, he returned to the airpark to buy a ticket. Having a quarter of an hour until boarding, he made use of the services of a barber who had set up shop by the ticket office to service customers wanting to arrive in Barral or Leratia looking their best.

His pulse raced with both fear and anticipation. He'd never

travelled in an aircarriage before and it gave him a buzz of satisfaction to be doing so at Kilraker's expense. Unlike the professor's aircart, the chassis of the aircarriage was large enough for several passengers to travel inside, protected from the cold air. Single seats ran along each side with an aisle between them. Tyen tried to hide his excitement as he stepped aboard and was led to his seat by an usher. He was the last passenger to arrive so he was directed to a seat not far from the back.

Soon he felt a swooping sensation as the tethers were released and the aircarriage gently rose into the sky. Looking out of the window by his seat, down through the glass roof of the station, Tyen saw that another railsled had arrived and passengers were spilling out into the street. One of the distant figures stopped to look around. It was impossible to recognise anyone at that distance, but Tyen could not help imagining it was Kilraker. Another figure walked over to meet it, then both turned to regard the one-seaters arriving to carry passengers away.

Or are they looking beyond, to the airpark, Tyen thought. The whirr of the propellers grew louder as the driver set them spinning faster. As the aircarriage turned to face the south, the station passed out of Tyen's view. He turned away from the window and leaned back in his seat, hoping he looked more relaxed than he felt.

CHAPTER 13

I was only worried about where we would go, not whether we'd have trouble getting out of Leratia, Tyen confessed.

At least that is no longer a problem.

We'll reach Wendland by midnight.

Will the Academy have people there waiting for you?

Probably. They have contacts there, and the treaty between our countries states they must detain any criminals and send them home.

But you think they won't expect you to arrive by aircarriage.

No message the Academy sends can arrive before us, as it would have to go by sea or an aircarriage following this one. It is a good thing Leratia is an island. If we were connected by rail I'd have no hope of outrunning a message, or the distribution of the Leratian Daily.

You think the picture in the *Leratian Daily* doesn't look much like you, too.

It does a little, but I look like most other young Leratian men my age. For once, having an average, unremarkable appearance is to my advantage. I wonder how many young men are going to be approached or avoided in case they are dangerous sorcerers because of me. I hope none will be treated badly as a result.

He sighed. How much effort would the Academy expend in finding him? Would there be a point at which the time and expense of searching were not worth finding a mere

255

ex-student and a book they never wanted to keep in the first place?

A great deal of effort, considering the secrets I contain about them.

Tyen felt a chill run down his spine.

They're that bad?

The professors thought so. In other times and other places these matters would have been considered petty and unimportant, but in this time and place people take such things more seriously.

Don't tell me anything.

I will not be able to stop myself, if you ask a question to which the answer reveals their secrets.

Then . . . warn me before answering, so I can look away.

You are concerned that, if you learn their secrets, they will never allow you to resume your old life even if you prove your innocence?

Yes.

Yet I think you also know that they will not believe you, if you tell them you never discovered their secrets from me.

Tyen bit back a curse. She was right. But that meant . . . His skin prickled. He was in a worse position than he had realised. They were willing to destroy Vella to hide their secrets even if it meant losing a valuable magical artefact. He wasn't valuable.

But theft wasn't a great enough charge to warrant execution. Unless Kilraker set him up for someone else's death. Or the Academy persuaded the Emperor to charge Tyen with treason.

No, surely they wouldn't go that far. But whatever they did, they'd want him unable to communicate their secrets to anyone, and that probably meant prison at the very least.

I can never go back, he thought.

Not if you wish to avoid that fate, Vella agreed.

Tyen's chest contracted painfully and for a second he couldn't breathe. He was suddenly conscious of the other passengers. Forcing himself to relax and inhale slowly, he surveyed the passengers nearby from the corner of his eye. His blood ran cold as he realised the man across the aisle appeared to be looking his way. Had his agitation attracted the man's attention?

Not wanting to turn and meet the stranger's eyes, he looked up at the window instead, hoping to catch a glimpse of the man in its reflection. Sure enough, he could see the man sitting on the other side of the aisle. And immediately they locked gazes.

The man's eyes dropped to the folded paper on his lap.

Tyen's heart froze, but when he looked closer he was relieved to see the paper was not the *Leratian Daily*. From the images and headlines about aircart racing, it looked like a sporting paper.

If I can see his reading material, can he see mine?

He looked at the reflection of Vella, her words reversed in the ghostly mirror copy. He'd thought it safe to read her because there was nobody behind him to catch sight of her over his shoulder, never thinking that she might be visible in other ways.

Sorry, Vella. Closing her, he slipped her into the pocket of his jacket and pretended to gaze out of the window. The other man glanced his way a few more times, but mostly he remained immersed in his paper.

The next few hours passed slowly. Tyen watched the shadows far below lengthen as the sun dipped slowly towards the horizon. Darkness finally shrouded all but the lonely windows of farmsteads lit from within or the clustered lights where villages lay. With so many people filling the narrow chassis of the aircarriage the air stayed warm, though a slight draught indicated a ventilation system that ensured the air remained fresh. A conversation between two passengers in the seats in front sounded oddly muffled, but he guessed that was because he'd grown used to the noise of the propellers.

Eventually a bigger cluster of lights appeared directly ahead of the aircarriage. Beyond it was an expanse of darkness, mostly free of lights. This, he guessed, was the sea. He watched it draw slowly closer, anticipating the moment they left the coast and his homeland.

When the propeller noise abruptly lessened he and the other passengers looked up and around in surprise. The usher started down the aisle from the front.

"We're making an unscheduled stop at Sacal Bay," he told them.

Tyen's stomach plunged far below the aircarriage.

"Why?" one of the passengers demanded.

"We don't know yet." The usher shrugged. "The signal lights are limited in what they can communicate."

"Will we be delayed long?"

"We won't know until we learn the reason we are stopping."

"Can we get off?"

"Yes, but stay close to the aircarriage. We don't want to be delayed any longer than necessary."

Tyen drew in a deep breath and let it out, trying to steady his nerves so that he could think clearly. The sensation of his heart beating too fast was growing far too familiar. He wished he could confer with Vella, but he dared not risk it.

I hope the usher is telling the truth about not knowing the reason, he thought. *If he knew a wanted man was among the passengers surely he would insist we all stay on board.*

But it would make no difference, if the police were waiting when the aircarriage arrived. Tyen would be trapped. Unless . . . hadn't he noticed a door at the back when he boarded?

"Are you well?"

Tyen started as he realised the usher was leaning over him. He met the man's gaze then quickly looked away.

"Um . . ."

"Perhaps a little airsickness? Don't worry, it happens to a lot of people." The young man reached into his pocket and brought out a folded piece of brown paper. "Here. Just in case."

As the usher continued past, Tyen examined the gift. Unfolding it, he saw with amusement that it was a bag, the inner surface coated with a glossy varnish. To avoid a mess if he happened to throw up, he guessed.

He looked back down the aisle past the usher, who was doing something at the end of the chassis. There *was* another door, with a large sign reading "Service Employees Only". Turning away, Tyen looked down at the bag and realised he had the beginnings of an escape plan. A desperate one, but that was better than no plan at all.

The aircarriage descended so gradually towards Sacal Bay that Tyen began to wonder if the driver was deliberately torturing him. He badly wanted to hear the usher announce that the signal had changed, or had been misread, and they were heading straight to Wendland after all, but if they were going to land, he wanted to get it over and done with. As they drifted over the town he tried to memorise the lie of the land. The airpark was brightly lit, drawing the eye and making the surrounds seem darker. From the pattern of street lamps and house lights he could see that the town was a crescent shape, curving around the bay. The streets followed the same arc. Even from the air he could see that the land sloped steeply down to the water except at the centre of the town, where the scant level space had been reserved for the airpark and a small open public space. Connecting streets were not square to the main roads but angled to reduce the steepness of the descent for vehicles, while staircases cut a more direct path for pedestrians. The houses were almost like staircases themselves, each peering over its neighbour below. It would look pretty from the sea, Tyen guessed.

At last the aircarriage pulled up above the airpark loading bay, hovering as if having second thoughts. The usher hurried to the rear again and Tyen heard the sound of hatches opening and cables unravelling. A shudder went through the chassis as the cables were snagged, then it vibrated as it was cranked into position. As the roof of the loading bay passed Tyen's window he caught a glimpse of a small number of people waiting. Most were aircarriage staff waiting to welcome the passengers, but the rest wore the uniform of the police.

Tyen sagged forward, clutching the paper bag and keeping out of sight of the window. As the aircarriage settled into place and the rest of the passengers rose, he turned away from the window. He gathered his satchel and pogbag, then leaned his shoulder against the back of the seat, a hand pressed to his forehead.

The usher hurried to his side. "Are you unwell?"

Tyen nodded. "I need some air," he said.

The young man grimaced in sympathy. "Hold on there. You'll be out soon."

Tyen looked beyond him. "Does that open?"

The usher glanced at the door and pursed his lips.

Puffing out his cheeks, Tyen cast about, satchel and paper bag caught in one hand and pogbag in the other. He let the paper bag slip from his fingers.

"Yes, yes, come this way," the usher said. He beckoned and turned to the service door. "Go down the stairs. If anyone asks why you're there tell them Dila Nailer sent you. The men's room is to the right, down the passage."

"Thank you," Tyen gasped, then closed his mouth and gulped as he passed. The door opened onto an open metal framework that gave access to the aircart for the workers who serviced the aircarriage. He stepped out onto a platform. A narrow set of stairs spiralled down the little tower, taking him under the loading bay and out of sight of the police above. And of the usher. He took in his surroundings quickly. It was an area for the workers who tethered and serviced the aircarriages, and it was empty but for five men leaning against a wall nearby. They watched him hurry down the stairs, but didn't appear concerned.

"Men's room's that way," one called out, pointing to a gap between the main airpark building and a smaller one. "Second door along. Don't go too far or you'll end up in the dock-workers' quarter."

Tyen tapped his hat in gratitude and hurried in the direction they'd indicated. Once in the passage he glanced back to make sure nobody had followed him and the dockworkers weren't watching, then continued on towards the rectangle of light where the smaller building ended.

At the end he stopped, surveying the area beyond. A narrow but clean street crossed his path. To the left it met a wider road, which he guessed was the one that ran along the public entrance to the airpark. To the right it continued for a short distance before coming to a dead end. Directly ahead was a narrow, unlit alley. He walked across the road and slipped into the shadows.

A small measure of weight lifted from him. He had evaded the police, but how long would it be before they learned of the sick passenger who had left by the rear of the aircarriage to use the men's room below and not returned? Once they did, they would guess he had come this way. They would follow.

And he was dressed as a wealthy man in what was probably one of the poorer parts of the town.

If the locals saw him they'd know instantly that he did not belong. While he could use magic to defend himself against robbers, it would make him stand out even more. And the *Leratian Daily* would have arrived hours ago, so it would not take much for anyone to connect an out-of-place sorcerer with the fugitive the Academy sought.

I need to change my appearance again, he thought. He needed clothing and somewhere to hide until he worked out how to get out of Sacal Bay.

First things first, he told himself. Sticking to the shadows, he tried to keep his footsteps quiet. He heard occasional voices from within the houses on either side, but the streets were quiet. Perhaps the dockworkers were early risers. Perhaps they knew better than to roam the area at night. A staircase appeared between two houses, leading down. It was unoccupied and he needed to get off the street that led so directly from the airpark, so he began to descend. He had to slow, as the stairs were in a bad state of repair and loose treads were concealed in the shadows. It crossed another narrow street. The street was empty, so he turned onto it.

Several steps later he noticed a man standing in the doorway of a house. It would have appeared suspicious to stop and go back so Tyen kept walking and pretended not to notice. He felt the man's gaze on him as he passed. After twenty or so more steps he heard footsteps behind him.

He took the next stairwell, though it was occupied by some children. They stopped their play to watch him. This time he could not pretend not to have seen them, so he smiled as he skirted around them.

Even before he'd reached the next street he could hear it. Slowing, he realised that he was approaching a busy thorough-fare of the area. His heart sank as he saw that the stairway did not continue on after it. He would have to walk along it or go back. Glancing over his shoulder, he saw the shapes of the children still sitting on the stairs. Beyond them was another figure, descending towards him.

The man from the doorway? A chill ran down his spine.

Perhaps it would be better to be among a crowd, even if he did stick out in his fancy clothes. Turning away, Tyen continued descending. He briefly considered stopping to open the pogbag and change into his student coat, but as people on the street below passed the bottom of the stairs he knew it would make no difference. He'd still look far better off than the locals.

Reaching the corner, he stopped to survey the street. People were walking to and fro, many with the weary look of workers heading home at the end of the day. A small, loosely spread crowd had gathered several paces along in front of a drinking house. More such establishments were spaced along the street.

Hearing footsteps drawing closer behind him, Tyen took a deep breath, stepped out and started walking. He tried to look relaxed and purposeful, and unconcerned when a few drinking house patrons noticed him and their eyebrows rose. More faces turned towards him as he passed, but he ignored them.

Once he'd passed he could do nothing more than stroll onward. Shops, their windows securely shuttered, followed the drinking house. Far ahead there appeared to be a gap between two that he hoped was a staircase heading uphill again. Before then, he had to pass another, smaller drinking house. As he drew closer he realised that it was actually a cheap travellers' hotel with a drinking room at the front. The thought of a bed to sleep in tempted him, but he dared not go inside. The story of the rich traveller stopping at the hotel would surely reach the police before the night was through.

The customers were a quieter lot, he noted as he passed. A small group outside appeared to be exchanging farewells before they parted ways, and barely glanced at him. He was drawing curious looks from the workers he passed, however. The sooner he got off this street the better. He fixed his gaze on the stairway gap ahead and lengthened his stride.

"Ren!" a woman shouted somewhere behind him. He heard

the sound of someone running behind him, coming rapidly closer. "Stop, Ren! It's me, your little half-sister! Sezee!"

A hand caught his arm. His heart lurched. He considered resisting – pulling away and making a run for it – but the good manners drilled into him by his father, and the fear of attracting more attention by shaking her off, made him turn.

Immediately he saw three things: the woman was unfamiliar, she was foreign and she was rather beautiful.

"I'm sorry, young la', you are mis—" he began.

"Oh, Ren. I'd know you anywhere. But you haven't seen me since I was a child, and the light is behind me." She smiled and hooked her arm in his. "Come over to the street lamp."

Perturbed by her overt friendliness and certainty, he did not know what to do. Across the road, the small group had separated, one half entering the travellers' hotel, the other walking away, and neither paying attention to the apparent reunion. Less than a hundred paces behind him a small group of men approached, and they *were* paying attention.

She leaned closer and murmured. "Come with me. They won't dare follow you inside the hotel."

He obeyed. There was no time to consider his misgivings. Either she was leading him into a trap, or rescuing him from a mugging. He noted that her clothes were neither shabby nor designed to be seductive, so if she was a whore she was no ordinary one. Her skin was a warm light brown in the lamplight, and her hair a glossy black. She guided him across the road and to the hotel door, which he opened for her. As he stepped inside the other patrons glanced up, then looked again as they noted his fine attire. Sezee – if that was her name – immediately unhooked her arm from his and wove between the tables as if there was no question he would follow.

He could not go back outside, so he trailed after her to a small table by the front windows, occupied by another, older woman. This woman looked to be of the same race – perhaps from the West Isles. The smell of food sent his stomach growling, and he was glad it was too noisy for them to hear it. His rescuer, Sezee, sat down and pushed an empty plate and glass to the centre of the table.

"You remember Aunt Veroo, Ren?" she asked.

Perhaps, if she was keeping up the pretence, she had reason to. He bowed. "I . . . it was a long time ago."

"It was," the woman replied, her eyes crinkling with humour. "Let's get you a chair."

"Do not trouble yourself," he told her. He glanced out of the window. The thugs were gone. No police. Yet. "I cannot stay long."

Sezee ignored him, rising and moving to a nearby table to ask if she could take an unoccupied chair. The couple sitting there eyed her suspiciously, but as her gesture led their attention to Tyen the dislike in their faces disappeared and they nodded.

"Thank you," Tyen said as he took the chair and Sezee settled down again. Sezee leaned towards him and lowered her voice.

"Forgive me for asking, but what are you doing in this part of town?"

"I confess I was lost," he told her.

"So you just arrived in town?" she guessed. "Looking for your hotel?"

"Yes."

"Which hotel were you seeking?"

He shrugged. "Whichever had a room free. I hadn't made a booking."

She smiled again. "You have an adventurous spirit. I like that. Perhaps a little too adventurous if you thought you could come into this part of town looking like that." She leaned a little closer. "What will you do now?"

"I don't know," he admitted. "I fear I must risk heading back to the centre of town, or all the rooms will be taken before I arrive."

"You could stay here. It's not glamorous, but it has a clean reputation." Her gaze shifted over his shoulder then back again. "I wonder . . . would you be willing to continue pretending to be my wealthy Leratian half-brother Ren?"

He looked from her to the older woman. Sezee appeared hopeful and perhaps even a little embarrassed, but Veroo was frowning. Was this some kind of trick? Had they worked out who he was and were they trying to delay him?

On the other hand . . . if they were willing to pretend to be relatives, it might prove to be the disguise he needed.

"Why do you want me to be?" he asked.

"We've been trying to find a decent place to stay since we got here this morning, but all Sacal Bay's hotel were full, despite what their signs said." Veroo's scowl told him how likely she thought that was. "This has been so often our reception. I do not know if it is because we are foreign or two women travelling without a male companion, or a combination of both."

Tyen blinked as he realised what this meant. "You do not have a room here?"

"No. Fortunately they were happy to sell food and drink to us. We were about to leave when I saw those men following you."

"You want me to come with you to try another hotel?"

She shrugged. "We've tried all the rest. So I guess if you don't help us we'll have to find somewhere quiet to wait out the night."

Which was what Tyen had planned to do. But they were not fugitives, like him. They were two innocent, defenceless women.

He ought to leave them to their own troubles. He ought to find a place to hide and a new disguise. Looking out of the window, he saw no police. No pursuers. Had they not worked out where he'd gone? Did they fear to enter the dockworkers' quarter at night? To search it thoroughly they'd have to go from house to house, hindered by disgruntled residents. Perhaps it would be easier and safer to do so in daylight.

"The manager wasn't around when you came in," Sezee told him. "If you ask for rooms for yourself and two women . . ."

"You think he'll give them to me," he guessed.

Sezee nodded. "It's worth a try. You don't look like someone he'd dare refuse."

He didn't. But for the same reason, he couldn't stay here. Still, it was the least he could do to see them settled in a room. Perhaps there was a rear entrance to the hotel that he could leave by, rather than the very public street in front. And if he could somehow find a change of clothes . . .

"How many nights do you wish to stay?" he asked.

"Just the one. We're leaving early tomorrow."

"What does the manager look like?"

"Large. Bald. Smells like pipegrass."

Tyen found the manager at the back of the room, smoking with two equally large and hairless men. When the man saw him, his eyebrows rose with amusement.

"Have you a couple of rooms free?" Tyen asked.

The man blinked in surprise, then got to his feet. "We have one. It's a standard double room. Nothing fancy."

Tyen shook his head. "There are three of us, and the la'es require a room of their own." He began to turn away.

"Well, if you don't mind sharing, I have a free bed in another double."

Looking back, Tyen pretended to consider. "Very well," he said, then sighed. "It will have to do."

The man demanded the fee up front and refused to haggle. Tyen insisted he inspect the women's room before paying anything. Once out of sight, he quickly explored the nearby passages and found a door that, though locked, appeared to be a way out. Then he returned to the drinking room. The manager looked more amused than annoyed when the women turned out to be to Sezee and Veroo.

"How are you related?" he asked as they made their way towards Tyen.

"My father travelled a lot when he was young," Tyen replied drily.

The manager chuckled, then recounted the coins Tyen gave him before handing over two keys. "Yours is next door to theirs. Number five."

Sezee followed Veroo into their room, then turned and startled him with a kiss to each cheek. "Thank you. I hope you manage to sleep."

She glanced at the door to room five and grimaced. Even through the door they could hear the other occupant snoring loudly.

Tyen found his voice. "Have a pleasant trip . . . wherever you're going."

"I'm afraid after our reception here in Leratia, anything would seem pleasant in comparison. But you, at least, have proven that some Leratians are decent people. May you find your hotel without mishap, tomorrow." She smiled, then closed the door.

The snoring quietened as Tyen unlocked the door to number five, but resumed with gusto after a moment. The other occupant looked a few years younger than Tyen. A familiar smell flavoured the air, but Tyen couldn't place it. As his eyes adjusted to the faint light coming through a small window, he made out more details. Something lay on the empty bed. He quietly stepped forward.

A shirt. Trousers. All laid out ready for the next day. On the floor below was a pair of shoes. Work boots. The smell was suddenly very familiar. Shoe polish. Tyen shook his head at the luck of it, fighting a sudden urge to giggle. Slowly, so as to make as little sound as possible, he took off his fancy clothing and dressed in the stranger's clothes, slipping Vella into a pocket. Then he laid out his expensive woollen trousers and jacket, over which he placed the fine shirt. The stranger would be surprised indeed to find his clothes transformed into fine garments overnight.

The man's boots were a size too big. Tyen silently apologised for the blisters his new shoes would cause, the thought he was actually stealing from the man sobering him. It made it easier to leave the pogbag and his old student clothing behind. But he kept the satchel. Though it looked too new, he could scuff it up a little.

Hanging from a hook on the back of the door was a jacket and the sort of hat favoured by one-seater drivers and morni carers. It smelled of the animals, too. Tyen took both, then opened the door and slipped out into the corridor. Not wanting to risk making any more noise than necessary, he left the door ajar.

He encountered a drunk man swaying back from the men's room, who barely registered Tyen's presence. Reaching the locked rear door, Tyen placed a hand on the wall beside it and drew a little magic from within, where the Soot left behind would not be noticeable unless someone with the ability sought it. He used it to cut through the latch, hiding the damage. Opening the door, he looked out.

And cursed under his breath. Before him were a couple of

steep steps and a short wooden pier surrounded by water. The hotel façade was part of an unbroken wall curving away on either side, windows and little piers extending from neighbouring houses.

He hadn't realised they were this close to the water's edge.

Voices from behind caught his attention. Raised voices, but not in drunken disregard for the other hotel customers. He turned to listen, recognising the hotel manager's voice.

". . . if you're wrong he's not going to be happy. Do you want to talk to the two women he was with? He said they were relatives."

"No. If he isn't the one we're looking for, there's no need to disturb them."

Tyen's blood went cold. The second voice was all too familiar. *Kilraker!*

He stepped out of the door and closed it, then backed down the stairs. He had only a moment to decide what to do before his absence was discovered. Breathing quickly, he looked to either side, realising that he had very few options.

Maybe even none.

CHAPTER 14

Through the door Tyen could hear footsteps growing louder, then quieter, then louder again. Looking to one side, he considered whether he had enough skill with magic to lift and carry himself to the neighbouring pier. All elevation required a stable surface to orientate to and push away from. He didn't know if it was possible over water.

He briefly wished he'd learned to swim, then realised a dunking would ruin all the money he had but the coins and might damage Vella. Even if he got to the next pier, he'd still be in full view once Kilraker and the police stepped out of the hotel door anyway.

Something moved under the far side of the distant pier. Looking closer, he recognised the shape of a rowing boat. A shot of hope went through him. He moved to the edge of the hotel pier and looked down. Sure enough, a small boat was tethered there. A ladder descended into the water. He slung his satchel strap over his shoulder and carefully climbed down. The boat was tethered by a rope. He grabbed it and pulled the craft close. As he stepped into it the boat moved under him and he fell forward, his chest slamming into the seat. The hull bounced off a pylon and back underneath the pier.

From above came the sound of a door opening. Tyen froze, not daring to move, or even turn to look up.

"He couldn't have gone out this way," a voice said.

"No," a more familiar voice agreed.

"He must have left again. I knew there was something odd about him."

"If he's left, he can't have gone far. We should hurry," said another, quieter voice inside the building. The door closed.

Allowing himself to breathe again, Tyen remained still in case someone had remained outside. He'd heard no tread on the steps or pier decking. Looking up, he peered through the cracks between the slats but could see no sign of anyone standing there. He pushed himself up into a sitting position and considered his next move.

He couldn't go back inside, even once the police and Kilraker had left. The women and the manager would recognise him, and the owner of the clothes he was wearing would spot them. No, he would have to use the boat to get away.

He considered waiting in case someone stepped out onto the pier again, perhaps to search more thoroughly, and saw him rowing away. But if they did come out they might also think to look under the pier. No, he'd best get away now.

Sitting up, he located the oars and untethered the rope. Awkwardly, trying in vain to avoid splashing, he began to row, wishing that when he'd observed the layout of the town from the air he'd taken note of the waterside features as well. Staying near or disembarking at the neighbouring houses would be foolish, since the police were still searching the area, so he struck out into the bay. Fortunately it was a calm night, the waves mere ripples on the bay's glossy surface. Ships were moored across the width of Sacal Bay. He wondered if he could sneak on board one, but as he drew closer he saw men aboard, and some appeared to be looking his way.

How suspicious was it for a single man to be rowing a boat in the middle of the bay at night? He had no idea. The crews could be Leratian or foreign. Some might have just arrived and not yet heard about the dangerous sorcerer the police were looking for, but he had no way of knowing which ones they were.

Feeling too exposed, he changed direction, angling back towards the shore and hoping he looked like someone heading home after a late-night visit. The exertion had him breathing hard and eventually he had to rest. Taking the opportunity to survey the bay, he noticed that he could see the ridge that surrounded it and the town, black against slightly paler clouds. He'd noted, while in the aircarriage, that there was one road in and out of the town. The only way out by water was through the bay entrance, which would take him into the sea channel between Leratia and Wendland. Not a good place to take a tiny boat.

He was, he realised with a sinking heart, cornered. The four ways in and out of Sacal Bay – air, sea, rail and road – were each limited to one route that was easily monitored. He would not get away with pretending to be a rich aircarriage traveller again and the airpark would be guarded too closely for him to steal an aircart. The main road and docks would be watched, all railsleds and ships searched.

The ships were the most numerous and varied of the forms of transport. They ranged from cargo carriers to passenger liners, small private vessels to company fleet ships, wind-powered craft to magic-driven steamers. Sacal Bay was a busy port, but it wasn't considered a main one. Larger, magic-powered passenger liners did not stop here. Sturdy enough to weather storms, they only berthed at major cities like Belton. He suspected that Sacal Bay was too shallow for the newer ones, too. Smaller passenger and private vessels might use the port, but most of the shipping coming through here was prob-ably cargo. And from the number of lights bobbing in the darkness of the bay, there was plenty of it.

He didn't know a lot about ships, but the fact that most here were moored out in the bay might signify that they must wait for the tide to come in to access a dock. He'd noted from the aircarriage that there appeared to be two docks, one near the airpark and one further from the centre of the town. If he was right about the tide, the ships moored here would have a limited time to unload and load. Their crew would not want to wait while the police searched them, one by one.

In such a situation there might be an opportunity. Perhaps he might slip aboard during the mayhem.

He sought the other dockyard. From his vantage point he could see that the sea wall the hotel was built upon stretched around the water's edge, the surface lighter where the tides reached less often or never at all. Above this the buildings varied in size and shape. In front of the airdock a large pier extended for the passenger ships' customers. Far to the right of this the wall was divided into a higher and lower section. The lower was supported by pylons and on the higher stood several larger buildings. Warehouses? Cargo ships needed somewhere to store incoming or outgoing goods. This, he guessed, was the wharf.

He set to rowing again. He couldn't stay out here in the boat all night, and he would have to find somewhere to hide it once ashore again. By the time he reached the wharf he was shaking with weariness. Avenues of pylons supported a deep wooden pier. He found a ladder leading up to the pier and, more carefully this time, stepped off the boat onto it. With a push of magic, he sent the boat into the darkness under the pier.

Once it had disappeared into the gloom he climbed to the pier. The timbers creaked under his boots, but the sound blended with the other dockside sounds. He walked to the end, to the first of the tall warehouses. Testing the high, broad double doors he found them closed firmly against the night and intruders. Walking along to test the rest and finding them all similarly locked, he began to fear there would be no access to the docks other than through the buildings.

At the other end he found a narrow gap between the last warehouse and a neighbouring building, blocked by a gate. Climbing the gate took the last of the energy out of him and he slumped against a wall before he found the will to stagger onward. How long had it been since he'd eaten or drunk anything? Not since the train journey that morning. Which seemed like months ago. Could he risk looking for food now? No. He may as well stay here, if he was going to try finding a ship in the morning. But was it safe? He reached a recessed area filled with broken crates and empty sacks and sat down to rest and think.

Something took hold of his shoulder and shook him.

Opening his eyes, he blinked in surprise to see the narrow passage bright with daylight. A man with tanned and leathery skin from a life in the sun was smiling down at him.

"Wake up, son," he said. "What yr doing here?"

Tyen ran his hands over his face and smoothed his hair to give himself time to wake up and think of an answer.

"I'm . . . hoping to buy passage."

"Got in early, did you?"

"Ah . . ." Tyen looked around. "Yes."

"Passengr dock's back in town." The old man turned and began to gesture with his hands as he gave directions.

"Wait . . . They said if I wanted a cheap passage I could try my luck here."

"Then yr need to see the dockmaster. Queue's this way."

The old man ushered Tyen out of the alcove and down the narrow passage. Tyen didn't resist. If the only way he'd get on the ship was by seeing the dockmaster then he'd have to risk it. A line of people had formed, perhaps waiting for access to the docks. Mostly men – crew, he guessed – but also a woman and two small children dressed for travel. Near the end he saw two women and something about them sent a tingle of apprehension through him. Were they . . .? Surely he couldn't be so unlucky as to . . .

Looking up as he and the old man approached, their eyes widened in recognition. Tyen forced his mouth into a smile and bowed as he reached them.

"Good morning, la'es."

"A good morning to you," Sezee replied.

"Wait here," the old man instructed, and Tyen turned to see him turn on his heel and stride away.

"I thought we'd seen the last of you," Sezee added in a quieter voice. Tyen turned back to her. He would have to leave, but not so quickly that anybody would guess that something was wrong.

"I found it impossible to sleep," he told them. "So I sought more genial accommodation."

"After acquiring less conspicuous attire?" Her gaze dropped to his clothing and her eyebrows rose.

"I am ashamed to admit it." He lowered his gaze. "I hoped the swap proved advantageous to both parties."

As he met her gaze her eyes narrowed, and he read from her expression both suspicion and amusement. *She has considered who I might be*, he guessed. *They can't have been oblivious to the police searching the hotel.*

If she wanted to expose him she could have done so straight away. But she hadn't. Why not? Was it gratitude for his help the night before? Did she figure Leratian problems were for Leratians to worry about? Could she be overcome by the mystery of a bold and misunderstood renegade, like the women in foolish romance novels? He doubted the latter: he'd never managed to mystify a woman before, let alone charm one.

"Well, I'd best be—" he began.

"Leaving? You are not seeking passage?" Veroo interrupted.

Tyen shrugged. "I—"

"You'll need papers." She lifted her bag and began looking inside. "You have papers?"

"Yes," he replied even as his stomach sank. He had papers, but they were in his name. Looking around, he saw that any mayhem he'd thought he'd be able to take advantage of clearly did not exist. He couldn't see himself slipping onto a ship unnoticed. The whole idea seemed crazy now. He bit back a curse. His escape plan was never going to work.

"But you can't use them," Veroo guessed. "How about these?"

She drew from her bag a leather wallet of the kind that travellers used to store their papers and tickets, and handed it to him. Puzzled, he opened it and examined the sole document within. It was an identification paper.

"Aren Coble," he read aloud. "Porter." The description was for a taller, younger man who had been born in a northern district, but at least his colouring was right.

"Are you sure about this?" Sezee asked in a low voice. Tyen looked up to see her frowning at Veroo.

The older woman shrugged. "As you said: a small revenge."

Sezee snorted softly. "Now you're the risk-taker. What does that make me?"

"The less compassionate one?"

"Never."

"Well, we can always say he tricked us, if they recognise him." Veroo looked at Tyen and smiled, but her gaze was challenging.

"You could," he acknowledged. "I am entirely in your power. And I will be in your debt."

"Only if this works," Sezee added in a murmur. "In return you must agree to two conditions."

"Three," Veroo inserted.

"You will pay your way – you can, can't you?" Sezee asked. He nodded. "And?"

"You will not harm anybody."

"Of course not."

"And you will tell us the truth," Veroo finished. "Who you are and what you've done."

"That's fair. I agree to your conditions."

Sezee smiled. "So, Aren. You are, as you will have noted, our porter. So pick up our bags and do not speak unless you are addressed." She gave him a lofty look, then walked away. Veroo followed, leaving him with their bags. The gate had opened, he noted, and the line of people had begun to move. He quickly lifted the luggage and caught up with the women.

A man with a notebook stopped and asked them their names and business.

"We are Sezee and Veroo Anoil of the West Isles. We have arranged passage to Darsh on the *Nightstar*."

The man waved them on, never giving Tyen a second look as he passed. They walked through the gate into docks now loud with activity. The doors to the warehouses were open and goods were being carted to and from the ships. Tyen and the women had to dodge men carrying heavy loads as they picked their way along the wharf. Sezee walked confidently, Veroo keeping protectively close, while Tyen hurried after, fighting a return of the weakness of the night before that made his legs feel shaky and his head spin.

Instead of approaching the dockmaster, Sezee strode up to a ship and led the way up the removable ramp onto the deck. The crew eyed them, but none seemed surprised. All but one continued with their tasks – currently carrying barrels on board and down a ladder into the hull of the ship. The man directing them smiled and came over to greet the women.

"Captain Taga," Veroo said in greeting.

The conversation that followed was spoken in a language Tyen didn't recognise, so he tried to guess its meaning from expressions and gestures. Sezee did most of the talking, though the comments that Veroo inserted here and there gave the impression she was, ultimately, the one in charge. Captain Taga clearly knew them already, but though his skin was also browner than the typical Leratian he had the distinctive lean look of a Great Archipelago man, not a West Islander.

Catching the name Aren, Tyen looked expectantly at Sezee, but she continued talking to the captain. The man gave Tyen a quick look over, then shrugged and held his hand out to Tyen.

"Give him your papers, Aren," she said, without turning.

"Yes, la' Sezee." Tyen took the wallet from where he'd tucked it under one arm and handed it over. Taga skimmed the document then nodded and shrugged again. Sezee then gave him her most dazzling smile and posed a question. The captain shook his head. A little wheedling followed, then she sighed, brought out her bag of coin and counted out what Tyen guessed was his fare. That settled, she beckoned to him and set off along the deck. He quickly picked up the bags and followed. The captain chuckled as he passed.

"You're a brave man joining those two."

Wondering what the man meant, Tyen followed the women across the gently rocking deck, through a narrow door, down a corridor with a low ceiling and to a tiny room with a bunk with two beds. At this last effort, or perhaps at the relief of finally finding a way out of Sacal Bay, his head started to spin again.

"Leave the bags here, Aren," Sezee ordered. She gave him a look he could not decide was a smile or a grimace. "I'm sorry, but you're going to have to sleep with the crew."

He opened his mouth to say that it was fine. But the world had begun to tilt alarmingly.

"Aren?" Veroo said. "Are you ill?"

He shook his head, but that only made it worse. A numbing darkness crammed in on him. Someone grabbed his arms and was guiding him to . . . somewhere.

CHAPTER 15

A t least you chose a private place to faint.
Tyen winced as the words appeared on the page. He looked up at the sea and his earlier melancholy returned. Beyond the horizon lay his country, a day and a night's sailing behind him. Every hour that passed he travelled further and further away from home. The uncertainty of his future stirred fear, but all he could do to ease that was turn his intent towards his destination and overcome the obstacles that lay between him and reaching it.

He'd risen early so that he could catch some time alone to talk to Vella. Though she would have learned of all his ordeals since the aircarriage as soon as he'd touched her, he'd felt a need to relate the whole adventure stage by stage in order to get it straight in his mind. He looked down at the page again.

I didn't "faint". I "passed out", he protested. *But even so, it wasn't very manly of me.* What was it that Sezee had said? "According to your novels, women are the ones who are supposed to fall over at the slightest fright." By "your" she'd meant Leratian. But she'd apologised for teasing him after she'd learned how long he'd been without food or drink. "Such things don't bother literary heroes," she'd added, with no trace of mockery. "The real world is not so convenient."

281

He'd passed out for the briefest moment, but it had changed the women's attitude to him instantly. Veroo had disappeared to find some food and water, returning so quickly he imagined she had simply snatched both from the hands of the first person she'd found bearing either. Sezee had drilled him on his symptoms, their duration and how long they'd been occurring for.

Fortunately, the chunk of plain bread and cup of water had restored him. They'd insisted he stay in their room and get some sleep, and since it was wise to remain out of sight until the ship left Sacal Bay he didn't argue. He'd lain awake, stomach twisting with anxiety, until the ship began to dip and sway with the swell of the sea which had it protesting for an entirely different reason. He emerged on deck in the hope that it would reduce his sea-sickness to a tolerable level. Aside from a night sleeping in a sling bed in the crew's quarters, which seemed to reduce the nauseating effect of the rocking, he'd spent most of his time since then on deck.

How much should I tell Sezee and Veroo? he asked Vella.

You promised to tell them the truth.

Yes, but I didn't promise to tell them the whole truth.

A lesser man would simply lie.

I'm willing to become a lesser man, if it means we don't die. But I'd rather not lie. It's too easy to forget what I've already told someone.

They will have guessed that you are running from the police and Academy. They may have seen the article in the Leratian Daily warning of a dangerous sorcerer. The article didn't say you had stolen something, however.

So I don't need to tell them that. But they'll expect there to be a reason the Academy is chasing me. Theft is better than some other crimes they might fear I have committed.

If you wish to avoid lying, then all they have to do is keep asking questions and they will get all your secrets out of you.

Which was a problem Vella knew all too well. Fortunately, there hadn't been any opportunity for the women to ask questions. The little room they shared was too small for three people to squeeze into for a private conversation and it would look odd, possibly scandalous, for two women and their porter to do so anyway. He wasn't sure how thick the walls were, either. On deck there were always crew about. So far he'd been able to keep to two of Sezee and Veroo's conditions: he hadn't harmed anyone and he'd paid them for his passage. Which was for the short crossing to Wendland, as it turned out.

"Aren."

Sezee's voice cut over the constant whine of the wind. He turned to see her making her way past crew and various obstacles towards him. Closing Vella, he slipped her into the inside pocket of his jacket.

"La' Sezee."

She smiled at the honorific, used when addressing a female superior.

"How are you feeling? Did you sleep well?"

He shrugged. "The advantage of catching no more than a few hour's sleep over two days is that sleeping in a hammock feels like a luxury."

"A hammock, eh?"

"Yes. Seemed to help with the sea-sickness, too."

She grimaced. "Do you think they'd let us try it?"

"Bad night?"

Her nod was followed by a shudder. "But we'll be arriving at Darsh soon and things will improve. Well, all travel has its discomforts but I prefer something other than endless water to look at while I'm enduring them."

"Have you ever travelled by air?"

She sighed. "Not yet. I was rather hoping we'd get the

opportunity while in Leratia. I guess we can add that failure to our list of disappointments."

"Are you free to divulge your purpose for visiting Leratia to a mere porter?"

"I suppose I am." Her lips twitched into a lopsided smile. "I think you will find it amusing. Veroo sought to join the Academy. I came along for the adventure."

He frowned. "I gather they did not accept her."

"No. They barely acknowledged her existence." She scowled. "Apparently when they say women of means and status are welcome they don't mean foreign women. Or any women, if they want to learn sorcery. Apparently we can't be trusted with magic, as our heads are full of superstitions and our bodies can't take the strain."

Tyen winced. He'd heard such views expressed by some of the more conservative professors, but since there were women in the Academy he'd assumed those men did not have undue influence in the admissions approval process.

But, then, I know of no female sorcery students. I assumed there had been none with enough ability to qualify.

"I'm . . . sorry to hear that," he said.

"What are you apologising for?" she asked, her eyebrows shooting up but her eyes narrowing. "Did you have anything to do with this policy?"

"Er . . . no, but—" He stammered to a halt as a crewman passed them.

Sezee smiled. "You feel you must apologise for your countrymen," she finished for him. Looking away, she shrugged. "Never mind. It is their loss. I've never seen a setback diminish Veroo's determination and curiosity. She will find other ways to increase her knowledge and skill. And we *have* had quite an adventure." She turned to him. "Whereas yours is only beginning, I suspect."

He nodded. "Are you travelling directly home?"

"Yes, unless we hear of another source of magical learning. I don't suppose you know of any?"

"No." Tyen frowned as he remembered Gowel describing the lands of the Far South, of a place called Spirecastle where the sorcerers knew a few techniques unknown to the Academy. "Though I have recently heard a story told by an explorer about the lands below the Lower Latitudinal Mountains. He said there was a small school of sorcerers."

Sezee's eyes lit up. "Do they train women?"

"I don't know." Her excitement died as quickly as it had sparked, but her expression became thoughtful. "Still, we could make enquiries."

"It is a difficult place to get to. The mountains are impassable by land and difficult to cross by air, though by all estimations the lands within are vast."

She grinned. "I so like it when you sound like an academic."

He heard a smothered chuckle, and turned to see another member of the ship's crew hurrying past.

"Well, a porter does tend to pick up a few insights from his employers," Tyen replied in the hope the man didn't realise one of the passengers wasn't who he was supposed to be, though he was probably too far away to hear now.

"I'm looking forward to the insights you provide." Sezee's eyebrows rose with meaning. "When Veroo and I have a moment to drill you on your reasons for leaving your former employer." She moved a little closer. "Do you think you might be able to teach her a few things?" she asked in a quiet voice.

He frowned. When it came to sorcery, the Academy had strict rules about teaching. Only members of the Academy could be trained in magic, and students weren't supposed to teach at all. Breaking yet another rule would not help his chances of being accepted again as a student . . . but then he remembered the conclusion he'd come to, in the aircarriage, about his likely fate should he fall into the Academy's hands.

"It depends . . ." He did not finish, as another crewman had moved close enough to hear them.

Sezee's mouth twisted into a smile. "Of course it does. Well, we'll have to see if we can afford to keep you on after we reach our destination."

He opened his mouth to protest, then thought better of it. Kilraker's money – which he'd had to trust them to mind in their room while he slept among the crew – would not last for ever. And the prospect of continuing on in their company, whether as teacher or porter, wasn't unattractive.

"Tell me more about your homeland," he said.

She blinked in surprise, then he saw understanding in her expression. Turning to lean back on the railing, she stared past the ship's rigging into the distance.

"We come from Bleze, the largest of the West Isles," she said. "From Loire, one of the larger forts before the Leratians conquered us over fifty years ago. Now it is our main city."

"Conquered? I was taught that the West Islanders handed over administration of their lands peacefully."

"Your historians don't count possession by occupation as a form of conquest but we do. It is as effective as it is insidious. But I'm sure you do not wish to discuss the evils of the Leratian Empire's past, so I will stick to the present. The West Isles' main income comes from what we grow. My grandfather – a Leratian colonist named Tomel Firegard – made his fortune growing lall, and we still grow some of the best lall in the world."

"I shall have to try some."

"You must. It is excellent. You're probably wondering how a granddaughter of a Leratian colonist could have my colouring. Well, good old Tomel Firegard acquired half of his land by marrying the daughter of the West Islander queen. Which

makes Aunt Veroo the eleventh and youngest of his offspring
and the daughter of the deposed heir of Bleze."

"But . . . deposed? The royal family is still recognised in
the West Isles."

"A line of the royal family is, but not the legitimate one.
The colonists recognised the first *son* of the queen as the ruler,
but until then inheritance always passed along the female line."

Tyen shook his head, both at the treatment of her people
– though after seeing Mailand he wasn't surprised to learn of
another land unhappy at the Empire's methods of control – and
at the realisation that Veroo was, by her people's reckoning,
royalty. And Sezee, as her niece, was too. He understood now
where she had acquired her boldness and confidence. Though
she would never have the authority her ancestors possessed,
her family was still a powerful one.

Suddenly Leratian society, which didn't allow women to own
anything but their clothing and jewellery, seemed far more
primitive and uncivilized. *Perhaps this is why Leratian women
surround themselves with such elaborate rules of manner and protocol.
It gives them a sense of control and respect. Interesting, then, that I
find Leratian women confounding but am at ease with Sezee.*

Were all women of her country like her? Maybe it was
simply that Sezee was a confident and outspoken woman. Much
like Vella, he realised. Which was an interesting thought . . .

"So if you are royalty, how is it that you were allowed to
leave and travel on your own?"

Sezee didn't answer. She was looking at something behind
him, frowning. "That one's flying low."

He glanced over his shoulder to see an aircart buzzing past,
close enough that he could see that the driver's face was turned
towards them. Aircarts and aircarriages had been a common
sight since they'd left Leratia, but this one was flying unusu-
ally close. Fear pulsed through him and he turned his back.

The ship had been following the northern coast of Wendland since he'd emerged that morning. They would arrive in Darsh, the capital, soon. When they did it was possible – no, likely – Academy sorcerers and local police would be there, watching to see who disembarked.

His stomach twisted. He'd had a brief respite on the ship. A chance to eat and sleep. But it would soon be over.

"What will you do when we arrive?" Sezee asked.

"I don't know," he confessed.

"You'd better stay below for now. Stay out of sight." She pushed away from the railing. "Let's collect Veroo and ask for something to eat."

For the next few hours he pretended that they were doing nothing more than embarking upon an interesting voyage. They ate, then Sezee insisted that he stay in the little room to rest and guard their belongings while she and Veroo watched the approach to Darsh from on deck. His thoughts circled uselessly around the problem of disembarking without being seen. Would his disguise as the women's porter work? Was there any other way he could slip ashore unnoticed? Could he bribe one of the crew into changing clothes with him and the others into letting him pretend to help them offload goods?

If Kilraker was there, or anybody from the Academy who could recognise Tyen, no disguise would work. Could he use magic to fight his way free? He had escaped Kilraker before. Perhaps he could do so again. But even if he managed it, there would be no aircart nearby to steal. Only ships. And a ship needed more than one person to sail it.

At last the door to the passage opened and light, rapid footsteps could be heard approaching.

"Aren!" Sezee's voice was low and urgent.

He rose and stepped into the passage. "Yes?"

She placed a hand on his arm. "We're pulling in to the

docks. There are Darsh police everywhere and men we think are from the Academy. How much money do you have?"

He picked up his satchel and opened it, keeping it tilted so she would not see Beetle. "I don't know. A few hundred levees, I think."

"Are you prepared to give a hundred to the captain, if he hides you?"

Tyen's breath caught. It was no small amount and the loss would mean survival would get tougher sooner, but there could be no surviving at all if he was caught. He nodded.

"Stay here."

She hurried away. As the passage door closed behind her, Tyen sagged against the wall, assailed by nausea. *What if it doesn't work?* he thought. *What if the captain takes the money and turns me over anyway?*

The door opened and this time one of the crew entered. He smiled thinly at Tyen.

"Follow me."

Did that mean the captain had agreed? As the man passed him and continued down the passage, Tyen hesitated. Then he shrugged and followed. What choice did he have but to trust him?

At the end of the passage was the door to the water closet. The man opened this, then grasped the seat of the latrine and lifted. The entire thing popped out of the floor like a cork. He stepped back and jerked his head towards the hole.

"There's handholds. Try not to knock the outlet pipe. Someone outside might see it move."

Tyen had read in history books that, in ships of the past, one of the punishments for mutinous crew was to be locked in the chute under the latrine with predictably unpleasant results. Trying not to let his dismay show, Tyen stepped up to the hole and peered down. An enamelled copper outlet pipe curved down and to the left, carrying away the waste. There wasn't much space around it, but the cavity below was large enough for a man to squat in, and it was clean. The walls were rough wood, with chunks of timber nailed on to provide hand- and footholds for access to repair the latrine.

He dropped his satchel inside, then stepped through to the first handhold, squeezed around the pipe and climbed down as quickly as he could manage. As soon as his head descended past the floor, the crewman, without another word, shoved the latrine back into place. Tyen crouched in the dark, tiny space and listened to the man's footsteps as he hurried away.

The air grew warmer and heavier. Instead of growing used to the smell from the latrine pipe so close to his head he found it was intensifying in the small space. He listened to the muffled stomp of many feet and occasional heavy thump – perhaps of cargo. Then all went quiet. When the signs of life returned the nature of the noises had changed, and as footsteps approached the room above the difference was suddenly fright-eningly obvious. Instead of the thud of the soft partree soles of the crew's shoes, designed for grip, he was hearing the clack of hidesole boots worn by people whose job entailed walking the cobbled streets of cities.

The Wendland police were on board, and no doubt there were Academy men with them. Searching for him. The foot-steps drew closer. The door above opened. He kept his breath slow and quiet. The floor above his head creaked. He waited for the door to close again, but it didn't. Surely it only took one look for an unsuspecting searcher to confirm the water closet was unoccupied. Did that mean the man suspected there was more to the little room? Was he looking closer, searching for evidence of trapdoors? Had he, like Tyen, heard of the old punishment for mutinous crew?

CHAPTER 16

A faint trickling noise came from the pipe beside his ear. From above he heard a man speak and it took a moment for Tyen to remember enough Wendlandish to translate.

"What are you doing?"

"Checking that it works."

"There's a law against using the privy while in dock."

"You going to arrest me?"

"Well . . . hurry up then."

Tyen let out his breath as the sounds stopped and footfalls retreated from the water closet. Then they both returned in reverse as the second man took his turn. By the time the searchers had done their business and left, no other hard footsteps could be heard echoing around the ship. A long silence followed, then the earlier noises of goods being unloaded resumed and he allowed himself to relax a little.

He could do no more than wait until someone came to release him. When nobody did, he guessed that they were planning to leave him there until the ship reloaded and left the dock. He hoped they weren't intending to stay overnight.

At one point Tyen thought he heard a familiar female voice beyond the hull. He realised that Sezee and Veroo would have left the ship to continue their journey home. He would never get a chance to thank them. Perhaps he could send a letter.

He had no specific address, but if Sezee's family was as well known as she described it would probably still get to her.

The thought of never seeing Sezee again saddened him. He had never got the chance to fulfil their last condition for helping him: to tell them the truth about his reasons for fleeing Leratia. It would have been nice to know that someone in the world knew the whole story. Other than Kilraker. Or most of it, anyway. As Vella had advised, he would not have told them what he'd stolen. It all made him more determined to get a letter to his father somehow.

He wished he knew exactly what Sezee had arranged with Captain Taga. Where was the man going next? Not back to Leratia, Tyen hoped. Had Taga accepted the hundred levees as the bribe, or demanded more? Without Sezee to confirm or deny the amount he could tell Tyen anything and there would be no way of knowing if he was lying. Tyen might evade the Academy another day, but he would not survive long without money.

Overhearing the police speaking in Wendlandish had also reminded him that whatever money he did keep, if any, might have to be exchanged for local currency. Leratian levees were used in all the Empire, but he suspected it would be easier to hide from the authorities if he mingled more with humbler locals. But exchanging money meant records would be made that the Academy might be able to trace, especially if he was required to produce identification papers. Thanks to Sezee and Veroo, he had alternative identification papers (and they had never explained why, he recalled) but if the Academy worked out that he was posing as Aren Coble they'd be as useless as his own.

As time stretched on, he grew bored. He abandoned an attempt to pick his satchel up off the floor when he found it meant making a lot of scraping noises. Remembering that he'd put Vella in his jacket pocket, he took her out. He cupped his hand over her and drew enough magic to create a soft glow, then lost himself in her stories of other worlds and powerful sorcerers, and was only jolted back to reality when the ship began to move again.

They were leaving. He went to put Vella back in his jacket pocket, then thought better of it and slipped her inside his shirt. Whatever happened next, at least she would be able to see and hear it.

He didn't have to wait long. Footsteps once again echoed in the passage above. He heard the water closet door open, then the scrape of the latrine as it was lifted. When it came free he had a view of the water closet ceiling. Then a familiar face peered down at him.

"Oh, it's not at all as bad as it sounded," Sezee declared.

He smiled in surprise and relief. "You stayed on board!"

She shrugged. "Yes and no. We had a quick look around town like the tourists we're supposed to be would, then we came back."

"Thank you. I hope I have not unduly spoiled your travel plans."

"Not at all. Besides, you haven't yet told us why you're running from the Academy. Are you coming out, or have you got too comfortable down there?"

With some effort, he managed to manipulate the satchel with the toe of one boot so that it lay against the wall, then squatted far enough to grab it. Lifting it up, he handed it to her, then climbed out. The crewman stood behind her, holding the latrine. As soon as they'd squeezed past him he slotted the seat back into place.

"Stay down here," he advised. "The cap'n wants a chat, once we're 'way from shore."

Then he hurried back down the passage, passing Veroo

standing outside her room, and disappeared through the door to the deck.

"Well, then." Sezee grabbed Tyen's arm. "It's time you explained why the Academy is after you."

Tyen did not resist, letting her haul him along to the doorway of their room. Veroo did not smile as he approached. Her eyes narrowed at him. Sezee, still apparently as cheerful as before she'd changed her plans for him, pointed at one of the beds.

"Sit," she ordered, like a bossy child. Or princess.

He obeyed.

"Talk."

He chuckled. "How much detail do you want?"

"Not so much that we're left none the wiser when Captain Taga gets here."

"Very well. I am – I was – a student of the Academy. I was learning history and sorcery. On a research expedition recently I found something. It was . . . hard to determine its value. We were meant to hand over all our finds, but it was a rule that was often overlooked and I . . . I knew the Academy would not see the potential in it that I did, but I thought I could find a way to persuade them. But they discovered and took possession of it before I could. It was then stolen – but not by me. By Professor Kilraker, a man I once admired and trusted. He arranged it so that I would be blamed."

Sezee watched him intently as he spoke, and continued to after he fell silent. Then she shook her head.

"But surely, if you don't have this thing, nobody can accuse you of stealing it."

"They would suspect I had hidden it. Or sold it."

"Suspicions are not proof. Not in Leratian law. And if you are so sure this professor stole it then why not tell them?" Her eyebrows rose. "Ah! But the thief no longer has the object either, correct?"

He nodded.

"Do you still have it?"

"You only asked me to tell you why the Academy is chasing me."

"Our condition for helping you was that you told us the truth."

"But not the whole truth," he replied.

"That's—"

"Sezee," Veroo interrupted. "Leave it."

The young woman turned to the older, who shook her head. Frowning, Sezee narrowed her eyes at him. Her gaze dropped to his satchel, still in her hands, then widened.

"Is it that mechanical insect guarding your money?"

He gave her a level look. "Couldn't resist taking a peek, could you?"

Veroo smiled as a blush reddened Sezee's cheeks. "I might have," Sezee replied. "We weren't completely unaware that we might be helping a man who might turn on us."

"And what did the contents tell you?"

Her bottom lip pinched upward. "Nothing we hadn't guessed already. You have money. You're from the Academy."

"How did my bag contents tell you I was from the Academy?"

"The shaving implements have the 'A' on them."

"Oh." He smiled and shook his head. He'd never noticed. He reached out for the satchel and she reluctantly gave it back to him.

"So." She smiled. "Am I right?"

He looked up. "Is it Beetle? No."

At the sound of its name, Beetle stirred. Tyen thought of her assumption that it was there to guard his money. It wasn't a bad idea. If he found the time he would make a few changes so it could function that way. An alarm would be easiest. The instructions would be similar to the alarm he'd trained it to make when Miko had approached his room. Though perhaps he could add pins or blades to its front legs so it could sting anyone who reached inside.

"I told the captain you would pay him half now and half later," Veroo said.

He looked up and nodded. "Thank you. Thank you both for helping me." He paused. "What exactly did you arrange? Where are we going?"

"South," Veroo answered. "Captain Taga trades up and down the coast. He seems an honest enough man, so far as any independent trading captain can be."

"What of your plans to return home?" Tyen asked.

"Well," Sezee said, in that way people did when they were about to try winning you over to an idea they'd had. "You're going to the Far South and since—"

Tyen's heart skipped a beat. "Wait. What makes you think I'm going to the Far South?"

Sezee's smile widened. "You are, though. Right?"

"I might be."

"It is one of the few parts of the world not under the influence of the Leratian Empire, after all."

Tyen shook his head. "Then I shouldn't go there, if it's so obvious."

"Anywhere else you go, you'll be turned over to the Academy as soon as anyone works out who you are."

"*If* they work out who I am."

"The further you go from Leratia, the more obvious it's going to be that you're different from the people around you. In the Far South that won't matter. They have no agreement with the Empire."

"That doesn't mean they'll stop the Academy hunting me down and taking me home."

"They might. And the Academy have to find you first. It

seems to me your chances are better there than anywhere else. And didn't you say the only way to reach the Far South was by aircart?"

"Yes."

"You can operate an aircart."

"Can I?"

"Don't all Academy students learn to drive one?"

"No."

She paused and frowned. "Can you?"

He smiled. "Yes."

"And you can build one?"

He nodded.

She grinned. "So, will you take us with you?"

He looked from her to Veroo. The older woman smiled, but her gaze was sharp and unwavering. *Of course*, he thought. *She wants to seek out the school of sorcery Gowel mentioned.* The thought of this woman learning all that the Academy had denied her gave him an odd feeling of satisfaction.

"I would be glad to," he told them.

Sezee clasped her hands together and said a strange word. She turned to Veroo, who grudgingly repeated the word. Tyen guessed it was some expression of satisfaction or victory in their native language. Then Veroo's head snapped to the side.

"The captain's coming," she warned.

Sure enough, the door to the deck opened and Tyen heard footsteps approaching. He got to his feet as Taga stepped into view.

"So," the man said. "It's Tyen Ironsmelter now."

"Yes, Captain," Tyen replied.

"Come into my room." He beckoned and led the way back a few paces, to a door on the opposite side of the passage. Opening it, he ushered Tyen through. "The women have told you of our arrangements?"

"Yes."

He followed Tyen into a small room with a table and two chairs to one side and a bed on the other. The captain closed the door, leaving Sezee and Veroo outside.

"Did you kill anyone?"

Tyen looked at the captain, at first surprised and then a little offended. But it was a reasonable question to ask, he supposed – though the captain wouldn't know if Tyen's answer was the truth.

"No."

"Steal anything?"

Tyen sighed. "That's . . . complicated. What they say I stole . . . I was set up as the thief. But I did steal an aircart to escape and there happened to be a large sum of money on board."

The captain regarded Tyen in silence for a while, then nodded. "Fifty levee."

Tyen blinked, surprised that there were no more questions. He opened his satchel and drew out a few bundles of money, counting out half of the bribe the women had arranged.

"Thank you," he said, handing it over.

The captain took the money. "I want no trouble with the Academy," he warned. "You're to stay aboard and out of sight when we're in port."

"Of course."

"We only go as far south as Carmel."

Tyen nodded.

A knock on the door diverted the man's attention. "Come in."

One of the crew stepped inside. "Aircart. Looks like it's tailing us," he said.

The captain scowled and turned back to Tyen. "Stay here." He led the way out of the room, walking past the women and out onto the deck.

Glancing around, Tyen saw a small window on the opposite side to the door. He approached cautiously, but could see nothing but clouds and birds and a small part of the deck. The ship altered direction slightly and the rocking increased, forcing Tyen to brace himself. After several minutes he gave up and moved to one of the chairs.

Perhaps hiding and waiting for someone to tell him what was going on was the way things were going to be from now on. It was a small annoyance to endure, if it would keep him out of the Academy's hands. All he could do was sit quietly and hope that he was safe.

PART FOUR

RIELLE

CHAPTER 11

Rielle reluctantly peeled Izare's paint-stained hands from around her waist and slipped out of his embrace. "Enough of that. Get back to work."

His lower lip protruded. "But—"

"You told me to do this," she reminded him, backing towards the chairs. "You said I was too much of a distraction and I should shoo you away. I don't want to be the reason you're late delivering the spiritual. Later than you already are, that is."

He smiled and followed her. "But I finished it last night."

She glanced at the easel. The back of the board he was painting faced the stairs, so she had not yet seen the progress he'd made. Keeping out of reach, she approached the front of the painting.

It was a narrative based on the story of Sa-Azurl, the Doubting Priest, who chose to believe the Angels did not exist rather than that they had not saved his village from flood, but eventually came to see his mistake and was welcomed by the Angels when he died. Rielle had suggested it, as the man who had ordered it was a melancholy old widower of one of the city's oldest families, who was very self-critical. Her guess that he might appreciate a story of forgiveness had proved right.

As with all Izare's spirituals, the scenery and format were

traditional, but the figures were so extraordinarily real she almost expected to see them blink.

Izare took her distraction as an opportunity to slip his arms around her waist from behind, resting his chin on her shoulder. "What do you think?"

"It is beautiful, as always."

"As always," he repeated. Then he sighed. "And the same every time. I would like to change so much more. Why must they always be a story? Why are they always set outside?"

"How would you do your own spiritual?"

He hummed and the vibration of his voice penetrated her shoulder bones. "Like a portrait. One man – or woman – but not looking at the viewer as if knowing they are watched. Instead absorbed in their own mind. Praying, perhaps. Perhaps to an Angel. Perhaps unaware of being observed by an Angel, who is barely visible in the shadows."

Rielle shivered. "You should try it."

He pulled away. "And risk that the priests would find some outrage in it?" He shrugged. "If I'm going to do that, I may as well paint naked women. At least I'd have fun *and* earn money." He glanced at the window. "And in matters of income, I had best start doing the rounds of temples to see if I can attract some new commissions."

Something tightened within Rielle's stomach. It was not quite a knot of anxiety, but it was close. Izare turned her around to face him.

"Don't worry. I told you, customers change their mind all the time. I have always found new commissions when I looked for them. It's just been a while since I sought them. That's all."

She smiled. "Perhaps I should seek my own."

"Not yet." He moved away to a box he kept full of small, square samples of spiritual scenes. "I know you'd like to sell your work, but people are strange when it comes to women artists. They may feel it is not proper to hire you. You might be better off helping me with the spirituals without them knowing, but you'll need more skill with the oily paint first."

Suppressing a sigh, she nodded and moved to the table. "Then I had better continue practising."

He grimaced. "Yes . . . but not today? I am a little low on paint."

Turning back, she headed for the chairs instead. She settled by the window and watched Izare gather his things. Along with the box of samples, he pulled together some cheap paper and chalk. He tied his money bag to his belt then walked over to kiss her.

"You will be fine on your own?" He asked the same question every time he left the house.

"Of course," she told him, then watched him head for the stairs. It was a lie, and he knew it. If the priests or her family came to drag her home she would not be able to stop them. But neither would he have been able to.

I'm almost offended that they haven't tried, she mused. *I guess Mother and Father think I'm spoiled goods now. Nobody in the families will marry me so I have no worth to them.*

She had stayed in the travellers' house for two quarterdays. Izare had hidden in Greya and Merem's rooms. The priests had found him there but though they questioned him at length they had not attempted to force her whereabouts out of him. When it was clear he wouldn't offer up the information they had ignored him.

Izare could not afford to pay for her rent for long, so she had moved to his house in the middle of the night and hadn't dared leave it since. He'd arranged with a few of the locals he trusted to warn her if priests entered the area. She would have to leave and come back when the priests had gone.

Hearing the door below shut, she watched Izare through

the window as he strode away along the street below. He looked unconcerned and cheerful. It was easy not to worry when he was so relaxed, and she did not yet want to burst the bubble of happiness she was caught within.

It was not a perfect bubble. She missed Narmah badly and felt terrible about hiding so much from her aunt. She could not help feeling guilty about disappointing her parents, brother and cousin, and causing a scandal that now blemished their names. And she was no fool; she knew a life with Izare was likely to be hard.

She was determined to be a help to him, all too aware that he had two people to feed and clothe now. Since she had moved here she had begun a mental tally of his expenses and, during the lessons she insisted he still give her, pressed him on what was a fair price for different kinds of paintings. She sought ways she could be useful, like grinding paint and preparing boards, though he did not have enough work at the moment for that to save him time. When it was safe to leave the house she figured she could fetch him art supplies and food. Maybe she could learn to cook. He seemed to prefer buying meals already cooked from bakeries and drinking houses, but it was an expensive way to eat all the time. Perhaps one of Izare's friends could teach her, though that would mean cleaning up the grimy corner that passed for a kitchen on the ground floor and hoping there were cooking pots in among the piles of dirty dishes and the mess.

She grimaced and told herself it was more important to hone her skills, since cleaning and cooking wouldn't earn them anything. If she couldn't paint she'd draw. Rising, she found some chalk but no paper, then realised that Izare had taken the last of it with him. With a sigh, she sat by the window again.

Well, it's not like there's anything here I haven't already drawn.

She felt a pang of guilt then. She had used most of his supply of paper without knowing it. Izare had brought some to her at the travellers' house to fill the hours she'd spent hiding there. Later she'd practised by drawing him, the corners of his house and the view from the window. Though she'd known good paper was expensive, what he used was low-quality, cheap stock and he'd not said anything about her consumption of it. Too late she'd noticed that he often used a piece several times, dusting back the chalk and drawing over the top, and using both sides.

Is it possible to make paper at home? she wondered. *Would it be cheaper than buying it?* She resolved to find out, once she was free to leave the house.

A movement outside the window caught her eye, and her heart skipped as she saw one of Jonare's boys running towards Izare's door. Leaning closer to the glass, she saw his mother following, daughter and two nieces at her side and baby in a sling across her chest. The door below opened then slammed shut.

"'Zar!" the boy called, thundering up the stairs. Rielle smiled as he reached the top and halted, searching the room.

"Izare is out finding new customers," she told him, wishing she could remember the boy's name.

The boy stared at her, caught by the revelation of someone strange in a familiar place. The door below opened again.

"Perri!" Jonare scolded. "I told you to wait!"

Perri spun around and hurried down the stairs. Rising, Rielle walked over to the railing.

"Hello, Jonare."

The woman looked up and smiled. "We thought you might like some company."

"Thank you." Rielle beckoned. "Come up."

Two of the girls were carrying a basket between them. Jonare took it from them, freeing them all to run up the stairs and into Izare's studio. Rielle winced as they began to tear around, then hurried to catch the finished spiritual as one of them collided with the easel. She set it aside in what she hoped was a safe place.

Jonare moved to the chairs and sat down with a sigh. Guessing it was the woman's turn to look after her sister's twins, Rielle sat at the edge of a stool, ready to rescue anything else they might upset and thinking that, while she appreciated the company, the sudden introduction of five children was a bit of a shock after the isolation of the last few quarterdays.

"So he's on the hunt for commissions," Jonare said, nodding. "He hasn't had to do that for a while. Usually people compete for his work."

"Is that so?" Rielle asked. Perhaps things weren't as bad as she'd been told to expect.

Jonare frowned. "Yes. People are more frugal after the festival, though. They spend too much."

"Then it wasn't good timing, me coming here." Rielle sighed. "An extra mouth to feed when work is scarce. I've been trying to think of ways I can help."

The baby had woken and was beginning to fuss. Jonare lifted her tunic and began to feed it. Averting her eyes, Rielle looked at the children instead, then leapt up and extracted a tube of paint from the mouth of one of the girls. Thankfully the twists hadn't come apart at the ends yet.

"You mustn't eat paint," she told the child. "It's poisonous, and could make you very sick." She turned back to find Jonare looking surprised.

"Poisonous? Izare never said that."

Rielle shrugged. "Maybe he doesn't know." She caught the hands of the girl, who had reached towards more colourful things on the work table. "It might be safer for us to go downstairs."

Jonare nodded, then rose and called the children to her.

They all stomped down to the ground floor. The room below was slightly smaller than the studio and the only furniture it contained was a bed, a single rickety chair and a narrow work bench over by the stove. Though Rielle had made some attempts at tidying, all she had achieved was slightly more organised and less dusty piles of belongings. As the children began to jump all over the bed, she cast about in vain for a better chair to offer. This might be a safer place for children to play, but all the seating for adults was upstairs. Perhaps she could suggest Izare move some down.

"I guess I'll have to sit on the bed," she said, moving the chair over for Jonare.

Jonare shrugged and sat down. "Is paint really all that dangerous? Mele once got blue paint all over her face. We thought it was funny and called her an Angel."

Rielle grimaced. "Well, it depends on the colour. The reds and greens are the worst. My family has strict rules on how to handle dyes and pigments. We – they – don't want any of the workers getting sick or dying."

"Izare has paint on his hands all the time."

"It is hard to paint without getting a little messy. I'm trying to get him to clean up afterwards, but the oily paint requires soap and he says it's cheaper to wipe your hands on rags."

Jonare nodded. "Try ashes. It absorbs the oil, then you rinse it off."

"Truly?" Rielle glanced towards the stove. "Do you know how to cook?"

"Of course. Nothing fancy, though."

"Could you teach me?"

The woman looked amused. "You never had to, did you?"

Rielle shook her head. "Not beyond simple preparation for feasts. It looks to me like it would be cheaper to make food than pay others to."

Jonare nodded. "It certainly is – and you'll need to know how to feed a bub soon enough, I'd say."

At the woman's smile, Rielle looked away, feeling her face heat and her heart shrivel.

"Not until we're married," she mumbled.

"No?" Jonare laughed. "I don't think you'll have much choice about that!" But when Rielle said nothing, she reached forward and patted her on the knee. "Don't worry. I've never seen him so besotted with someone, and he's the sort of man who treats women fairly, but making it official isn't cheap."

Rielle frowned. "But you don't need money to get married."

"You need a willing priest," Jonare pointed out. "And in these parts, willing means well persuaded."

"What? Truly?" Rielle shook her head. "I can't believe how corrupt the priests have proven to be. Sa-Baro . . ." The old priest would surely not demand money from her. But he might refuse to do it, telling her to go home to her family instead.

Would he, if I was with child? He always said that parents should take responsibility for their children, even those born outside marriage. He wouldn't want to split us up, if we became a family.

But she couldn't have a child. At least, not without undoing what the corrupter had done to her. And that meant using magic.

The sound of a door opening and closing drew their attention, then steps going upward. Rielle rose and hurried over to the lower room's door. She peered out to find Izare nearly at the top of the stairs.

"We're down here," she called.

"'Zar!" a small voice yelled, then Rielle was shoved aside as four children pushed through and raced up the stairs. Izare grinned. Perri reached him first, and was rewarded by being lifted high in the air.

"You're getting heavier, little man," Izare told him before

setting him down. Then he let the boy grab his hand and guide him back down. As he reached Rielle he kissed her firmly then moved on into the lower room. "Well, well. Two women in my bedroom. I could get to like this."

Jonare snorted softly. "Not if you knew our plans. I'm going to teach Rielle how to cook."

Izare's eyebrows rose and he turned to regard her with a thoughtful expression. "Well, don't go out and buy any pots and pans quite yet," he told her. "It's going to take a little longer to find work than I hoped."

"What happened?" Jonare asked, her voice suddenly deep and serious. At her tone Rielle felt her stomach sink.

"Just the priests of the city letting me know how displeased they are with me," he said, looking from Jonare to her. "They are refusing to give out my name to potential buyers, discouraging anyone from commissioning my work, and a certain family has insisted their local temple cover up and replace its wall painting."

Rielle gasped. "They can't do that! It would be a great waste of money and a loss of something beautiful and sacred. And . . . all that work you did."

He smiled, then walked over and encircled her waist with his arms. "I don't mind. They've paid me already, and I have something even more beautiful and sacred right here."

She could not help but smile at that. The bubble of happiness returned. Until she remembered what Jonare had said about the priests demanding payment to perform marriages. If they could be persuaded by her family to replace an entire temple wall painting, she doubted any could be bribed into marrying her and Izare.

They could only hope the priests' willingness to bow to her family's wishes would weaken with time. The problem was what to do in the meantime, if Izare could get no work.

"Spirituals aren't all I paint," Izare reminded her, no doubt reading the worry in her face. "We will be fine."

She nodded, feeling some of the tension leave her. Remembering his portrait of her and how it had revealed his weakness at painting cloth, she smiled. *If he lets me, there is a way I can help. I just have to convince him I can do it.*

CHAPTER 12

L ooking at the piles of dirty dishes, paint-stained rags, soiled clothing, long-dead flowers and old vegetables covering the kitchen bench, Rielle considered where to start. Dividing it all into items worth keeping or to be thrown away would be a beginning. She considered separating the former based on whether the object needed to be cleaned or not but realised that there was nothing that didn't.

She couldn't venture outside to collect water, however. When Izare returned she would get him to do it. Then she would burn some of the rubbish in the stove to heat the water and use the ash, as Jonare had suggested, to help clean the dishes.

Yet she hesitated, afraid that if she disturbed one item the rest would topple over. Would that be such a bad thing? Most of the dishes looked chipped and cracked anyway. The trouble was, they could hardly afford to replace them.

Better start from the top, then, she told herself. Stepping forward, she began to lift an old shirt draped over half the mess. It peeled away, so stiffened with grime and oily paint that it retained some of the shape of the items beneath it. Underneath she found a plate of mouldy sunmelon slices. She sighed out a small prayer to the Angels. No wonder this corner of the room smelled so bad.

A knock came from the main door. Looking over her shoulder

towards the sound, then back at the blue-crusted melon, she sighed and replaced the shirt. She hurried out of the room, hoping that whoever had come would fetch her some water.

The heavy main door swung inward to reveal a familiar, kind face set in a frown of sternness and determination.

"Ais Lazuli," Sa-Baro said. "May I come in and speak with you?"

She could not answer for a moment, first because she had frozen with alarm, then because she was biting back a curse at her own stupidity at answering the door at all, and finally because she was unsure what she should do. He could have so easily forced his way in with magic, but he hadn't. He had *asked* to come in.

Would he go away if she refused to talk to him? She was tempted, just to see what happened.

She thought of Narmah and the urge to rebel faded.

"Are you here to take me home?" she asked.

It might have been her imagination, but his expression appeared to soften a fraction. He shook his head.

"Why should I believe you?"

"I swear it is true," he replied solemnly. "I swear it on the Angels' names."

She opened the door fully, gesturing for him to enter the lower room. He looked around as he entered, his gaze moving from the bed to the piles of mess, no doubt comparing it to the tastefully decorated receiving room in the dyeworks. She pushed a pile of dirty clothes off the old chair and waved at it, though she could not imagine him, in his perfect blue robes, looking anything but out of place. He shook his head.

"I won't be staying long." He turned to face her. "Are you well?"

"Yes," she replied. "Is my family well?"

He nodded. "Anxious for your wellbeing, of course."

"Of course." By thinking of Narmah, not her mother, she managed to keep sarcasm from her voice.

He looked down at the floor, his brow furrowing, then regarded her directly.

"I apologise for my bluntness but . . . have you . . . is Izare your lover?"

She held his gaze, surprised at how easy it was. Perhaps because her answer would have been different if he had done what he had promised to.

"Yes," she answered.

He looked away, shaking his head. "Foolish girl."

A surge of anger went through her. "If my choice was foolish, then you are to blame for forcing it by betraying my trust."

His eyes narrowed. "You dare to judge me, when you have been lying for so long?"

She shook her head. "I did not lie to anyone."

"No? But you concealed the truth. From your family. From me. How was I to advise you well, if I did not know all that troubled you?"

She closed her mouth. He was right. Would he have told her parents of his suspicions about her and Izare if she'd admitted to him how fondly she had come to regard Izare? Perhaps he'd have guessed she might choose to leave her family, if faced with losing him.

He must have believed their relationship was a shallower thing. He hadn't thought the prospect of being married off to one of the great families' reject sons was enough to drive her into running away, because he'd assumed she had nowhere to go.

Or perhaps he'd assumed she wouldn't give up the wealth of her upbringing to live with a poor artist.

Sa-Baro sighed. "Your aunt would like to see you. Will you meet her?"

Rielle's heart leapt. "Yes."

"She hopes to establish friendly relations," he told her. "Make peace between yourself and your parents. Are you open to such a thing?"

"I am . . . with conditions."

"I'm sure she will have some of her own." He nodded. "I will let her know."

He started for the door. She stepped aside and followed him out of the room. He let himself out, pausing once to look at her, his expression sad, before stepping outside.

After the door had closed, Rielle drew in a deep breath and let it out, willing the anger and regret to whoosh out with it. Hope warred with fear. It would be wonderful to see Narmah. So long as the meeting *was* with Narmah, and not some attempt by her family to capture her and take her home.

Abruptly, from out of nowhere, a thought sliced through all others.

I spoke with a priest and never once thought about how I'd learned magic.

She shivered. All she'd thought about was how Sa-Baro had betrayed her. Next time she might not be so lucky. It was going to be hard, meeting the eyes of a priest while thinking about what she had done. Hopefully, many years of hiding her ability to see Stain would help her keep this new secret.

But for now she had more pressing problems. Pushing the thought aside, she turned to look at the lower room, seeing it as Sa-Baro must have and feeling ashamed. Izare did not mind the mess and had no servants to do the work. Nothing would change here without her making it.

Since it was clear that the priests knew she was here and weren't about to drag her home, she was free to fetch water for herself. Straightening her shoulders, she walked over and picked up the metal basin she and Izare used to wash themselves and their clothes. Setting it on the stove, she picked up the large pitcher Izare used to carry water in from the fountain and headed for the main door.

As she stepped out into the courtyard her skin prickled. She hadn't been outside in two quarterdays. The neighbours knew she was there. She'd seen them peering up at the windows of Izare's house and heard them ask after her. While she was not dressed in the fine clothes she had always worn at home – Jonare had sent some skirts and tunics from before her first pregnancy – she felt conspicuous. Reaching the fountain, she filled the pitcher then hurried back inside.

When she returned to the fountain, she was not surprised to find Monya filling some glass bottles.

"Hello, Rielle," the woman said, smiling and glancing up. "Are you well? I saw the priest leave. It was uncommonly sneaky of him to slip past our lookouts."

Rielle smiled. "I'm well, thank you. He did no harm. Only wanted to ask a few questions. How are you and Dinni?"

She looked pleased. "We're getting by. Dinni is carving again, thanks to the generosity of our latest customer. She heard what happened and withheld her usual festival donation to pay for replacement materials."

"Sounds like a nice customer."

Monya nodded. "She is. A great appreciator of art and a champion of women. I should introduce you."

"I'd like that." Perhaps this customer wouldn't mind a painting by a woman.

"Doing a little cleaning?"

"Yes, though probably more than a little."

"Tam, the old weaver who lives over there . . ." – she nodded to a nearby house – ". . . used to wash Izare's clothes every quarterday for a few copee."

"Does she still?"

"She figures you'll be doing it now. But if you'd like her to, I'm sure she'd be happy to."

Rielle nodded, noting the shift in tone that suggested Monya was hinting at something more. Most likely the old woman needed the income. Trouble was, she didn't know if Izare could afford it now.

"I'll see what Izare means to do," she said. "He's out trying to find new commissions."

Monya looked thoughtful. "He hasn't had to do that for a while."

"So I hear." Rielle grimaced and looked down at the pitcher. "I'd better get started."

She headed back to the house, and made two more trips before the basin was full. Hours later she had removed everything from the kitchen bench, made a pile of reusable items and scrubbed the plates with ash and an old rag. She tossed the garbage she couldn't burn into a shallow pit in an alley all the locals used. When it was full everyone put money together to pay garbage collectors to empty it.

She was tipping the last of the dirty water into a bucket to empty down the drain outside when the main door opened and Izare strode in, carrying a cloth-wrapped rectangular bundle and a loaf of bread. He paused in the lower room doorway to stare at her, then put down his burden and hurried forward.

"Let me help you with that." Grabbing the bucket, he carried it outside.

"Any luck?" she asked when he returned.

He shook his head. "Monya said you had a visitor."

"Sa-Baro."

Izare's eyes widened. He stepped forward and seized her hands. "What did he do?"

"Nothing. Except ask if I'd meet with my aunt."

He looked thoughtful. "What did you say?"

"That I would."

"It could be a trap. He might have come here hoping to surprise you, and told you your aunt wanted to meet you so you'd stay put while he went to inform your family of your location. They could be on their way right now."

She shrugged. "It was hours ago. If they were going to do it, they'd have done it by now. No, I'm damaged goods. Nobody in the families will want to marry me now. It's better for them if I stay away rather than be a burden and a constant reminder of scandal."

"No!" He brought her hands to his mouth, kissing one after another. "You are not *damaged*, nor were you ever goods to be traded."

She drew a deep breath, steeled herself and looked at him directly. "Do *you* want to marry me?"

He smiled. "Want to? Yes! Afford to? Not yet."

She pulled her hands from his. "Jonare told me about the priests' bribe. If I could get my parents to approve of a marriage they wouldn't dare ask for one."

"But your parents won't."

"They might, if it blackened the family name a little less."

The corner of his mouth quirked up. "Rendered it in grey instead?"

She smiled at his joke. "It would look better if their only daughter wasn't living in poverty, too."

He scowled. "I don't need their charity."

"You don't *want* their charity," she corrected. "And neither do I. I don't want you to starve because of me, either." She looked down at the bundle, which he'd dropped on the bed. "What did you buy?"

He grimaced. Unwrapping the bundle, he revealed several sheaves of cheap paper, a bottle of oil and some jars of pigment.

"That must have cost a bit."

"Yes – but don't worry. There's one kind of artwork that always generates a reliable income, but I can't do it if I don't have paint." He smiled. "I'll start tomorrow. But for now . . . it looks like you've done enough work for today. Your hands are all red. Let me take care of the clothing."

Picking up the bundle of dirty clothes she'd tossed on the bed, he headed for the main door. "I'll be right back."

Rielle opened her mouth to object, but closed it again without speaking. *Old Tam needs money, too*, she reminded herself. *Perhaps some day we'll need a favour from her.*

CHAPTER 13

As Rielle woke she realised she had thrown the bed coverings off and was lying completely naked and exposed. Not that it mattered. Izare had seen her unclothed many times now, and in the warm air of the lower room she was perfectly comfortable. For now she was too sleepy to bother reaching for a blanket. Parts of her were tired that she had never known could be, until that first night with Izare.

Thinking of that, and the many times since, she smiled.

And then she did want to wake up properly. Opening an eye, she looked at the kitchen bench, now clean and bearing a tidy, diminished stack of the least chipped dishes. Though Izare obviously wasn't bothered by the way it had been, he also appeared to like what she had done. Or perhaps he liked the idea of eating home cooking.

They'd spent a few hours tidying the room and washing the floor. Afterwards he'd accidentally dumped a pitcher of clean water over her, and that had led to removing wet clothing, which had led to things that kept them well occupied late into the night.

Was he awake? She listened for his breathing. Instead, she heard a soft, familiar sound of scraping and dabbing. She turned over and saw that she was right: he was standing behind his easel facing her. Painting.

"Don't . . ." he said. "Roll back to where you—"

"What are you doing?" She grabbed a blanket and drew it up around herself.

"Painting."

"Obviously." She rose and, holding the blanket close, strode over to him. Rounding the easel, she turned to see a small board, barely larger than her two hands held together. The bed was sketchily laid down, but the woman on it was already taking on the magical lifelike quality of all his figures.

"Narmah warned me this would happen," she muttered.

"That you'd run away to live with me and I'd be forced to paint nude women in order to pay the rent?" he asked, raising his eyebrows in a challenge.

She narrowed her eyes at him. "You plan to *sell* paintings of me *naked*?"

He sobered. "Of course not. Nobody can tell it is you. Your face is hidden and . . ." he grinned ". . . and it's not like anyone else would recognise the rest of you."

Turning to look at the painting again, she noted how the woman's head was turned away. *Her* head. Only the profile of a breast showed. It was mostly a view from behind. Which meant her buttocks were clearly in view. She frowned. *I don't like it.* But they needed the money.

"People will buy this?" she asked.

"Yes. Readily. Though more eagerly if more was showing."

"A painting from the front."

"Yes. I could conceal your face. Or paint in another face, from memory."

She thought of herself posing naked and shrank from the idea of standing exposed for so long. "Why can't you do all of it from memory?"

He chuckled. "Despite what you might think, I've not spent

that long staring at women's naked bodies in my short life. And certainly not one as beautiful as yours."

She raised her eyebrows. "Flatterer. Don't think I missed the admission that you have spent *some* time staring at women's naked bodies."

"It's a hazard of my profession. How can I convey beauty if I have not seen it?" He set his brush and palette down. "And how can I see it daily and resist the artist's urge to capture it in paint?" He snaked an arm out and, before she could dodge away, caught the edges of the blanket. Pulling it out of her grip, he spread his arms wide, exposing her. "Surely it is selfish to keep this sight all to myself?"

She covered her breasts. "But what if I don't want to be shared around like a . . . like a . . .?"

"A whore?" He shook his head. "No. This is entirely different. When a singer sings does it diminish her? When a storyteller tells his tales does it cheapen him? No matter how many times I painted you, you would remain unmarked by the brush. Still you." He pulled the blanket edges, drawing her closer and wrapping them both in the cloth. "The physical you." He leaned down to kiss her neck. "The flesh and blood." The kisses were soft surprises, moving down into the shadows cast by the blanket and making her pulse race. "That is for me alone."

She bit her lip, caught between wanting to argue and wanting very much to say nothing more, then nearly drew blood as a loud pounding came from the main door. Izare stilled, then cursed and emerged from the blanket.

"The bastard is early. Well, at least he didn't barge in." He stood up and Rielle quickly drew the blanket around herself again.

"Who?"

"Errek. He's going to introduce me to a few customers he

doesn't want to work with. Ones he holds grudges against. A few he doesn't trust." He moved to the easel and put it behind the lower room door, so it would be hidden when it opened.

"If he doesn't trust them, should you?"

He walked back to her. "I'll insist on part payment in advance. If they fail to pay the rest, at least I have some income." Giving her a firm kiss, he smiled and turned away. "If I run into Jonare I'll let her know you're ready for cooking lessons."

Rielle let out a short laugh. "She'll have to bring the pots. And the ingredients."

He looked back and smiled at her before closing the door behind him. She heard the main door open and Errek's muffled voice. Then the sound of the door closing reverberated in the stairwell and silence followed.

Sighing, she turned away and got dressed so she could fetch water and wash. Once clean and clothed, she moved over to the easel and examined the painting.

Izare could not have been painting her for long, and yet he had captured her so well. The naked form was so luminous that the eye barely registered that the rest of the scene was sketchily painted. *It's perfect as it is. I wish I could keep it.*

But they needed money. In order to sell it, the painting needed to be finished.

Well, I can do something about that. Izare can hardly complain if I work on it. It's not like he wants to establish a reputation as a painter of indecent art.

Picking up the easel, she set it back in place and set to work.

Since the painting was small and she was only finishing the background and drapery, enough paint was already made up that she did not have to stop and prepare any. An odd mix of contentment and agitation filled her. She was not familiar enough with the new medium to be confident with it, yet it was wonderful to set her mind to the challenge again, and every success was like a victory. After a few hours she stopped, deciding that though it wasn't completely to her satisfaction, it had progressed well enough that she was happy for Izare to see it.

As she was wiping her hands clean, a light but urgent tapping came from the main door. She answered it to find a small, grubby child hovering outside.

"Priests coming," he whispered loudly, then pounded away.

Her heart skipped a beat. Sa-Baro had said he'd return with a time and place to meet Narmah. She looked back at the lower room, pleased that he would see how clean it was now. The easel blocked her view.

The painting! She would die of shame if he saw it. Running forward, she grabbed it, the easel and paints and carried them upstairs. Setting the easel down, she took the nude off and cast about for a place to hide it. The stacks of paintings leaning up against the walls were much smaller than they had been before she'd moved in with Izare, and his portrait of her was gone. He'd told her he'd moved it and many others to a safer place. Recalling how he used to hide paintings within the frame of larger ones, she hurried over to the nearest stack and flipped them forward until she found one with a partly torn backing. Carefully holding the gap open so the fresh paint wouldn't smudge, she slipped the nude inside.

As she straightened, a pounding came from downstairs. She took a deep breath, then forced herself to descend to the door. As she'd feared, the memory of the corrupter and the knowledge of what she had learned filled her mind. Swallowing shame and fear, she opened the door.

The man who stepped inside was dressed in blue, but he was not Sa-Baro. It took her a moment to realise where she had seen his face before. This was Sa-Elem, the priest who had caught and punished the tainted who had abducted her. Another man pushed through, his shoulder sliding across her chest in a way that was neither rough nor polite. She stepped back and glared at him. Sa-Gest, the young priest the temple girls disliked so much, smiled at her, his eyes gleaming with a peculiar satisfaction.

The older priest frowned at his companion, but said nothing. He turned to her.

"Ais Lazuli, is Aos Saffre home?"

"No, Sa-Elem."

He nodded. "This would be your first inspection, then?"

Inspection. Not a message from Sa-Baro, then.

"No, the dyeworks has been searched a few times, though not for many years I believe."

He turned towards the lower room. "I expect your parents would have kept you out of the way."

"Yes." She followed as the two men entered the room. "Can I help in any way?"

He looked around then he waved at Sa-Gest. "Go upstairs."

She stepped away as the younger man passed, anticipating an attempt to brush up against her again.

"Have you seen anything suspicious hereabouts?" Sa-Elem asked.

Rielle caught her breath as she realised what he meant by suspicious. "*Another* tainted?"

"Yes." He almost appeared to smile. "While you are not as safe here as you would be at the dyeworks, he or she is as likely to hide in this part of the city as any other of the lower parts."

"That's reassuring," Rielle replied, letting out a wry laugh. "No, I haven't seen anything suspicious, though I haven't been out except to fetch water from the fountain and take out the garbage."

He nodded. "Well, let us know if you do." He walked back into the stairwell. "Done?" he called.

A moment passed before Sa-Gest answered. "Yes."

Rielle heard footsteps move towards the stairs. They seemed to come from near the stack of paintings. She forced herself to breathe slowly and her expression to stay the same – a little concerned but not *too* concerned. The young priest appeared and started down the stairs, his hands tucked into the sleeves of his robes. Sa-Elem turned away, moving to the door. As he did, Sa-Gest looked at her and grinned.

Her stomach flipped over. She permitted herself a frown, then stepped back so that she was well away when he passed her. Sa-Elem held the door open for his companion, then followed him out and closed the door without saying anything more.

She waited, heart racing, until she had counted to a hundred before she ran upstairs. Looking around the room, she saw nothing disturbed. She moved to the window, searching the street below. The priests had gone.

Hurrying over to the paintings, she found the one she had slipped the nude inside. Carefully opening the tear in the fabric, she looked inside.

The painting was gone.

Sitting down on the floor, she pressed her hands to her mouth. How had he known where to look? What would he do with it? She was still sitting there some time later when Izare returned. He came upstairs when she didn't answer his call, then hurried over to her side. She gasped out the awful news.

"Don't worry," he said, drawing her into his arms. "Nobody can tell it's you."

"But he'll have guessed."

"So? He can't prove it. If he shows anyone they'll think he bought it for himself. Which is not something a good priest ought to be doing. Since you worked on most of it I can deny that I painted it. A good artist will be able to tell the difference between our work." He rubbed her shoulders.

"At least he didn't break anything, or take something more valuable."

She looked up at him. "I don't think I can pose for you again."

He smiled. "You won't have to. I have a commission."

Hope filled and lifted her like a gust of cool air. "What is it?"

"A portrait." He grinned. "The first time someone has walked up to me on the street and commissioned one based entirely on my reputation."

"Can they pay?"

"Yes."

"Who is it?

"A young woman of one of the families. About your age."

The lightness vanished and Rielle's stomach plunged to the floor.

"Who?"

"Her name is Famire, and she will be coming here next quarterday afternoon for her first sitting."

CHAPTER 14

The scarf draped over Rielle's head smelled faintly of cheap perfume and someone else's sweat. Izare had borrowed it from Greya, since Rielle had only the scarf she had worn the day she had fled the dyeworks and it was the wrong colour.

The right colour was a dark red, the most subdued hue that Famire owned. The hope was that if anyone was watching Izare's house and saw Rielle leave, when they saw a woman wearing similar clothes arrive later they'd assume it was also her. It would be better if nobody saw Famire visiting Izare in case they guessed he was painting another scandalous portrait.

Rielle was half relieved that this meant she would not be present. Famire had always been unpleasant company even when she was in a good mood, and she had expressed nothing but dislike towards Rielle. It was hard to believe that the girl only wanted her portrait done. More likely she wanted to see how far Rielle had fallen in situation and gloat.

To Rielle's relief, it had occurred to Izare that Famire might not be being honest with him. He'd asked for half of the painting's worth in advance. If Famire was truly interested in seeing Rielle's misfortune for herself then she would find some excuse to leave once she'd had a look around, not stay and pay him the first instalment.

As it turned out, Rielle had a good excuse to be absent.

Sa-Baro had stopped by the house the previous night to let Rielle know that her aunt would be waiting at a juice seller's shop the next afternoon, if she still wanted to meet her.

The shop was not far from Izare's house, at the same group Izare often bought bread from. Rielle approached cautiously, keeping out of sight. The usual collection of seats and tables graced the edges of the little courtyard. She spotted her aunt sitting on a bench built into the side of the juice shop wall. Her insides twisted with guilt, then abruptly loosened again as she saw the woman was not alone.

Mother. Sa-Baro didn't say anything about her being here as well.

Perhaps Mother had discovered Narmah's plan to meet Rielle and insisted on coming. Perhaps there was something else afoot. As Izare had suggested, Rielle slipped away and approached the shop from another direction, looking for any other people from the dyeworks in the area. She peered into shop windows but saw nobody familiar.

Skin prickling, she finally took a deep breath, steeled herself and stepped out into the courtyard. Narmah's frown disappeared as she saw Rielle coming. She leapt to her feet, coming forward with open arms.

"Ah! My little niece! Are you well?" Grabbing Rielle's hands, Narmah began a quick examination. "You look different."

"It's the scarf," Rielle said. "Not mine. How are you, Aunt?"

Narmah grimaced. "Worried about you." She leaned closer and lowered her voice. "Everyone's concerned about you. Even your mother, though she doesn't like to show it."

Rielle looked over Narmah's shoulder to find her mother sitting stiffly, watching them with an expression of disapproval. Only a small twinge of guilt came at the accusing look her mother gave her. *What a terrible daughter I am,* she thought. *I should care more about the trouble I've caused, but I don't.* The dyeworks was the best in the city and would always make money, and in seeking to marry her into one of Fyre's families her mother had been aiming too high above her station.

"Come and sit down," Narmah ordered. Holding onto one of Rielle's hands, she led her over to a chair placed opposite the bench.

"Mother," Rielle said, for the sake of good manners.

Her mother stared at her, then looked away. "So it was more than having lessons, then."

Rielle frowned, then remembered her objection when they'd confronted her about her visits to Izare.

"It was mostly that," she replied. "I can see now that I was already in love with Izare, but I had no plans to . . . to run away."

Mother turned to regard her. "Why did you, then?"

"Because the other choice was worse."

"Who told you that? The girls at temple classes?" Mother shook her head. "Another reason I shouldn't have sent you. They've put foolish ideas into your head, no doubt to stop you considering anyone they wanted themselves."

"It wasn't just the temple girls," Rielle said. "It was obvious at the parties and gatherings I went to that I didn't belong. And Sa-Baro agreed with me."

"Sa-Baro would never—"

"It doesn't matter," Narmah interrupted, her tone sterner and more determined than Rielle had heard before. "What's done is done. What matters now is what we do next." Mother closed her mouth and nodded. Narmah turned to Rielle. "You've made a brave choice, but it need not mean breaking ties with your family. If your parents agreed that you would not have to marry anyone you didn't like, would you come home?"

"Perhaps. What if I want to marry Izare?"

As Mother shook her head, Narmah frowned. "You surely

see that you will be poor if you do. What of your children? How will you afford to feed and clothe them?"

"We'll manage. He may not be wealthy, but he's not as poor as you fear. He is healthy and clever and hard-working." Rielle shrugged. "Like most other people in this city who make and sell things. Besides, even if I was willing to leave him, do you think any man in the families would still consider me?"

"I doubt it," her mother said, scowling.

"Then I may as well marry Izare."

Narmah's shoulders sagged, yet she nodded. "Well, if your mind is made up . . . maybe I can talk your parents into it. Would you come home until the wedding? If he loves you as much as you love him, he should be willing to wait for you."

"What is the point?" Mother muttered. "It won't save her reputation." She narrowed her eyes at Rielle. "Are you pregnant yet?"

Rielle glared back at her mother, the heat of embarrassment followed by anger, then an echo of horror as she remembered the corrupter. "No."

"It'd be too soon to know for sure," Narmah said in a hushed voice, looking around to see who might have overheard before leaning towards her sister. "And what if she was? Would you have the child remain nameless and fatherless?"

Mother's expression darkened, but she shook her head. Narmah turned back to Rielle.

"Will you consider coming home?"

Rielle looked down at her hands, dry and red from cleaning. She hadn't minded the work, but it wasn't earning them money. There were few ways she could help Izare and too many ways in which she was a burden. Her old daydream of introducing Izare to her family, him winning them over and them offering him a place in the dyeworks had long been discarded. Perhaps it could be salvaged.

"I will consider it."

Narmah's smile was bright, but vanished as Mother abruptly stood up.

"Well, that hasn't got us very far," she said, and with a last disapproving look at Rielle she began to walk away.

"Wait, we haven't paid and . . ." Narmah sighed and shook her head. "She is angry, but she will get over it. Unlike your father, she can't be angry and practical at the same time."

Rielle felt a pang of affection at the determination in her aunt's expression. "Thank you, Narmah."

Her aunt smiled again.

"I had better go. Take care of yourself." She touched Rielle's cheek briefly, then hurried away to pay the juice shop owner and follow Mother.

The meeting had ended sooner than Rielle had expected. She considered what to do now. Izare didn't want her to return until Famire had left. Two women wearing red scarves arriving at his home would make it obvious one wasn't Rielle. She decided to sit down again, order a mug of juice and think over what Narmah had proposed.

Would her parents let her come home and still marry Izare? What if they changed their minds about Izare after she returned?

It would be harder for them to, if I was pregnant. Having a child outside of marriage was considered much worse than simply having a lover. Which was silly, because the latter often resulted in the former. Fathers were not required by law to provide for illegitimate offspring, which could be hard for both the children and the mother. She thought of Jonare and her sister, taking it in turns to mind the other's children so that each could work. How would they cope if they did not have each other?

She sipped at the juice. It was sticky-sweet, and she regretted buying it, but she made herself drink it anyway. *If I move back to the dyeworks it would be better if I was already pregnant. If I stay with Izare, eventually he will wonder why I haven't fallen pregnant.* Either way, she needed to reverse what the corrupter had done to her. Which meant using magic.

"Angels forgive me," she whispered. The last and only time she had used magic, she had been in pain, so shocked and frightened of the corrupter that she had followed the woman's instructions without protest. What she was contemplating now was deliberate.

Yet she would be fixing the damage the corrupter had done. Putting things back the way they were supposed to be. Undoing the evil.

Would the Angels agree with her? Her other choice was to be childless for the rest of her life. While the thought of having a child so soon was a little frightening, she'd rather have one now than never at all.

Surely the Angels wouldn't deny her that? Surely they would see that she had intended to help the priests find the corrupter, and paid a terrible price for her failure?

If they did, they would also see that I haven't told the priests what I discovered. That I am unwilling to sacrifice myself in order to rid the city of evil.

Suddenly she was too nauseous to finish the drink. She rose and paid the juice seller, then started walking. With plenty of time to fill, she wandered the streets of the city. Having time on her hands was a situation she rarely encountered. Though her family was wealthy, she'd always had studies or painting to do or they had set her to work helping in the shop. She decided she did not like being idle. It left her too much time to worry. It was time wasted in which she could be earning money.

Turning a corner, she looked up and froze as she recognised the street she had entered. A man leaned against a wall, strumming a baamn. Nearby, scarves tied to a shop front fluttered in the breeze. She hadn't meant to return to the courtyard. In fact, she was approaching it from a different direction, which was why she hadn't realised she was about to. Which meant that . . .

Her blood froze. Slowly she turned to her right.

The alley where the corrupter's covered cart had waited was empty.

Relieved, but with heart pounding, Rielle retraced her steps, turning into a side street as soon as she encountered one. As she put more distance between herself and the scene of her tainting she began to breathe a little easier.

Of course she isn't there. She probably moves constantly in case one of her customers informs the priests. Or, like me, they came to see her in order to betray her.

Rielle shook her head. It was yet another way in which her attempt to find the corrupter had been a stupid mistake. The woman had said a tainted shouldn't return to a place where Stain had been created. They should use magic somewhere unpleasant so people wouldn't look too closely or stay long. Somewhere dark, because Stain appeared black to those who could see it, though they could sense it in other ways. Somewhere it wasn't strange for the tainted person to be.

The only dark and unpleasant place Rielle might plausibly go was the garbage pit in the side alley of the courtyard. It stank, so the neighbours came and went as quickly as possible. Garbage collectors spent the longest time there, shovelling the muck into a cart to be taken out of the city. If Rielle used magic there just after they'd visited, the Stain would have faded by the time they returned.

It was close to home, however, and she would have to return to it whenever putting out the garbage. If the Stain was noticed, it would draw more suspicion on the artisans living there, reinforcing the prejudices against them.

But she was part of that community now. If she went elsewhere and her use of magic was discovered, it would still reflect badly on all artisans. To find a place far from her home meant roaming around the city to parts where she was a stranger, and would draw more attention. Better to stay where her presence and movements were so familiar they would be ignored.

Her feet were now taking her towards Izare's house. Glancing at the buildings, she estimated by the angle of the sunlight that bathed them that, if she walked slowly, she should not arrive too soon. When she neared the streets leading to the courtyard she spotted one of the neighbourhood's children. The boy was happy to take a message to Izare and bring one back. She told him to deliver one word: "Now?"

The boy came racing back to her and panted out the word "Yes!" He took the coin she offered, grinned and ran off. Relieved, Rielle headed for home, wondering as she had many times during the afternoon if the wait had even been necessary. She expected to find that Famire had, after collecting observations about Rielle's new life to relate to the other temple girls, claimed she did not want her portrait done after all.

As Rielle pushed through the front door she smelled the familiar scent of oil, strong enough to suggest Izare had been at work on something or simply preparing more paint. A glance in the lower room told her he wasn't there, so she started up the stairs.

Emerging into the studio, she looked over to see Izare standing before a new painting. He turned to her, but she did not see his expression as the image before him caught and consumed all of her attention.

Famire stared back at her, a sly smile puckering her lips. She wore no scarf, and though her clothes were roughly sketched in it was clear by how much skin of her neck and shoulder was visible that her tunic was partly unfastened. Izare waited in silence as she stared at it.

"It's horrible, isn't it?" he finally said.

She tore her eyes from the painting and looked at him. His smile was rueful, but not from self-doubt. *He looks ashamed. I suppose I should be grateful that he's not trying to pretend otherwise.*

"So she stayed," was all she could think to say. Stating the obvious.

He nodded. "And paid half in advance."

She turned back to the painting, but found she could no longer look at it. Her eyes slid off it as her mind shied away from the thought of how Famire might have got into that state, and why she looked so smug.

It doesn't mean anything happened. It's only a painting. And we need the money.

That didn't make her feel better. What if one of Famire's conditions had been for him to do more than paint her? Was that the true reason he'd suggested Rielle should leave for the afternoon?

"How did the meeting go?" he asked.

She shrugged. "Well enough. I'm . . . I'm going to get something to drink."

He said nothing as she walked back downstairs. She heard him moving about as she entered the lower room. The pitcher she'd filled from the fountain that morning was empty. Picking it up, she turned towards the door, then froze as she saw the bucket they collected their garbage in, half filled.

If I was pregnant, he'd never touch another woman for fear that I'd go back to my parents, and he'd never see his child.

The thought brought a sour taste to her mouth. Was this all that she was? Was being a vessel for making children all that was valuable about her? She had been, for a short time, a hero when she'd helped the priests capture the last tainted, but that time had been finite and short. She had been a source of inspiration and passion for Izare, but now she was just another mouth to feed. She had dreamed of painting alongside him, but nobody was ever going to commission art from her. Nobody even knew or cared that she was good at it.

Oh, stop feeling so sorry for yourself. You chose to come here. It must have been hard work for Izare to gain his skills and reputation, and he's clearly had to do work he doesn't care for along the way. I will have to do the same, even if that work is raising children.

If all went well, she would have the support of her family as well. At that thought she almost smiled. Narmah would be very happy to look after little ones while Rielle worked.

But it will never happen if I don't fix things.

Straightening, Rielle put down the pitcher, picked up the bucket and headed outside.

As she neared the alley and garbage pit, fear stirred within her. She held onto her determination. She was glad to find nobody else there and that the pit had been emptied a day or two ago. Most people threw their garbage in from the front so they didn't have to go far into the alley, though that resulted in a mound that overflowed into the street. Rielle grimaced at the smell, slipped down the side and tossed the contents of the bucket into the back of the hole.

She looked around. There was nothing to sit on. It wasn't as dark as she thought, and she began to doubt that Stain would be so hard to notice here. Still, her eyes had probably adjusted to the dim light whereas anyone coming in from the street would be dazzled by the sunlight outside.

"Angels forgive me," she breathed. "I only seek to put things back to rights."

Moving to the very back of the alley, hoping that nobody would come in, she closed her eyes and thought about what the corrupter had told her. Some nights she had lain awake, worrying that she would forget the instructions and repeating over in her mind what she wasn't supposed to know.

"*When you see Stain, you don't see it with your eyes,*" the woman had said. "*You are sensing it with your mind. What you are sensing is nothing. An absence. It is where magic has been removed. And that means . . .?*"

It meant that magic was everywhere else. Around her. Inside her. It had taken a tiny shift of awareness to sense the *something* rather than the *nothing*. Even remembering that revelation was enough to make Rielle aware of the magic around her now. It was like being aware of sunlight, except instead of the sensation being detected by her skin it was felt by her mind.

She had only to stretch out and take it.

What was an even spread of magic became condensed power held by her will. She realised she was shaking, but it was not an effect of holding power. It was fear and panic.

Get it over with before someone comes along and wonders what you're doing, she told herself.

"*Your body will know what it needs,*" the corrupter had said. "*Feed it and it will heal itself.*"

Turning her awareness to her body, she directed the magic into her belly and let it go. A tingling sensation filled her abdomen, making her want to scratch deep beneath the surface. It lasted a few breaths before fading away.

Then . . . nothing. She felt no different from before. If something had changed then it was so subtle that she could not sense it.

"Rielle?"

She jumped, her eyes flying open. A young man was standing in the alley entrance, peering at her.

"You've been gone a while. Are you upset?" he asked.

Izare. Hearing the concern in his voice, her heart warmed. A traitorous relief followed. He probably thought she had come here to seethe or cry over the painting of Famire. *Well, it's not far from the truth*, she thought.

"No," she replied, knowing that he'd hear the lie and misinterpret it. She walked around the pit to join him, noticing that he held the pitcher. "Just thinking."

He put an arm around her. "Don't worry about Famire. She's petty and ugly. She spent the whole time here sniping about other people. I had to imagine what her mouth would be like when it's not all twisted."

"While her clothes were half off," Rielle reminded him. She resisted the temptation to look back into the alley for a sign of Stain.

He led her away, towards the fountain. "Not half. A little skin, that's all. It's what she wanted. I suspect it's what she thinks your portrait is like."

"Did you show it to her?"

"No."

"Why not?"

He smiled. They had reached the fountain and he dipped the pitcher in. "Because there's more mystery about it now. Apparently it's very romantic of you to sacrifice all to be with me, which has made getting a secret portrait done the new fashion."

"Secret?" Rielle frowned. "You said she'd got permission from her parents."

He chuckled. "I doubt it." He took her hand and drew her towards the door of his house.

"What if they find out and object? You lost spirituals as a source of income because of annoying my family, but they're not as powerful as Famire's family. They could have you driven out of the city."

He pushed open the door and they moved into the cool interior. "There are always risks when you're an artist. Painting spirituals in a different way was a big risk. Perhaps a bigger risk than a private portrait that could help a young woman attract the eye of the man she wants to marry. Which is a risk that pays a lot better, I have to say." He reached under his tunic to his belt and, after untying the cords of his money bag, drew it out and pressed it into her hands. It was heavy and full to bursting. She opened it and felt her heart skip. Gold and silver glittered softly.

If this was *half* the painting's price, perhaps it was a risk worth taking. *Another risk worth taking*, she added, thinking of the healing she had done.

"Then you're going to have to let me stay here whenever you paint them," she said. "You need someone to reassure their parents when they're finally found out that nothing scandalous happened to their daughters while they were here."

He smiled. "Famire won't like it, but she will have to put up with it. You, on the other hand . . . can you stand being around her?"

Rielle sighed. "I'd rather that than get run out of the city because of some silly rich girl."

CHAPTER 15

Izare frowned at the ceiling. Rielle waited for him to say something, but he remained as he was, lying on the bed with his hands behind his head, eyes fixed on the dusty undersides of the flooring above. Keeping her eyes from wandering over his lean, brown chest, she fixed her gaze on his face, determined not to be distracted or to back down. He'd had several days to think about Narmah's proposal. He'd seemed pleased by her family's wish to be on good terms.

She'd thought he was being sensible deciding to think about it for a while, but if she didn't give her family an answer soon they might assume she'd rejected the offer. Now, as time stretched and Izare said nothing, she felt as if her insides were shrinking and contracting with doubt and fear. Then they seemed to reach a limit and expanded with sudden hot anger.

"You said you wanted to get married," she reminded him.

He rolled over to face her. "I do," he said gently. "But I don't want you to move out. I like having you here."

Her heart flipped over and she quickly looked away, not wanting him to think that he could win her over with a few, admittedly wonderful, words.

"I like being here, but I would like to be on good terms with my family, too. It would not have to be for long. My parents will probably want us married quickly. The sooner we are, the sooner the respectability of the family will be . . . well, not so much restored as patched up. The last thing they'll want is their daughter having a child out of marriage." She looked at him. "And it's not something their daughter would be all that happy about, either."

He smiled, reached over and laid a hand on her belly. "The priests have been known to lower the bribe, if the bride is with child."

She rolled away and swung her legs over the side of the bed, rocking into a sitting position. "It seems no matter what we do, we won't get very much time together, the two of us," she lamented. "It's a pity what Famire paid you wasn't enough to pay for both the bribe and the rent."

"We can be married and homeless or unmarried with a house to live and work in," Izare said. "Such is the life of an artist."

She shook her head. "I still can't believe the priests are so corrupt." She sighed, stood, and moved over to the shuttered windows to peer through the slats. From the angle of the shadows outside she guessed it was mid-morning.

"It's later than I thought. I had better clean up and go. Jonare said to come over before midday."

"Me, too. I'm meeting Errek at Dorr's house."

Izare stretched, the muscles under his skin shifting in all too interesting ways, then threw off the blanket and stood up in one smooth motion. She averted her eyes, still not used to his unhurried attitude towards dressing of a morning.

"Anything planned?"

He shrugged and began to put on his shirt from the day before. "We'll probably sit and talk. You and Jonare could bring over the results of your cooking lesson later on."

Rielle rolled her eyes and handed him the empty water pitcher as he finished tying his trousers. "I suppose we could. If there's anything edible."

He took it and grinned. "I'm sure it'll be a feast worthy of the Angels."

After he'd returned with water for the wash basin, they cleaned up, dressed and set out together. As they passed the garbage pit alley, Rielle resisted the temptation to stare into the shadows to see if the Stain she must have left was visible. She was sure she could feel a wrongness down there, but she dismissed that as her anxiety stimulating her imagination.

It's done, she told herself. *Hopefully it worked, and I'll never have to think about magic and Stain ever again.*

A few streets from the artisans' courtyard they parted, Izare taking advantage of the quiet, narrow streets they had taken to give her a brief but firm kiss. Smiling and enjoying the lingering sensation of his lips on hers, she headed towards Jonare's home.

Her thoughts went immediately to the conversation they'd had that morning. It was wonderful to hear him say he didn't want them to be apart, and she didn't want to be either, but surely he could see that in the long term it would be better if they were on good terms with her family. There could be benefits for him, and not all of them financial.

She began to consider how she might persuade him, but her thoughts scattered and her blood went cold as a familiar grey-robed man stepped out of a doorway to block her path.

"Ais Lazuli," he said, falling into his habit of staring somewhere below her chin and above her waist.

"Sa-Gest," she replied. A buzz of apprehension came as thoughts of magic arose, but she pushed them aside. "What brings you into this part of the city?"

"Well," he said, then paused. "I was looking . . . looking for you."

"Me?" The uneasiness grew stronger. Did he know? Had he found the Stain? But he hadn't been back to the courtyard since . . . her stomach twisted as the awful memory of his visit crashed over her. *Since he stole the painting. The nude.*

"You're . . . you're very beautiful, Rielle," he said, edging closer. His hand extended towards her face.

"Thank you," she replied stiffly. She leaned backwards to avoid his hand, but it snaked down to grip her arm.

"Don't go," he said. He pulled her closer. "I could help you, Rielle. A word here, a word there, and I could make your life a lot easier if you did some things for me." His gaze shifted higher and stopped at her mouth. Fingers moved towards her face again and she flinched away.

"What are you doing?" she asked loudly, pitching her tone between puzzlement and outrage.

He paused and looked around, but didn't let her go. The narrow street was still empty. *It won't be for long*, she told herself. *If I delay, or can get loose . . .* Sa-Gest was thin but his grip was strong. He might be able to hold her if she struggled, but would probably let go if she hit him. *But I can't hit a priest!*

"Only suggesting," he said, his gaze returning to her mouth. He grabbed her chin. "Just making an offer. You can refuse it, of course, but I wouldn't if I were you. I could be very *un*helpful as well."

He leaned towards her and she realised that he intended to kiss her. Revulsion rose up and she yanked her arm away. He overbalanced and stepped towards her. Dodging his outstretched arms, she twisted around and ran.

No footsteps sounded behind her. She heard a humourless laugh.

"I'll give you time to think about it," he called after her.

A few turns and crossroads later, she emerged onto a wider thoroughfare. Heart racing more from alarm than exertion, she stopped and looked back. She'd heard no sound of pursuit. It didn't surprise her. A running priest was an unusual and alarming sight. People would definitely gossip if they saw a priest chasing a young woman. And she couldn't imagine him going to the effort.

No, he expects his threats will bring me to him.

Her stomach plummeted. What would he do when they didn't? How much more trouble could he cause for her and Izare? She drew in a deep breath and let it out slowly. Whatever he planned they would have to endure. The idea of letting him kiss or touch her . . . or worse . . . was unthinkable.

She shuddered and continued on her way. Her heart was still beating quickly when she arrived at Jonare's home. The yells of children spilled over her as the door opened. Shadows circled Jonare's eyes, but she smiled.

"Come in. I've been up half the night nursing Perri. How are you?"

"I'm fine."

Jonare frowned. "You don't look fine." She waved Rielle inside. "What happened?"

"We . . . I . . . Sa-Gest stopped me on the way here and . . ." Rielle stopped and shook her head, not sure if she wanted anybody to know about the encounter. Nothing had happened and perhaps this sort of thing occurred all the time. After all, she hadn't known about the searches and bribes. "It's probably nothing. Is Perri ill?"

Jonare led her over to her small kitchen setup. "Oh, he'll be fine. The fever broke this morning and, as you can see, he's back to his old self." She looked back at Rielle and frowned. "But it's clearly not nothing." She waved at a chair, then sat down on a stool. "Tell me."

Rielle sat down and sighed. "I don't know if it's bad or normal. Sa-Gest tried to . . . to kiss me and threatened to make our lives difficult if I . . . if I didn't do *things* for him." Her face warmed and she hoped she wouldn't have to elaborate.

"Ah," Jonare said, looking away as her niece came over to ask for something. She replied to the girl in a quiet voice, then turned back to Rielle. "If this is the priest I've heard about, he has a reputation for harassing women. Mostly whores. He thinks those robes he wears give him the right to take what he wants without payment." Her mouth twisted in a humourless smile. "He's aiming a bit higher this time. Quite a bit. But I suppose he figures your family won't or can't do anything, or that nobody will believe you, or you'll want to avoid further trouble."

"What should I do?"

Jonare shrugged. "Go home. Or do as he asks."

Anger and indignation rose at Jonare's blunt advice, but Rielle pushed it away. The woman was being honest, which was better than vague reassurances.

"Surely there's something else I can do."

Jonare shook her head. "The priests hold the power in this city. You might think it was the families, but they'd have nothing without the priests' support." She looked thoughtful. "It could be that the priest is doing this for your family's sake, to frighten you into leaving Izare. They might have guessed you'll only leave him for his benefit."

Rielle's heart skipped. "So it's a bluff?"

"Might be. Can you take the risk that it's not?"

"If it is, it's a strange move to make. I met with my mother and aunt not so long ago. They said if I came home they might let me marry Izare. Why would they say that, if they meant to scare me into leaving him?"

"What did Izare say?"

"He doesn't want me to leave, even temporarily."

"And you?"

347

"If there's a way we can be on good terms with my family, it would be better for everyone. Especially in the long term." Rielle tapped on the seat of her chair. "Perhaps I should tell my family that the priests are trying to scare me into coming home and see what they say."

Jonare pursed her lips as she considered. "That's a risk, too. If the priest's motives are purely selfish he will act on his threat, and if your parents won't believe that a priest could do something like that they will think less of you for making up such a thing."

"They probably won't believe me. I could tell Sa-Baro." Rielle decided against it even as she said the words. "No, he'd be as unlikely to trust me."

"Well, whatever you decide, there's one thing you can't do," Jonare told her.

"What is that?"

"Tell Izare." The woman's gaze was direct and full of warning. "He will do something foolish that will get him in trouble with the priests, and that will make everything worse. For him, for you *and* for your family."

Not tell Izare?! How could she keep something like this from him? And whether she returned to her family or defied Sa-Gest and endured the consequences, he would need to know the reason. Rielle stared at Jonare, but though she opened her mouth to protest no words came out because she realised that if she took the third option – inconceivable as it was – she definitely couldn't tell Izare.

It's not going to come to that, she told herself. Standing up, she looked at the kitchen bench on which vegetables, grains and other foods were arrayed.

"So, what are you going to teach me to cook?"

CHAPTER 16

A familiar ache drew Rielle out of sleep. She sighed. Sometimes she thought the Angels must have a cruel sense of humour, to inflict regular discomfort and weakness on women. Her aunt had always reasoned that it was their way of telling a woman she wasn't pregnant.

Not pregnant.

The thought jolted her into full waking. She opened her eyes and stared at the ceiling. In a few days she would be meeting Narmah and her parents. Izare would be coming with her. She had hoped to convince all of them that she and Izare should marry as soon as possible. The news she was carrying a child would guarantee everyone's agreement.

She grimaced. Maybe they would still agree to it. Maybe it wasn't too much to hope that she could be with the man she loved, be on good terms with her family and salvage some of her integrity without bearing children so soon.

But will I ever be able to have them? The question frightened her. If only she could see inside herself and know whether the pathways the corrupter had severed had been repaired. The woman had said it would happen spontaneously.

Unless . . . unless she knew I wouldn't be able to do it. Unless she meant to force me to go back to her and pay to have her fix me.

She shuddered. Going back to the corrupter was not an

option. She had risked too much the first time. If the other choice was to seek that woman's help, then perhaps she would have to accept that childlessness was her punishment for using magic.

But Izare . . .

He wanted children. Lots of children. How could she deny him that? Her heart constricted. Why should he be punished for her mistake?

Don't panic yet, she told herself. *This might be normal. Not every woman conceives in the first cycle.*

Thinking back, Rielle recalled how the corrupter had made her *see* the change she'd made. If she could remember how to do that, she would at least know if her healing had worked. She had not needed to use magic to do it.

Closing her eyes, she laid her hands low on her belly. She slowed her breathing and concentrated on the area below her hands. A thrill of hope went through her as she found she could sense . . . but what was she sensing? Pulsing, shifting, twisted things that she did not understand. A confusion of areas that were *her* mixed with those that were not. The cramping distracted her, demanding she pay attention to it. Concentrating on it did ease the pain. Then she felt a far more familiar sensation.

She was up a moment later and seeking to stem the flow with her store of clean rags. Izare remained asleep, to her relief. She was not used to any man being near when she had to deal with this and he preferred to be absent when she did. Looking at the bed, she mouthed a silent curse as she saw the red stain on the bed sheet. Then her whole body went cold.

Floating above the stain was a *disturbance*.

Stain. She must have used magic when looking inside herself. For all that it had gained her. She stood paralysed. *"The worst places you can use magic are those you and others frequent,"* the corrupter had said. It was a tiny blot, though. It would soon fade away. But what to do in the meantime? It was in full sight, too high above the bed for the bedding to cover it.

A loud knock on the main door made her heart nearly jump out of her chest. Izare started awake. He glanced around the room, blinked at her, then his gaze moved to the door of the lower room. He cursed.

"Famire. She's early. Or we slept late."

Rielle found her voice somehow. "Probably a little of both. You'd better get dressed and answer the door."

He turned back to the bed and her heart froze as his gaze settled on the stain. But he only grimaced in sympathy and began to pull on his trousers from the night before.

"Let Old Tam take care of it. I'll get some water and send Famire upstairs." He grabbed the pitcher and slipped out of the room shirtless. Rielle winced as she heard a young woman's voice. While she was relieved it was Famire, she knew the girl would either be scandalised or enjoy the sight of his bare chest a little too much.

Looking back at the Stain and the red blotch below it, she had a flash of inspiration. If it was washday, then she had a way to cover both. Grabbing everything that needed cleaning, she piled it on top of the bed. She could still sense the Stain if she searched for it, but if she hadn't known it was there she'd have never noticed it. Hopefully it would have faded in a few hours, when she took the washing to Tam.

Izare returned with the pitcher, put on a shirt, then headed upstairs. Rielle took her time cleaning and dressing, then started preparing a simple meal of bread, salted preserves and sliced melon. They both needed to eat, but it was rude to do so in front of a guest without inviting them to join in. She ate the ends of the bread and melon as she worked. By the time she was done her sense of calm was almost completely restored. Only when she saw the pile of washing did she feel anxiety rising, so she avoided looking at it.

Using an unfinished, long-ago-rejected painting as a tray, she carried the food upstairs. Famire was already in position, her clothes artfully dishevelled. The girl's eyes snapped to Rielle.

"Oh, it's the woman herself. Ais Lazuli. Talk of the temple."

"Ais Famire," Rielle replied. "How are you? How are the girls?"

Famire shrugged and the shoulder of her tunic slipped even lower. Izare made a low noise of annoyance and she hoisted it up again.

"They're the same as always. You gave them something truly exciting to talk about for a while there. Ooh, is that for me? I'm starving!" She was peering at the food. Izare sighed and put down his brush, but when he looked at Rielle his expression was grateful. He gestured towards the chairs.

"I'm afraid you caught us before we'd eaten," he said. "But you're welcome to join us."

Famire hoisted her tunic up but didn't retighten the ties. As Rielle and Izare sat down she flopped into a chair.

"This posing is harder than it looks," she said. Not waiting for a response, she leaned forward and plucked some bread from the plates and began piling preserves on top. "I had a morning meal, but I'm already hungry again."

By the time she was done, half of the food remained. Izare nodded to Rielle, inviting her to serve herself next. She shook her head. "I'm not that hungry," she lied, figuring she had eaten a little during the preparation but he'd had nothing. He began grazing, but soon Famire was done with her first serving and was feasting on the rest, leaving little behind for him. A meal that should have fed two had been gorged by one who ought to have had the good manners to share, even if she couldn't comprehend that her hosts had to eke out what little money they had until the next commission.

Or couldn't she? Famire had hardly been warm and friendly since Rielle had arrived. She had always been antagonistic and disdainful, and Rielle could see no difference in her manner now.

I thought I'd escaped this, and here she is back in my life. The thought sent a bolt of anger through her.

"You *are* hungry," Rielle observed. "Your morning meal must have been *very* meagre."

Famire shrugged. "Oh, I can't eat much in the morning."

"You have a delicate stomach?"

"No, I'm used to eating as much or as little as suits me at any time of day." Famire spread her hands. "I guess it's my upbringing. I can't imagine what it's like to adjust to a different way of life, such as you have."

Rielle nodded in mock sympathy. "No, I don't imagine your imagination would stretch that far."

Izare slapped his thighs. "I think it's time we got back to work."

"Oh, yes!" Famire agreed. "I will be able to concentrate much better now that I am not so distracted by hunger."

Rielle smiled. "Sitting quietly is a skill not everyone possesses. There are good models and bad models, or so Izare tells me. The good models get the better portraits, naturally."

Famire glanced at Izare and smiled. "Izzy is so strict. He really doesn't like it when I move. But," she paused to look at him from under her eyelashes, "I find it hard to stay still when someone's looking at me so much."

"Because it makes you self-conscious?"

"No, I quite like it actually."

"Well, then, we'll have to make sure you don't enjoy yourself. For the sake of a good portrait, of course." Rielle picked up a chair, moved it closer and sat down. "I'm sure your father doesn't want to pay for a bad portrait."

Famire tossed her head. "Oh, Father won't be seeing it. He gave me the money to buy a gift, but doesn't care what I buy so long as he doesn't have to take me shopping or hear me talk about it."

So I'm right. Rielle looked at Izare. He turned to meet her gaze, then shook his head.

"I'm in agreement with your father," he said. "But only because I can't concentrate when you two are talking. I regret that I must cut short your reunion and," he turned to Rielle, "I also need my dear Rielle to fetch something for me."

Rielle opened her mouth to object, then closed it again. *I suppose I asked for that. He can't exactly ask Famire to leave.*

"Something downstairs?" she asked.

He shook his head, put down his brush and walked over to her. "I need you to buy some food and iquo for when Errek and the others come over tonight." He reached into his money pouch for the coin. "Buy yourself a treat, too," he whispered. "I know you lied about not being hungry."

She nodded, though her blood had frozen. He wanted her to go out. Alone. She had avoided venturing into the city by herself since Sa-Gest had accosted her. Once she had seen the priest lurking in the shadows of a side alley, watching them. Another time, when she and Izare were eating out with his friends, Sa-Gest had sauntered past, his eyes locking with hers briefly before she had looked away.

Izare led her towards the stairs, picking up some paper and chalk along the way and pressing them into her hands with the money.

"I haven't seen you drawing for a long time," he murmured, his head close to hers. "Don't let me be the reason you stop."

In that moment she loved him more fiercely than at any

time before. When he kissed her, she pressed her lips to his firmly, then stepped away. She held onto that feeling as she walked down the stairs to the lower room. Averting her eyes from the pile of washing on the bed, she slipped the coins into her money bag and strapped it on under her tunic. Then she closed the lower room door firmly and headed out into the courtyard.

The courage she held onto drained away. Standing in the shadows of the doorway, she looked all around, searching for a thin grey-robed figure. Though she didn't find one, her fear remained as she forced her legs to carry her away from the safety of home.

When Sa-Baro had visited to arrange a second meeting, this time with her parents, she had thought of telling him about Sa-Gest, but Izare had been there and she had remembered Jonare's warning that he might do something foolish. She was not sure telling Sa-Baro was a good idea. Or her family. Once she moved back in with them Sa-Gest wouldn't dare continue pursuing her anyway.

Yet once she was married to Izare she would be vulnerable again. Sa-Gest could still make their life difficult.

Angels save me, she thought. Out of habit, for surely they would take one look at her tainted soul and leave her to the fate she deserved.

All the worrying took too much energy and thought. It was better not to think at all. She concentrated on making her way through the city quickly, checking ahead for a grey-robed priest when forced to use the smaller, less populated streets. She found places to wait out the hours until Famire left, but couldn't risk focusing her attention on drawing in case Sa-Gest sneaked up on her. Eventually she bought food and iquo for that evening's gathering but nothing else, as she felt too much turmoil inside to eat, and made her way home.

When she reached the door of Izare's home a wave of dizziness forced her to tuck her purchases under one arm and grab the frame for support. Though her head cleared, a weariness remained. And nausea.

If I didn't know better I might think I was pregnant, she mused. That thought caused her mouth to twist into a bitter smile. Would Sa-Gest find her so attractive all swollen with child?

Would Izare? *No, he loves me.* She smiled as she remembered his words. *"Don't let me be the reason you stop."* He didn't want her to give up that part of herself, but what wouldn't she give up for him?

Would I give in to Sa-Gest?

Would he lie with Famire to keep the commission they so desperately needed?

These thoughts are not making anything better, she told herself, and pushed through the door.

Three men stood in the stairwell. Her body went rigid with fear as she recognised the man she had dreaded encountering all day. Then she saw Izare and the fear ebbed a little.

And then went weak as she took in the third man.

Sa-Elem. That could only mean one thing: an inspection. They had searched the house while she was gone.

Had the Stain faded? The door to the lower room was open. It took all her will not to look through it to the bed. Glancing at the three men again, she noted that Izare wore his usual expression of forced tolerance during an inspection. Sa-Elem regarded her coolly. Sa-Gest smirked.

"Ah . . ." she began. "Forgive me for interrupting, Sa-Elem, Sa-Gest. Have . . . have you just arrived or are you about to leave?" She stepped forward and handed some of her purchases to Izare, who smiled at her as he took them.

That's a good sign, she thought. *He wouldn't be smiling if the priests have found—*

"We just arrived, Ais Lazuli," Sa-Elem told her. He turned towards the door to the inner room and her heart stopped. "I have received a report of suspicious activity in this area."

"Activity?" she asked.

"The use of magic," he said. "Stain was found near the garbage pit, so we are searching the surrounding houses."

She swayed and caught the frame of the door behind her. "Are we in danger?"

Angels, please let the Stain be gone. I will do anything. I will accept my barrenness . . .

The priests stepped inside the lower room. Izare followed. Not wanting to be left with Sa-Gest, Rielle followed. The younger priest waited in the stairwell, most likely expecting to be ordered to search upstairs.

As before, Sa-Elem's gaze swept the room quickly. She relaxed at the careless examination. He looked up, taking in the ceiling, then down at the floor. And then he stilled. His head turned slowly, his attention moving back to the bed. Abruptly he broke into motion. Her mouth went dry as he strode to the bed and knocked the pile of washing off with a swipe of one hand.

The Stain was still there, a tiny blot hovering above a now dry bloodstain. Sa-Elem looked up from the sheets to stare at Rielle. *Not accusing*, she realised. *Knowing.*

Another wave of dizziness came. Hands grasped her arms.

Oh, how embarrassing, she thought. *I'm going to faint.*

But she didn't. Izare and Sa-Gest guided her to the old chair. She nearly laughed at the irony of the priest helping Izare assist her. Then Sa-Gest placed a hand firmly on her shoulder, and she realised he had done so as much to stop her attempting to escape. Izare glared at the man, then squatted beside her.

"Did you eat anything?" he asked.

She could not meet his eyes. She couldn't speak, so she shook her head.

"Eat something now." He rose and moved to the bed, where he had tossed her purchases.

"I think it can wait a short while," Sa-Elem said, though without malice. He looked at Rielle. With a great effort, she made herself meet his eyes.

"You can see it, can't you?" Sa-Elem asked.

Rielle frowned as if in puzzlement or concern, her mind whirling with urgency. Could she deny it? She could claim to have nearly fainted because she hadn't eaten much all day, not because of seeing the Stain or knowing her crime had been discovered. But once he told her what was there, how would she explain how it got there? If neither she nor Izare had made it, who else could have? It might have been easier to direct suspicion elsewhere if the Stain had been upstairs in the studio rather than above the bed.

Or was it? Famire had been here. The portrait upstairs would seem to confirm something scandalous had been going on here, with Rielle absent.

Izare would be hurt at her distrust if she suggested it, and if Famire had not entered the lower room in the entire time she'd been here then he would *know* she couldn't be the cause.

"What can you see?" Izare asked Sa-Elem.

The priest looked at Izare. "Stain." He leaned down and traced the shadow with his fingers. "Here."

Izare stared, his eyes wide with horror. "There. So close to . . ." He looked at Rielle, his brow tight and lined. "You can see it," he said, moving over to crouch before her again. "I can read it in your face, Rielle. There's no crime in that." He touched her cheek, tracing her jaw with his fingers. "I've known people who could. I understand. A lifetime of hiding is a hard habit to break. However it got there—"

358

"It wasn't there early this morning," Sa-Gest said. "When I did the first sweep."

Izare's blink was more like a flinch. His eyes went dark with realisation, and she knew then that nobody had entered the lower room since she'd left it. Izare knew that the Stain could only have come from her. Horror came next, and she knew that he would never be able to accept what she had done. She clutched at his arms as if that would stop the truth from driving him away, but he was not moving away. Instead he grabbed her arms tightly.

"What . . . what were you doing?" he demanded. "Did you . . . Did you . . .?"

"Getting rid of a child is one of the most common reasons women seek to learn magic," Sa-Gest said, his voice laced with mock sympathy.

"No!" Rielle protested. She could not bear for Izare to believe such a thing. "There was no child. I want a child. I didn't even *mean* to use magic."

"You tried to make yourself fertile?" Sa-Elem asked.

"No. To see if the damage she'd done had healed." She looked up at Sa-Elem. "She hurt me so I would have to heal myself. I was tricked."

Izare let her go, rising and staggering backwards, but she barely noticed as a memory flashed into her mind. "*I was tricked*," her abductor had said. Yet he'd still been paraded through the city and sent wherever the tainted were sent. She saw Sa-Elem's face relax into sadness and sympathy. *He knows the corrupter does this. He knows.*

"Why didn't you tell us?" he asked.

She looked away. "I was going to, but I couldn't see how I could without . . ." She sighed. "The result would have been the same."

He said nothing to that. Moving away from the bed, he

walked over to stand in front of her. With him before her and Sa-Gest behind, she felt surrounded – caged – by priestly robes. The potential of their magic, for all that it was sanctioned by the Angels, was no longer awe-inspiring or comforting.

"Ais Rielle Lazuli," Sa-Gest said. "You are to accompany us to the temple."

PART FIVE

TYEN

CHAPTER 17

Leaning on the ship's railing, Tyen stared out into the darkness. Dark clouds blocked the stars and the lights of the shore were far beyond the horizon. Only the occasional froth of a cresting wave broke the blackness beyond the ship's lights.

"Such a lovely, calm evening for a party,' a quiet voice said.

He turned to smile at Sezee as she joined him at the railing. "It is."

"Of course, it's not really Veroo's birthday," she added.

He frowned, surprised at the lie.

"Don't look at me like that," she said, then raised her glass to her lips and sipped. Her dark eyes glinted with mischief. "Her birthday passed when we were back in Leratia, when we weren't in the mood for celebrating. This gives us something to do while on board and it's far nicer to share such occasions with friends."

"Captain Taga shared a bottle of his finest wine with us," he reminded her.

She shrugged. "He didn't have to. We provided one we bought while on shore. And I doubt it's his very finest."

Tyen looked away and sighed. He'd not set foot on land for several weeks. Though the women were happy to purchase things for him whenever the ship docked, and had mailed a letter to his father for him, he envied them their freedom. He dared not spend any more money than he had to either, knowing that if he did his supply would run out sooner.

No doubt guessing the reason for his miserliness, Sezee and Veroo kept giving him presents. He'd abandoned the habit of reading fiction after joining the Academy, having too much studying to do, but after boredom had driven him to try the novels they bought they'd found a few more to his taste. They criticised every book thoroughly, and each time the ship stopped they sought out another bookshop at which to buy more and sell those already consumed.

"Taga said we are a few days from Carmel," Sezee reminded him. "What should we do then? Find another ship or stop to build an aircart?"

Tyen had thought about this many, many times since their sea journey had begun. "If I am to build an aircart I'll need the right materials. The further we are from cities and larger towns the harder it will be to find them."

"What do you need that we won't find in a small town or village?"

"Propellers."

"They're made of wood, aren't they? Small towns have carpenters."

He looked at her, and smiled at her determined frown. "I doubt they are asked to make aircart propellers very often."

"Can you instruct them?"

"Yes, but that is not the issue."

She pursed her lips. "You're worried such an occurrence would be unusual enough to attract the Academy's attention?"

"Yes."

"Can you make the propellers yourself using magic?"

"Perhaps, if I had quality materials. Buying those might attract notice as well."

"Can we buy something made of the right wood and adapt

it?" Her eyes narrowed as he smiled. "You've thought about all this already, haven't you?"

"Of course. I'm surprised you hadn't thought of it sooner."

She gave him a coy, sidelong look. "Who said I hadn't?"

He chuckled. "I have noticed it is not your habit to store questions away, unasked."

"Oh, I store." She gave him a lofty look. "I'm quite capable of storing, if there is an advantage to be had from it."

"So what advantage did you see in this case?"

"It would have made you chafe to be ashore even more. Though I may as well have asked anyway. You've been quite unbearably irritable these last few weeks." She shaded her eyes as one of the ship's lamps suddenly brightened.

He crossed his arms. "I have not—!"

"Tyen," she interrupted, squinting at something behind him.

Belatedly it occurred to him that no ship's lamp could produce light as brilliant as the one that now bathed them. His heart lurched. Turning, he flinched at the brilliance of a white flame floating beyond the ship's deck, so fierce that it obscured whatever lay beyond it. *Whatever* hovers *beyond it*, he corrected as a voice boomed out.

"CAPTAIN TAGA. YOUR PASSENGER, TYEN IRON-SMELTER, IS A FUGITIVE WANTED BY THE ACADEMY." The voice was distorted in a way that suggested the speaker was using an amplifier cone. "YOU ARE TO PROCEED TO SHORE IMMEDIATELY."

The buzz of aircart propellers followed. The sound penetrated Tyen's gut, turning it to liquid. He took a deep breath and willed his racing heart to slow. *So someone has found me. But they haven't taken me prisoner yet.*

"But . . .? Where did he come from?" Sezee protested.

"He must have stopped the propellers upwind of us and let the breeze push him to us." Tyen extended his senses and immediately detected the Soot surrounding the aircart. There was no trail. The driver hadn't taken any magic, either, in case Tyen noticed it.

Footsteps drew near and they turned to see Veroo approaching.

"He's a clever one," she said. "Sneaking up on us like that."

Tyen nodded. "Clever, but if I was in his position I'd have tried to rob the area around us of magic before drawing attention, so we couldn't attack him. I suspect that's as much reach as he has." Which made the stranger seem far less threatening. Unless . . . he shaded his eyes and managed to catch a glimpse of the aircart. "I think he's alone, too." He smiled as he realised the situation wasn't as bad as it first appeared.

Sezee moved a little closer. "What are you thinking?"

"That I could disable the aircart. Force him to return to shore."

A man cleared his throat behind them. "I'm afraid we would have to follow."

They turned to face Captain Taga.

"But—" Sezee began.

"I want no trouble with the Academy," the captain said, looking at Tyen. Then his voice and expression softened. "I am sorry. They would confiscate the ship and ban me from trading in the Leratian Empire."

"You're going to give in just like that? You treacherous b—" Sezee began.

"Sezee," Tyen interrupted, giving her a look that, to his surprise, actually silenced her. "Would you have him lose his livelihood?"

She scowled. "Are you going to let him sail to shore?"

"Yes." He nodded to the captain. "You will have to sail directly to the coast then have your men row us to a suitable landing place."

The captain nodded.

"Suitable doesn't have to be populated. An isolated bay would do."

A spark of understanding entered the other man's gaze.

"Plenty of those this far south," he said. He began barking instructions to the crew. Tyen hunched his shoulders and sat down on a nearby barrel.

"Do you mind fetching my satchel?" he asked Sezee. "I fear if I disappear below our discoverer will grow anxious and do something foolish."

Sezee stared at him in disbelief. Veroo placed a hand on her arm.

"He knows what he's doing," the older woman said.

With a huff, Sezee turned away and stalked across the deck, Veroo following. As Tyen waited for them to return, he watched the crew working. The aircart circled the ship, then followed at a safe distance as it headed towards shore. Tyen ignored it, not wanting to be so dazzled by the bright light that he would be blinded when they reached land. He wondered who the driver was. It might have been his imagination, but the shouted words had had the trace of an accent. Perhaps Wendlandish. Had the aircart driver followed them all the way down the coast? Was it the one that had circled the ship the day then retreated after they'd left Darsh?

Sezee and Veroo emerged carrying their bags and his satchel. He smiled as they plonked them down next to the boat the crew were preparing to lower into the water when neared the shore.

"Not staying on board?" he asked.

"No," Sezee replied. "We're coming with you?"

"All the way back to the Academy?" He raised his eyebrows. "I thought you wanted to go to the Far South?"

"Well, we can't get there without an aircart, can we? So we may as well head home."

Tyen looked at Veroo. The older woman smiled faintly and said nothing. He shrugged, picked up his satchel and considered his possessions. The women had bought him clothes more appropriate for a porter, including a second set they kept in their bags for him to change into when the first was being washed. He had no idea what had happened to the clothes he'd stolen.

He slung the satchel strap over his shoulder and tucked Vella and his wallet inside. At his order, Beetle shifted position to place itself between the new items and the satchel's opening. He'd filled some time on the ship modifying it to obey the command to guard an object. It would adopt a threatening posture, buzz loudly and give anything that came near it a nip with new pincers.

For the rest of the way to shore they remained silent, watching the captain, crew and, once it came into sight, the approaching lights of the coast. A lighthouse beacon shone to the north, reminding all how dangerous approaching the coast could be at night. To the aircart driver's credit, he began to fly ahead of the ship, his light illuminating the water ahead, but from the way the captain was scowling and shading his eyes, Tyen suspected the light's dazzling brightness was as much a hindrance as a help.

At last Taga called a halt. The anchor was dropped, sails were turned out of the wind and the ship's rowing boat was lowered into the water, the women's bags securely strapped within. A rope ladder was tossed over the side of the ship where there was a gap in the railing.

"Again, I apologise," Taga said to Tyen. He turned to Sezee and Veroo. "Are you sure you don't want to continue with us, at least to the next port where you may disembark more easily?"

"I am sure," Sezee replied, though with a hint of doubt in her voice as she peered over the railing.

"We are sure," Veroo repeated firmly. "Thank you, Captain Taga. I hope the Academy believes you when you say you had no idea who Aren Coble really was."

Three men climbed down the rope ladder, scaling it effortlessly. Perhaps reassured by their agility, Sezee approached with sudden determination. She turned her back to the sea, took hold of the railing and extended a foot to the first rung, having to kick away her skirt when it got in the way. Worried that, being so encumbered by her clothes, she would slip, Tyen drew a little magic to catch her if she fell. But she reached the end of the ladder safely and the sailors below helped her into the rocking boat.

Veroo insisted on descending next, first hitching her skirts up to her knees and tying them. Tyen wasn't sure what the proper manners were in this situation – did the man go first or last when alighting from a ship by rope ladder? When Veroo was safely aboard the rowing boat, Tyen stepped up to the ladder. A hand grasped his arm and he looked up to see Taga frowning at him.

"Best of luck," the captain said. He nodded towards the aircart. "And don't be too hard on the driver. He thinks he's doing the right thing. There's quite a reward on offer for you."

The women had not mentioned that. Tyen smiled. "Thanks for not cashing in on that reward."

The captain let go and stepped back. "Not worth my reputation."

Tyen found the first rung and began to climb down. It wasn't as easy as it looked and he felt even more admiration for Sezee and Veroo for managing it without complaint or mishap. Getting into the rowing boat was even more challenging, as the swell was greater than it had appeared from above. All too soon he was hauling on an oar, perspiration breaking out all over at the unexpected exercise. Sezee and Veroo gripped the sides of the boat and their seats, eyes wide as the boat bucked and dived. From time to time a wave hit the side, spraying them all with salty water. The women's luggage did not look particularly watertight, he noted.

Above them, the aircart hummed, lighting their way.

After an even wetter and rougher ride through some breakers, the bottom of the boat vibrated as it scraped on a hard surface. Tyen turned to look behind him. They'd reached a small, pebbled beach. The sailors sprung from the boat and hauled it as far out of the water as they could as the waves swept in. When the vessel stilled, Tyen rose to help Sezee disembark and steadied her when she stumbled on the slippery, smooth stones. She yelped as a wave rushed in and wet them to their knees. The water was bracingly cold.

Veroo's skirt was still tied up. As Tyen helped her, the sailors lifted the luggage and carried it beyond the reach of the waves. Veroo hurried over the slippery pebbles, outrunning an incoming wave to avoid a wetting.

The sailors then began pushing the boat back into the water. Tyen drew a little magic and moved it for them. They ran after it and dived inside, then began to battle the incoming waves. Taking even more magic, he shoved the vessel even further away, wanting the crew gone before the aircart landed and he had to face the driver.

The aircart remained in the air, however. When the sailors were safely beyond the breakers, Tyen shaded his eyes against the light, trying to see the driver. The sound of the propellers changed and the light began to rise.

Either he's having second thoughts or he's leaving us here for someone else to collect, Tyen thought. *Either way, he should have left earlier.*

"Go," he told Sezee and Veroo. "Shield yourselves with magic or get behind some rocks."

"Wha—?" Sezee began, but Veroo muttered something and dragged her away.

Stretching out, Tyen robbed the air around the cart of magic. Some of it he used to still the air around himself to form a shield. Some he used to take hold of the vehicle's chassis and begin moving it downward.

The light blinked out. Tyen braced himself for an attack, but instead felt the natural buoyancy of the cart increase. The driver was using magic to move it upward. *Fool*, he thought. *If we fight over the cart we'll tear it apart.* The vehicle was close enough to the ground that the driver might survive a fall, so long as the cart didn't crush him. *Then it would be better if he fell before the cart did*, Tyen thought. He sent a ball of stilled air at the driver and watched in surprise as the man tumbled off the chassis and landed on the beach. The man hadn't even been shielding himself.

The propellers stopped spinning, and in the quiet that followed, the sound of the driver's cursing was audible. Two figures emerged from the darkness and hurried towards him. Tyen opened his mouth to call out a warning to them, then closed it again. Veroo should still be shielding them both. He could feel the cart growing less buoyant as the air in the capsule cooled. He turned his attention to it, guiding it down until it hovered several paces from the driver, next to the luggage. Sezee hurried over to him, leaving Veroo crouching by the man's side.

"He's alive," she said. "Veroo thinks he has a broken arm, and he'll have some impressive bruises. There are lights moving up on the ridge behind us, so whoever's up there will find him soon enough. So . . . do we get on the aircart now?"

Tyen laughed at her eagerness. Relief washed away his fear that the driver was badly injured, though he could not help feeling guilty about what he'd done, and was about to do. "Yes, and quickly."

Sezee helped him lift the luggage onto the chassis and tie it down. A bag was already strapped on near the front. Tyen removed it and inspected the contents – some small packets of food, the man's papers, and clothing. He pocketed the food and put the bag on the ground.

"Veroo!" Sezee shouted. "Come on!"

He turned to see that Veroo was leading the driver up the beach. The man was limping, but not badly. He was a few years older than Tyen and definitely Wendlandish. Veroo reached a rock and helped him sit down. She stepped away and hurried to the cart.

"I don't think he'll be any trouble now. He's terrified of you." She looked amused. "All set?"

Tyen nodded. "Get on board."

They ducked under the rope railing and stepped up onto the chassis. He let go of the aircart, allowing it to rise again. The women gripped the capsule support struts uneasily as the cart began to rise.

"Sit down," he advised as he moved to the front. He climbed into the driver's seat then glanced back to check that they were in place. They were sitting either side of the capsule's front support strut, legs straddling the canoe-shaped chassis. "And hang on." Sending a trickle of magic to the capsule, he heated air and sent them rapidly upward. Below, the driver watched, pale face tilted. Tyen felt a pang of sympathy.

Losing an aircart is bad enough, but losing it through such misjudgement has got to sting. The driver ought to have demanded the ship take them to the nearest port. Or at least have brought another sorcerer with him. He'd probably been acting on his own in the hopes of getting the reward, and not considered what he'd do if Tyen proved to be a stronger sorcerer.

What would I have done if he hadn't been so foolish and weak? Would I have been willing to kill him? He wasn't sure. As far as he knew, the Academy's reward was for his capture, not death. If the worse he faced was a lifetime in prison, was he justified in ending someone's life to avoid that? A life in captivity was a wasted life, but it wasn't death.

He sighed. He'd been lucky this time. The last stroke of luck he'd enjoyed had been followed by a setback. *I'm not safe yet,* he reminded himself. Setting the propellers whirring, he turned the aircart towards the sea.

"Tyen."

He turned to see that Veroo had shuffled along the chassis to get closer to him and be heard over the propeller noise.

"Yes?"

"You're not making the sea crossing now are you?"

"No, just getting some distance between us and the driver. We need to head further south, where the eastern and southern continents are closest."

"How long until we do?"

"A few days."

"And how long will the crossing take?

"Three days, if the weather is good and the wind in our favour."

Veroo frowned. "Then we're going to have to stop somewhere for food and warmer clothes for you."

Tyen's heart sank. "Yes. We will have to be careful. Land at night to sleep and buy food in small villages."

"And you'll have to teach me how to fly so we can take turns."

He shook his head. "Women don't fly."

"They don't learn sorcery either," she retorted. "Do you think I'm too weak and emotional for it?"

He laughed. "No, not at all. But the sight of a woman driving an aircart will be talked about from here to Belton."

"You can teach me after we start crossing, then. You can't fly for three days straight."

She was right. He could stay awake for three days, but by the time he reached land again he'd be exhausted. Not a good state to be in, if he had to make a difficult landing. Yet teaching her to drive when they were far from shore would be dangerous, too. A big enough mistake could force them to land in the water, far from help.

But it was a small danger compared to what they'd face if they were caught up in bad weather. He only needed to teach her how to drive in a straight line. Launching, landing and manoeuvring were trickier, as they involved timing and avoiding obstacles, but unnecessary in the middle of sea crossing.

"You'd better get comfortable, but not so comfortable that you fall asleep and slip off." He turned back to see them both regarding him with fearful expressions. "I'll keep low so you don't get too cold. Otherwise . . . I'm afraid it's going to be a long night."

CHAPTER 18

Veroo has picked up flying so quickly, Tyen told Vella. *The Academy was foolish for turning her away.*

Hoarding magical knowledge is a common form of defence.

But her country is part of the Empire, not an enemy.

It is a conquered land. Rebellion is always possible.

Surely that's more likely if it is denied the benefits of belonging to the Empire. And even if everyone in the West Isles with the ability learned magic, there wouldn't be enough sorcerers to overthrow the Leratian Empire.

If all lands colonised by Leratia were to do so, would there be enough?

Tyen frowned. *Perhaps. But . . . Veroo is no threat on her own. Just one woman . . .*

Who can teach others. Her gender is no obstacle in her country, either.

Yes, I see your point. It seems like a waste not to teach her, though, and anyone with magical ability.

It is. It may be sensible for the Empire's defence, but it is limiting for the Academy. Restricting knowledge slows the pace of development. The fewer sorcerers free to learn and teach, the less time is spent experimenting and making new discoveries.

And yet this last century has been a time of great advancement.

For the Empire. Every time it conquered new lands it absorbed new knowledge. Even small discoveries, like a more efficient way to record information, can lead to great change.

Like printing presses. Their earliest form was a system used by the equatorial tribes. Their inventor always said he couldn't accept full credit for it. Tyen smiled. *I guess you would have had the same effect, if he'd read of the system from your pages instead of the tribes'.*

Yes. That was Roporien's intention. Most of what he knew he'd learned in the first few hundred years of his life. The older he got, the longer it took to discover new information until it was more profitable to him to wait for geniuses to be born, grow up and make new discoveries than for him to travel in search of them.

Why did he continue looking for new knowledge?

He took a certain pride in knowing more than anyone else, perhaps anyone who had ever existed. That way nobody could defeat him simply by being better informed.

And yet that didn't protect him. He still died. So . . . how did he die?

I don't know. Nobody I have encountered knew. There was a rumour that it was a more powerful sorcerer. A man they called the Successor.

Successor? Roporien's son?

No. His replacement. There is a belief held in many worlds that a sorcerer as powerful as Roporien is born once every thousand cycles — a cycle being a unit of time a little longer than this world's year. When this Successor comes to full strength he will kill the old one. It is known as Millennium's Rule.

Do you believe it to be true?

I believe nothing. I only store information, and I do not contain enough to prove if the Rule is correct.

Was there a powerful sorcerer before Roporien, who he killed when he was young?

Yes. A sorcerer tried to kill him who was stronger than any he'd encountered before. He defeated the man, despite being far less experienced in magical duelling.

Then Roporien's Successor is still out there?

If my calculations are correct, it is a little over a thousand cycles since Roporien died. His Successor will have already been defeated by his own Successor, if the Rule holds truth.

Do Successors ever fail?

I have no record of one failing. It is possible that one may be killed before acquiring the knowledge of agelessness, or from inexperience or simple bad luck.

Tyen looked up from the pages, barely registering the sea stretching below and around the aircart as a sudden longing filled him to see these other worlds and know if Roporien's Successor still lived. Though if the man was that powerful, it would be safer to find out without actually meeting him. Roporien had been a cruel man. Who knew what his replacement was like? Or the man who might already have defeated him? Either way, a Successor had to have killed at least one man.

"Tyen."

He looked up to find Sezee making her way along the aircart towards him. Unlike Veroo, she had not grown used to riding on the narrow chassis. Standing up in view of the sea far below made her head spin, so she crawled up and down the chassis on all fours. Before they'd set out across the ocean she had changed into a bodice and jacket that buttoned up to her throat for warmth. While that prevented the view of her crawling towards him from being distractingly indecent, she had also donned a pair of pantaloons, which made watching her crawling *away* from him an entirely different matter.

She had also insisted they attach some strong netting between the rope railing and the chassis on both sides for most of its length to reduce the chances she'd slip off the side of the aircart. He'd chafed at the delay, but came to appreciate the netting's value as a more comfortable safety measure to the usual straps that held a passenger in place when sleeping.

Closing Vella, he slipped her into his coat pocket.

"It's my turn to drive?" he asked.

"Yes, but that's not what you need to see." She stopped, settled onto one hip and smiled. "Have you noticed the lites?"

He looked around. Sure enough, several species of the winged creatures were visible, gliding above or skimming the water below. Some were migratory, or spent most of their life over the ocean. Others were coastal, visiting the sea only to feed, which meant . . .

"Land," he said, shading his eyes and peering towards the west. "We must be close."

"Yes." She grinned. "We're nearly there."

He got to his feet, holding the capsule support strut for balance. "Oh, we have a long way to go still. We have an entire mountain range to cross."

Carefully stepping past her, he made his way to the front of the aircart, where Veroo sat with her skirts hitched up and stockinged legs dangling over the edge of the seat.

"Tyen," she said. "Warfare was part of your aircart training, wasn't it? Do you have any aerial battle experience?"

He laughed. "Yes to the first, no to the second. Why do you ask?"

She let go of the wheel with one hand and pointed towards the north. "Is that what I think it is?"

His heart skipped a beat as he turned to stare northward. It took him a while to find the tiny shape, and if they had not been flying so low he would not have seen it easily against the sea. It, too, wasn't more than a few hundred paces above the water. The capsule was pointed at the front and seemed larger than the average aircart's, though not as big as an aircarriage capsule. Though he was seeing it from nearly directly front on, something about the shape of the propeller arms was familiar. His stomach sank as he realised what it was.

"That," he said, "is a Dart, one of the Empire's fighting carts. Designed for speed. There'll be two sorcerers on board – one to fly and shield it so the other is free to fight."

"Will they have seen us?"

"Definitely."

"Are they hunting us?"

"It would be wise to assume so."

"Will we reach the shore before they get here?"

"I don't know. We have no choice but to try. Increase the speed of the propellers."

She looked over her shoulder at him. "You want me to keep flying?"

"Do *you* have any fighting training or experience?"

She smiled grimly and turned back to grip the wheel with both hands. Tyen made his way back to Sezee.

"Did you hear that?" he asked.

She nodded, her eyes wide. "Most of it. Should I strap myself in?"

He shook his head. "If the cart falls, try to leap off and outward before we land, or you might be caught and dragged under the water. Can you swim?"

"Of course." She gave him a lofty look. "Everyone on the islands learns to swim. Can you?"

He grimaced. "No. If we cut the capsule off before it sinks the chassis should float. It's mostly wood."

"But the capsule is full of air."

"If we hit the water it's unlikely it will be." The buzz of the propellers had steadily increased and the vibration began to shake the chassis. He could hear the capsule support struts creaking. "No more, Veroo," he called. "Or the cart will shake itself apart."

Looking northward, he noted how much closer the other cart was. He could see enough detail to confirm his suspicions

379

were right. It was a Dart and it was flying at full speed, directly towards them. Looking over Veroo's shoulder, he saw a jagged blue shape above the horizon and his heart leapt. Mountains.

The wind was still at their back, driving them towards land. He looked from the mountains to the Dart and back, again and again, trying to gauge the advance of both. As time crawled by, the peaks slowly grew and joined at the base to form a coastline, while the Dart doubled and tripled in size. He shook his head. It was going to be close. Even if they made it to land in time they'd still have two sorcerers experienced in aerial conflict to deal with. All they'd gain was a chance of landing on firm ground if the aircart was damaged.

They had a little time to ready themselves, fortunately. Tyen moved to the back and untied his satchel from where he'd kept it bound onto the chassis, transferred Vella to it and slung it over his head and one shoulder. It wouldn't save Vella or Beetle from a dunking, but he'd be less likely to lose them than if he put them in his pockets. If they survived this, he decided, he would modify Beetle so it could swim.

He then transferred most of Kilraker's remaining money to Sezee's bag. The paper notes would be ruined by water and the coins would weigh him down. The Empire's coinage would probably be worthless in the Far South anyway, which no doubt had a money system of its own. For a second he was a little breathless, wondering how he would survive in a strange land with no money.

I should have bought some gold and gemstones to exchange. There hadn't been any time or opportunity. At the least, he might be able to use Kilraker's remaining money to bribe the sorcerers into letting them go.

Sezee had unlaced her boots and was tying them together, looped through her belt. Since she knew about swimming, he decided to follow suit. Veroo had done nothing, her attention no doubt taken up with driving the aircart.

He glanced to the north and felt his heart skip. The Dart was closing in faster than he had guessed. Watching it approach, he tried to ignore the fluttering within his stomach.

What will they do? The Academy wanted to keep its secrets safe. To do that it needed to destroy Vella and silence Tyen. The sorcerers in the Dart had probably heard about the aircart driver who had ordered Tyen to shore only to receive a broken arm and lose his aircart. So they knew their quarry would put up a fight. The Academy may even have decided that, if Tyen couldn't be captured, it had no choice but to order its sorcerers to kill him.

But what of Sezee and Veroo? Surely the Academy would not risk the lives of the two women, even if they had not worked out the pair were of the West Isles' royal line. It might consider the women accomplices and therefore criminals, or even rebels. Tyen might have told them the Academy's secrets. Nobody would hear about their deaths if they happened out at sea, unobserved and leaving no evidence.

He shivered. It was better to be prepared for the worst, he decided. At that thought the press of responsibility settled on his shoulders like a heavy coat. Sezee and Veroo were here because of him. They would not now be in a stolen aircart heading to the Far South if they hadn't helped him. They might still have learned about the distant land by another means and sought to go there if they hadn't met him, but they would have travelled in safer company.

I must make sure they make it safely to shore at the least, he thought. *Even if it means being captured. Even if it means being killed.* But what of Vella? He frowned, then nodded to himself at the obvious answer. He must find a way to slip her among Veroo's belongings.

That decided, he turned his thoughts back to the coming battle and considered what he knew of magical fighting.

It all came down to using as little magic as possible to the greatest effect. Moving and stilling were the least taxing ways to use magic in battle. Heating and cooling were those two actions intensified, but the greater the temperature change the greater the magic required. Attacking by heating the air and throwing the resulting "fire" ball was much less economical than projecting a missile at the enemy.

The most common weapon in a fighting aircart was a stock of arrows. They were small and sharp and didn't add much weight. Cannon and shot were too heavy. A skilled sorcerer could launch hundreds of arrows at once. A sprung bow or two were kept on board fighting aircarts in case the sorcerer ran out of magic or flew into Soot, though they were less useful as they could shoot only one arrow at a time.

Unfortunately, he did not have a supply of projectiles on board. At least, nothing that would cause his enemy any discomfort. Throwing his, Sezee's and Veroo's shoes might cause a few bruises, but they didn't have a large supply of those either.

He was probably better off saving magic for defence, anyway. The first thing an attacker would do was attempt to take hold of the enemy aircart, as Tyen had done when he'd stolen this one. To prevent that he could take hold of it himself, but that took more power than simply creating a shield of stilled air the enemy couldn't reach through. And the shield had the twin purpose of repelling missiles.

Reaching out to either side, he took in magic and used a little of it to still a thin layer of air before and above the aircart, about twenty paces away on the side facing the Dart. He made it strong enough to slow an arrow rather than stop it, to conserve magic, and orientated it with the cart so it moved along with it. The other cart was close enough now that he could make out the shapes of the two occupants and sense the trail of Soot streaming behind their vehicle. As he watched he saw black emptiness billow out on either side as the sorcerers prepared to attack.

Glancing towards the coast, he saw that it was now a line of green below mountains grown darker and more distinct, with paler peaks visible behind them.

We're not going to make it.

A shock went through him as something passed through the barrier. An arrow tumbled down and landed in the sea. He muttered a curse.

"What?" Sezee asked. "You stopped it."

"Yes," he agreed. "But I should have caught it. We have nothing to throw at them."

"What about this?"

He tore his gaze from the Dart and looked down. She held a small knife with a curved, notched blade. It was a surprisingly nasty-looking weapon.

"You've been carrying that all this time?"

"It comes in handy. Especially when Veroo and I are separated."

"Do you know how to use it?"

"If you mean in a fight, then yes."

He shook his head. "Then keep it. If nothing else, you might need it to cut ropes or something—"

At a further shock he looked up again. Another arrow tumbled towards the water. This time he reached out and caught it with magic, moving it to his hand. Before he could send it back towards the Dart, however, the air between the aircarts filled with thin, dark lines. Trying to catch several at once was like trying to grab a handful of twigs. He settled for grabbing them one at a time, but had caught only three when Veroo called out:

"We're dropping."

It was subtle, but now that Veroo had pointed it out he could feel it. With a sinking feeling he looked up at the capsule. The front appeared unharmed, though he could only see the bottom half. As he turned to examine the rear, Sezee made a small noise of surprise. She was staring up, crawling backwards away from him.

Following her gaze, he froze, startled to see a long blade suspended a mere hand's width from his nose. It was attached to the end of a spear, protruding from the belly of the capsule.

He cursed as he realised his mistake. He'd been taught that it was better to save strength by protecting only the side of a cart facing the enemy. Moving something in a direct line only required that a sorcerer propel it that way, while sending it on an indirect path meant controlling it for the entire journey, which took more magic and concentration.

Which was effort worth expending if one simple strike brought the enemy down. The sorcerers in the Dart had moved the spear behind Tyen's aircart then propelled it through the capsule. With the capsule blocking the view upward, Tyen could never have seen it coming.

He cursed again, then apologised to Sezee.

"Oh, this is no time for manners," she told him. "Are you going to pull that out?"

He shook his head. "If it didn't come all the way through it might have barbs." Drawing more magic, he extended the barrier around the entire aircart so it formed an elongated bubble. No longer helped along by the wind, the aircart slowed a little.

"So there's an even bigger hole in the top of this?"

"Probably." He felt sick with disappointment. It had been a stupid mistake, not protecting the whole aircart. *But it's what I was taught to do. It's not like I've done this before*, he reminded himself, but he felt no better.

"Tyen," Veroo called, her tone full of warning.

He whirled around to see that the Dart was angling towards the coast, clearly intending to head them off. Then he saw that the land ahead was closer than he'd dared hope. Trees covered it – a forest larger than any he'd seen before stretching towards the mountains. It grew right to the water's edge, where a small cliff outlined the break between water and earth.

"There's nowhere to land," Veroo pointed out.

"We'll find a clearing. Open all of the lower valves of the capsule and move air inside, heating it as you do."

"Already am," she replied.

Which was why they weren't rapidly heading for the water. Tyen turned his attention back to the Dart, which was steadily drawing closer and ahead of them. Soot was blossoming all around it as the sorcerers took the magic he and Veroo would need to drive and defend the cart.

He saw, then, the Dart occupants' ploy. They would fly in front, robbing the way ahead of magic. The obvious reaction would be to turn the aircart to avoid the Soot. The Dart would turn the same way, slowly circling around until they had the aircart trapped within a ring of Soot, spiralling in until Tyen and Veroo had used up all the magic within.

Tyen could try to bluff them, turning one way to begin with, then dashing the other way across the Dart's Soot trail in the hopes of escaping the trap. But the Dart was faster and would soon be circling around them in the other direction.

They could keep weaving back and forth in this way, but with a torn capsule the aircart would soon end up in the sea. They needed to fly directly to shore.

Then we'll have to fly in the Dart's Soot trail. He and Veroo could do it for a while if, before they reached it, they gathered enough magic to drive the cart and hold the shield. He looked closer at the blackness. If the trail's width was an indication, his reach might be a little greater than the sorcerers'.

He moved past Sezee again to stand close to Veroo as the Dart moved between the aircart and the coast. The sorcerer not driving the Dart moved to the rear of its chassis, a large cylinder tucked under one arm from which he was pulling arrows. He sent them in multiples, each time sending one or two arrows on an arching path to strike Tyen's shield from the side or back.

"What do you want me to do?" Veroo asked.

"Keep flying straight."

"Into the Soot?"

"Yes. Take as much magic as you can from all directions before we reach it."

"That means there'll be nothing for you—"

"Don't worry about me."

Soot surrounded them as Veroo drew in magic, moments before they entered the void.

It always seemed to Tyen that the air was cooled and sound dampened within Soot. He had enough magic left to hold the barrier in place as he reached out in all directions, beyond the edges of the void. He sensed magic within his grasp. Felt it drifting towards him, naturally flowing in to fill the gap the sorcerers had made. He seized it.

Veroo gasped and looked up at him. He kept his attention on the Dart. Looking closely, he saw that he had even managed to rob the magic from around and beyond the other aircart.

He straightened, surprised. "Well . . . that worked better than I expected."

"Are all Academy sorcerers like you?" Veroo asked.

He shook his head. "I have no idea. There's so little magic in Belton that we're only allowed to use it in the Academy grounds, and nobody uses more than they have to." He shrugged. "I'm starting to suspect I may be a bit stronger than the average."

"It was a waste you being there," she told him.

He blinked, remembering his own thoughts about the Academy's rejection of her. Before he could think of a way to tell her this, she looked ahead and cackled with glee.

"Their propellers have stopped! They're descending."

His heart skipped as he saw she was right. But the Dart was coming to *a level* with them which meant . . . He looked down. The sea was a lot closer than it had been before the capsule had been damaged. Disturbingly close.

"So are we," he muttered.

"We'll make it to shore," she assured him.

He looked ahead and shook his head at her optimism. More likely they'd crash into the trees, or the low cliff. He could try to push the aircart higher with magic, but he needed solid ground to push against, and the capsule support struts weren't designed for such stresses. If they were going to repair the capsule and use it to cross the mountains, the less damage done to it the better.

The attack from the Dart had stopped. The driver had abandoned his seat and had joined his companion, both moving about hastily.

"We're gaining on them," said a voice at Tyen's shoulder. He looked back to see Sezee standing behind him, the rope railing gripped in white-knuckled hands. "Will they shoot at us as we pass?"

Tyen nodded. "Probably. How much magic do you have left, Veroo?"

"I'll get us past them, I think."

He was relieved to hear it. Though he could drive the cart and hold a barrier at the same time, he'd rather not have to when he needed to keep his attention on the sorcerers. Veroo shifted direction, obviously intending to give the Dart a wide berth.

"No, pass them as close as you can," he told her. "The sooner we reach land the better."

The front of the aircart drew level with the rear of the Dart. The two sorcerers were no more than twenty paces away. They turned, each steadying a large sprung bow resting on the struts of the Dart's capsule. Twin arrows shot towards Tyen. As they reached the stilled air of his barrier they passed through, but their path had slowed so much they dropped towards the sea. He caught them with magic.

The sorcerers notched and cranked two more arrows. Tyen couldn't tell if they were holding a barrier, but it was likely they had put all their remaining magic into one. He turned the arrows to face the Dart. Yet he hesitated. The sorcerers were no danger to him right now. He did not want to kill anyone needlessly.

But what will happen when – if – we reach land? Will I regret not taking advantage of this opportunity?

They would have sensed him taking magic. They knew he was stronger. If he were in their position, he'd withdraw and return with more sorcerers.

He could ensure they took longer to do so.

Propelling the arrows towards the Dart and through his own shield, he gave them an extra push when they neared the capsule. They encountered a weak barrier but broke through it and pierced the Dart's capsule. As the sorcerers sent more arrows he did the same, but this time their barrier repelled the attack. They did not send more. When the aircart overtook the Dart, Tyen propelled the arrows he'd collected earlier towards them. These encountered no barrier at all, and made splashes as they broke through the other side of the capsule and landed in the sea.

"They're out of magic," he said.

He smiled as Veroo and Sezee cheered. The holes he'd made would bring the Dart down slowly, allowing it reach land but forcing the sorcerers to stop and repair their cart before seeking reinforcements. He watched one of them set down his bow and hurry back to the driver's seat. The wind would still push the Dart towards land. To keep the sorcerers disabled a little longer, he took more magic downwind from the cart, ensuring they would not be able to follow easily and attack the aircart's rear.

"I'm done," Veroo declared.

Tyen heard the propellers slow to a stop. "Stay there and steer," he told her as she began to climb out of the seat. He concentrated on warming the air within the capsule and setting the propellers spinning again.

"We've made it!" Sezee exclaimed. Looking down, Tyen saw they had finally passed over land. He let out a sigh of relief and looked back at the Dart. It still appeared to be following them, steering with its rudder.

"Ah . . . Tyen," Veroo warned.

Turning back, he saw a wall of foliage blocking their way.

"I can't see any clearings," Veroo said.

"Aim for the widest gap between the trees." Tyen drew more magic and, using the ground below to orientate it, gently took hold of the aircart chassis and moved it upwards. The support struts creaked as they pushed up against the capsule, which bulged and rippled.

The cart rose a little, but too slowly. The raking fingers of a tall branch scraped over his shield where it protected the propellers, jerking the aircart sideways. As it broke through Veroo spun the steering wheel to turn them back towards a too small gap in the trees ahead. Tyen sent out magic in a chopping force, snapping off limbs. Foliage whipped back and forth as they scraped past, then the aircart emerged into branch-free space.

Only to face a high, treed ridge. Tyen noted that it angled towards the mountains.

"Follow the valley," he instructed.

"We won't get far," Veroo told him. "We have to find a place to land."

"I know, I know." He looked down, but found no open space. A narrow thread of water glinted in the sunlight. A river . . . but with trees growing right to the edge.

The cart tilted as it changed direction. Now that the capsule was side-on to the wind the ride became rougher and slower. Tyen felt his stomach lurch as they began to descend quickly. Perhaps the rent in the capsule was being blown wider.

"Tyen," Veroo said.

"Just keep flying, as long as possible."

Sezee grabbed his arm. "They're still following us."

He looked back. The Dart was cresting the ridge. *Why aren't they hurrying away? Are they staying to see where we land?*

"Tyen!" Veroo shouted.

He turned back to face a wall of branches and leaves.

"Hold on!" he shouted, and strengthened the barrier around the aircart. They plunged into the foliage, branches scraping over his barrier, then burst through.

And fell, nose first, into the waiting heart of another tree.

CHAPTER 19

The impact tore the railing from Tyen's hands. He heard a gasp from Veroo, but nothing from Sezee. He fell forward, sliding head first over the side of the chassis. Throwing his arms out, he caught a strut and managed to hook a leg around the railing support. The shoes tied to his belt swung up to strike him in the chest. His satchel's strap scraped his nose as it slid over his head. He snatched at it but his hand clawed at the air as it fell.

"Beetle!" he called. "Fly!"

The flap opened and the insectoid emerged, wings blurring.

"Guard bag," he ordered. Beetle zoomed downward. He didn't wait to see it land. The aircart's forward momentum had stopped. Its nose – or, rather, the front of his shield – was planted in the tree, but with nothing supporting the rear it began to fall. Tyen strengthened the shield below the cart, but when it was almost level it caught on something and, after bouncing a few times, went still.

He hauled himself up, the movement setting the cart swaying, and looked around. Sezee was cradled in the netting. She met his eyes and smiled grimly, which he took to mean she was unhurt. Veroo was muttering darkly as she climbed out of the driver's seat. He sighed in relief. The driver's seat, at the front of the aircart, could have sustained the most damage but his barrier had protected her.

The rear of the aircart capsule had settled onto a branch of another tree. Only his barrier was keeping it in place, however.

"Keep your movements slow," he said. "The cart could still fall."

Sezee looked over the side. "How are we going to get down there?"

Tyen followed her gaze. The ground was too far away to risk jumping down to. It was covered in vegetation, so he couldn't guess how even or rocky it was. He considered the rope ladder that all aircarts carried, attached to a strut. He doubted it would reach the ground. He examined the tree the cart had plunged into. The branches were too widely spaced to climb down. But a combination of both . . .

"We'll go down in stages," he decided.

"Wait. Can you hear that?" Veroo asked.

They fell silent. A distant, throbbing noise was barely audible over the sound of the wind in the leaves.

"The Dart?" Sezee wondered aloud.

"Probably. If it is we'll be safer on the ground," Tyen told them. Using magic, he brought the ladder to him rather than risk unbalancing the chassis. He created a hole in his barrier and stepped out into the nest of branches the cart's nose had plunged into. Looking down the trunk, he chose another cluster of branches well within the ladder's reach to aim for. He secured the ropes and started to descend.

"What happened to women going first?" Sezee asked, looking down at him through the netting.

"Do you want to be the one who tests my knots?"

She shook her head. "No."

"And if you fall I'll catch you much more easily if I'm

standing on something firm." Safely reaching the cluster of branches, he looked up at Veroo. "Your turn."

"Sezee should go next," the woman said.

Tyen nodded. "Then get onto a branch. I don't want to have to catch you both if the cart falls."

He stilled the cart as Sezee crawled along it to the tree. Soon she was climbing down the ladder, Tyen putting his weight on the bottom rung to keep it from swinging around. Veroo followed, then Tyen untied the ladder with magic and secured it so that they could descend the rest of the way to the ground.

Firm ground had never felt so welcome. As the women descended he looked up at the cart. With no air being sent into it and heated, the capsule sagged.

"Can you bring it down without damaging it further?" Veroo asked as she joined him and Sezee.

"I hope so." Sezee had already replaced her shoes, he noted. He sat down on a large exposed tree root and began putting his own back on.

"Can you repair it?" Sezee asked.

"I'll answer that when I've seen the damage."

Taking a deep breath and a little more magic, he used the barrier around the cart like a cupped hand, gently cradling and guiding the cart downward. It slid off the branch abruptly, then he had to let it tilt away from the tree it had landed in to come free at the front. From there he had to support the full weight of it, which forced him to take even more magic. The struts creaked as he set it down and the capsule collapsed in on itself with a whoof of air.

They moved closer. Sezee stopped, then parted the wide leaves of a plant.

"Here's your satchel." She bent then recoiled. "And Beetle."

Tyen started towards her. "Beetle," he called.

A familiar buzz sounded as the insectoid rose up from among the undergrowth. It flew over to him and the pressure of tiny metal legs settled on his shoulder. Sezee stared at it in fascination.

"I've never asked – is it a he or she?"

He blinked in surprise. "It's just . . . Beetle. It doesn't have male or female, er, parts."

She reached out and stroked its head. "I reckon it's a she, based on the pretty wings. You wouldn't have made them decorative and colourful if you'd meant it to be male."

"Some men like to adorn themselves," Veroo pointed out. "And wear bright colours."

"Not in Leratia, and Tyen's Leratian."

Tyen shook his head. "Why does it have to be male or female?"

Sezee shrugged.

"I don't hear aircart propellers now," Veroo interjected.

They fell silent, listening intently. The only sounds Tyen heard were of the forest. He let out a sigh. "They've marked where we landed and are probably looking for somewhere safer to stop and fix their capsule." He looked under the plants, found his satchel and picked it up. Opening the flap to check if Vella had survived, his heart froze as he saw she wasn't in there. He began searching around the plant.

"Lost something?" Sezee asked.

He grunted in reply.

She began parting vegetation. "What is it?"

"A book."

"The one you were reading during the— Ah! Here it is!"

She crouched, her hands disappearing under the leaves of another plant. When she straightened she was holding Vella. She looked at the worn old cover, turning it in her hands. Tyen kept his expression unconcerned as he walked towards her,

extending a hand. To his relief, she did not flick through the
pages but handed it over.

"Thanks," he said, tucking it away in the satchel. "Now,
let's see how bad the damage to the cart is. If we're lucky the
owner kept a patching kit on board for the capsule."

"Where will it be?" Veroo asked.

"Inside the chassis."

They followed him over to the aircart. Part of the capsule
was draped over the support struts, so he pushed the thick
fabric back inside the cradle. His heart sank as jagged ends of
wood appeared.

"It's worse than I thought," he said. The hole in the top of
the capsule appeared. It was not as bad as he'd feared, but the
damage to the struts was bad news. He'd need to carve new
ones and attach them somehow. Holding the edges of the hole
up, he looked inside and found the spear that had caused the
damage. As he'd guessed, it had a barbed shaft. He pulled it
free, tossing it onto the ground.

"Nasty-looking thing," Sezee said, eyeing it critically. "And
to think it came so close to putting a hole in your head."

Tyen shivered. "I'd rather not contemplate that."

"Is this the patching kit?" Veroo held up a small, familiar
bag – the standard kit sold to aircart drivers by the main
aircart outfitters, Lawson & Sons.

"Yes." He shook his head and sighed. "It'll take longer to
fix this than the Dart will. They'll be back before we're
finished."

"Tyen," Veroo said, in the same warning tone she'd used
when they'd been heading for the trees. He turned to see her
attention was on the stream nearby. "We have company," she
told them.

Surely the Dart's sorcerers hadn't arrived already? It took
him a moment to make out the two figures standing in the

dappled shadows of the trees, and he was relieved to see these were not his pursuers. A man perhaps ten years older than Tyen stood with arms crossed, scowling. Beside him was a wide-eyed youth, who kept looking from the aircart to his companion anxiously.

"Who are they?" Sezee whispered.

"I have no idea," Tyen replied. The pair wore tough, well-worn clothing. The man was carrying an axe. They were probably local, possibly foresters. Would they be willing to help? Though it was a risk to put their trust in strangers, whether or not Tyen repaired the aircart or abandoned it, he and the women needed food and shelter. Taking a deep breath, he took a few steps towards them.

"Good day," he said. "Please, could you tell us where we are?"

The man's frown deepened. "The Greening," he said. "Southernmost edge of Rymuah." His eyes narrowed. "You're Leratian."

Tyen nodded.

"But the women aren't."

"They are from the West Isles." Tyen turned to each of the women and introduced them. "I am Tyen. We are . . ." Fugitives? Escapees? He couldn't tell them that. "We are adventurers."

The man tilted his head briefly towards the coast. "I've seen your type before. But I've not seen the Empire try to shoot one of you out of the sky before." He tramped towards him and held out his hand. As Tyen extended his, the man seized it and squeezed firmly then let go.

"Welcome to Rymuah. Orn Lorgen," he said. "This is my son, Ozel."

The women came forward and were treated to shallow bows. Both men eyed Sezee's trousers uneasily. Tyen smiled in sympathy.

"So," Orn said. "These Empire men are chasing you. Did some damage." He nodded at the aircart.

There was no point denying it. Tyen nodded.

"Their cart was damaged, too. How long do you think we have before they fix it and return here?" Veroo asked.

"Not long enough," the stranger said. "There's a village not far north-west of here. The Empire's men will land there. You have a couple of hours, no more."

"Are there more sorcerers there?" Tyen asked.

Orn nodded. "There've always been arguments about who owns what land around here and has the right to fell the trees and sell the wood. The Empire's sorcerers settle them for us. Always in their favour of course."

Sezee turned to Tyen. "Could you fight them off?"

Tyen grimaced. "I don't know. Depends how many there are." And what then? He didn't want to have to kill anyone. "We should leave. We can build another aircart."

"It'll take time," she protested. "They'll tell the Academy where you are and send more sorcerers and Darts here to hunt for you. By the time we can fly again it won't be safe to take to the air."

"If I was you, I'd continue on foot and get some distance between you and here," Orn said. "I'll advise you on the route."

"Thank you." Tyen sighed. "Trouble is, we can't get where we're hoping to go on foot."

The man's eyebrows rose. "Over the mountains, eh?" He walked towards the aircart, the young man close behind. "How much damage?"

"Some struts need replacing, and the capsule has to be patched."

"Can you help us?" Sezee asked. "We can pay you."

The man pursed his lips, then puffed out his cheeks. Finally, he let out a soft pop of breath and nodded. "I think we can. If I get word to some friends who live hereabouts they can take the cart apart and move it. The Empire types will think they're scavenging it. You can come back when they're gone and put it back together again."

Tyen looked at the man in amazement. That he was willing to go to so much effort for them was humbling. He met Orn's eyes. "Are you sure you want to risk helping enemies of the Empire?"

Orn nodded. "I don't know why you're running from them, but that's enough for me to want them not to find you. An enemy of the Empire is a friend of the Rymuan."

Tyen smiled. "I'm starting to think I should adopt a similar policy."

"Where should we go in the meantime?" Veroo asked.

Orn paused as he considered. "You are welcome to stay at my home. It is some hours' walk away but well hidden."

As the man moved away to inspect the aircart, Sezee touched Tyen's arm.

"Are you sure about this?" she murmured.

He shrugged. "No. But even if he somehow managed to fix the aircart in time, they'll spot us as soon as we fly above the trees and the chase will start again. They'll catch us before we can cross the mountains."

"No, I mean trusting him."

"I don't see we have much choice."

She turned to Veroo, who nodded. "He's right. We should get our bags."

With a sigh of defeat, Sezee moved to the cart and began removing their bags from within the chassis.

"I hope you don't intend to carry all of those," Tyen said.

She shot him a dark look. "No. You will. After all, we hired you as our porter."

"Sounds like it's time I quit."

Sezee looked down at the bags. "But . . . can't you use magic to carry them?"

Veroo chuckled. "And create a clear trail of Soot to track us by?"

"Then we shall take the smallest bag," Sezee decided. "Let's repack."

"Quickly," Veroo added.

In a few minutes the women had stuffed a few items into the smallest of their bags. They handed it to Tyen then stuffed the larger bags inside the chassis. The man spoke quietly to the youth, who nodded and raced away.

"Follow me," Orn said, and started walking.

Tyen looked at Sezee and Veroo. They frowned back at him, but did not object. Straightening his shoulders, he tightened his grip on their bag and set off after the Rymuan.

Orn set a steady pace, not hurried but with few pauses. He chose a trail so slender it was barely wider than his shoes in places. Other paths crossed it, so often that Tyen wondered if the forest floor was one huge maze. Several times he saw the imprint of some sort of animal. Fallen trees occasionally lay across the path. At first Tyen stopped to help the women over them but Sezee, unencumbered by skirts, had no trouble negotiating most obstacles and stayed close to Veroo, offering the older woman a steady hand when needed. He settled on walking behind, the rear guard, ready to help if they asked for it.

The further they walked the more often they travelled uphill than down, and the steeper the path became. They crossed rough wooden bridges, first spanning narrow streams then the vertical sides of steadily deepening, vegetation-filled ravines. Whenever they crested a rise Orn slowed and searched the sky.

None of them spoke for a long time, until Sezee called out to Orn and asked if they could stop for a drink soon. He nodded, eventually halting before a rock face down which water trickled, fresh and cold. He offered them some strips of salted meat and in return Veroo produced some dense cakes made of nuts, grains and dried fruit bought before starting the sea crossing. Orn enjoyed these more than the women did the hard meat.

The forest slowly darkened as the last rays of the sun retreated from the treetops above. When the air grew chilly, they buttoned up their coats and drew gloves from the pockets. With the starlight obscured by trees, they were soon tripping over roots and rocks in the darkness. Orn stopped again.

"I know my way well enough," he said. "But you can't go on without a light." He looked at Tyen. "We've passed between two arms of the mountains, so they'd have to be above us to spot it, and we'd hear their propellers if they were that close."

Tyen nodded. He created a tiny flame and set it hovering just above the ground. Another flame appeared beside it and he looked up at Veroo. She shook her head then looked pointedly at Orn.

So he can use magic, Tyen thought. The man gave Veroo the same assessing look as Tyen was giving him, no doubt because Tyen had clearly assumed the flame was hers. She shrugged and a third flame appeared. Orn smiled and set off into the forest again.

Though Tyen suspected the rest of the journey was shorter, it did not feel like it. The chilly darkness pressed in on all sides. The constant rustle of leaves and wind far above was a constant reminder of the trees, which had become a looming presence now that they couldn't be seen. The forest seemed noisier, too, with deep, guttural growls to high-pitched shrieks and peeps echoing around them.

The path took ever tightening turns and grew ever steeper. He could hear the women's strained breathing over his own noisy panting, until all was obscured by the sound of gushing water. In front, Orn's flame began to rise in the air as he started to climb a flight of rough stone stairs. Sezee and Veroo stopped, breathing hard. When Tyen reached them they smiled and waved him on before them.

By the time the stairs ended Tyen's throat was raw from the breath rushing in and out of his lungs, and his legs were shaking. He stumbled to a halt as he saw that Orn was waiting for him, the air misting before his face the only indication that he was breathing faster than usual.

Then Tyen realised Orn was standing on the porch of a house built into a crack in a rock wall. Beneath the porch ran a stream, which plunged into a crack in the ground. The source of the sound of running water.

A woman and two younger men stood with Orn. Tyen could hear them speaking but only caught half of their words. Muffled by the cascade, footfalls behind him told him that Sezee and Veroo had arrived. His legs felt stronger, so he turned and offered them an arm each to sag against as they recovered from the ascent. Mist from their breath combined into a cloud as they mutely gathered their composure.

Sezee was the first to move, a little unsteady as she pushed forward. Veroo immediately followed. Tyen joined them as they approached Orn and the house. The Rymuan and his family stepped down from the platform to meet them.

"Welcome to my home," he said. "This is my wife, Ael, and my older sons, Onel and Onid." He introduced Tyen, Veroo and Sezee to his family.

The woman smiled. "Come inside. You'll be safe here. We'll see you rested and fed."

After the long walk, everything seemed to happen quickly and efficiently. Ael and one of the sons prepared them a meal. A small girl appeared briefly, gazing at Sezee shyly before she was shooed back to bed. When asked how they came to be chased by the Empire's sorcerers Tyen told them that he'd been set up by one of the Academy professors to take the blame for a theft. Sezee interjected that he'd have been caught if she and Veroo hadn't helped him escape.

"Why come south?" Onel asked.

"They're headed over the mountains, of course," Onid replied. "The only place the Empire hasn't conquered yet."

"Which is why you need the aircart repaired," Orn finished, smiling.

Tyen nodded. "Or we could make a new one."

"If all goes right, there'll be no need," Orn said. "I sent Ozel, to Kel," he explained to his family. "He and the boys should be able to move the cart somewhere safe and out of sight."

Sezee smiled. "Thank you so much for your help."

Tyen nodded. "I am in your debt twice over," he said, humbled by these people's generosity. "As Sezee said earlier, we can pay you. I have some remaining money, which I doubt will be legal currency in the south."

"There is no need t—" Orn looked at his wife, who had elbowed him in the ribs gently. He sighed and turned back to Tyen. "If you want, we'll put any coin you don't need to good use helping the local people put out of work or off their land by the Empire."

Tyen smiled. "I can think of no better use for it."

"Well, looks to me like you could all do with a good sleep," Ael decided. She rose and began arranging for the others to bring bedding into the front room of the house. Soon the family had disappeared into rooms deeper within their strange home, leaving their guests stretched out on mattresses on the floor.

Which were more comfortable than the aircart chassis, Tyen mused. But though tired, he lay awake, hearing Sezee's breathing deepen into the slow rhythm of sleep, then Veroo's.

Meeting Orn was another great stroke of luck, but would it be followed, as it had the last two times, by another setback?

As he drifted towards sleep it occurred to him that most of the good luck he'd had was really only meeting people who disliked the Empire enough to help him. Perhaps luck didn't come into it.

But if that was true, what would he do once he reached the Far South, where most people either didn't know of or had no reason to hate the Empire?

PART SIX

RIELLE

CHAPTER 17

For the first hour or so after admitting her crime, Rielle felt lighter and, strangest of all, *freer*.

She had been hiding something for as long as she could remember, and now she didn't have to. Since the day Narmah had realised her niece could see Stain – and Rielle had few memories from before then – she'd had to be careful. Now that she no longer needed to it was as though her limbs moved more easily, or the air was less resistant, or she had access to energy that had previously been spent keeping secrets.

She knew it would not last long, but it did not fade when she entered the temple or when Sa-Elem related her crime to the other priests. Nor did it go when he led her down into the passages below the building, guarded by a young priest. It only died when the gate of her cell clanged shut.

Sitting down on the cell's single piece of furniture – a plain wooden bench – she'd let the fear and guilt flood in and accepted it as deserved and inevitable.

All she could guess of her likely future was based on what she had seen others suffer. Yet she hadn't been subjected to torture with magic as her abductor had, probably because she hadn't resisted capture or tried to use magic. If she continued to co-operate, would they spare her the parade of shame through the city streets, as they took her away to who knew where?

Surely the priests would arrange a more private exit for the daughter of a wealthy merchant family. The great families would not want to draw attention to the possibility that richer members of society could be tainted.

But they might also use this opportunity to distance themselves from the Lazuli family, pointing out that dyers were artisans and therefore more likely to be drawn to magic. After all, dye was another form of stain.

It would ruin her family.

Or would it? Her parents had fought against the stigma of being dyeworks owners all their lives. Her father tolerated nothing but the most respectable behaviour from the workers. Her mother could be, as she knew all too well, ruthless in promoting their business. They would do all they could to salvage their reputation, and if that meant casting out Rielle, they would do that, too.

Though it hurt, Rielle hoped they would. She did not want her own mistakes to harm them or the people they hired. And if they blamed her, they wouldn't blame Izare.

They might anyway.

The sound of a door opening saved her from contemplating that. The guard priest closed his book and stood up as Sa-Gest walked into view, carrying a lamp. Rielle's stomach sank.

"I'm to relieve you," Sa-Gest said.

The guard nodded. He picked up his own lamp and left without glancing at Rielle. Sa-Gest's expression was blank until the door closed, then his face relaxed into a lazy smile.

Though her heart began to pound as he walked over to the gate she kept her face as still as possible, hoping that no fear showed and thankful that the cell was large enough that he couldn't reach through and touch her.

"Well, well," he murmured. "I've never had a woman go

to such extremes to avoid me before. It's actually rather flattering."

She stared back at him and said nothing. Chuckling at his own joke, he took hold of the bars. The memory of how deceptively strong those fingers were made her shudder. He grinned and shook the gate. Its rattling made her jump. He had magic. He could force his way through to her. He might even have the key.

But he wouldn't. The other priests wouldn't allow harm to come to a prisoner, even a tainted.

Sa-Gest smirked. "Just checking you're securely caged. Wouldn't want you escaping on my watch." He leaned closer. "Though if an opportunity comes, I might be persuaded to help you," he whispered. "In exchange for a few favours."

She kept her stare level and cool. He would not suggest such an exchange if he was free to assault her.

"On the other hand," he continued. "If you say anything about me approaching you and the favour I asked of you, I will ensure you, your family and your lover suffer all the humiliation and—"

A clunk and a voice calling his name covered his last words. He let go of the bars and stepped back, a flash of alarm crossing his face, then composed his expression and slowly turned to face whoever had interrupted him. It was the young priest who had been guarding her earlier. A frown of annoyance creased his forehead.

"Sa-Elem wants to speak to you at once."

Sa-Gest nodded. "Thank you."

With unhurried steps, he strode away. When Rielle heard the door close she drew in a deep breath and slowly let it out.

The guard examined her, eyes narrowed in suspicion or thought, then took the book he had been reading earlier out of his robes and resumed ignoring her.

She thought about Sa-Gest's offer and threat. *Well, that confirms it. He was working on his own, not trying to scare me into returning to my family.* She considered if this made it worse or better. She decided on worse. Nobody would believe her if she told them of his threat. At least imprisonment gave her some protection from him, and once she was gone from Fyre there was no point in him making Izare's life harder.

Izare. Even thinking of his name was like a stab through her chest, leaving an awful twisting ache. What did he think of her now? Had he believed her, or did he still think she had tried to abort a child? She longed to tell him everything, to make him understand why she had done what she'd done, and to tell him she was sorry.

Oh, Angels. Am I never going to see him again? The turmoil and pain were too much. She closed her eyes and willed herself to stop thinking and feeling. After a while she found that, if she imagined herself painting, she could stop her thoughts spinning and find a kind of fragile calm.

The sound of a door opening again jerked her out of it, however. She cursed silently, wondering who had come to torment or gloat now. When Sa-Elem walked into view her heart froze. The priest's gaze snapped to hers, and his mouth thinned into a disapproving line. Another, older priest accompanied him.

"Wait outside," he said to the guard, his eyes never leaving Rielle. The young priest closed his book and left.

Sa-Elem picked up the chair, carried it over to the gate of the cell and set it down, then indicated his companion should sit. The older man was carrying a book, pen and a small inkwell with a flat spike attached to the side. Settling on the chair, he opened the book and slipped the spike of the inkwell down into the spine.

Rielle could not help feeling a twinge of fascination.

410

How ingenious. I could use such an arrangement to paint outdoors with—

"Ais Rielle Lazuli," Sa-Elem began.

The sound of a pen scratching followed, as the other man began recording their conversation. So this was to be her interrogation.

"Yes, Sa-Elem," she replied.

"Earlier today you admitted to using magic."

The words sent a shock of cold and fear through her. She swallowed, finding her mouth suddenly dry. There was no point denying it. Sa-Gest and Izare had witnessed it. One might lie to save her, the other to ruin her.

"Yes," she croaked.

"How did you learn to use it? Speak slowly."

It was good finally to be able to tell the whole story. Everyone must know that her intentions, though foolish, had been good. So she described the old woman who had baited her when she stumbled upon Stain. Then she told how the inspections had spurred her to risk returning, in the hope that if she helped the priests find the corrupter the artisans might be left in peace. Sa-Elem listened silently as she described meeting the old woman again, the directions, the scarf seller who did not appear to know what she was a part of, and then how she had been ready to give up.

"But then she was there, behind me. I had nothing useful to tell you, and I feared that if I ran away she would know I'd tried to find her and use magic on me. So I played along and went into her cart."

"A cart?" Sa-Elem interrupted. "Tell me about this cart."

Rielle described it, the scribe priest writing quickly. "I can draw it, if you wish. I can draw the corrupter, too."

Sa-Elem looked at his companion, then down at the book. The scribe's eyebrows rose and he shook his head slightly.

411

"We will bring you paper later," Sa-Elem decided. "Tell us what transpired in the cart."

"I pretended to want a way to prevent conceiving, thinking that she would tell me how to do something before or after . . . it was needed. She asked if I was already pregnant and grabbed my stomach, and I . . . it was so quick. I felt pain and she told me she had cut something inside me." Rielle flinched as she remembered. "I would have to learn magic to fix it. So I . . ." Her throat stiffened, refusing to let her admit it.

"You did," Sa-Elem finished. "Because you wanted to undo what she had done."

"Yes." Rielle frowned. "Actually, no. At the time I was too afraid of her to refuse."

"Yet you did try to repair the damage later."

Rielle looked down. "Yes."

"Why?"

She sighed. "There were . . . so many reasons. It would have brought Izare and my family together and made them co-operate."

"And you wanted a child."

She looked up at him in surprise. "No."

"So you *did* want a way to avoid conception?"

She frowned. "Well, if there was a way to do it without using magic or making myself sick I would have tried it. It would make sense to wait until Izare and I had more money and were on good terms with my family before having children."

The other priest glanced up from his writing. "Did you succeed in undoing what she had done to you?"

Surprised by his sudden interest, she turned to look at him. "I don't know. I was trying to find out this morning. She said that looking inside myself didn't use magic."

"So it was accidental?" he asked after recording her answer.

"Yes."

"This morning was the third time you used magic," Sa-Elem pointed out.

She turned back to him and nodded.

"The garbage pit was the second, when you tried to heal yourself," he guessed.

She nodded again.

He drew in a deep breath, and let it out, his lips thinning as he exchanged a look with the scribe. Her spine tingled. Their looks suggested there was significance to this, and it wasn't good.

"Anything else?" he asked the man.

The scribe nodded and turned to Rielle. "For how long have you been able to see Stain?"

A shiver ran down her spine. Would the answer harm her family? Though seeing Stain wasn't a crime, families were supposed to report if a member had the ability. It was a law many ignored, however.

"Since I was a child," she told them.

"Can you be more precise?"

She bowed her head. "It was after the funeral procession of Sa-Imnu."

The scribe drew in a quick breath, and the two men exchanged another look. This time they looked more surprised than grim. The scribe looked down and resumed writing quickly, while Sa-Elem returned his attention to her.

"Have you used magic other than these three times?"

"No."

"Have you seen the corrupter since?"

"No."

"Did anybody other than the corrupter and yourself know you had learned magic?"

"No."

413

"Do you know anybody other than the corrupter who has used magic?"

"No."

"Did anybody other than yourself know you could see Stain?"

She winced. "My aunt." *Sorry, Narmah, but someone must have taught me not to react to it. Angels, please let her not be punished too severely.*

"Not your parents?" Sa-Elem asked.

"No."

His eyebrows rose in disbelief.

"Narmah felt the fewer who knew the better."

"Is there anything else you wish to tell us?"

She paused to consider. Only Sa-Gest's threats remained unspoken of.

"What will happen to me?" she asked.

"That hasn't been decided."

"But it's likely I'll be sent away."

"It is."

"Where?"

"We can't tell you that."

She nodded, then bowed her head.

"However, it will not be for some days," Sa-Elem warned. "If you need any . . . basic necessities for a woman, you may request them of your guard."

Rielle felt her face warm. To ask a man – a priest – to bring her such things would be humiliating. But she needed them and she'd rather ask the guard, or anyone else, than Sa-Gest.

At a signal from Sa-Elem, the scribe packed up his book and writing instruments and stood. Sa-Elem returned the chair to its former position. Rielle watched them leave, telling herself that they wouldn't believe her if she told them of Sa-Gest's threats. Though if there was no chance they would, why did he feel the need to threaten her?

414

What if they did believe her? She doubted priests were given harsh punishments. He'd still find a way to harm Izare and her family.

She hung her head. Without her around, Sa-Gest would have no reason to cause them trouble. It seemed the best thing she could do for Izare now was to go far, far away.

CHAPTER 18

Not all of the necessities Rielle requested were provided. At first she thought the list had been too long for the young priest to remember, but when further requests for bedding, soap and a change of clothes were ignored she understood that what they considered necessities did not match her own.

They did supply her with rags, water and a bucket that smelled faintly of the leavings of a previous user. She worked out how to keep herself clean and relieve herself without undressing, her back turned to the young guard and the older priest who took the day shift – Sa-Gest did not return. The narrow bench was her bed. Meals were a humble bowl of broth, bread, or stewed grains – probably the same fare priests ate during their times of isolation and prayer. She counted the days by the meals, as she suspected that the cycle of lying awake worrying followed by exhausted sleep she'd fallen into did not match the rising and setting of the sun.

Sa-Elem returned once, with his scribe, to give her paper and chalk to draw the corrupter and to ask a few more questions.

"When did you meet the corrupter?"

"The day Sa-Baro told my family I was visiting Izare," she told him.

"The day you left them," he observed, nodding. "Before or after?"

"Before."

She'd watched him turn to leave, her drawing in his hands, a thousand questions crowding behind her tongue. None she thought he would, or could, answer. But she had to try.

"Can you tell me anything?" she finally blurted out.

He looked back. "A few more days."

Another two quarterdays passed before he returned. A different priest accompanied him. The way they moved, all efficient and tense, suggested something was about to happen. Her heart began to race with a sickening anticipation.

"It's time for your examination," Sa-Elem said, confirming what her instincts had told her. "As always, those who were closest to you will be questioned, but due to your family's status and co-operation we have agreed to hold it in private."

The thought of being subjected to scrutiny before a crowd of strangers had made her stomach clench. Gratitude and relief did little to ease the nausea, however. She wanted her story and reasons to be known, and to see her family and Izare again, but the price for that was to face them. To feel their disappointment and anger. *But I would pay that price ten times over if it meant seeing Izare again.*

Sa-Elem unlocked the door and indicated that she should follow him. Her guard and the other priest walked close behind as they made their way through the passages beneath the temple. She felt all too conscious that she hadn't run a comb through her hair or changed her clothes in several days, and probably smelled like it. The journey did not take long. Sa-Elem stopped at a door and opened it, then ushered her inside.

Her first impression was that she was in another cell. A simple metal lattice stretching from floor to ceiling caged her into the corner of a large room, shaped and furnished in a way similar to the public hall of a small temple. Rows of wooden seats filled the main space, with an aisle between. In place of windows were rows of oil lamps, and where the priest ordinarily stood to address the gathering a long table and five chairs had been placed.

At the table sat three priests: the head priest of Fyre, Sa-Koml, Sa-Baro and a priest she had never seen before. The rest of the hall was empty. For now.

She hadn't realised it was possible to feel exposed and trapped at the same time.

"Stay away from the bars and remain silent unless addressed," Sa-Elem instructed, then closed the door.

She looked at the priests again. Sa-Baro had been watching her, but he looked away as she turned towards them. Sa-Koml's attention was on the papers before him. The stranger had also been watching her, but he turned away as Sa-Baro murmured something.

As he did, she saw that his face was marked on the left side by a scar, and she shivered as she realised she *had* seen him before. He'd been with Sa-Elem and Sa-Gest when her abductor had been paraded through and out of the city.

He will be the one taking me away, she guessed. He was the youngest one there, though many years senior to Sa-Gest. She could not help trying to read something of him from his face and manner. Would he be harsh, kind or indifferent towards her? His posture did not hold the tension of the other two, but then it was not a citizen of his city and a former student of his temple being judged. If dealing with tainted was his role he'd be used to attending examinations. She took comfort in his demeanour being neither menacing nor forbidding. Though if he were sympathetic she would feel unworthy of it. Indifference would be easiest to endure.

The sound of an opening door made her heart skip, but it was not the main doors. Sa-Elem and the scribe priest entered from a door at the other corner of the room. They joined the others

418

at the table and Sa-Elem, after speaking quietly, picked up a bell and rang it. All looked towards the far end of the room.

One of the large entry doors opened, admitting three people. Rielle felt her heart sink as her parents and Narmah took in the room, the five priests and the cage. It was hard to see their faces, and by the time they drew near enough for her to see them their expressions were composed. They stopped before the priests. Only Narmah's gaze shifted towards Rielle, though she kept her head facing the table.

"Ens Lazuli, Ers Lazuli and Ers Gabela," Sa-Elem began. "You have been summoned here to assist our examination of the circumstances surrounding the tainting of Ais Rielle Lazuli. We are not here to judge her. She has already admitted to the crimes of learning and using magic. Have you all read the transcript of our conversation?"

"Yes," they replied in unison. The scribe's pen made a single scratch on the page of his record book.

"Was there any part of it that you believe to be false?"

Rielle's father glanced at her mother and aunt, who shook their heads.

"No."

"So, Ers Gabela, you admit to knowing that Rielle could sense Stain from a young age, and that you concealed this fact?"

Narmah bowed her head. "I do."

"Why did you do so?"

"I . . . I knew her mother had plans for her to marry well. Her ability would have made that impossible."

"Not impossible," Sa-Elem corrected. "Only if it had been publicly known would it have influenced her prospects. That is why we conceal the identity of those who possess the ability."

Narmah looked up, her eyes wide with surprise and horror. "I didn't know."

"Your distrust and ignorance are unfortunate," he told her,

but his tone was mild. "Your fear of society's prejudices is understandable, and since your family has not sacrificed a son to the temple you do not have the benefit of his guidance. We have discussed this and decided that no malice was intended. The loss of a niece you were fond of is punishment enough."

Rielle winced. Sacrificing a son to the temple was a glorified way of saying a family member had chosen to become a priest, and since most priests were related to the city's great families, Sa-Elem had essentially pointed out her family's lesser status.

"She is leaving Fyre to live with her son."

Catching her breath, Rielle moved a little closer to the bars. Her mother's voice had been hard and cold. Narmah's expression was pinched, and her gaze lowered to the floor. Anger stirred within Rielle. By punishing Narmah, her parents suggested that they blamed her for Rielle's mistakes. *At least she gets to see cousin Ari.* Rielle's heart shrank a little. *Who I will never see again. Or my brother. What will they think when they hear—*

"Do you have any information to add to this examination?" Sa-Elem asked.

Rielle's parents exchanged a glance then shook their heads, but Narmah's chest rose as she took a deep breath.

"We were going to meet with her," she said. "She wanted to come home. She knew we were willing to consider her choice of husband."

"I know," Sa-Elem told her. "Sa-Baro was assisting you," he reminded her.

She shook her head. "Something must have forced her to do it. Why else would she risk everything?"

A short silence followed, in which Sa-Elem regarded her without speaking, perhaps only so she felt she had been listened to. Then he looked at his fellow priests, who shook their heads.

"That will be all," he said, turning back.

As her family turned to leave, Rielle's stomach sank. Narmah paused and looked back at her niece, her expression open and anxious. Then she jerked away. Rielle saw her mother's hand on Narmah's arm, guiding and pulling. She watched her family walk away and disappear somewhere beyond the hall's main doors.

The bell rang again. Rielle watched, holding her breath, but the three who entered next were dye workers. People she had known all her life. People whose children she had played with when she was young. Unlike her family, they stared at her, showing curiosity, disgust and even fear. Sa-Elem asked if they had suspected anything. They replied that they had not.

Her heart beat quickly as she watched them leave. Three more people answered the next ring of the bell. She felt a shock as she recognised them.

As Tareme, Bayla and Famire walked to the front of the hall they stared openly at Rielle, but their expressions were not what she expected. Tareme's mouth opened in shock as she saw Rielle and Bayla's eyes widened. Famire wore a haughty smile, but as Rielle stared back at her, the girl's smirk looked forced and unconvincing.

Sa-Elem's introduction and questions were the same. Tareme and Bayla responded honestly. Famire agreed that she had never suspected Rielle of having the ability to sense Stain, but said she later came to wonder if she could. When Sa-Elem asked her to elaborate, she looked at the other girls pointedly. The priest sent the twins away.

Once alone, Famire sighed. "I heard that Stain had been found near the courtyard where Aos Saffre lived. I was curious. It had been years since I'd seen any, and I wanted to know if I still could. Of course, it would have been rude not to drop in on my old friend Rielle. As you know, it was while I was there that I sensed the Stain in their house."

A shot of cold pierced Rielle's body. *She can see Stain!* But it was followed by anger. Not at Famire's admission that she had reported the Stain in Izare's house. It was the lie that she'd visited them out of social obligation and friendship. *She hasn't told them she was there for a portrait.*

Rielle opened her mouth. The need to speak the truth welled up like an irresistible force inside her.

But if I tell them, what will happen to Izare? He would lose the commission. She closed her mouth. *I doubt Famire will return for him to finish her portrait anyway. She can't afford to be seen with someone known to be so close to a tainted, especially if she can see Stain.* She drew in a breath to speak then stopped again. *But as long as nobody knows about the portrait she won't dare ask Izare to give back the first half of the commission.*

She let out a sigh. Famire's lie would at least protect Izare. *And the truth will do me no good.*

Rielle barely heard the rest of Sa-Elem's questions or Famire's replies. First Sa-Gest's threat, then Famire's true purpose for visiting Izare: how many more facts would she have to conceal that she'd rather were known? So much for being free from the burden of secrets.

A bell rang out and she jumped. Looking between the bars of her cage, she saw that Famire had left and another three people were entering the room. At once her gaze fixed on the central figure. Even at a distance, with low lighting, she knew him. His walk, though not his usual relaxed stride, was so familiar.

His head turned towards her and did not move away. She saw his lips move. The person to his left hooked fingers around his arm. The one to his right placed a hand on his shoulder. Somehow she registered that the first was Jonare and the second Errek, but she could not tear her eyes from Izare.

A longing filled her. *I must be mad. I'm about to be sent to prison but all I can think of is what it would be like to touch him again.* To feel the warmth of his skin against hers. To hear his voice. To see his smile.

Izare continued staring at her until he stopped before the priests, then he turned to regard them. She could not tear her eyes away from him. She waited for Sa-Elem to repeat his introduction, but different words echoed around the hall.

"Move away from the bars, Ais Lazuli."

She blinked and registered cold metal against her palms. Looking down, she realised she was gripping the bars, her face pressed into a gap between them. With an effort, she let go and stepped backwards.

Perhaps it would be better if I don't look at Izare. She backed up to the wall and set her gaze on the floor.

Sa-Elem returned to the routine. Hearing Izare reply that he had read the transcript of her conversation with Sa-Elem sent a flood of gratitude through her. *He knows why I did it. He knows I didn't try to kill a child of his.* To hear him say he did not believe anything she'd said to be false was like food after a long fast, or a cool breeze in summer. She smiled, barely listening as Sa-Elem continued, until a different question disrupted the previous sequence.

"Aos Saffre, did you persuade Rielle to use magic to fix the damage done to her by the corrupter so that she could carry a child?"

Breath caught in Rielle's throat. She looked at Izare. He was glaring at Sa-Elem. Jonare and Errek looked equally shocked.

Hasn't Izare confirmed everything I said was true?

She expected an angry denial, but Izare's expression softened and his voice was quiet when he spoke.

"No. And I'd have told her not to, if I had known. If she had t . . ."

A shiver ran down her spine. She could hear his voice in her mind as she finished the sentence for him.

If she had told me.

Why hadn't she? She loved him. Why hadn't she trusted him?

It was too terrible. What I'd done. What it meant for our future. He would have rejected me. And she would have deserved it. She had never longed to share the burden of her mistake with him. Surely, of all people, he would have been the one to tell, but she had never even considered it. Why not?

Because I don't love him enough to risk everything for him.

She heard a name spoken that roused her out of her thoughts. Looking up again, she saw Izare's mouth twist in contempt.

"Famire lied," he said. "She was there to have her portrait done. I can show it to you, if you want proof."

Rielle felt sick. Did he think it worth losing the commission for the sake of punishing Famire? *I'm not worth it,* she wanted to call out to him. *Don't sacrifice yourself for me.*

"I do," Sa-Elem replied. He looked at Sa-Baro, who was frowning. "Bring it to the temple at the first opportunity."

Somewhere in the back of Rielle's mind something clicked into place. Of course they would want to know if Famire had lied to them. Lying was a worrying habit in someone able to see Stain.

Sa-Elem let out a heavy sigh. "Do either of you have any information to add to this examination?"

Errek shook his head. Izare looked over at Rielle and her heart stopped. *If I don't love him, then why do I feel like this?*

"No," he replied.

"I . . ." Jonare began. Izare looked at her and frowned.

"Yes?" said Sa-Elem.

The woman grimaced. "Rielle told me something a few quarterdays ago. She said someone was blackmailing her."

Rielle caught her breath. It hadn't occurred to her that

Jonare might tell them of Sa-Gest's threat. After all, she had advised Rielle not to tell Izare in case he did something foolish. Surely she would not risk more trouble for her friend for the sake of his tainted ex-lover?

"Did she say who?" Sa-Elem asked.

Jonare frowned. She looked at Rielle, then back at the priests. Rielle could not breathe. If Sa-Gest was named and punished he would think Rielle had told them.

"No," Jonare lied. "She never said who it was."

"The corrupter?"

"No, it was a man. Someone powerful."

"Someone from her family, perhaps?"

Jonare shrugged. "We did consider it might be an attempt by her family to scare her into leaving Izare and return to her parents." She grimaced. "I advised her not to tell anyone. I wish I hadn't now."

Izare was scowling at Jonare. She glanced at him, her expression guilty. "I'm sorry. It seemed wiser at the time that you did not know."

Sa-Elem drummed his fingers on the table, then nodded. "If there is nothing else, you may go."

She ought to have been relieved, but Rielle felt empty as she watched the trio leaving. Every step Izare took towards the far door was one closer to her last sight of him. Something in her chest tightened painfully and she knew she could not let this last opportunity slip through her hands. The priests would tell her to be silent, so she would have to be quick.

"Izare!" she called. He froze midstep. "Izare, I am sorry! I—"

"SILENCE!" Sa-Koml bellowed over her last few words, but Izare had heard. He turned and looked back at her but it was too dim in the back of the hall for her to see his expression. She caught a movement in the edge of her vision, in the direction of the priests. Errek took hold of Izare's arm.

425

Abruptly turning away, Izare strode towards the doors and out of sight.

When the door closed, silence filled the room. Turning to the priests, she found that Sa-Elem was watching her. Sa-Koml was scowling but the scarred priest looked, if anything, a little bored. Sa-Elem glanced at the scribe, then turned to his companions.

"I wish it to be recorded that I believe Izare's shock on discovering Rielle had used magic was genuine. I regard her story as likely to be true, though I suspect omissions."

The scarred priest hummed. "It often appears there is more going on. Sometimes there is a deliberate attempt to mislead or distract."

Sa-Koml shrugged. "It does not matter. Ais Lazuli has admitted to stealing from the Angels three times. At first unwillingly and later unintentionally, but once deliberately."

"The punishment for all instances is imprisonment at the Mountain Temple, but the latter requires she also be made an example of by a public expulsion from the city," Sa-Elem reminded him.

Sa-Koml nodded, his expression grim. "We allowed the family a private examination, but we cannot stretch the law any further."

A shock went through Rielle. It left her weak and shaking. She grabbed at the bars to steady herself as a memory of the tainted, covered in rags, rose to block all vision of her surrounds. She heard the sound of the crowd, saw the missiles flying . . .

Hands gripped her upper arms. Her knees bent and she heard a grunt behind her as someone took her weight. Dragging in a breath, she managed to get her legs to support her again, then let whoever was holding her guide her out of the cage.

In the passage, she sagged again. Sa-Elem's voice boomed in the passageway but she could not make out what he said. There was someone on either side, supporting and guiding her through the dim, cold ways. Doors opened and closed. Hinges creaked. She was lowered onto a hard surface. A lock clicked. Footsteps faded away.

Eventually she recovered enough for one word to creep into her thoughts.

When?

How long would it be before she was paraded through the city? How long before she was taken from everything and everyone she'd ever known? The question repeated in her mind until she heard the door open. Looking up, she saw that the guard had been there all along. Now Sa-Baro stood beside him. The guard left and the old priest turned to regard her.

He wrung his hands as he approached her, his eyebrows knitting together.

"Rielle," he said. "Ais Lazuli. I am so sorry. I know now the terrible timing of my actions. If I hadn't spoken to your parents when I did you might have trusted me enough to reveal what had happened to you. You might not have run away from your family."

His apology sent a bitter anger through her. Rising, she came closer to the gate, but not so close he might think she would try to escape. "So you get to ask for forgiveness, but I don't."

He grimaced. "It's always better not to expose family and friends to—"

"Tell me one thing," she interrupted. "When do I leave?"

He winced. "Ah. I don't know exactly."

It was a lie. She could tell from the way he avoided her gaze. Perhaps he had been warned not to tell her. Perhaps they feared she would try to escape if she knew. To use magic. After all, what did she have to lose now? Her soul? It was already condemned.

"Sa-Baro?" another voice said.

The priest turned and she saw that the scarred one had entered the room. Sa-Baro nodded and retreated from the gate. He started for the exit, but as he passed the scarred priest he stopped.

"Sa-Mica," he said quietly. "Keep a close eye on Sa-Gest."

The scarred priest nodded. "I will."

"You know . . .?"

"Yes. Rest assured, the Mountain Temple is the only appropriate place for men like him, isolated from the innocents he would harm here."

Rielle staggered back, recoiling as if struck by the words. *Sa-Gest is coming with us. Sa-Gest will be working at the prison.* She could not breathe. She fell back onto the bench.

Then she realised what this meant. Sa-Gest would not be in Fyre. Surely he could not cause trouble for Izare and her family from afar. A mad hope filled her. Once he had left Fyre she would be free to speak of Sa-Gest's threats.

Except that he could always return to Fyre, or make arrangements from afar. So long as he was alive, he was a danger. At least she could ensure he was only a danger to her.

"What is wrong?"

She looked up. Sa-Mica stood at the gate, his dark eyes narrowed with suspicion.

Taking a deep breath, she gathered what control she could and laughed bitterly.

"What isn't?

"It was something Sa-Baro said, wasn't it? He's gone now. You may speak."

She looked away so that he would not see her anger. *So I can talk now, can I? Well, too bad. You'll get nothing out of me. After all, I've been told to be quiet, not to complain or criticise, to stay silent all my life. I've had plenty of practice at it.* It was a pathetic kind of resistance, but it was all she had.

When her refusal to answer outlasted his patience, he sighed.

"There is more to this. Don't think that I will not discover it."

She ignored him, and remained immobile until he left.

CHAPTER 19

The most Rielle managed that night was a fitful doze. Every time she raised her head to look, the young priest was still reading his book. The only gauge she had for the passing of time was how far through it he'd read. It was a large book, but she had no idea how fast he was reading, or if he skipped sections when she wasn't watching. He had been near the start when she'd lain down to sleep. When she roused herself and found he was reaching the end she began to anticipate the day. Then she wished she hadn't thought to note his progress, as she spent the next unknown measure of time fully awake and expecting the door to open at any moment.

When it did, she wished that it hadn't.

The guard snapped his book shut and stood, turning to face the visitor. Rielle's heart began to race as Sa-Elem entered. She swung her legs off the bench and sat up. The scarred priest from the day before followed Sa-Elem. He approached her, his face set and grim, and pushed a bundle of fabric through the bars of the gate.

"Remove your clothes and shoes and put this on."

She took it. As it unfurled in her hands she felt a wave of nausea. It was a long tube of fabric – little more than a sack – with holes cut in the sides and top. The edges were unfinished. A memory rose of her abductor dressed in ragged, dirty trousers,

429

filthy from the rotten food and muck thrown at him. Her stomach twisted.

There would be no more waiting. They were taking her from Fyre today.

At least I'll be covered from the shoulders down, she thought. She looked at the priests nervously. Surely they weren't going to watch her dress. They exchanged a glance, then turned their backs. She breathed a sigh of relief.

She changed quickly, hoping they wouldn't notice that she'd kept her undergarments on. The rough sacking only came to her knees and her arms were bare. She'd never felt so exposed while still wearing clothing. Shivering, she replaced her scarf and turned around.

"I'm done," she murmured.

They turned to face her. Sa-Elem unlocked the gate and handed her a pair of sandals. They comprised simple hide soles with rope straps. She slipped them on and tied them. Sa-Elem beckoned, and as she stepped out of the cell he pulled off her scarf. She opened her mouth to object but was shocked into silence as he lifted a blade. Before she could shy away he stepped behind her, grasped her hair in one hand and pulled firmly. She felt the pressure and heard the shush of the blade slicing through hair, then her head was free to move again.

A familiar weight was gone. She saw it held within Sa-Elem's hands, glossy, black and straight, before he dropped it into a wooden bowl held by the guard. Her throat closed at the loss. Then she heard a metallic rattle and a shiver ran down her spine.

Sa-Mica stepped forward holding heavy chains.

She swallowed hard. "I am co-operating," she forced out. "I won't try to run. Are those truly necessary?"

"They are to convince others that you are no danger to them," he told her.

She stared at the chains, feeling sick. The priests paused, then Sa-Elem took her arm and lifted it. A loop went around her left wrist and was fastened with a lock. Another encircled the right, then Sa-Mica bent to do the same with her ankles. The two chains were linked by a third. Finally, the cold weight of metal settled around her neck, the length of "lead" draping against her spine. She shivered violently.

"Keep the leg chain off the ground and you'll be less likely to trip," the scarred priest recommended in a neutral tone, as if he was teaching her nothing more alarming than how to dance in a long skirt.

Looking down, she found it too easy to picture how pathetic she looked. Like the abductor . . . but not exactly. He'd had his hands bound behind his back. Was this some strange sort of kindness, or had they made a mistake?

What did it matter? The end result would be humiliating either way.

The two priests exchanged a look. Sa-Mica nodded, then started towards the door. Sa-Elem placed a hand on her shoulder, gently pushing to indicate that she should follow. Lifting her hands so that the connecting chain to her legs rose from the floor, Rielle stepped forward.

It was easier to walk than she'd expected. Her abductor had shuffled awkwardly, his steps shortened. She couldn't have made a full stride, and certainly not run, but she was able to walk without trouble. Sa-Mica led her through the door and along the underground passages. All too soon they reached the stairs to the building above. These took a little deliberate co-ordination of the chains to ascend. The priests did not hurry her.

At the top she entered the splendour of the temple. A fresh, familiar scent filled her nose. First they entered a short passage, then passed through a carved door into the main hall. It was, thankfully, empty but for a few priests with mops and buckets. A sloshing behind her told her they had resumed cleaning the floor. They chanted as they worked. Something about cleansing the taint from the temple. *How appropriate*, she mused.

Sa-Mica set a stately pace as he led the way down towards the main doors. The chanting did not fade as they walked. Were the priests following? She resisted the urge to look back until Sa-Mica slowed to meet more priests standing at the main doors. When she did, it was like a blow to her gut. They *were* following her. They were sweeping their mops over where she had walked. It was *her* taint they were washing away.

Before she could stop herself, she looked up at the huge painting covering the back of the hall. Her gaze snapped to the Angel punishing the tainted and something inside her shrivelled, but she could not look away. What was it going to feel like to have her soul shredded to nothing?

The sound of the door opening jolted her into motion. Tearing her eyes away, Rielle forced herself to turn and face whatever waited outside, telling herself that it could not be as bad as her final moments would be. Sunlight streamed into the hall, dazzling her. As it had so often before, when she and the temple girls had left after their lessons. As it had the day she'd been abducted by the tainted.

Sa-Koml's voice boomed from somewhere close by as he announced her crime and called on the Angels and citizens of Fyre to cast her out. As her eyes adjusted, she saw a crowd watching. That didn't surprise her, but it was a smaller crowd than she had expected considering how large the one that had followed the abductor had been. How long ago had they heard that a tainted was to be driven from the city? Surely not long. But news spread fast and would soon bring more hecklers.

The people who stared at her looked more curious than

angry, but as they took in her appearance she saw ugly scowls appear, and a chilling kind of glee. She saw herself in their eyes: chained, shorn, partially dressed in rags. Reduced to a shameful sight so that they might imagine they were safe. A reminder of what would happen to them, should they be tempted to steal from the Angels.

To one side was a small cart and as she saw who stood behind it she shuddered. Sa-Gest's expression was sober, but his eyes glinted with expectation. She looked away, reminding herself that so long as he was far from Fyre her family and Izare were safe.

From somewhere Sa-Elem produced a bell and swung it. The sound echoed in the hall behind her and spilled out into the courtyard.

"Go," he said.

Glancing at him, she found him watching her expectantly. The abductor had walked before the priests, she remembered. So must she.

That means I can set the pace, she realised. *Well, then. Let's get this over with.*

Hoisting the chain, she started down the stairs. As she hoped, the crowd shrank back, allowing her through. Without hesitating, she strode forward. People tripped over themselves in their haste to get away. She saw malicious glee turn to fear.

Something flew past her head. She flinched from it, too late to have avoided it if the thrower's aim had been better. Catching an oncoming object in the corner of her eye, she threw up her hands to block it. But the chains pulled her arms up short and something soft and wet smacked into her forehead. The smell of rotten fruit turned her stomach as liquid spilled down her face. She shook the drops off before they could drip into her eyes.

Cheers burst from the crowd, then more missiles. She paused, crouching, her arms raised in self-defence, and felt a patter against her back and shoulders, some strikes harder than others. When the attack slowed she straightened again and forced herself onward. A moving target was harder to hit. It would be impossible to avoid all of the missiles, but perhaps if she kept an eye out for anything coming straight at her she could protect her face in time.

The crowd seemed to surround her completely and she realised she had become disorientated. Looking back, she noted the priests walking behind her, Sa-Elem holding the end of the chain and Sa-Gest pushing the cart. A quick, careful search of the buildings ahead told her where Temple Road began and she headed towards it.

She realised then that she could not set the pace. If she walked too quickly more was thrown at her. At most she could manage a steady walk. The crowd grew bigger and nastier. Not long after she had started down Temple Road something solid hit her shoulder and she yelped with pain.

A voice boomed out behind her.

"NO STONES," Sa-Elem ordered.

She took a few steps before any more missiles flew towards her. Those that did exploded a handspan from her body as if hitting an invisible wall. *Magic!* She shivered and resisted the urge to look behind. Stain would be radiating outwards from a priest like an Angel's halo. She didn't need a reminder of either. After several steps the missiles began to strike her again, and the crowd cheered in response.

The same had happened when the abductor had been driven out of the city. A conversation rose from her memory:

"Why don't they protect him the whole time?" she had asked Izare.

"They must keep the crowd happy."

She looked at the buildings but if she was near the place they had watched from she couldn't tell. The crowd lined the streets. People stood in doorways to get a better view. Others hung out of windows. Was Izare among them? She searched the faces, realising that she had been looking for him ever since she'd left the temple.

Would he come out to watch? Or would he hide away, afraid that people would turn on him for harbouring her? Something trickled out of her hair into her eyes and she wiped it away. She had hoped at first that he would come to see her one last time, but now she hoped he wouldn't. Something inside her shrank at the thought of him seeing her with her hair cut off and bound with chains.

Would he visit her in prison? Would her parents? Was it allowed? She had no idea how far away the Mountain Temple was. She'd never heard of it before the examination. Nobody knew where the tainted were taken. Nobody except the priests, that is.

Four more times she was stung by hard objects. She learned to take advantage of the brief respite that came after to lengthen her stride and cover more ground, though the rope straps of the sandals began to chafe her feet and the weight of the chains made her shoulders ache.

It was during one of these rare moments of protection that she reached a section of Temple Road where the crowd had thinned out on the left. A few steps later there was nobody linking the street on that side and she saw why.

The wall of the dyeworks stretched before her. Words had been painted across its surface. She froze in horror.

TAINTED FILTH.

Something hard hit her forehead and her sight went dark. She clasped a hand to her head and swayed but managed to keep her feet. She would have a lump there later. There was a lump in her throat, too, though she could not remember a stone striking it. The pain was making her eyes water.

"It's not their fault," she said aloud, though nobody could hear. *No, it's mine.* After all the years of hard work her family had put into establishing the dyeworks as the best in Fyre, she had ruined it with one stupid, foolish mistake.

The missiles had stopped. She forced open her eyes and looked around. Nobody had emerged from the dyeworks. The front door, usually open to welcome customers, was firmly shut. She dragged in a breath and let it out, then forced herself to start walking again.

They will rebuild, she told herself. They would wait until it was safe then paint over the words. If necessary, they would do it over and over again. After all, they made paint. They had plenty of it. They would also publicly disown her. They probably already had. They had to, if they were to survive this.

Her parents would not be visiting her in prison.

Her feet and her head ached, and everything between. At least it would be over soon. It wasn't far from the dyeworks to the edge of the city. She quickened her pace, ignoring the missiles that added to the muck covering her. Temple Road took a sharp left turn and began to slope upwards. Ahead she could see North Bridge and beyond that the pink- and blue-tinged sand of the desert. The crowd was suddenly determined to use every last rotting vegetable and fruit and fistful of muck it had gathered, but as her feet finally met the wooden surface of the bridge the rain of missiles abruptly stopped. She paused then and turned to look behind her. The priests scowled at her, but she ignored them.

Fyre, her home, lay before her. She had always wanted to leave, though only to accompany her brother or cousin on one of their business trips, and never permanently. Now she would not see it again. The crowd watched her, jeering and making rude signs. She turned away and started across the bridge.

It was empty of traffic. Warned about her approach, people waited on the other side. She could hear the priests' footsteps and the creak and trundle of the cart behind her. Nobody called out to her to stop as she stepped off the bridge, so she continued on down the desert road. It stretched straight towards the horizon, disappearing into the glare and dust long before reaching it. It, too, was empty. Most traffic across the bridge came from the houses that lined the other side of the river, or from towns up- and downstream.

The road edges were marked by two rows of stones. The surface was paved, but further away the sands covered it in places. That would probably be easier on her feet, though it would make the sandals chafe even more.

The sounds of the city faded and a quietness settled around Rielle. The sun's heat radiated from the sand, drying the muck on her. She felt sticky and sore, and was already thirsty, but she did not stop. She found herself listening for the sound of the priests' breathing and the squeak of the cart, just to know they were still behind her. Finally, after several long minutes, a voice spoke.

"Stop, Rielle."

Obeying, she turned to see that the city was now a low shadow behind the priests. Sa-Mica had spoken her name. The priests closed the distance between them and her. Sa-Gest's face was slick with sweat from the effort of pushing the cart, she noted. Priests did not abuse the right to use magic given them by the Angels. She felt a small satisfaction at that.

Sa-Elem came forward and removed all the chains but the loop around her neck. He said nothing. Sa-Mica removed a metal basin from the cart and set it down on the ground, then lifted a large, round-bellied pot and, uncorking it, poured water into the basin. She caught the same faint scent used by the priests when cleaning the temple. Sa-Mica set a bundle down next to the basin.

"Wash and change," he ordered.

Once again, he and Sa-Elem turned their backs. Sa-Gest

followed suit. Glancing around, she confirmed that there was nobody else on the road, or in the sands on either side. As quickly as she could, she tore off the rag shift, knelt and washed herself down. The bundle was a simple tunic, skirt and scarf made from undyed cloth. She dressed, threading the chain through the neck of the tunic, then, bending over, tipped the last of the water over her hair. There was not enough water to clean away all the muck, but it would have to do. Perhaps later she could use sand to scrub away any lingering filth. At least the scarf concealed her tangled, greasy hair.

Sa-Mica seemed to know when she rose to her feet. He turned and handed her a pack. Behind him, Sa-Gest was shrugging into one as well. The weight that settled onto her shoulders didn't seem too great, though they ached from carrying the chains. She could feel water sloshing in a container within the pack.

Sa-Mica had returned the basin to the cart, but ignored the rag shift. He nodded to Sa-Elem.

"It is done."

Sa-Elem nodded. "Safe journeying, Sa-Mica." He turned to Sa-Gest. "I hope you find the Mountain suits you, Sa-Gest." Then without even glancing at Rielle, he turned and strode back towards Fyre.

The scarred priest moved to stand in front of Rielle.

"We have a day's ration of water each. If you run you might escape us, since it is very easy to lose someone in the dunes. Should you return to Fyre they will know you by the chain. If you head in any other direction you will soon die of thirst. With no water, no amount of magic will save you in the desert."

Then he gestured to the road. "Walk," he ordered.

She knew from the countless stories of desert survival from her brother that he spoke the truth. Turning around to face the desert, she set her gaze on the dust-obscured horizon and began to walk.

PART SEVEN

TYEN

CHAPTER 20

Tyen gripped the wheel of the aircart tightly. Neither Veroo nor Sezee had spoken for a long time, their chatter dying away the first time the capsule had come close to colliding with one of the snow-wrapped peaks. He had lost count of the moments they'd nearly encountered some feature of the high mountains over . . . what must be several hours now.

It must look as if his driving skills were lacking to anyone who had never tried to steer an aircart. Steering was not a precise art, not even on a calm day. The propellers and rudder provided a limited amount of control, but their efficacy depended on the wind. Flying with the wind was easiest. Flying into it was a matter of power against the wind's force. Flying side-on to the wind made arriving at a particular destination a matter of compensation and guesswork.

When the wind was prone to change direction constantly it was like guiding a drunken man through a dense forest. Tyen might steer a little more to the right to allow for a wind in that direction then find he was now being buffeted from the left. Magic was often needed to nudge or push the cart away from obstacles. Unfortunately, Veroo had too little experience to predict where and when such assistance might be needed. Only Tyen could feel the effects of a wind shift and know if non-magical steering would be enough.

The temptation to pump the capsule full of more air so that they could rise higher was strong, but he dared not try it. If they passed out in the thinner air the capsule would rapidly cool and the cart descend, and he might not wake in time to stop it plunging into the icy heights.

A ridge now blocked their path, sharp and jagged like the side of a knife turned to face them. He steered towards the lowest point, then, as the nose of the cart was blown left, he turned the wheel to the right to compensate.

"More heat," he said.

That, at least, was one task he had been able to give Veroo. His stomach swooped a little as the cart began to rise. He watched the ridge draw closer, trying to judge if he was approaching too quickly for them to ascend in time. He'd knocked snow off such obstacles before to gain more clearance, but the top of the vertical face ahead was too narrow and steep to hold any. Using magic to push left and right was easier than moving the entire cart upward.

The top of the ridge bore down on them. It looked about the height of the cart's nose, then at a hundred paces or so away it seemed about the level of the chassis' base. The wind shifted to come from behind them, speeding their approach. There would be no steering away now. He created a shield under the chassis and moulded it close to allow them as much clearance as possible. It would protect the cart, but bouncing off the rocks could still do damage, to the cart and its occupants.

A sudden gust of wind pushed them to the right and Tyen cursed. The cart wobbled as he span the wheel to the left. A vibration went through the cart as the rocks passed beneath it, dragging along his shield and slowing them down. He held his breath.

And then they were over the ridge. Tyen let out a sigh of

relief and behind him heard Sezee and Veroo do the same. He turned to grin at the two women, and they smiled back.

Turning back, he realised that, for the first time since they'd left in the early hours of the morning, no high peaks stood in their way.

"We've made it," he said. "We're on the other side of the range."

The arms of a valley widened before them. The further they reached, the gentler and smoother they were, eventually shrinking to a flat plain. Threads of reflected light converged to form a river meandering below. It was tempting to follow the valley, but, from what Vella had recorded of Gowel's map of the south, Spirecastle was built into an outcrop of a cliff somewhere to the west of where the adventurer had crossed the mountains. If they had crossed near to where Gowel had, they need only follow the line of the range and they would reach it. It was there that Veroo would most likely find a source of magical training.

"You've been driving for hours. Would you like me to take over?"

He turned to see Veroo standing behind him and nodded. The driving from here should be easy, and it would be good to consult Vella again before they encountered any of the southerners. He'd had no chance to talk to her for days. Orn's younger children had been relentlessly curious about everything he and the women possessed. He'd caught them trying to get into his satchel several times after he had, perhaps unwisely, taken Beetle out of it to show them. Though they had left it alone after the insectoid had stung one of them, Tyen decided it was better Vella stay safely out of sight.

Once out of the seat, he helped Veroo take his place, freeing her skirt when it caught on a protruding bolt. She looked down, unperturbed by the view below her boots.

"Where should I head towards?" she asked.

"Follow the mountains."

"Keep this high?"

"A little lower if you like, but well out of the range of arrows," he said. "I don't know if all the locals are friendly."

Which was another reason to head for Spirecastle. It was one place in the Far South Tyen knew of where people from the north would receive a friendly welcome, thanks to Gowel's previous visit. He started for his favourite reading position, back against the rear struts. Sezee was sitting within the netted section; she smiled as he stepped over her but said nothing.

Taking Vella out of his satchel, he straddled the chassis, leaned back on the rear struts and opened her cover.

Hello, Tyen. I see much has happened since we last spoke.

Yes. He thought back to the last time he'd communicated with her. *We were chased and attacked by Academy sorcerers, but made it to shore.*

Where you landed the aircart in a tree. Sezee found me, remember?

Ah, that's right. He felt a twinge of curiosity. *Did you read much from her mind?*

Yes.

I shouldn't pry, but . . . is there anything important I need to know about them? Some secret that could prevent me making the south my home? Such as . . . Veroo is an Academy spy or Sezee plans to rob me?

Veroo is no spy, at least as far as Sezee knows. The women pose no danger to you. Sezee is, however, in love with you.

He stared at the words, reading them again, then once more. Before he could stop himself, he looked up at Sezee. Sensing his gaze, she glanced up but he quickly looked down again before he was forced to meet her eyes.

For how long?

It is hard to pinpoint the beginning of affection. She realised it for herself when you brought down the aircart and stole it, but she liked the look of you since she first saw you.

An odd mix of gratification and disbelief replaced his surprise. This self-assured, good-looking woman liked the look of *him*? And more. She was *in love* with him? Surely it couldn't be so.

But if Vella says so, he thought, *it must be true*.

An urge to look up at Sezee rose again, but he resisted it. Schooling his expression in case she was watching, he closed Vella, slipped her in his pocket and looked towards the mountains, hoping he appeared lost in mundane thoughts.

So Sezee loves me. It was a not unpleasant surprise. She was a bold, admirable woman. Attractive, too. Once he would only have considered another Leratian woman a suitable romantic partner, but now that seemed ridiculous – another stuffy Leratian attitude that he'd not questioned until recently. Compared to all the women he'd met in his short life, Sezee was warm and approachable, smart and interesting. But, then, he'd never had the chance to know Leratian women as well as he had come to know Sezee. Perhaps given the chance, he'd have found someone who was as good company. But that chance would not come now – and he didn't care that it wouldn't. He would be proud to have Sezee as his wife.

And yet, even as he thought that, he knew something was missing.

"Good company", "approachable" and "interesting" got nowhere near the words he'd heard other men use to describe the women they were infatuated with. Words like "fascinating", "adorable" and "enchanting". While he liked and admired her a great deal, his feelings towards her were not strong enough to be described as true, passionate love.

He considered the weight of Vella in his pocket. He'd put her there partly to be alone with his thoughts, partly to shield her from them – as if he feared she would be jealous, even though he knew she could not feel any such emotion.

I promised I would search for a way to free her, he remembered.

How can I put all my efforts into fulfilling that promise and at the same time give a wife the attention she deserves? He would feel a little as if he was being disloyal. To both of them.

Abruptly, Miko's words flashed out of his memory. *"It's like she's your girl. Like you're in love with her. With a book. Mad."*

Was he in love with Vella? He paused, searching for the emotions he found lacking when he thought of Sezee. Something stirred. Not passion. Something more like loyalty. And protectiveness. He cared about her. He wanted to help her.

And, strange as it may be, he thought, *I really want to meet her. I don't think that I am in love with her but . . . I want the possibility of it.*

He drew in a deep breath, let it out again and felt acceptance settle within him. He did not love Sezee. Neither did he love Vella, at least not in the usual sense, but he was dedicated to protecting her and seeking a way to free her. Knowing that she would see this when he touched her, he took her out of his pocket and opened her cover again.

Are you sure, Tyen? Love could grow from what you feel for her. You may be throwing away a chance of happiness for the sake of an ancient object occupied by an incomplete person.

I am sure.

If you change your mind it will not hurt me. What you seek to do may be impossible.

I know. But I must satisfy myself that I have given it my best effort. You know you can't convince me otherwise. Perhaps we'll find the answer here in the Far South. And while I know you don't have much information about this place, there are other questions you can answer. Like: what might be the best ways to establish friendly communications with a people who don't speak our language?

For the next few hours Tyen consulted Vella, pausing only to survey the land they were flying above. Sezee brought him and Veroo some food and water, then returned to the security of the netting.

She is more frightened by heights than she wants to admit, Vella told him. Sezee smiled as he glanced up at her, but when he sneaked another glance he saw her look downward, shudder, then close her eyes.

"Look!" Veroo called, her arm extending as she pointed towards the mountains.

Tyen peered under the railing, searching in the direction she had indicated. The lowering sun brightened the face of a cliff wall with a warm light. The sheer surface undulated like a ribbon standing on edge, growing wider the further west it stretched. Details were revealed as they flew closer, and along the wall. In places, erosion had left isolated fragments of this wall behind, sometimes as a narrow spit, sometimes a spire joined by a curtain of rock, and sometimes a lone spire.

"I see it," Sezee said. She grinned at Tyen. "Spirecastle!"

He frowned as he searched for the castle. It would be one of the smaller spires, he decided. His eyes were drawn instead to unnaturally straight lines below: roads, the square edges of fields, and forest giving way to the patterns of human inhabitation and cultivation.

The larger roads all led to a great cluster of buildings around a pinnacle that had once been a part of the cliff, but now stood alone. Large birds spiralled around the spire. In the creases of stone were numerous openings and some of the birds swooped into these. A movement at one of the openings made him look twice and he finally saw what Sezee and Veroo had noticed.

The openings were windows or doorways onto balconies. People stood within both, watching the aircart.

This enormous pinnacle was Spirecastle.

Though Gowel had said it was carved out of a rock spire, Tyen had imagined it shaped to look like a building. As they drew closer, he made out clusters of ropes strung between the pinnacle and the cliff face. Standing up, he slipped Vella into his shirt so she would continue to see their approach. He moved past Sezee to stand near the front.

"Don't drive into the ropes," he advised.

Veroo nodded, but her attention was elsewhere. "Those people," she said. "They're flying."

He looked closer and caught his breath as he realised she was right. What he'd assumed were birds were actually humans, gliding from dark opening to dark opening. As he watched he saw one leap from a balcony, but instead of their dive taking them downward they soared to one side, circling the tower. A faint trail of Soot followed, amazingly small for the amount of magic they must have used.

"They're children," Sezee said, behind him. She sounded shocked. "Why children?"

"Because they are smaller and lighter so don't use as much magic?" Tyen suggested.

"It seems a very dangerous pastime."

"Can you sense it, Tyen?" Veroo asked. She looked up at him. "The magic . . ."

As soon as she said it, he felt it. The magic around the tower was subtly different. Was more *condensed* there than anywhere else. It radiated outward and slightly towards the cliff.

"What do you want to do?" Sezee asked.

Tyen considered the crowds gathering on the balconies. It was impossible to judge whether they were friendly or not. If the flying children were able to venture away from the spire's face with weapons they could easily damage the aircart. Yet Gowel had said they were friendly.

"Circle around and climb higher than the spire so we avoid the ropes on the cliff side."

"You mean the bridges?"

He looked again. The scale had confused his perceptions again. The tangles of ropes were larger and more organised than he'd first guessed. Many did form bridges, others appeared to be part of a pulley system, perhaps to transport large objects. On the cliff side he could now make out paths carved into the face and a large cave opening where the ends of three of the bridges were secured. He turned back to Veroo.

"We'll land if they invite us to, though I doubt there will be a place large enough to put the aircart down. We could tether it, I suppose, but if we have bad weather it could dash itself to pieces against the spire."

"Do you want to take control?"

He shook his head. "No. It'll be safer if you steer us close and then leave it to me to land the cart with magic. Leave the heating of the capsule air to me."

Nearly all of the openings in the upper part of the spire were occupied by people now, from the largest opening to the smallest. None appeared to be carrying weapons, Tyen noted. He heated the capsule further, sending them upward. As they passed over the top of the spire a wide, flat area, sheltered and hidden by walls on three sides, came into view.

The men occupying this place wore armour and at their waists hung the sheaths of what were either long knives or short swords. Their weapons weren't drawn, however. They stood in two lines on either side of two men. One of these central figures had the stature of a short but fit man, midway between Tyen's age and his middle years. He wore a generous coat of a rich, dark green with fur around the collar and cuffs. The other man was grey-haired and a little broader around the middle, wearing a simple dark grey coat with no adornment. Both were staring up at the aircart. The younger man lifted an arm towards them and waved.

"Ooh, that would be the king," Sezee exclaimed.

449

"How do you know that?" Tyen asked.

"You said they had a king. Who else would be on top of the spire, waiting to greet us, but the person in charge?"

"He appears to be inviting us to land," Veroo added.

The man Sezee assumed was the king had brought his arm down in a sweeping motion to gesture at the space between the guards.

Tyen looked back at Sezee. "Shall we land? We have to trust that Gowel was telling the truth about them being friendly."

"Or that by the time he left they hadn't learned to feel less friendly towards northerners," she added. "He doesn't sound like a particularly honest man."

"I can't see why he would deliberately anger them, when he was here to try to establish trade."

Sezee nodded. "I think it's worth the risk. If they don't like northerners, it won't matter where we land, will it? Better to make friends with the people at the top and hope that everyone else will follow suit."

The green-coated man made the gesture again.

"Steer us in, Veroo," Tyen said, then hurried back to the rear to uncoil the landing ropes.

Veroo did a good job of it, and would have entered the sheltered alcove exactly in the centre if a gust of wind hadn't pushed the cart to the side at the last moment. Tyen steadied it with magic. The guards hurried forward to grab the ropes. Clearly they had done this before. Tyen let air out of the capsule, but not all of it in case they had mistaken the benevolent intentions of the locals and needed to make a quick exit. Though if the guards turned on them and slashed the capsule open they'd be stuck.

The man who might be the king and his companion were smiling broadly as the chassis settled onto firm ground. Tyen stepped off first and, as Vella had advised, bowed as he would

have if visiting the Emperor. He then turned to help Sezee
and Veroo to alight. They followed his lead and curtsied.

The old man took a step forward.

"Ffelcome to Tyeszal, ffissiters of the north," he said. He
gestured to the younger man. "I introduss you to Mzelssa Cryll,
leader of Sseltee."

Gowel and his crew must have taught this man some Leratian,
Tyen thought. *Or at least a few formal phrases.* He bowed again.

"Thank you for the warm welcome," he replied, speaking
slowly. "It is an honour to meet you, Mzelssa Cryll, leader of
Sseltee. I am Aren Coble of Leratia." They had agreed that he
should use the name Sezee had given him, just in case the
Academy did guess he'd crossed the mountains. "This is Veroo
Anoil and Sezee Anoil, of the West Isles."

The old man translated for the king. When he was done,
the young ruler stepped forward. He held out his hands, palms
outward, to Tyen. As Vella had advised, Tyen imitated the
gesture tentatively, indicating his willingness to oblige as well
as an apology for his ignorance of custom. The king smiled
and pressed his palms lightly against Tyen's, then turned to
Veroo and Sezee.

After they had participated in the greeting he then stepped
back and spoke, glancing at the old man as he finished.

"Cryll ffishes to know ffat you sseek in Sseltee," the old man
told them.

"We seek knowledge," Tyen replied. "Veroo seeks training
in magic and Sezee has travelled with her as a companion."
He paused, still unsure how to communicate what he wanted.

"And you?" the old man urged.

"I seek the same and more. I wish to learn about the Far
– the Sseltee."

The old man nodded. "As did the Leratians who last came
here."

451

"Yes. They sought to trade with you. I only wish to . . . learn."

The man's face brightened. "A true erafhei," he said. "People seeking for the seeking . . ." He touched his forehead, then gestured all around them.

"Those who learn for the sake of learning," Tyen agreed. "True scholars."

The old man turned to the king and an exchange followed in which the younger looked, to Tyen's relief, quite pleased.

"Cryll asks that you stay here days of three or more so he might learn more of you and your places?"

Tyen nodded. "We would be honoured."

The old man communicated that to the king, who smiled at each of them then walked away. Tyen looked to the translator, who extended his palms to indicate they should stay where they were.

"Cryll will speak to you later. I show you place to rest and sleep and tell you law of city," he said. He placed a hand on his chest. "I am Ysser. Sorcerer to Cryll." He looked at the aircart. "This ffill need . . ." He made gestures that expressed remarkably well the collapsing and tying of the capsule.

"Yes."

"We ffill help."

The old sorcerer had clearly participated or watched an aircart being packed up before. When Tyen untied the women's bags two guards came forward to carry them. Soon the capsule was deflated and the cart had been moved to one wall, where it could be tied to metal rings rammed into the rock. Satisfied that it wouldn't blow away in the wind, Tyen nodded to the sorcerer to indicate his satisfaction and that they were ready to go inside. The old man smiled and led the way into Tyeszal.

CHAPTER 21

The trouble with living in a tower was that it meant a lot of walking up and down stairs. Ysser seemed determined to show Tyen everything, which meant Tyen had been doing a lot of ascending and descending over the last day.

"Tyeszal has many ffays in and ffays out," Ysser said as he led Tyen down yet another stairway. "The . . ." he gestured to the treads and looked at Tyen.

". . . stairs?" Tyen said.

"Stairs! Yes." The sorcerer was old, but he was as quick to pick up words as any younger student of language. Perhaps even quicker. "Stairs are . . ." He drew circles in the air with a finger, slowly moving his arm downward.

"The slow way," Tyen said.

Ysser nodded, then quickened his steps. At the end of the corridor was a railing, beyond which was a hall of some sort, lit by a warm glow that suggested lamplight. As Tyen followed the sorcerer out to the railing, his heart skipped as he saw the true size and dimensions of the hall.

It was vast. A smooth domed roof stretched above them, but the floor was far, far below. Spirecastle was hollow.

The inside walls were lined with balconies and staircases. Great beams criss-crossed the space a few levels below. From these hung enormous pulleys through which ropes as thick as his arms were looped. As he watched, a wooden platform was slowly hauled upward by one of the devices. As it drew level with one of the balconies, two men stepped upon it. He could not tell if it was operated with magic. There was no Stain within Spirecastle, as by law everyone who used magic had to take it from outside the structure.

"This ffay more fast than stairs."

Tyen tried to count the levels, but they extended so far he could not make out the details far below. "How many people live in Tyeszal?"

The old man held out both hands, then pointed to one finger of the other hand then held out both hands again.

"Ten times ten . . . a hundred?"

Ysser held out one hand again.

"Ten times ten times five," Tyen guessed. "Five hundred."

"Many more below."

"The city at the base of Tyeszal."

"City?"

"Place where many people live."

"City," Ysser repeated, memorising the word.

The two men on the rising platform stepped off at the uppermost level. They stared at Tyen, but not in an unfriendly way, as they approached. Though both were shorter than he was, as most Sselts appeared to be, their face shapes were very different. He'd seen people similar in appearance to both, and others who looked different again, and surmised that there were regional differences in the peoples of the far south.

As had happened many times with others, the men held out a palm to him and Ysser as they passed. Just one and with no effort to touch palms, so perhaps this was a less formal greeting. The old man returned the gesture, so Tyen followed suit. One carried several bolts of fine-looking cloth under his arm.

"What do the people living in Tyeszal do?" Tyen asked.

"Few help Cryll lead. Many make. Many, many makers."

"Make? Those men . . . they are tailors. They make clothes." Tyen patted the soft trousers and long, lavishly embroidered shirt, given to him by the Sselts that morning.

Ysser nodded. "Many making. Only good making."

"So the castle is full of craftsmen and artisans, but only the best," Tyen concluded.

"And they make magic. Make Tyeszal most magic place in Sseltee," the old man said with obvious pride.

Tyen felt a chill run down his spine. *There it is again. This belief that making something generates magic.* The idea did not repel him as it once had. Most likely Gowel was right, and magic had some relationship with people rather than with any specific activity.

"Is there less magic in the city below?" Tyen asked

Ysser shrugged. "Less magic for so many people. Many ten hundred people."

A little less magic but a far greater population, Tyen translated. He felt a little thrill as he realised this was exactly the sort of arrangement that would prove or disprove the theory. If no relationship existed between magic and creativity then isolating a group of mostly craftsmen and artisans from the rest of the population would result in their surroundings being poorer in magic than the far larger city below. Instead, Tyeszal was richer in magic. *Could Vella be right and the Academy wrong . . . ?*

"I show you."

The old sorcerer led Tyen back to the stairs. "All above stairs is Cryll place," he said.

"The palace."

"Palace," Ysser repeated, committing the word to memory.

I'm staying in a palace, Tyen mused. *Miko would never believe it. Neel would be jealous.* And his father would be amazed and proud. At the thought of his father, Tyen felt a pang of both sadness and guilt. *I hope he got my letter. One day I will go back and see him*, he told himself. *When the Academy has given up looking for me. But, oh, how I wish I could show him this place.*

The room he had been given was richly decorated. From Sezee and Veroo's description the previous night at dinner, theirs was equally sumptuous. They had eaten with the king, his family and several people who looked and sounded important. All were very curious, but their inability to speak Leratian or for the visitors to speak Sselt kept Ysser very busy translating, and at the end of the night the old man looked strained and tired. By the next morning, when Ysser had come to Tyen's room, he was bright and energetic again and deter-mined to give his guest a tour of the castle. Sezee and Veroo had not been with him. No doubt they had turned down the offer, had a better one, or were being shown around by others and he would hear all about it over dinner that evening.

Ysser's pace slowed on the stairs, but he lengthened his stride when they reached the level above the one containing Tyen's room. He steered Tyen down a corridor to a large door, then pushed through. Following, Tyen entered a large room lined with cabinets filled with objects both familiar and strange. A collection of skeletons and bones of humans and animals filled one, and stuffed animals loaded the shelves of another. Instruments and vessels of various shapes reminded Tyen of the Academy's experimentation rooms. Rolls of paper and books took up at least half of the cabinets, or were stacked on the floor.

In the centre was a table on which a plan of some sort had been placed, the corners weighed down by an ink pot, a rock, a goblet and a shoe. Tyen would have paused to examine it as they passed if a much bigger, stranger object hadn't caught his attention. Like the aircart, it had a chassis of wood mostly covered in fabric and a kind of rudder at one end, but instead

456

of a capsule another fabric-covered framework had been fixed above, at right angles. Flatter than it was tall, the front edge curved and the rear tapered to a point. If Tyen hadn't been at the top of a castle carved out of a spire of rock and far from the sea, he would have thought it some strange sort of sailing craft, and assumed the flat edge swivelled up to catch the wind. Wheels were fixed to the chassis, and the whole contraption rested on a wooden platform, sloping towards a pair of large doors.

"Mig," Ysser called, then spoke a few rapid words in Sselt.

A head rose from behind the vehicle's chassis. Tyen caught a glimpse of a boy's wide eyes, then the head disappeared again. After a moment the owner, who looked old enough soon to be venturing into adulthood, shyly crept out into view.

"I introduss you to Mig," Ysser said. He turned to the boy and Tyen heard his false name "Aren Coble". The sorcerer turned back. "Mig is . . ." He paused, then pointed to his forehead. "Good here."

"Smart," Tyen offered. "Clever. Your apprentice?"

Ysser frowned.

"You teach him magic?"

The old man straightened and shook his head. "No. He has no magic. So he is . . . smart." Ysser reached out to touch the vehicle. "He made this."

"What does it do?"

"It fly. No magic. It . . ." He said a word in Sselt and moved his hand like a bird gliding. "He make many for people in Tyeszal so they go ffay out faster." He smiled and moved to the doors. Mig hurried over to help. Unbolting them, they swung them inward, letting in bright sunlight. They latched them to the walls to prevent them swinging in the wind that now rushed into the room, making the rolls of paper rustle in their cabinets.

Ysser beckoned, then walked outside. Following, Tyen pulled up sharply as he found himself on a balcony with no railing between him and a drop to the land far, far below. Though he was not usually bothered by heights, the lack of protection and the wind buffeting him roused an instinctive fear.

As if intended to disorientate him more, a flyer swooped past, the girl's arms outstretched. The Soot that marked her path began to shrink. He'd never seen it fade so quickly. It would be gone by the end of the day, he estimated.

He moved back into the room and examined the flying vehicle. It would take a precise aim to bring it back inside the doors. And with no capsule to lift it . . . "How do you get it back up again?" Tyen asked, mimicking the hand movement, but bringing his hand up.

"Un-make and . . ." The sorcerer mimicked carrying something under his arm.

Tyen nodded to show his understanding. It was a one-way flight, and not one the driver would want to take on a whim when it took so much effort to return home. But it could be brought up on the platforms, he supposed, if it could be dismantled into small enough pieces.

Moving closer, he saw that the driver actually sat within the chassis on a simple seat, a set of levers in front of him. He wondered how much skill it would take to keep it airborne and control the direction it flew. There would be no hovering. It seemed a far more limited vehicle than an aircart in that respect.

The boy watched silently, shyness and pride radiating from him as Tyen examined his invention. When Tyen tried to ask him a question, the lad looked uncomfortable. Considering how he might win Mig over, Tyen remembered Beetle. He'd slung his satchel over his shoulder as he'd left his room, as much from habit as not wanting to leave his most precious possessions behind. Opening the flap, he looked up at Mig and smiled.

"Beetle," he said. "Fly."

At once the insectoid stirred into life, wings buzzing as it launched into the air. The boy's eyes went wide and jumped back, then he gaped in fascination as Beetle whirred around Tyen's head.

"Rest," Tyen said, and the insectoid landed on his shoulder. He took hold of it and held it out. Ysser and the boy came over to peer down at it, both wearing the same expression of curiosity and excitement.

Tyen had been explaining how it worked for only a short time when a piping sound drew their attention to the balcony. A girl around Mig's age stood between the open doors, with what Tyen guessed was a whistle between her teeth. Her fitted clothing was a flier uniform and he guessed its green colour indicated she was a messenger of the king. She stared at Tyen with a bold curiosity that he suspected he would have to grow used to as a stranger in this land, then spat the whistle out, held a palm outward towards Ysser and said something. Tyen recognised the word "Cryll".

The old man turned to Tyen and smiled apologetically. "I must go. You go to your room no guide?"

Tyen nodded. "I will find my way there."

The boy looked disappointed as Tyen placed Beetle back in the satchel.

"Beetle, sleep," Tyen said. At once the insectoid curled up its legs and went still.

He followed Ysser out, then made his way back to his room alone. There he found a generous meal laid out on a table. His stomach growled when he saw it, though his morning meal had been no small affair either. The tour must have taken far longer than he had realised.

After he had sated his hunger he rose and walked over to one of the small windows. He estimated it was about mid-afternoon. For a while he gazed out at the world so far below, then he returned to the chair.

What should he do now? Though nobody had told him he must stay in his room, knowing he was living in the palace made him reluctant to roam around without a guide or reassurance that his exploration would be welcome. He could seek out Veroo and Sezee, but they were probably in the middle of their own tour of the castle. He would see them when they were done.

So he drew Vella out of the satchel and filled her in on what he had seen and learned.

The king said we could stay a few days. What should we do then? Tyen asked.

To remain longer would be to outstay your welcome, and you should keep moving in case the Academy does cross the mountains in pursuit, she replied.

If any sorcerers did, it would take them a few days to prepare for such a journey. A Dart was too large and heavy for the crossing, so they'd need to find a smaller aircart or two and provisions.

The king or Ysser may be happy to suggest where you would be well received in Sseltee, Vella said. *And a solution to the problem of money. You have the aircart so transport is no issue, but you still need food and, where necessary, to pay for a bed each night.*

Yes, I will have to ask if they will exchange their currency for mine – what's left of it. He'd given the foresters who'd helped him repair the aircart all of the heavy coinage and most of the paper money left from Kilraker's bags.

Someone may buy the money as an item of curiosity.

I wonder how Sezee and Veroo plan to overcome this problem. If Veroo is accepted into the school of magic, how will they pay their way?

From what I picked up in her mind, Sezee has some jewellery to sell and is confident she will find a way to earn money as a singer.

Singer? She sings?

Yes.

Tyen frowned. In all this time he'd never heard Sezee sing. He was filled with a sudden curiosity to hear her. Perhaps he'd ask her about it later. He turned his attention back to the question of what to do next.

I will ask Ysser for maps and suggestions for places to explore, he said. *Perhaps . . . perhaps I should show you to Ysser before leaving. You would learn a lot from him. But should I trust him to give you back? I've only just met him. He seems nice enough – but Kilraker seemed nice enough until he set me up. What if Ysser tries to steal you, or tells the king about you and the king decides he should own you?*

You must weigh the advantages against the risks.

Tyen shook his head. It would be foolish to trust the old man so quickly. He would have to make his own way. He could go with Veroo to the school of magic. Gowel didn't think the sorcerers were as advanced as those of the Academy, but if he was to find a way to restore Vella he had better seize every opportunity for a magical education.

Would that be the best way to improve my skills and knowledge? he wondered.

The best way would be for you to leave this world and its limitations, and seek out the best teachers of the worlds.

He chuckled. *That's not very helpful advice.*

No? I can teach you how to travel between worlds. All you need to find is enough magic.

But there isn't enough in this world, is there?

There might be. There is more magic here at Tyeszal than anywhere else I have been in this world and time.

Tyen's skin prickled at the thought. Travel the worlds? Was it really possible?

However, the locals may object to you depleting so much of what they have generated. You may find other places in the south where magic is being created but not used.

So you are saying that I shouldn't go to the school, but should seek out one of these places so I can leave this world?

That would be the best way to improve your skills and—

A knock at the door snatched his attention away. He took a deep breath, slipped Vella inside his shirt and walked over to answer it.

No sooner had the latch clicked open than the door was pushed inward. Sezee bustled in, taking in his surrounds with a critical eye. She had changed her clothes to the local garb since arriving but was wearing her warm jacket, scarf and gloves on top.

"Nice room. Ours is bigger, but has two beds. Where have you been all day?"

Tyen followed her to the centre of the room. "Ysser took me for a tour of the castle. Well, until he was interrupted by a summons from the k—"

Sezee whirled to face him. "A tour? And you didn't come and get us?"

He stared at her. "Um. No. Well, I expected you'd join us but when you didn't I thought they must have taken you out separately."

She pursed her lips, then smiled and shrugged. "Yes, they did. But it would have been nicer to look around together, wouldn't it? When we asked if you could come along they went to fetch you, but you'd already gone. Didn't you ask if we could come with you?"

"I . . . um . . ."

She tsked and moved to the window. "Well, it doesn't matter now. I've come to say goodbye."

He stared at her in surprise. "Goodbye?" he repeated.

She turned to face him. "Yes. Veroo and I are leaving. A group of young Sselts set off to the school two days ago, as they apparently do twice a year, but they're travelling slowly and we should catch up by midnight."

"You're leaving *now?*"

"Once I'm finished talking to you." She walked over to him. Her gaze moved everywhere except his face. "It takes a few months to get to the school, which will give us time to learn the language."

"But . . ."

Her eyes rose to meet his. "But?"

"So soon. We've only just got here and I . . ."

She smiled – or, rather, her lips widened but her eyes showed no humour. "You?"

"I haven't decided what to do next."

Her half-smile faded and a crease appeared between her brows. She took a step closer and reached out towards his face. The soft hide of her gloves brushed his cheek.

"Dear Tyen," she said softly. "That confirms all my suspicions. If you felt for me as I do for you there would be no decision to make."

He looked down, heart twisting with both guilt and sadness. "I'm sorry," was all he could think to say.

She sighed. "There is nothing to apologise for. I don't mind. How could I? But it is no fun being with someone you love when the feeling isn't reciprocated." Her voice caught and he looked up to see her blinking quickly. She stepped back. "We are going to the school. You can't. If the Academy follows you here it's the first place they'll look. So we were always going to part. It has been a grand adventure, Tyen. For that Veroo and I thank you. You brought us across the uncrossable mountains. You taught Veroo to fly."

He followed and caught up one of her hands. "I owe you a

greater thanks for helping me leave Leratia and escape the Academy. Please, pass on my gratitude to Veroo for helping drive the aircart, too. She did very well. I think she may have a natural knack for it."

She smiled, squeezed his hand then pulled hers away. "I will tell her. She'll be quite chuffed to hear that. And sorry she didn't get the chance to say goodbye herself."

He frowned. "Where is she?"

"Packing. We really do need to leave quickly if we are going to catch up with the recruits." She turned towards the door, then paused and looked back. "By the way, the king gave us quite a generous exchange rate. He wants to have some money on hand for when the next lot of northerners turn up. Which I think is a good hint of how soon you need to leave, Tyen. And don't tell anyone where you are going."

He nodded. "I won't."

She gazed at him for a moment longer, her expression sad, then managed a smile. Without another word she headed for the door. A few steps and she was gone.

He stared at the back of the door. *Am I mad for letting her go?* he wondered. He nearly hurried after her to ask them to wait for him to pack and join them. But her warning kept him still.

"*. . . don't tell anyone where you are going . . .*"

Tonight he would find out as much as he could about the Far South from Ysser, and let the man know that he was keen to begin his exploration as soon as possible – if not tomorrow then the day after. He would either have to avoid saying where he would go, or lie about his intended destination.

But for now there was nothing he could do but wait until Ysser returned. The old man was the only person who knew enough Leratian to tell him what he needed to know, and he was currently attending to the king. Frustrated, Tyen kept himself distracted by tossing objects towards the bed and teaching Beetle to fly after and catch them. He found himself imagining Sezee and Veroo making their way down endless stairs to the city below, despite knowing they had probably ridden one of the wooden platforms at the centre of the spire. Though Sezee would not have liked that. Not at all. *Hmm, I wonder if her dislike of heights was part of the reason for her eagerness to leave.*

Finally, a tapping came at the door. He grabbed Vella and ordered Beetle into the satchel, then went to answer it. A messenger greeted him with open palm. While the flyers were all girls, the messengers who worked inside the spire were all boys. This one held up a piece of paper.

"The Cryll requests you join him for dinner," he said, slowly and with great care. "Bring Beetle. Follow me."

Tyen slung his satchel over his shoulder, stepped out of the room and nodded. At once the boy turned and started down the corridor.

As he followed his young guide, Tyen considered how he should approach his questioning of Ysser. If he was to ensure nobody knew where he'd gone, he could not show too much interest in any places the old man suggested he visit. Or else he should show interest in destinations he didn't want to visit and a lack of interest in those that appealed. Though the next time the Academy came visiting the old man would learn that Aren Coble was actually Tyen Ironsmelter and perhaps guess he'd only been pretending disinterest.

The boy, with the thoughtlessness of youth, dashed up the last flight of stairs with enviable speed. Tyen followed, but had to pause to catch his breath at the top. More guards stood along the corridor leading to the rooms in which the king entertained and met visitors. They regarded him with wary looks, so he pushed himself on.

The boy did not lead him to the dining room, but towards a pair of large, ornate doors. A guard opened one for Tyen. The boy gestured to the opening then hurried away to his next task. Still breathing quickly, Tyen stepped through.

The room he entered was not large, but made up for it in grandeur. Tall windows allowed in the afternoon light, currently a deep red from the setting sun. The colour reflecting off the gilding on the paintings and plasterwork made it look as if the room was on fire. It also cast the occupants of the room into russet-edged shadows, so Tyen had to squint to see their faces.

When he did, his blood froze.

"Tyen Ironsmelter," Professor Kilraker said. "We've been looking for you everywhere."

PART EIGHT

RIELLE

CHAPTER 20

The merchant's camp surrounded the well. Firelight threw warped, elongated shadows of men onto the sand, stretching to join with those of long-legged kapo, their burdens still strapped to their narrow backs. Even the steam rising from the pot the cook carried to his fellows cast a shadow.

Sa-Mica turned away and led the way back down the road. In the distance the dune that they'd climbed over was a pale crescent. Nobody could stop the sands shifting in the winds, but the road was straight so wherever dunes covered it a person only had to walk onwards and they would easily find it again on the other side.

"We aren't going to join them?" Sa-Gest asked.

"They would not rest well knowing a tainted was close by," Sa-Mica replied.

"What about refilling our flasks?"

"It can wait until morning."

"Mine's empty."

"You must drink more slowly."

"I would have if I'd known, but . . ."

Ignoring him, Sa-Mica turned off the road and climbed a dune. Rielle followed. Sa-Gest paused, then hurried after them. The scarred priest reached the top of the dune and paused to look around. Starlight bathed the desert in a deep, cool blue.

It softened the edges of everything, turning the gritty texture of the dunes into smooth sculptures. Sa-Mica waited until Sa-Gest caught up, panting, then started down the other side. Rielle felt soft sand change to hard ground as they reached the bottom.

"We will sleep here tonight," Sa-Mica said.

He shrugged off his pack. Pain lanced through Rielle's shoulders as she tried to do the same. Holding still until it eased, she considered how else she might remove it. Sitting down, she felt the weight lift off her shoulders as the base of the pack met the ground. With a wriggle she was able to extract her shoulders from the straps. After stretching and rubbing the stiffness out, she pulled the sleeping mat free and spread it over the ground a few steps away from Sa-Mica's.

They had been walking for three days now. Each night they had camped at a well, sleeping on mats with nothing but their clothing between them and the stars. As soon as the sun rose they ate a quick meal then set off again. Sa-Mica stopped only to eat and they did not halt when the sun set. The day's trek ended when they reached whichever well Sa-Mica chose to rest at – which could be soon after sunset or closer to midnight.

The rope sandals had chafed Rielle's feet until they bled, so she'd walked barefoot on the hot sand. The heavy chain about her neck rubbed, too, and the weight of it gave her headaches, but she could do nothing about that. Her scarf kept the sun off most of her face, but wherever her skin was exposed – hands, feet and above the neckline of her tunic – it burned.

Sa-Mica approached and opened her pack. Though they each carried their own sleeping mat and water, the rest of their supplies were divided among them. Rielle had noted that Sa-Mica removed food from her and Sa-Gest's pack more than his own. Perhaps he had other items stowed in his. Perhaps he figured they should use up the food in her pack first, so she was less tempted to run away.

She touched the chain at her throat. Thanks to her brother's stories and advice, she knew better than to venture into the desert with less than a day's water. How would she get away from the priests, anyway? They took it in turns to watch her through the night. Even if Sa-Gest fell asleep during his watch, she doubted she'd be awake to notice. When she lay down she slipped into an exhausted slumber, only broken by the rising sun.

Perhaps they feared she'd use magic to get away, but what chance had she, ignorant and unskilled, against two priests? No chance at all.

Yet despite the impossibility of escape, contemplating it drew her out of the sadness and despair she'd felt since her capture. She knew she could not survive in the desert, but it did not go on for ever. Her family's maps showed that there was a long line of mountains on the other side of the sands. She was being taken to a place called the Mountain Temple, not the Desert Temple. Perhaps, if she was lucky, Sa-Gest would fall asleep on his watch and she'd slip away before either priest noticed.

Would I use magic if I had to?

Her soul was already tainted. What would it matter if it became more tainted? The Angels would tear it asunder when she died anyway.

I have nothing left to lose but the last years of my life. This thought had occurred to her a few days ago, and it had returned many times since. She had lost her family, her lover, her future and the regard of the Angels. Even if she managed to run away, she would still feel the terrible weight of guilt. Part of her wanted to be punished, if that would somehow make things right. *And I still love the Angels and don't want to steal what's rightly theirs.*

471

Interrupting her thoughts, Sa-Mica handed her a lump of stale bread, a stick of dried meat and a handful of salted beans.

"Tomorrow night's fare will be fresher," he promised as he gave the same to Sa-Gest, with an added bundle of sweet preserved fruit.

Rielle's heart leapt. Did that mean they were nearing the end of the desert? She did not dare ask.

With such a dry meal, she was glad to have saved half of her water. After she had eaten she still had a quarter of her flask left. As she went to slip it back into the outer pocket of her pack, Sa-Mica extended a hand to her.

"Give it to me."

She obeyed. He handed the flask to Sa-Gest, who immediately guzzled the rest. As she received it back she wiped the mouth of it thoroughly on her skirt. His eyes narrowed, but he said nothing.

On the first night she had been all too conscious of him watching her. Every time she'd glanced his way he'd smirked at her, so she'd tried to avoid looking at him at all. The next morning the sound of voices had roused her. She realised the two priests were talking and she'd come fully awake when she heard her name spoken.

". . . harmed in any way. You will find your new superior will not be as forgiving as your former ones."

"I have never forced myself on a woman," Sa-Gest objected.

"You prefer to trick them into compliance. Yes, I know why they were so anxious to send you with me."

There was a pause. "They said I was better suited to a life there."

"You may be, but you must still adhere to the rules."

"I understand."

"And common sense should tell you it is easier dealing with a co-operative tainted. It is clear she fears you. Keep your distance unless I tell you otherwise."

It had not stopped Sa-Gest smirking at her when Sa-Mica's attention was elsewhere, but he did stay away from her. Their conversation had filled her with questions and doubts, however. It suggested that Sa-Gest had caused trouble in other ways than threatening her, and some of the priests in Fyre had known of it, and perhaps tolerated it. But it also sounded as if his behaviour would not be accepted at the prison. So why, then, was Sa-Gest not dismayed to be going there? And why was life there better suited to him? The questions worried at her when there was nothing else to distract her.

Perhaps it was knowing he would be at the prison that made her think about escaping so much.

Now, as she saw Sa-Mica bring out a little lamp and his book, she felt a contradictory mix of eagerness and dread. Every night Sa-Mica had read a story from a small book. *Encounters with Angels* it was called. She'd never heard of it before, or the tales he'd read. While any distraction from her thoughts would be welcome, she suspected these readings were meant to remind her what her ultimate fate would be, as they were often about the tainted. Still, he had a lovely deep voice that she could have listened to for hours, and not all of the stories had grim endings.

The lamp snapped into life. Behind her, she heard Sa-Gest sigh.

"The Scribe," Sa-Mica began.

"Many years ago lived a man named Lem. He was a writer of documents and keeper of accounts, taught by his father who had also been taught by his father and his father before him. But Lem's hand was steadier and his skill greater than any of his ancestors'. Flattered by the compliments and praise of customers, he grew ambitious. He vowed to learn all there was to know of the art of beautiful writing. He left his father and a young wife and set out to become the greatest calligrapher in the world.

"He travelled far, and for many years. He visited many lands and met people very different from himself. Wherever he went, he sought those who had elevated the work of the pen to an art, and all shared their knowledge with him.

"He learned how to carve pens of reed and wood, of spines and feathers. He even found a jeweller who could show him how to shape pens from gold and silver, or carve them from glass or gemstone. Each of these pens produced writing of a different quality, their shape and form altering letters in a subtle and unique way, and he mastered them all.

"He learned how to make paper from grasses and leaves, from hide and hair, from mud and cloth. He even learned how to write on living skin, writing words on the arms and legs and backs of those who sought such decoration. Each of these papers was more or less receptive to the application of ink, some welcoming, some resistant, and he understood them all.

"He learned how to extract ink out of bark and sap, out of fruit and flowers, out of insects and sea creatures, out of the glands of animals and from the humble earth. He even learned to write words that disappeared and could be made to appear again in the right conditions. Each of these inks must be produced with careful measurement and process, thinned or thickened to the right consistency to match pen and paper, and he mixed them all."

Sa-Mica paused. The desert seemed silent, though it was never completely so. The faint whistle of the wind was always present, as well as the squeak and chirrup of insects. Rielle had felt a quickening of interest at the lists of ink ingredients, but, brought back to the present, her stomach sank. Would she be allowed to draw in prison? Chalk was easy enough to come by, but paper was expensive. And what would she draw? Would she ever see anything more than the inside of her cell?

Taking a sip from his water flask, Sa-Mica cleared his throat and returned to the story.

"Twenty years passed and he longed to return to his home and family. But he knew he had not learned everything there was to know of his art, as he'd vowed. He'd heard tales told of a form of writing practised long ago, before The Restoration began. A form of writing now forbidden, for it required magic.

"If he returned home, he must admit he had not done as he had vowed or else lie. He was pious, but he was also proud. A man of his integrity did not hide behind such deceptions. He could not decide whether defeat or dishonesty was worse. Then, whether by his own design or at another's suggestion, he struck upon the idea that he only need *learn* the forbidden form of writing, not actually practise it."

Sa-Mica's eyes rose to meet Rielle's, then he looked away, reaching for his water flask. She watched him drink a single mouthful then carefully stopper it and put it aside.

"Returning to those places where he'd heard or read of the skill, he sought more information. He reasoned that if he could not discover anything then he could return home satisfied that he had acquired all the available knowledge of his art. But the forbidden secret was not lost and made the knowledge he had gathered in the last twenty years seem small and insignificant. For with this skill no ink would fade, no paper rot or burn, no knowledge be destroyed, no history be forgotten."

Sa-Mica chuckled. "That, I am told by a reliable source, is an exaggeration. Most likely Lem embellished the tale to make his choice appear more noble." He took another sip, then continued reading.

"Amazed by such an invention, he eagerly learned how it was done. Satisfied that he had achieved what he had vowed to achieve, he returned home. There he found his father weary with age and ready to hand over his business, his children grown and married. He set to work and gained great wealth by putting nearly all that he had learned to good use, and ensuring his family's wealth by teaching his sons.

"But as time passed he grew frustrated with inks that faded and paper that yellowed. The knowledge that his skill and effort could be preserved for ever, not lost to time, was like a burr in his clothing that he could not find. Most of all he lamented the deterioration of his greatest work, a decorated copy of the Book of Angels. How could the Angels protest if magic was used to record their deeds and wisdom for the teaching of countless souls to come?

"And so he conceived a work of such beauty and grandeur that might stir an Angel's heart to forgiveness — perhaps even gratitude. He set out to use forbidden knowledge to create a copy of the Book of Angels that would exist for ever.

"He laboured over every page, neglecting his family, business and even his appearance. He sought places where the Stain of his creation would not be noticed. When he could no longer find any, and was in danger of discovery, he left to seek a safer location. He found a remote house on a mountain where few travellers strayed. There he worked, year after year, existing on mountain herbs and magic. He forgot how to speak to others, driving away those few visitors who came his way. The more beautiful the book became, the more ugly and sick he grew.

"One day a great priest walked along that dangerous, weedy track. Dreams had sent him from his home, and along this path. When he arrived he knew why the Angels had sent him. The house existed in a great void, all the magic stolen by Lem to create his book. He prepared himself for a great battle, expecting to face a terrible sorcerer within. Instead he found a sick old man and the most beautiful Book of Angels he'd ever seen.

"So he nursed the old man back to health. As he learned what it had cost to make the book he recoiled from it. Lem heard of the dreams that had brought the priest and rejoiced, for he believed the Angels had sent him to receive the book. But the priest refused to touch it or take it away with him. Disturbed by what he had discovered, and unsure what to do about it, the priest left to consult with his peers.

"Lem tied the book to his back and followed, forcing his aged body to hurry. As he caught up with the priest the man regarded the book with fresh horror. Looking over his shoulder, Lem saw a trail of Stain stretching behind him. The book was drawing magic into itself.

"At last Lem saw the travesty he had created. Using magic one last time, he destroyed the book, casting the pages into the wind. Then he collapsed, sure that his soul would soon be torn asunder by the Angels.

"The priest, seeing that Lem was a good and pious man at heart, was saddened. He carried him back to the mountain house, then aided him in turning the place into a monastery. There Lem lived his last days teaching priests the art of writing so that they might spread the Angels' wisdom in more humble forms. And it is said that when he died, the Angels forgave him, for his and his pupils' work created more magic than he had stolen, and his art had inspired many thousands of souls. But only those who pass into their domain know if that is true."

Sa-Mica lowered the book, closed his eyes and was silent. Then he blew out the lamp, closed the book and put it away.

"Do you have any questions?" he asked quietly.

Rielle blinked. He was looking at her, not Sa-Gest. She considered the story and began to shake her head, then checked

477

herself. One question had been worrying at her since they'd left Fyre, and maybe now was the time to ask.

"How many days' travel do we have left?"

The unscarred corner of his mouth twitched upward. "Many quarterdays, but not all of them through the desert." He lay down on his sleeping mat. "I have not heard you praying, Rielle. You will meet an Angel one day. Ignoring them will make no difference to the outcome."

Rielle swallowed. Her mouth was dry and Sa-Gest had finished all her water. She lay down and considered Sa-Mica's observation. She had tried to pray while in the temple cell, but the words had stuck in her throat. It felt presumptuous to ask the Angels for anything after what she had done. Her crime was unforgivable, so what was the point of asking for mercy?

But perhaps there was some hope for her. After all, she had stolen far less magic from the Angels than Lem had, and they had forgiven him.

He had created more magic through his art. Though she had been taught that magic was generated by acts of creation she had always assumed that only the greatest of human endeavours produced any significant amount of it. Had she been making it by painting and drawing? If she was allowed to draw in prison, could she replace what she had stolen?

Whether praying was pointless or not, it would not do any harm. But as she opened her mouth the thought of Sa-Gest listening made her voice freeze in her throat. So instead she recited a simple prayer taught to children, praising the Angels and wishing her family good fortune.

That would have to do for now.

CHAPTER 21

Eight – or was it nine? – days later they left the sands behind them. A line of peaks had appeared on the horizon a few days before, growing ever taller as they approached. Ahead, the road wound between the claw-like toes of the mountains then climbed the more generous curves of their lower reaches before disappearing into a fold of the steep higher slopes.

That trek would begin the next day, thankfully. The sun hung low in the sky and a dark huddle of buildings shadowed the desert's edge not far ahead, the distinctive radiating lines atop a temple spire rising above the highest roof. It was the hour when people returned to their homes, and as Rielle and her guardians entered the village the locals stopped to stare, their gazes lingering on the chain around her neck before they continued on with more haste than before.

The same had happened at the few other villages they'd passed through. Rielle could not guess how common it was for priests to bring a tainted this route to the prison, but it was often enough for the locals to know exactly what she was. In one village three youths had followed them, jeering. In another the occupants came out of their homes to hiss curses at her. Sa-Mica had instructed her to walk between him and Sa-Gest. At first she'd assumed this was to prevent her dashing

479

away and perhaps using a villager as a hostage, but she soon realised it was mostly for her own protection.

It appeared that in this village all she would be subjected to was glares, and most of these from doorways and windows. The main road was the only thoroughfare, lined on either side by buildings. The temple was at the furthest end. Though taller than the rest thanks to the tower, the building was disproportionately small, which gave it a top-heavy, looming presence. Sa-Mica led them around it to two low brick buildings: one with two wings stretching forward from either side, the other nestled in the courtyard between them and barely bigger than the cell back in Fyre.

As she saw the gate set into the front of the little building Rielle realised there was more than a resemblance. All of the temples they had stopped at so far contained a cell, but this was the first she'd encountered with one separate from the other buildings.

A priest emerged from the central section of the larger building and walked forward to meet them. His expression was warm as he saw Sa-Mica, but his smile faded instantly as he examined her and Sa-Gest.

"Welcome again, Sa-Mica," he said. "I see I will be having a late night, tonight."

"Only a little later than usual, Sa-Jeim. This is Sa-Gest, who will be taking a position on the mountain. He will share the watch with me."

Sa-Jeim nodded to the young priest. It might have been an illusion cast by the thin light of dusk, but there was something about the calculating way he looked at Sa-Gest that sent a chill down her spine. She could not decide if she'd read dislike or envy, or both.

"Then we'd best get you all settled," he said, drawing a cluster of keys out of his robes and gesturing to the cell.

Rielle shrugged off her pack and handed it to Sa-Mica. The village priest opened the gate and she obediently stepped inside. Leaving Sa-Gest to guard her, the other priests headed into the house.

It was dark inside the cell, but the walls radiated warmth absorbed during the day. The only feature was a bench built into the back wall, of the same bricks that formed the walls. The floor was of stone covered in sand that had blown in through the gate. It smelled of stale urine and since she could not see well enough to be sure if the bench was clean, she took handfuls of sand and tossed it onto the bench hoping that it would absorb any lingering residue.

Sa-Gest waited beside the gate, his pack at his feet. It was not long before Sa-Mica emerged, bringing food and drink for them both. Her meal was stewed grains and a cup of water. She endeavoured not to look at Sa-Gest's, but it smelled of meat and agil, the herbed and spiced liquor priests produced for their own consumption and that was said to have healing qualities. Though her meal was flavourless it was, at least, not the hard and dry fare they'd been eating for many quarterdays.

Soon Sa-Mica returned carrying a bucket, a sleeping mat and a chair. After opening the gate briefly to give her the first two, he sent Sa-Gest to the house to sleep. He turned away while she relieved herself, then settled onto the chair and brought out his little book. It was fully night now, so he lit his reading lamp and held it over the pages.

Spreading the sleeping mat over the bench, Rielle sat and listened to his deep voice.

"Over a hundred years ago there lived a wealthy widow named Deraia who had five children. Though she could afford to hire servants to do all the domestic duties, she loved to cook and was famous for it.

481

"One day there came to her land a terrible plague. When the first of Deraia's children fell ill she turned to the healing lore passed down from mother to daughter in her family, but it proved ineffective and the child died.

"When the second child fell ill she turned to the physicians of the city, famous for their knowledge and skill from centuries of study, but they had not encountered this sickness before and the child died.

"When the third child fell ill she turned to the priests, but by then the temple was filled with victims of the plague and, with too few priests to treat them and not wanting to favour rich or poor, they selected who to cure by ballot. Her child was not selected and died.

"When the fourth child fell ill she prayed to the Angels for three days and nights and made offerings and performed all the rituals, but despite her piety the child died.

"When her last living child fell ill she turned to the oldest of the books passed down to her. There she found knowledge of magic long hidden, taught herself to use it, and the child lived.

"Afterwards she was seized by such guilt that her daughter should live while other children died. She knew her soul was already lost, so what did she have to lose by saving more? So she treated those of relatives and friends, hiding her method and persuading them to keep secret the fact she had done so.

"Yet the more children she saved, the greater and stronger her guilt became. Why should the less fortunate suffer and her wealthy friends not? So she ventured into the poorer areas of the city alone and soon the city was full of stories of the lady who cured with a touch, though none would say how.

"But when the priests heard of this they guessed the truth and set a trap to catch her. Once found she admitted her crime and submitted willingly to their judgement. She had done so much good, however, that instead of gathering to drive her out of the city, people came to protest and bar the way.

"Fearing rebellion against the Angels' wisdom, the priests sought advice from the ten most respected priests of the world. These men gathered and weighed the good the widow had done against the theft of magic. They knew that she must remain well guarded, lest she continue using magic. They knew she must be punished or others might seek to emulate her. They knew her punishment must be one the people would accept.

"They decided that she, and her daughter after her, must replace the magic she had stolen. When she was told this, and asked in which way she wished to work, she thought long and carefully. She had no skill but healing and cooking. If she could not help people with one, then she would do so with the other.

"So for the rest of her life Deraia and her daughter prepared meals for the poor and raised money for the temple. It was said these meals were astonishing, for to generate magic one must do more than simply combine ingredients by rote. People came from afar to experience them.

"And those who watched over her believed that she and her daughter had more than repaid their debt to the Angels before their deaths, and expected to see them in the spiritual realm."

Sa-Mica closed the book and, as always, closed his eyes for a little while. Rielle remained quiet, but her mind churned with questions.

What is he up to? While not all of the stories he'd told had been about people using magic and being forgiven, most were. Was he trying to tell her that she could redeem herself? If he was, and she did, what happened then? Would she be freed when her debt was paid?

Yet whenever she asked him about the prison he would not

give her details. It had occurred to her a few nights ago that he might be unable to speak of it around Sa-Gest, though she couldn't guess why.

"Do you have any questions?" he asked.

"None you have not already refused to answer," she said, failing to keep the hope from her voice.

"Then may the Angels watch over you this night," he said, and stood up.

She sighed and shook her head. Why did he ask, when he was not going to answer? *Perhaps because I'm not asking the right questions.* He chuckled. It was a comforting sound, but an odd expression of warmth given their respective roles and situations. "A few more days, Rielle." He blew out the lamp. "Go to sleep."

Despite the hard bed beneath it, she comprehended nothing after her head met the sleeping mat until sound and light roused her.

Her body ached. *How can it be morning when I'm still so tired?* Opening her eyes, she frowned as she saw the cell was still dark. Yet she could see her shadow outlined on the wall above the bench, cast by a faint light outside the cell. It was moving, but she wasn't. So the source of light must be moving.

Then she heard the breathing. Rapid, slightly hoarse, coming from the gate. She turned her head, then instantly regretted it.

Sa-Gest was pressed up against the bars. His stare was intense, but as she saw him his teeth flashed, illuminated by a spark of light floating between them. One of his hands held something small and square. His other arm was moving in short compulsive jerks. Looking down, she saw a tangle of fingers and what they were holding and froze in shock. He laughed quietly.

"Come over and assist me," he invited. "And when we get

there I'll make sure you're treated . . . well . . . better . . ." He caught his breath. "Ah . . . too late."

Already tensing to stand, she managed to duck out of the way. He'd aimed for her face. If he'd aimed further down her body she might not have been able to dodge in time. Even so, his seed spattered over the sleeping mat.

She gasped in disgust, then wished she hadn't. It told him he'd succeeded in revolting her. Swallowing bile, she pushed the mat over and onto the floor, hoping the dry sand would draw out the moisture.

Vile, disgusting man.

"Never mind," he said. She kept her gaze averted as he fiddled with his robes. Tucking himself away. "I'm sure there'll be other opportunities. It won't hurt you to get some skill in it before we get there. They'll be expecting that and much more on the mountain."

Her head snapped up and her eyes met his before she could stop them. He smiled and nodded. "That's right. I'm trying to do you a favour. You don't want to arrive there unprepared. And friendless." He snorted. "And don't think Sa-Mica will help. He'll be heading off to collect other tainted."

Ignore him, she told herself. *He's trying to frighten you.* Yet what if . . . *No. It can't be true.* He was still holding the square object, she noted. Seeing her attention shift to it, he grinned and turned it out to face her. The magical light reflected off a surface coated with some kind of shiny paste. As the object turned further and she saw the colours and shapes painted upon it she froze in horror.

It was the nude painting Izare had started. The one she had finished. The one that had vanished after Sa-Gest and Sa-Elem had inspected Izare's house. Smudged at the edges where he must have held onto it, still wet when he'd taken it. Anger filled her and she tried to snatch it from him, but he pulled away too quickly and laughed.

"No, you can't have it. I still need it. It's kept me company for many a night," he told her. "Not as pretty as the one of your face, of course, but that was too big to fit in my pack."

Rielle's breath caught in her throat. *The portrait!* She had not seen it since the day she'd run from her family. Had Sa-Gest taken it when the priests had sought her at Izare's house? *He must have. I never saw it after that. Why didn't Izare tell me?* She clenched her fists. *If I had to kill him to escape, I wouldn't regret it*, she told herself.

A shiver went through her. Suddenly escape was no longer a fantasy but something she craved. Everything that had been done and taken from her had been justified, but if she had to spend the rest of her life in the control of this man . . . she did not deserve *that*. Nobody did.

Then why not now? Why not take magic and try to break free? Sa-Mica was in the house. Fighting one priest was better than two . . .

"What is going on?"

Sa-Gest jumped away from the gate and the cell was suddenly dark. Lit from behind by the house light, a figure strode towards them. Though his face was in shadow she instantly recognised Sa-Mica by his walk. Sa-Gest turned and shrugged.

"Nothing."

"What have you got there?" Sa-Mica demanded. "No, I saw what you were holding and that is *not* it. Give it to me."

Something passed between the two priests. A new spark appeared and Rielle glimpsed the painting in Sa-Mica's hands before the light vanished again. Then flames replaced it, and the burning square fell from his hands to the ground. She stared at it. The only painting she and Izare had worked on together was gone, yet all she felt was relief.

"Fool," Sa-Mica said. "Tell me why I shouldn't send you back to Fyre?"

"I didn't touch her," Sa-Gest protested. "I was just . . . talking to her."

"Blackmail or taunting?"

"Neither! I just—"

"Go to bed. Wake Sa-Jeim and tell him we need him to start his watch early. Tomorrow you'll carry her pack as well as yours."

Sa-Gest hunched and walked away. A short time later the local priest emerged, yawning. Sa-Mica moved away a little and lowered his voice as they began talking. Rielle strained to catch the words.

"Sorry . . . this," Sa-Mica said.

"Is she . . .?"

"No. I think he knows. I don't know how." The scarred priest's voice quietened.

Sa-Jeim shook his head and murmured something. Rielle edged closer to the gate, closing her eyes and listening.

". . . do you do this?"

"Because I must." Sa-Mica's voice had grown forceful. He stilled and glanced her way.

"It gives me hope that you, born and raised in that terrible place, came out a better man than most," Sa-Jeim said firmly, then asked a question she could not make out. Sa-Mica shook his head. Sa-Jeim sighed then started towards the cell.

"I will get the truth from you eventually, Sa-Mica," he called over his shoulder, the warning softened by the affection in his voice. When the old priest neared the cell she was able to make out his expression in the starlight, and she shivered at what she read in his face.

Pity.

PART NINE

TYEN

CHAPTER 22

Tyen rubbed his face, yawned and leaned back against the struts of the aircart. It had been a gusty night and, with the wind making the capsule bob and jerk against the tether, he'd not slept well.

Looking down, he watched children flying around the spire and recalled what Ysser had told him about them. The first flyer had come to Tyeszal a few hundred years before. A child of acrobats who travelled the land performing for money, when the king of the time had seen her fly he had given the family a room in the tower and paid them to stay and teach other children. Soon their usefulness as messengers was noticed and, in the way of so many small tasks undertaken for royalty, laws and traditions were created to restrict the selection of trainees, the method of training and the length of service.

Equally fascinating to watch was the Soot that formed in the flyers' wake. Every time they zipped past he marvelled at how quickly magic seeped in to fill the void.

This must be what it is like in other worlds, he thought for the hundredth time. Which always led to wishing he could ask Vella if that were true, and wondering if she was lost to him for ever. *At least Kilraker and Gowel don't have her*, he told himself. He looked down at the two aircarts safely bound to either side of the platform, thought about the confrontation

491

in the Sselt king's audience chamber and wondered again if he could have done anything differently.

Kilraker, Gowel and two other Leratians had moved to encircle Tyen when he'd entered the room, but their plan to surround him was thwarted. Ysser had stepped between them and ushered Tyen away, leading him over to the king. The ruler sat on a wide, deep couch that could have seated four or five people – a kind of throne that favoured visitors could be invited to sit upon as well. Tyen had extended his palms, but the king had not returned the gesture.

"These men you know?" Ysser had asked.

Tyen nodded.

"Your name is Tyen Ironsmelter? Not Aren Coble?"

"Yes."

"They say you steal a thing. Is it true?"

"No," Tyen had replied, then, "Yes." At Ysser's confused look, he had gone on to explain. "Professor Kilraker stole something from the Academy," he said, turning to nod at his former teacher. "He made it look as if I had taken it. I took it from him, but I could not return it to the Academy. It was too valuable and they wanted to destroy it." He began to add that he'd stolen the aircart – two aircarts – but Ysser interrupted.

"Destroy?"

"Break. Kill."

Ysser nodded. He turned and translated for the king, who frowned and looked from Tyen to the professors and back, then spoke.

"What is this thing?" the sorcerer translated.

Kilraker scowled. "Tyen—"

"They didn't tell you?" Tyen asked Ysser.

"No."

No doubt Kilraker had hoped to avoid revealing what Vella

was, in case the Sselts decided to examine her and discovered the secrets she contained. Tyen had been very conscious of the satchel hanging at his side as he'd weighed up his chances of keeping hold of Vella. He'd guessed that all four Leratians were sorcerers. Kilraker and Gowel would not have weighed down their aircarts with anyone who wasn't. If it came to a confrontation, Tyen doubted he would win. But they hadn't attacked him. He guessed doing so without the king's approval risked spoiling trade between the Empire and the Sselts in the future.

"The king wants you treated rightly," Ysser had told him. "But he will not defy the laws of another land if he not know good reason for it. These men's claim must be shown to be right. Before then we will keep the thing you stole safe."

So he had given Vella to Ysser and told him what she was: a book that collected and stored knowledge from those who touched her.

Kilraker and Gowel hadn't been very happy about that.

Ysser had wrapped the book in a cloth before taking it from Tyen and giving it to the king. From a pocket of his coat the king had produced a drawstring bag made of a translucent material. He held it open so that Ysser could drop Vella inside then pulled the string tight. Then he had hung it on the back of the throne.

"It will stay there until we decide what is to be done," Ysser had translated.

He had then outlined how the trial to decide whether Tyen and the book would be handed over to the professors would proceed. Kilraker had warned the king that Tyen was powerful and it would be difficult to prevent him escaping, and offered their help in restraining him. The king did not accept. The discussion that followed led to Ysser declaring that Tyen would remain in his aircart with the propellers and rudder removed, tethered to the spire.

It was a strange form of captivity, but it was effective. Tyen could sever the rope and go wherever the wind blew him, but Kilraker would soon follow and retrieve him. Guards watching Tyen's every move ensured he could make no attempt to steal Vella back. Ysser had probably guessed that Tyen would not leave if a chance remained of reclaiming Vella, too. As the sorcerer had led Tyen out to the aircart he'd given Tyen a sidelong look.

"Why do you call it 'her'?" he'd asked.

"She was once a woman, changed against her will. Part of her remains in that book. I have promised to find a way to give her human form again."

"That is a . . . I think you call it a noble task."

Tyen had nodded. "Do you know how it might be done?"

"I am sad to say I do not."

They had given him warm clothes and extra blankets, and every day Ysser or another Sselt sorcerer lifted baskets of food up to him with magic. Tyen had to keep the air in the aircart capsule heated, but the only hardship in that was waking throughout the night to maintain it.

Twice they'd brought him down to the spire to answer questions. Each time he'd been reassured to see the bag hanging above the king's strange throne, Vella visible within. The last time, Ysser had assured him that a decision would be made soon, so as the door to the palace opened and the old sorcerer emerged with two guards, Tyen felt his heart lift with hope. He let some air out of the capsule and it began to descend. The two guards began to pull on the ropes, guiding the cart down to the platform.

As Tyen stepped off, Ysser smiled at him.

"Are you ffell?" he asked.

"Yes, though last night was a bit cold."

The sorcerer nodded. "I concern for you." He beckoned and turned back to the door.

The air inside was warmer, so Tyen shrugged out of the fur-lined coat he'd been given, took off the hat and unwound the scarf. Ysser did not stop at the audience room door, but continued on to another. The room within was smaller than others Tyen had seen on this level, but no less elaborately decorated. Two large couches similar to the king's throne faced each other, between them a long, low table.

On one of the couches sat Gowel.

The adventurer smiled. Tyen scowled and turned to look at Ysser.

"What is going on?"

"Gowel ffant to talk to you," he said. "I ffill be close, but not hearing talk. Speak if you need me," he added, giving Tyen a meaningful look. He walked out of the room, closing the door behind him.

Tyen turned to regard Gowel, who waved at the other chair.

"Sit, Tyen," he said.

"Why should I listen to you?"

The adventurer smiled. "Because I am going to give you a chance to buy your freedom."

"I won't give up Vella."

"I'm not asking you to."

Tyen narrowed his eyes at the man, then moved over to the seat and sat down.

"Why should I trust you?"

Gowel chuckled. "Why indeed? Perhaps because the trade I offer is worth the risk."

Tyen snorted. "Trade with too much risk is gambling."

"I suppose it is." Gowel grinned. "You've grown up a lot since we last met, young Ironsmelter. Not so naïve." He rubbed his hands together and leaned forward, his gaze unwavering. "The thing is, we didn't come south to find you. We had another purpose. Searching for you was a fine cover for our true purpose."

Tyen said nothing, but his mind began to race. If Gowel wasn't lying, what could possibly have brought him here? Was there something he had discovered in the Far South that he had kept to himself until he could return with Kilraker and friends? After all, Kilraker had been willing to give up his connections and secure job at the Academy to join the adventurer before he knew of Vella's existence. Willing to frame Tyen for the theft of Vella, too.

"You know from the book that there are other worlds," Gowel said. "Worlds with more magic than ours. You know that it's possible to travel between them, using magic, and that it takes no more magic to move several people than it does one."

A thrill ran down Tyen's spine. He hadn't known that last detail.

"We thought it must therefore be like digging a tunnel," Gowel continued. "You only need to expend the energy to create a passage that one person can use, and the others can follow, one after another. Several days ago we tried creating a small tunnel, assuming it would use less magic, to send objects or little animals through. Do you want to know what happened?"

Despite himself, Tyen could not help leaning forward. "What?"

Gowel chuckled. "It didn't work. A sorcerer cannot *send* other things through the barrier to the next world, *he must go with them.* Kilraker guessed as much. He then managed to go some way out of this world. He faded before our eyes. But in taking himself out and moving back again, he used all the magic he had been able to gather. We needed a richer source of magic."

"So you came here," Tyen guessed.

"Yes." Gowel looked around the room. "Perhaps our ancestors' superstitions were correct about magic's source, perhaps it is because these people do not have machines gobbling up their magic. It doesn't matter – or it won't soon – because what we hope to do is tap the magic of another world. We think that if a sorcerer stops midway between this world and the next he will be able to send magic from one to the other. Or, failing that, you can cross over to the next world, gather magic and carry it back to this one. The other worlds are so much richer in magic then you should be able to gather more than what is required to return here, and release it on arrival."

A chill ran down Tyen's spine. "You're not using 'you' in the second person, are you."

Gowel smiled and shook his head. "Kilraker *might* be able to gather enough magic here to do it, but we know from your fight with him at the Academy that you have a greater reach than he. You would be more likely to succeed. And we may not get a second chance at this. It will take most of the magic around the spire."

A tingling sensation had been growing at the base of Tyen's stomach, but it ceased abruptly. "You want to do it *here*? Have you asked the king if he minds you using all the magic around his home?"

"Of course," Gowel replied. "He approves. It will make Spirecastle an incredibly powerful place. The magic you bring back will flow out from here to replenish the world, making this place the one always richest in it." He slapped his hands onto his knees and leaned towards Tyen. "Think! We'll be heroes, the men who saved this world from running out of magic. Think of all the machines that enable us to clothe and feed more people, and the sorcerers who heal the sick. Think of how vulnerable Leratia's cities are growing. How soon before uncivilised but less magically depleted foreign nations seek to take advantage of that weakness? All that the Leratian Empire has gained would be lost – and perhaps the Empire itself!"

Tyen's pulse was racing, but he held his excitement in check. Perhaps it would be better for those foreign nations if they were freed from the Empire's control. He thought of Sezee and Veroo's people, forced to change to fit Leratian ideas of proper royal inheritance. He thought of Oren and the Darsh people, their forests cut down and land taken. He remembered the Mailanders, their traditions ignored while archaeologists and students looted their tombs.

But such change would not come without war and death. The machines did much good and it would be a pity if the advancements of the age were lost. If change could be made to occur slowly, with time for people to adjust, would it happen without conflict?

If he brought magic into this world at a controlled rate, perhaps it would. But it might not work at all. They might use up all the magic around Spirecastle and find they could not replace it. Did the king really understand that risk?

I will have to make sure he does, if I'm going to agree to this.

If he did, he would have to confirm this was all that Gowel wanted – and what of Vella?

"What is in this for me?" Tyen asked.

A frown creased Gowel's brow. He leaned back against the back of the couch.

"We'll give you your book and let you go. You will have to promise never to return to the north. We won't tell the Academy you are in the Far South."

So much for being a hero. Gowel and Kilraker had obviously never intended to share the credit. He could live with that, if he was free to search for a solution for Vella.

"I'll do it, but I want Vella back before I try anything," Tyen told him.

"Kilraker might not agree to that."

"You have the advantage of numbers, and you're not the one blamed by the Academy for a crime you didn't commit. I haven't forgotten what happened last time you offered to help me."

Gowel pursed his lips, then nodded. "Fair enough. I will attempt to persuade him." He rose and moved towards the door, then stopped and looked back at Tyen, his expression serious. "I have always wanted us to be your allies, not enemies. While I regret what was done to you, it may have worked out for the better for you. It would have been such a great waste for someone as powerful as you to be stuck in the Academy, always limited by the lack of magic and the rules."

"Instead I am limited by a lack of training," Tyen pointed out.

Gowel shrugged and turned back to the door. "Nothing you can't learn on your own," he said, then pushed through to the corridor beyond.

Tyen sighed. *Am I a fool for agreeing to this?* he asked himself. As soon as he had Vella back he would consult her, and the two of them would search for tricks and flaws within Gowel and Kilraker's plan.

After a long wait the door opened again and Ysser entered. The old man smiled. "They forgive you," he said.

Tyen shook his head. "I don't think forgiveness has anything to do with it. If Kilraker agrees, they'll be giving me Vella and my freedom in exchange for helping them. Did they explain what they intend me to do?" he asked.

The sorcerer smiled. "Yes. You ffill take magic from outside the spire, go to another fforld, and return with much more magic."

"Yes, but we will be taking a lot of magic. Probably all of it. And we have not done this before. If it doesn't work Tyeszal will have much, much less magic. It is a big risk."

Ysser nodded, his expression serious. "Without risk ffe do not find new things. Tyeszal ffill make more magic." He patted Tyen on the shoulder. "You good man, to think of us. I am happy you are free. I take to room for new clothes and food now. Tomorrow I bring you book."

CHAPTER 23

A tapping at the door woke Tyen. He bolted out of bed and stumbled over to answer it, the fog of sleep quickly dissipating as he remembered Kilraker's plans for the day.

I am going to attempt to reach another world, he thought. *Or at least go partway to one.*

He opened the door a crack to find Ysser's protégé, Mig, waiting. The young man smiled, then hurried away without saying anything.

A wake-up call? Tyen guessed. He considered the light coming through the window. The brightness made his head hurt. He'd stayed up late talking to Ysser, who'd shared a sweet liqueur from the seaside village he was born in. By the time Tyen had crawled into bed he'd wanted to adopt the old man as his own grandfather or become his apprentice. Or both.

Looking around he ignored the fine clothes the Sselts had left for him and sought out the other set of simple porter's clothes Veroo and Sezee had bought for him – that felt like a lifetime ago now. He found them, freshly cleaned and folded neatly, on a chest. They seemed like more practical clothes for travelling between worlds.

Another knock at the door heralded the arrival of a servant bringing food. Tyen started eating heartily, but as his mind returned to the task he'd agreed to do his stomach clenched and he found he could only pick over and nibble at the rest.

His third visitor was Ysser.

The old man grinned at Tyen as he slipped into the room. "A big day ffor you!" he said. "Kilraker said to give thiss to you ffhen you join him." He took a familiar drawstring bag out from within his coat. "I give it to you now. You may ask it of how travel to other fforlds. If bad . . . big risk . . ." His expression grew serious and earnest. "I help you go from Tyeszal not seen, and be free."

Tyen gazed at the old man in amazement. "You would do that?"

Ysser nodded, then held out the bag. "Your story true."

"You talked to her?"

"Mig talk to her. He say Kilraker bad to you."

Taking the bag, Tyen frowned. "Do you still want to let them do the experiment here and use so much of your magic?"

"Yes. You take magic from outside, so magic inside left for us. Put magic you bring here outside, too." Ysser tapped the book within the bag. "She says she teach you how before you try with Kilraker." He took a step towards the door. "I now go make my room ready for you all."

"Thank you," Tyen said. He opened the bag and tipped Vella out into his hand. The familiar weight and softness of her leather cover brought a wave of relief. She was unharmed. She was his again.

He opened the cover.

Are you all right, Vella?

Words formed. I am. So you have struck a deal with Kilraker and Gowel.

Yes. Will I be able to travel to another world?

Perhaps. You are strong and there is a lot of magic here.

Will I be able to stop midway and draw magic from another world over to this one?

I doubt it. I have no record of anyone doing so.

What about going to another world, taking in magic, and bringing it back?

That is definitely possible, if the other world is rich in magic and your reach is great enough.

And if one or both are not?

You must use some of what you take from the other world to travel back. What you deliver to this world must be more than what you took, or you will have made the effort for nothing.

If I bring back less then this world will be poorer.

And if the other world is poor in magic, you might not be able to get back at all.

A chill ran down Tyen's spine. He would be stuck there.

Do you know anything about the worlds closest to this one?

Yes, but my knowledge is over a thousand years old.

A lot could change in that time. His own world had.

I guess I won't know until I get there. It's a risk I have to take.

It is not the only choice open to you. Ysser will help you escape Kilraker and the Academy if you ask him.

No. If there's a chance we could slow the depletion of magic in this world, then I must try it. For the sake of the people of this world – and for your sake, too. If this world runs out of magic you will perish. He moved over to a chair and sat down. *Tell me how to travel between worlds, Vella.*

First you must establish an awareness of the world you are in. Take in magic and push that world away. You will feel it when it happens.

Moving to the centre of the room, Tyen concentrated on the magic around him and carefully drew some in from beyond the outside wall.

What direction do I push in? Up? Down? Forwards?

None of those. You are thinking in terms of physical directions in this world.

503

You want to push away from the world itself. But first you must learn to sense it. Close your eyes. It helps to prevent the physical world from distracting you.

He did. At once he was more aware of the pressure of the floor under his feet, and faint sounds within and outside the room. Those were physical sensations, though. He sought something else. All he detected was magic. Was that a physical thing? He opened his eyes so that he could read the page.

It is not. It cannot be affected by physical forces.

But if I let magic go it will flow outwards. Is that a kind of pushing?

Not the kind you want.

I didn't think so.

Sensing the world is not unlike sensing magic. It has a presence that has been there all your life, like a noise you've grown used to, so you must learn to detect it.

He laughed and shook his head. *That's so vague!* he complained. *Can't you tell me something more specific?*

These are the limitations of my form, she told him. *I can only explain something to you in words you already understand. You can only read them. Outside this world it is common practice for an experienced sorcerer to teach this by letting his student watch his thoughts as he does it.*

He felt a flash of inspiration. *But when they wrote about it, how did they describe travelling through worlds?*

Like taking a step back from the world. Or retreating behind a curtain.

Which didn't sound any more helpful. Still, he had to give it a try. Closing his eyes again, Tyen imagined himself moving backwards. He tried actually stepping backwards in the hope that some sort of parallel shift would happen in sympathy with the physical movement, but none occurred. He tried using magic to still the air before him then pushing against it, and wound up stumbling backwards. Sighing, he looked down at the open page.

You won't succeed until you learn to sense the world, Vella told him. *Stay still. Be patient. Ignore what is physical and not relevant.*

Tyen did as she instructed. He felt the floor beneath his feet and the temperature of the air moving in and out of his lungs. Considering other senses, he noticed the lingering smell of the food and the lingering flavours in his mouth. His ears picked up faint sounds: wind outside his window, footsteps in the corridor. He stood there with closed eyes until he was sure there was nothing left to sense, then gave up and consulted Vella again.

What other words have sorcerers used to describe it?

Like pushing away from a rock when you're swimming, she told him. He snorted. Since he didn't know how to swim, that analogy didn't help one bit. Unless he imagined pushing against the side of a bath while immersed . . .

That's not so different from pushing against an obstruction to prevent the aircart from colliding with it, he realised. Which meant orientating the cart with something solid to push against. *Only I'm trying to orientate myself with a world.*

Keeping his eyes open, he focused his awareness on the limits of his body. This was more familiar. It was basic battle strategy. In combat you needed to be able to still the air around yourself to ward off a physical attack without thought or hesitation, so all students were taught exercises that refined spacial awareness and encouraged them to do them regularly.

This time he wasn't repelling a physical attack, however. This time it was the world that was still and his body that must be repulsed. So he must become aware of it as if it was his body.

As he sent his mind out he sensed magic. As in Leratia it was not stationary, but drifted around him like a translucent fog. In Leratia it came down from above, replacing the void created by the machines. Here it moved sideways. Ysser had said something about this the previous night. *He said magic goes to the north. I thought he meant the Empire was more advanced in magic, but he was being more literal.*

The magic here flowed to the north because it was naturally inclined to even out, like water finding a level, and there was less magic in the north than in the south. Much less. No wonder the king thought it was worth risking the depletion of Tyeszal's magic. The north was drawing it all away anyway. If Tyen succeeded he would be helping both the Empire and the Far South.

Tyen took a deep breath as renewed determination filled him. He considered the magic flowing around him. If he could draw it to himself, then could he do other things? Could he still it?

He drew on the magic he had taken and exerted his will. He felt a jolt. The magic did not stop moving, but its flow pulled at him and it was taking more magic to hold on. He grinned. This meant it *was* something he could orientate himself with. Something he could orientate himself with even though it wasn't solid or still.

The room had brightened, he noticed. He looked down. His feet were slowly gliding across the floor, but there was no sensation of movement.

Was that supposed to happen? he wondered.

"Yes, it is," a voice said. A woman's voice.

Startled, he let go. At once the room stopped glowing. He sensed the moment he returned fully. It was as if his head had just broken through the surface of a pool of water into the air again.

He looked down at Vella. Words formed on the page.

Congratulations. You have travelled out of this world for the first time.

He grinned. *I did it! But who spoke to me?*

I did. In the place between worlds my connection to the mind of whoever holds me is different.

You could have warned me.

It wasn't information relevant to what you need to know just now.

And I didn't ask.

You couldn't know to ask.

Will that always happen, when we are between worlds?

Yes.

Is it like reading minds?

No. The only advantage is to hear my voice. And this will be a disadvantage if it causes you to lose concentration. The worlds will pull you towards them if you do not resist them. But the further you are from a world the weaker the pull is. You are not breathing when you travel, though you are unaware of it. If you take too long you will suffocate.

Suffocate? You didn't tell me this earlier!

You would have been too worried about it to concentrate. When you are only a little way out of this world a failure of concentration will bring you back to it quickly, so there was no danger.

So I should take a deep breath before leaving for another world?

Yes.

What happens to people who suffocate between worlds?

Their body is eventually pushed out into the nearest world.

Dead people materialising out of thin air? He shuddered as he remembered creepy stories he'd heard as a child. Perhaps they had held some truth. The more he found out about travelling between worlds, the more dangerous it appeared to be.

A tapping sound interrupted Tyen's thoughts.

That could be Ysser, returning to take me to Kilraker. Is there anything else I need to know?

Nothing relevant.

He closed her and slipped her into his shirt, then put on his jacket and buttoned it. As he turned to the door his satchel caught his attention. Should he take it with him? What about Beetle? Maybe he should leave the insectoid behind, in case something happened. He was sure Mig would like to have it.

507

But it had been taught to respond only to his instructions and he didn't have time to fix that. Kilraker might decide to take it back to the Academy as proof Tyen had been dealt with so he could claim the reward, too.

The professors might think he was planning not to return from the other world if he looked ready to travel, so he opened the satchel and transferred Beetle to an inner pocket of his jacket. Then he hurried over to the door.

Mig was waiting outside again. The young man beckoned and hurried away. Tyen closed the door behind him and followed.

He wondered briefly if the king would be present, and decided it was unlikely. Nobody knew yet if this would work. Experiments with magic always had the potential to be dangerous. He was not surprised to find Ysser, Kilraker, Gowel and their two friends, but nobody else, waiting in the old man's room. Ysser came forward to greet him.

"Ready?"

Tyen nodded. "I think I know what to do."

"Good." The sorcerer patted Tyen's back. "Be safe. Only take magic and release magic outside Tyeszal's walls."

Tyen turned to Kilraker. The professor's eyes narrowed. He was holding a piece of rope.

"Ironsmelter," he said.

"Professor," Tyen replied. "Or is that no longer correct?"

"I haven't officially retired yet," the man said.

Tyen forced a smile. "Well, maybe I should call you 'Kilraker' so you get used to it sooner." The man's knuckles tightened around the rope. "I hope you're not planning to tie me up with that," Tyen added.

"Tempting though that may be, it is not our intention. We were curious to see if you could carry one end of it through with you."

Tyen shrugged. "I can see no harm in trying."

He walked over to Kilraker. Looking into the man's face, he searched for evidence of his thoughts. No guilt for having ruined Tyen's life at the Academy? No hint of apology? Kilraker stared back coldly. At least there was nothing obviously sly in his expression either. He mostly looked impatient and cautious, as if Tyen was the one given to betraying other people's trust.

Kilraker handed Tyen the end of the rope. Closing his fingers around it, Tyen took a few steps back.

"So," he said. "You want me to travel to another world, or as far as needed to gather magic from it and bring it back here. Anything else you want me to try?"

"No," Kilraker said. "Keep your mind on your task."

Tyen looked at Gowel and the others. They shook their heads. He looked at Ysser.

"The flyers are inside?"

The old man smiled and nodded. Mig stood a step behind him, face alive with excitement.

No reason to wait. Time to see if I can get all the way to a new world.

Taking a deep breath, Tyen reached out beyond the spire. He reached as far as he could, then he drew in magic from the furthest distance inward, leaving a column of magic within Tyeszal's walls. Though he was aware that he was gathering more magic than he ever had before it was no strain to hold it.

He took a deep breath and focused on the magic within the spire. Now that it was surrounded by a void it flowed gently outward in all directions. This made it a more stable thing to orientate himself with. He *pushed*.

Once more his surroundings grew brighter. The room slowly grew less distinct, as if a fog had spontaneously formed to fill it, or his eyes were losing the ability to see colour. As in a fog, sounds were softened and diminished, too. Looking down at his hands he saw that they were also fading out of sight. So was the rope.

Looking up again, he could see Kilraker's hands clawing at the other end. The man's fingers were moving through it. He remembered what Gowel had said: "*A sorcerer cannot send other things through the barrier to the next world, he must go with them.*" Clearly, whatever the sorcerer held came with them. Which was fortunate, or Tyen might arrive in the other world without clothing. Or Vella.

But there must be a limitation. Kilraker wasn't being taken through, only the rope. The professor was scowling. He spoke, but his voice was too faint for Tyen to make out the words. The others shrugged. Kilraker's expression hardened. Ysser's eyes widened and he strode forward. He placed a hand on Kilraker's arm and began speaking assertively.

What is Kilraker up to? Tyen wondered, slowing his push to watch.

Kilraker shook Ysser's hand off roughly, unbalancing the old man. Mig caught the old sorcerer's shoulders to steady him. Ysser's shock turned to anger. He came forward again, his voice loud enough to penetrate to Tyen.

"No! Do not take from inside! You break our law!"

"It's all or nothing," Kilraker barked in reply. A faint ringing noise reached Tyen. Ysser's eyes widened and he looked up at the ceiling. The old sorcerer turned back to Kilraker. His expression was pleading now, but Tyen could not hear what he said. He reached out to grab Kilraker's shoulder but his hand passed through the man.

Tyen stopped pushing and felt himself drifting back. Kilraker had moved out of the world. Why? Was he following Tyen? Why was Ysser so angry and frightened?

Should I go back? Vella?

"*If you do it may be a long time before the magic you've used is replaced,*" she replied. The sound of her voice, so clear and human made his heart sing.

He had to go on. As he was propelling himself away again, he saw Kilraker suddenly stumble, reach out and grab Gowel. Since his hand didn't pass through the adventurer, he must have returned to their world. Had he run out of magic?

The fading room abruptly brightened even further as a square of white appeared to one side. The doors to the balcony were open. Mig ran from the opening to the flying vehicle and climbed inside. His hand slapped the side and his mouth opened in a muffled shout. Ysser took a few steps towards Mig and paused to look back. He glared at Kilraker, raising a hand to point at the man, his mouth moving to words Tyen could not hear, though the tone was clearly accusatory. Then he turned and ran to the vehicle. As soon as he had climbed inside it slid forward and disappeared into the square of light.

Tyen stopped again, certain that Ysser would not have used the machine without good cause. Looking back at Kilraker and the others, he saw that they were staggering about, faces stretched with terror. Objects in the room were moving – swaying or toppling over. The whole scene was shaking.

What is happening?

"*Perhaps an attack on the spire?*" Vella said. "*Sseltee has no powerful enemies, but someone may be exploiting Tyeszal's sudden lack of magic.*"

How would they know? A traitor had told them, perhaps. *We have to go back and return the magic so they can defend the spire.* He stopped resisting the pull of his world and began drifting back. *Can I speed this up?*

"*Yes, you just . . .*"

A low sound surrounded Tyen, loud enough to penetrate into the place between worlds. Something passed across his sight, turning all to grey. He sensed himself drawing near to his world.

Then the grey disappeared and a familiar view of a far-distant land opened before him.

This time not framed by a window or a door.

Silence followed. He looked down. A dark, roiling cloud billowed beneath him. Instinct made him lock himself in place.

Tyeszal was gone. There was nothing where he had stood moments before but air. Below it had been replaced by a great cloud of dust. He stared down at it, too shocked to think. Then a wave of horror rushed over him.

They're gone. All the people . . . Why? What happened?

"*I don't know.*"

He thought of the ringing sound Ysser had been so alarmed to hear. Had it been a warning? If so, then the occupants of Tyeszal might have known something bad was about to happen when it rang. But what?

Something Kilraker had done. He remembered Ysser's words: "*No! Do not take from inside! You break our law!*" Kilraker must have taken magic from within the spire in an attempt to follow Tyen.

Kilraker was dead now. As was Gowel, and anyone who hadn't managed to evacuate the spire. He could not imagine anybody having time to escape. Except for Ysser and Mig. And anyone else who owned one of the gliding aircarts. Looking around, he felt his heart lighten as he saw them, circling around the dust cloud as they descended. But far too few to account for all five hundred residents of the tower.

The dust cloud was clearing below, revealing a stump perhaps half the height of the former spire. Hollow, with the twisted fragments of staircases visible within. He could see

512

ropes hanging down the outside, too. *The bridges!* Tyen looked up at the cliff. He could see the ropes hanging down where the bridges had once spanned the gap between cliff and spire. Tiny movements drew his eyes to long lines of people filling the narrow paths on the cliff face. People staring down, people huddled together, people covering their faces as if unable to face the sight below . . .

Tyen's chest constricted. If only he hadn't come here . . . but how could he have known what Kilraker would do? There was no undoing it. But perhaps, if he went back . . .

"You will fall."

I could try to use magic to stop myself. But all the lessons about aircart safety told him otherwise. He'd have to orientate himself with the ground, and it was too far away.

What can I do?

"Move as quickly as possible to the next world before you suffocate," Vella said. *"You are running out of magic. The longer you stay here, the less likely you will have enough magic to reach another world."*

But all those people . . . I should help them.

"You cannot stay here, you cannot return, you can only try to reach the next world."

She was right. He had to get out of the place between worlds before he suffocated. He had to hope he still had enough magic to reach the next world, and that the world he reached was rich in magic so he would be able to gather enough to return.

Closing his eyes, he propelled himself away from the scene of devastation and towards the unknown.

PART TEN

RIELLE

CHAPTER 22

Rielle had thought the long days of walking in the desert had been tiring, but they were easy compared to the relentless upward climb into the mountains. She had noted that Sa-Mica had slowed and lengthened his strides and she found by copying him, concentrating on one deliberate step after another, it made the ascent a little easier. Sa-Gest kept pausing to catch his breath, then hurrying after them, or was so distracted by the scenery that he tripped on rocks that had fallen onto the road from the slopes above.

Whenever they rested, Rielle looked down at the desert in awe. She had never seen the world from above like this before. The road wound back to the village like a pale ribbon, then vanished into the sands. The dunes were not randomly scattered across the desert, but formed crescent-like curves all facing the same way. She itched to capture it in paint. In her mind she saw the colours she'd mix to make the right hues and shades.

By the end of the first day they'd climbed above the level of the hills. A steep drop now always fell from their right and a rock wall rose on their left. As dusk saw them still walking, Rielle had wondered if they would camp on the road or keep walking through the night.

Just as the last glow of the sun had faded they'd rounded

a bend and come upon a small house built against the rock wall. It had looked too narrow to contain more than a corridor's space within, but when Sa-Mica had lit his lamp and led them inside they'd found extra depth had been carved out of the rock. The room was large enough to fit two narrow beds with a space between. At the back a small spring dribbled down the wall into a basin, then overflowed into a hole in the floor.

The priests had slept on the beds. Sa-Mica had given her all three sleeping mats to lie on, so the floor wasn't as uncomfortable as the brick bench had been the night before. Even so, the next morning she was as stiff and sore as she had been the first morning after leaving Fyre. Her legs were unused to walking uphill.

They'd risen early but walked slowly. Eventually Rielle's muscles had loosened and she began to walk more easily, but a gloom settled upon her and refused to lift. They were out of the desert, but it would be no easier to survive here than out in the sands if she managed to escape.

The thought of getting away was now a constant hum in the back of her mind. With Sa-Gest always there, strengthening her conviction that, while she deserved punishment, nobody deserved to be subjected to his depraved manipulations for the rest of their life. She had grown more and more convinced that the Angels could never have meant it to be this way. If they had, then she did not want to meet them in the afterlife. She would rather not exist at all.

As the morning wore on, the road took them along the left side of a steep valley between the arms of two peaks. She caught glimpses of buildings at the end of the valley. The sight sent a chill through her, and a growing panic. Was this the end of their journey? Would she never get an opportunity to try for freedom? If not then what could she do? Hope that what Sa-Gest had hinted at was a lie to frighten her into obeying him? *Then why won't Sa-Mica tell me anything?*

It wasn't until they were almost upon them that she realised the buildings could not be their destination. The structures were houses, their doors and windows open and people walking freely in, out and around them. None of these people were priests. It was just another village.

She braced herself as the first of the locals saw them coming, but instead of staring and cursing they simply continued with their business. A few nodded to Sa-Mica as he passed them. Their lack of concern ought to have been a relief, but Rielle suspected it meant they were nearing the prison. Why else would the locals be so familiar with the sight of a tainted that they could ignore one?

It was more of a hamlet than a village, too. Nine houses faced the high side of the road. The largest was in the middle, with a low wall extending from the front to encompass wooden benches and tables, and heavy wooden beams supporting a sheltering roof. The tables were empty. To Rielle's surprise, Sa-Mica led them through the gap in the wall and sat down at one of them.

A stocky man immediately emerged from the building. Dressed in warm clothes covered with a leather apron, he looked like a metalworker. He glanced at her, gave Sa-Gest a longer look, then smiled at Sa-Mica.

"Welcome back, Sa-Mica," he said. "Heading to the mountain?"

"We are, Breca," the scarred priest said. "We'll have the usual."

The man chuckled. "As if there was a choice."

He disappeared inside. The view of the valley, unobstructed by buildings on the other side of the road, captured her attention. She tried to commit all to memory. Perhaps, if she was to redeem herself with work, trying to recapture this would give her something other than her prison to paint. Or she would try to draw it in her mind's eye, if things became too unbearable.

The air was colder here, and now that they were at rest she began to shiver a little. Breca emerged with three plates of steaming food. On each was a generous serving of bread, baked meat and root vegetables. Sa-Gest frowned when he saw that Rielle had been given the same as he and Sa-Mica, but the scarred priest said nothing and began to eat, not even pausing when Breca returned with three mugs of iquo.

Nobody spoke as they ate. The meat tasted wonderful, though perhaps that was because she had craved it so long. Narmah . . . as the name entered her mind Rielle was pierced by guilt and sadness . . . Narmah had told her when she had her first bleed that regular servings of meat would help ease the weakness that could accompany it. That sent a twinge of concern through her that rapidly expanded to apprehension as she counted the days on the road. They had travelled for so long that she was overdue. Lack of good food and unaccustomed exertion could cause such a delay. Rielle drank the iquo quickly, trying not to consider the other possibility.

All too soon Sa-Mica had them walking out of the hamlet. The other effect of travelling for so long without sustaining food was that the iquo had affected her more than usual. Maybe that was the intention. Maybe it was meant to keep her so relaxed or off balance that she wouldn't attempt to escape at the last moment. But as the effects slowly wore off she realised that was not the case. Even in her weary state, she would sober up before she arrived.

The road wound back and forth as it climbed the end of the valley, then plunged through a crack in the left side to emerge into another, deeper valley. She could see it continuing on, carved into the undulating side of the steep right-hand wall, disappearing into folds then emerging again. Looking even further beyond, she could see where the wall was vertical, extending further out into the valley. The jagged shape at the outermost point was too regular to be natural.

The Mountain Temple, she thought, shivering at the sight. The gloom expanded within her until she was sick and bloated with it. *Where I'll spend the rest of my life.*

Something inside her rebelled and she had to resist a mad urge to run back down the road. *There's no point*, she told herself. *I wouldn't make two steps before Sa-Mica stopped me.* The chain around her neck felt heavy. She made herself look down and count her steps. She tried to keep her mind blank. When she failed at that, she tried to recall all the stories that Sa-Mica had told her. She imagined herself painting the valley from the hamlet, choosing colours, grinding pigment, mixing it to Izare's formula, combining colours, preparing the board, applying it . . .

A call shattered her concentration. Sa-Mica stopped and looked back. Turning, Rielle saw a young man hurrying towards them and felt an irrational pang of hope. A rescuer? *Don't be ridiculous.* She didn't recognise him, but he wore similar clothing to the man who had served them their meal. They waited in silence as he caught up with them.

"Sa-Mica," he panted. "A man named Dorth arrived soon after you left, and asked for you. He says he has a message for you. He's waiting at Breca's."

Sa-Mica frowned. He looked at Rielle, then at Sa-Gest, then at the messenger. Finally he sighed and nodded.

"I will go back." He waved towards the hamlet. "Please return and tell him I am coming to meet him, but can only stop briefly."

The man hurried away.

Sa-Mica faced Sa-Gest. "Wait here. I will be back as soon

as I have received the message." He added something else in a murmur.

"I will." Sa-Gest held the scarred priest's gaze, his expression all respect and obedience.

Satisfied, Sa-Mica set off after the messenger, his pace faster than before thanks to the downward slope. Rielle watched him until he turned a corner and disappeared. At the edge of her vision she could see Sa-Gest watching her, but she ignored him. Her heart was racing. Was this the opportunity she had hoped for?

The prison lay ahead. A cliff lay to her left and a sheer wall to her right. The only other way open to her was the road back to the hamlet, on which she was bound to encounter Sa-Mica.

"No sense standing around in the sun if we don't have to," Sa-Gest said, then removed his pack, walked over to the rock wall and sat down on a natural, if narrow, shelf shaded by an overhang. It was wide enough for two. He patted the space beside him.

Taking off her pack, she walked over to the wall a few strides from him and found a relatively smooth area to lean against. She stared out over the valley. Since it meant twisting around to look at her, the priest left off staring after a while and did the same.

The opposite wall of the valley was as steep, but without a road slicing into the rock it was featureless. She found herself wishing Sa-Mica had picked somewhere with a nicer view to leave them. Birds dipped and soared overhead and out in the valley. She had no idea what kind they were. A large one circled above, then swooped and plucked a smaller bird out of a flock. It then glided across the valley, shrinking to a tiny dot before landing on the opposite wall. Looking closer, she realised it had built a nest there.

"Not far to go now," Sa-Gest said. He was tapping his fingers on his knees in a quick, impatient rhythm.

Her stomach sank. He was bored, and whatever he thought up for entertainment was likely to be unpleasant for her, even if he did heed Sa-Mica's warning not to touch her.

"Not long before you know the truth," Sa-Gest continued. "Then you'll regret you didn't take my advice."

She ignored him. It would not dissuade him from taunting her, but if he wanted to bait her she would make it as hard as possible.

"You don't believe me, do you?" He chuckled. "Oh, you're in for quite a surprise."

He looked out over the valley for a while. Just as she began to think he had found something else to distract him, he stood and turned to her.

"It's not too late, you know. It'll take Sa-Mica a while to get back to that village and return again. If you follow my instructions we can be done before he gets back."

She looked away. Sa-Gest chuckled. He walked a little way past her, then back again. His gaze fixed on the prison. "We're so close," he said quietly, as if to himself. Then he turned and strolled downhill again. "There's really nowhere for you to go now. The road ends at the Mountain Temple. I doubt you can climb that wall behind you and the only other option is to throw yourself off the cliff. Which I won't let you do – and I'd enjoy having an excuse to restrain you."

He stopped pacing and crossed his arms. "So I can see no reason to keep the truth from you. After all, you ought to have a chance to ready yourself for your new life."

He took a step closer. Rielle kept her gaze averted and steeled herself for whatever lie he had come up with to taunt her.

"You want to know what happens to the tainted?" he asked.

"It depends on your sex. If you're a man you can pledge your life to the Angels and become a priest. There's a long and unpleasant cleansing ritual, of course, and they keep an eye on you. But they *want* tainted men to become priests. It keeps the magical ability in our bloodlines strong."

He took another step towards her. "But, of course, women can't become priests."

A step closer. "They can strengthen our bloodlines in other ways, though."

Rielle's body went cold despite her determination to disbelieve him. She held onto her composure. With gritted teeth.

Sa-Gest came a little closer and lowered his voice. "You see, the reason we don't kill the tainted, the reason we take you far away and keep your location a secret is that the Mountain Temple is a big priest-breeding whorehouse."

Nausea gripped her. It could not possibly be true. He was taunting her again. Trying to frighten her into doing what he wanted.

"Not at all worried, are you? Sa-Mica has done his job well, with his stories and his appearance of kindness. I have to admire him for it."

To her relief, he moved away. The tension in her eased a little. If he tried to touch her she'd fight him. He crouched by his pack, opened it and took out a folded piece of paper or parchment yellowed with age. Straightening, he turned to face her.

"I can prove it to you. This is a letter from the superior of the Mountain Temple that was delivered along with me to the Fyre Temple when I was a boy. It says my mother was chosen by my father for her strong magical ability. My father was one of the senior priests, my mother one of the prisoners. He says their offspring should become a powerful priest."

He unfolded it and held it out to her. With fear coiling in her stomach, she read it, then read it again. Then examined it closely. Was it a forgery? The paper was good quality. The ink had faded as much as good-quality ink would in that time, but the words they formed filled her with horror . . . *the woman named Derina, the tainted sent from Fyre five years ago . . . called him Gest . . . allowed to nurse him but as this is no place to raise a child . . .*

"Why do you think I was so eager to return to the Mountain Temple?" Sa-Gest told her. "I was born and raised here."

Rielle shook her head. It couldn't be. It was too incredible. Too horrible.

"Why do you think Sa-Mica hasn't told you anything? You wouldn't have co-operated. Those stories are meant to make you trust him and think he cares about you. It is easier dealing with a co-operative prisoner than one who isn't."

Which was exactly what Sa-Mica had told Sa-Gest on the second day of their journey.

Sa-Gest laughed. "Think about it. Why would *I* want to return to a remote prison up in the cold mountains if there wasn't a payoff?"

A memory rose of Sa-Mica's response to Sa-Baro's warning about Sa-Gest. "*Rest assured, the Mountain Temple is the only appropriate place for men like him, isolated from the innocents he would harm here.*"

Sa-Gest folded the letter and was putting it away. "They gave me this to make sure I knew which one was my own mother. Even I am not that depraved."

His words were barely audible over the sound of blood rushing in her ears. The corruption among priests she'd learned about since meeting Izare had been shocking, but this was both cruel and immoral. She could not imagine men like Sa-Baro condoning it. Unless he didn't know . . .

But the letter proved that the priests at Fyre *did* know. And Sa-Mica *must* know. What had the priest from the village down at the mountain's feet said? *"It gives me hope that you, born and raised in that terrible place, came out a better man than most."* Then he had said something about getting the truth from Sa-Mica.

The truth. That the prison was a place where women were forced to bear the children of priests. A fate that she was . . .

"But I can't have children . . ." she began, her determination not to speak shattering.

Sa-Gest straightened. "Can't you? Did you ruin your life and that of everyone you care about by using magic, and *fail* at healing yourself?" He shook his head and came closer. "The priests will have a go at fixing you. If it doesn't work," he shrugged, "I guess you'll become the fill-in when the other women are all fat and ugly with child. That's what they usually do with the infertile ones."

Rielle shook her head. "It can't be true." *It can't be true.*

"Oh, yes it is." He grinned. "I can't wait to see your face when you get there, and you see it all for yourself." He rubbed his crotch. "And Sa-Mica is likely to be back any moment. I'm afraid you've lost your chance to get on my good side."

Her heart stopped. She looked back down the road. If she confronted Sa-Mica, would he have another explanation for the letter Sa-Gest had shown her? What if he didn't? What if he lied and she arrived to find out Sa-Gest was right?

Then it would be too late. It was already too late. She had nowhere to run. The road led to the prison in one direction and to Sa-Mica in another. She couldn't scale the wall. The other choice was to leap off the cliff. She thought of the future that awaited her.

I have no future. None. I'd rather have oblivion than live with Angels that allow this to be.

Closing her eyes, she reached out as the corrupter had taught

526

her. This time she did not pluck magic from close by, but stretched unrestrained into the air and rock around her. She would need a lot of magic to get past Sa-Gest, and she did not need to hide the Stain. She felt her awareness expand until she was dizzy. Then she opened her eyes and drew all the magic into herself.

The world went black.

Her senses shifted, adjusting faster than her eyes could adapt to a dark room. Sa-Gest stood in front of her, his expression shifting from glee to surprise. He reached out towards her with both hands. She had no idea how to shape the energy coiled within her, so she imagined a great wind like those that sometimes battered Fyre, and thrust it at him.

The air ripped and tore, making a sound so loud it hurt her ears. Sa-Gest's head snapped down and his legs and arms shot forward. She blinked, and he had vanished.

Silence followed. A silence so complete she feared she had turned deaf. Not that it would matter, since she intended to die. Pushing away from the wall, she took an unsteady step forward, then another, slowly approaching the edge. She looked around for Sa-Gest, but he was not on the road.

The emptiness of Stain was everywhere. She could see no end to it.

I pushed him. Did I push him over the edge?

Reaching the precipice, she looked down. It was a long way to the bottom. She searched for Sa-Gest's body, but he could be any one of the dark points scattered over the valley floor.

If I did, then I've killed someone. Worse: I've killed a priest. With magic. A crime for which she would be executed. Not that it mattered. She stepped up to the edge, trying to gather the courage and will to lean forward and let herself fall.

"Rielle."

She started so violently she lost her balance. Terror filled her as she slipped, but something pushed her away from the edge, propelling her back onto the road. Staggering, catching her balance, she whirled around to face Sa-Mica.

He was several steps away, bent over with hands braced on knees, gasping for breath. He had been running, she realised.

"Where . . . is . . . Sa- . . . Gest?" he panted.

She opened her mouth to answer, then closed it again. A small step to the side and she'd be free. But before she did, she would have him finally answer a question.

"Is it true that the priests at the Mountain Temple force women to bear their children?"

He flinched and a look of pain and guilt tightened his face. Her insides turned to liquid. Sa-Gest had not been lying.

"It was," he told her. He straightened. "It no longer is."

Was? What trickery is this? "Sa-Gest said—"

"Sa-Gest doesn't know. I let him believe it so he would come here willingly. I cannot manage two prisoners at the same time."

"Prisoners? You were going to *imprison* him?"

He nodded. "For intimidating women into sexual encounters." He paused. "He was trying to blackmail you, wasn't he?"

"Yes. He said he would make trouble for Izare and my family if I . . . didn't co-operate."

He looked around. "Where is he?"

Rielle swallowed, then looked towards the drop. His eyes widened and he moved to the edge. After searching for a while he shook his head, but as his gaze rose he stiffened, staring across the valley.

"Oh, Angels. It really was you who used the magic," he said and turned to stare at her.

"Yes. Again," she admitted, her voice shaking. Far, far more magic than she could ever replace. "I had to prevent him stopping me from . . ." She shivered. Even if Sa-Mica was lying, she was still doomed. *I killed someone with magic.* But a traitorous shiver of hope went through her. What if he wasn't lying?

"You've stripped this side of the mountain," he pointed out. "There is no more magic left to take. When I encountered the edge of the Stain I drew in as much power as I could."

She nodded as she understood what he was telling her. He could stop her jumping off the cliff. He could force her to go with him to the Mountain Temple. Dread awoke and curled within her stomach. As he started walking towards her the gloom settled over her again.

"Why did you believe Sa-Gest when you knew he would say anything to coerce you?" he asked.

"He had a letter detailing his parentage." She pointed to Sa-Gest's pack.

He grimaced. "Ah. That. He was supposed to leave it behind." He sighed. "How can I convince you that the Mountain Temple is no longer the place he described? Such evil cannot last. The Angels would not condone it."

"Then why didn't you tell me?"

"Why would I? So long as you didn't know there was anything to fear it was more important to keep Sa-Gest co-operative."

"Would you have told me, if he hadn't been with me?"

"Not unless you'd heard of the prison's past." His lips twitched into a grim smile. "One thing is still true: the tainted must be brought here and there is no point terrifying them with stories of their predecessors' fate." His gaze moved beyond her. "You must trust me, Rielle. Or at least not lose hope."

Hearing a noise, she looked over her shoulder. Four priests were walking down the road from the temple, their faces creased with worried frowns.

"What hope have I now?" she said, turning back to Sa-Mica

and gesturing at their surroundings. "I am more tainted than ever and I . . . I just killed a priest. With magic. I'll be executed."

The unscarred side of his lips quirked upwards. "You defended yourself against a criminal we had already decided to remove from our ranks. And the magic . . . it can be rectified. Though it will take much longer than before. Still, that is all for the head of the temple to decide." He closed the distance between them. "The one who ended the evil. You will be judged, Rielle, but I promise you will be judged fairly and with mercy."

Rielle searched his face for some sign of deception and found none. *What choice do I have?* None, as usual. She had used all the magic she'd stolen and there was no more to take. She could not fight five priests. He gestured to the road and she began to walk, sick with dread and despair.

CHAPTER 23

T he void – the Stain – continued almost all the way to the temple. In the last hundred or so paces they passed out of the edge of it. Everything brightened, and she felt shame for creating so much ugliness and darkness.

Then it occurred to her that she could take magic again if she had to. That sent a rush of crazed determination through her. She would do it, if she had to. If Sa-Mica had lied to her she would have nothing to lose.

The Mountain Temple was as forbidding up close as it had been from a distance. The walls were an extension of the sheer face of the cliff, broken by tiny windows scattered in a disordered pattern over the walls. The entrance was a large, square opening, broken hinges indicating where doors had once hung. The road didn't meet this doorway. A wooden bridge spanned a deep crevasse between the two.

Looking up, Rielle saw faces in some of the windows. Male mostly. The few women wore the same expressions as the men: curiosity. She saw no children. As she, Sa-Mica and their escort passed through the doorway they entered a courtyard. Here a few more men and women were occupied in ordinary domestic tasks like drawing water from a fountain and boiling it to wash clothing. A priest appeared to be making furniture, and one of the women was spinning. All had paused to watch her. She saw speculative looks, smiles and knowing glances exchanged.

It didn't look like a prison. Yet a place this remote would need servants to look after domestic chores so that the priests' full attention could be devoted to their prisoners.

She shivered, remembering what Sa-Gest had claimed that meant.

Opposite the entrance was another wall. They approached a pair of intricately carved doors that looked relatively new. Another priest stood outside them. He smiled at her, then looked at Sa-Mica.

"Welcome back, Sa-Mica. I'm afraid he wants to see both of you straight away."

Sa-Mica nodded. "I expected as much."

The man stepped aside and opened the door. "Is everything . . .?"

"Ask me when I come out."

"Very well."

They entered a generous hallway. On the right were several closed doors, on the left a pair of grand, highly decorated ones. Sa-Mica stopped outside the latter. Halting beside him, Rielle looked back and realised they were alone. The scarred priest laid a hand on the door, then paused, drew in a deep breath and let it out slowly. A shiver of alarm went through her as she realised he was gathering his courage.

"His name is Valhan. Don't be afraid," he told her. "Remember the stories I read to you."

He pushed the door open. Rielle followed him into a temple hall. It was smaller than the temple her family attended. Rows of five seats fitted either side of a narrow aisle. Four narrow windows on either side let in the cold mountain light. At the rear was a faded spiritual.

A chair had been placed where the priest usually addressed the worshippers. As Rielle's gaze fell on its occupant she froze. In the edges of her awareness she knew that Sa-Mica had stopped beside her and she heard the door behind her softly close, but all of her attention was caught by what she was seeing. And sensing.

The finest radiating lines of Stain appeared and vanished around him. The spaces between them appeared white in contrast. His hair was black, but where the light touched it the strands shone a deep, impossible blue. His jaw, cheekbones and brow were both finely shaped and yet unmistakably masculine. His skin was paler than even Greya's had been, and without a crease or flaw. Yet he gave no impression of youthfulness. His eyes were black and *ancient*, and gazed into hers. Revealing nothing. Seeing everything.

She heard herself gasp. Disbelief clashed with all she had been taught. It lost. After all, she had painted him and his kind so many times. How could she not recognise and accept what he was?

Fear filled her then, but to her surprise it ebbed as quickly, leaving calm, acceptance and fascination. There was no escaping *this*. And she had been ready to meet his kind, less than an hour earlier.

He lifted a hand and beckoned. She obeyed, but as she drew nearer uncertainty filled her. Should she hurry or approach slowly? Bow or kneel, or more? Nobody had ever schooled her in the protocols of meeting an Angel.

"Bow," Sa-Mica whispered, following at her side. "But don't look down. He doesn't like you to conceal your face."

As they stopped in front of the Angel, she did as she was instructed, Sa-Mica following suit. The Angel's gaze shifted to the priest.

"Lord Valhan," Sa-Mica said. "This is Rielle Lazuli, formerly of Fyre."

The Angel turned his enigmatic gaze to her again. "The one who stripped the mountain of magic." His voice was not as deep as Sa-Mica's, but it was melodic and strangely accented, and he spoke with slow deliberation. There was no note of question in his words. He was an Angel. He must know everything.

"Yes," Sa-Mica replied. "I was escorting another – a priest who was to be stripped of his rank, but who I kept unaware of his fate so that he would come willingly. He was born here and believed us still to be as we were. When I was called back to the supply station I foolishly left him with Rielle. He told her what he believed to be the truth, and she . . . I believe she acted in her own defence."

Rielle lowered her gaze. Why was Sa-Mica telling the Angel this? Surely the Angel knew already.

"Where is this priest?"

"Dead. She pushed him over the cliff."

"Deliberately?" The Angel turned to look at her.

Rielle's heart skipped. "No. I . . . guess he wasn't expecting me to try . . . anything."

"Or you did not know your own strength." He smiled. Though warned not to, she suddenly could not breathe and had to look away. *Oh, to have the chance to paint that smile . . .*

"But you used magic before this," he said. "Tell me why. Tell me everything, Rielle Lazuli. From the beginning."

So she did. She explained that her aunt had taught her to hide her ability to see Stain. She skipped ahead to the day the tainted had abducted her. She spoke of her affection for Izare and her parents' ambitions. From time to time he spoke of something in her thoughts – something she intended to omit or skirt around – and she realised he could read her mind. Whenever he did, the delicate radiating lines of Stain would deepen enough that she could sense them, then slowly fade away.

Finally, there was no more story to tell.

"I am sorry," she said, hanging her head in shame. "I should never have tried to find the corrupter, or repair what she did to me."

"It took courage to approach her," he said. "And your intentions were selfless. Your mistake was in failing to inform the priests. Still, your reluctance is understandable. When laws are inflexible they may cause what they are meant to prevent. This land's laws would have you die for killing Sa-Gest with magic. That would be unjust and a great waste."

He leaned forward slightly and she resisted the urge to avoid his dark gaze. She could barely make out the line between corneas and pupils.

"You are forgiven, Rielle Lazuli. And I offer you this: if you vow never to use magic again, unless to defend yourself, I will give you a second life. You cannot return to your home. You must not contact those you left. You must travel to a distant land where you will be a foreigner and a stranger. You must work to replace the magic you have stolen. And you can never speak of me to anyone. Can you do this?"

Overwhelmed, all she could do was nod. It was more than she deserved. More than she had even imagined was possible.

"You have discovered a powerful ability today," he warned. "The memory of it will be a temptation difficult to resist."

She shuddered. "All it has brought me is trouble. I will not be tempted to use it again."

"I give you permission to, if your life is in danger and you have no other choice." He straightened and looked at Sa-Mica. "Schpetza will suit her talents. You will take her there."

The scarred priest nodded. She recalled his words to her as they had entered he hall: *Remember the stories I told you.* Determination filled her. She would paint every day for the rest of her life, she decided. First to replace the magic she had used, then in gratitude to the Angel. She bowed her head.

"Thank you, Lord Valhan."

535

"Go," the Angel said. "Rest. Eat. You have a long journey ahead of you."

Sa-Mica bowed. Rielle did the same, then followed him out of the hall, all the way resisting the temptation to look back over her shoulder at the Angel. Only when the priest paused to open the door did she steal a glance back. The Angel – Valhan – was watching them, elbows braced on his knees. While his eyes were shadowed, she could see that his lips formed a faint smile.

Tearing her eyes away, knowing that the most incredible thing that had ever happened to her was about to become just a memory, she followed Sa-Mica out of the hall. He closed the door and looked at her.

"How do you feel?"

"Astonished." She drew in a deep breath and let it out again. "And immensely grateful."

He nodded. "It will not be easy, starting a new life in a strange place."

She thought of Greya, constantly dealing with curiosity and hostility for being a foreigner and looking different, and nodded. "I know. But it's better than being locked away, or dead. And I have a chance to fix my mistakes. The right way. Did he truly say I could use magic to safe my life?"

"Yes. Only as a last resort."

"That goes against everything we've been taught."

"That *you've* been taught," he repeated. "Fyre is particularly strict. Other lands not so much."

"And this . . . Schpetza?"

"It would still be better to keep your ability a secret."

She nodded. "Well, I've spent so much of my life keeping secrets, I don't think I could break the habit anyway."

He smiled. "Let's get you a room and arrange for a bath and a change of clothes. It won't be long before we'll be leaving such luxuries behind again."

PART ELEVEN

EPILOGUE

TYEN

The first impression Tyen had of the next world was of a white shape hovering above a grey one, with a lattice of random dark vertical lines between. As the view grew more distinct the lines resolved into the trunks and branches of a tree, the grey into a sky. A pretty scene, though it was upside down.

Unfortunately, he was also arriving some distance from the ground.

There was no stopping his emerging into this new world, however. He did not have enough magic left to resist the pull. Looking up, he tried to estimate how far it was to the ground. Perhaps he could . . .

He felt fiercely cold air on his skin then the rush of it passing. He instinctively braced himself, curling his head towards his chest and wrapping his arms around it.

Then the breath was knocked out of him as he slammed into the ground, shoulders first.

He lost track of time then, as a sudden need to drag in huge gulps of air seized him. Pain lanced through his head.

What is happening?

Vella did not reply. Now that they were out of the place between worlds he could no longer hear her voice. The pain slowly subsided to a hovering ache, and he was able to think.

You can't breathe between worlds, he remembered. *And I was in there for quite a while.*

A different sort of pain was replacing the one in his head now. It spread down his back. The cold.

With difficulty, as his upper body had plunged some way into the snow, he got to his feet. He dusted flakes from his shoulders and back, and looked around. Mountains surrounded him. He was on top of a hill, within a broad valley. Trees spread in all directions. They were bare but for a coating of white.

He began to shiver. Ignoring the cold, he unbuttoned his jacket and shirt and pulled Vella out.

Recognise anything?

He watched the words form.

Not yet. The landscape is unremarkable. This species of tree grows in many worlds. The best way for me to identify a world is by the structures humans make, though after a thousand years there may not be much left standing.

Tyen shrugged. *I suppose it doesn't matter. All I need to do is gather more magic and go home.* Snatches of what he'd seen flashed into his mind. There was a dreamlike feeling to the memories, as if he'd seen everything through a white mist. Which he had, though not literally. He shook his head and began to rub his arms to keep warm. *What I don't understand is why Ysser didn't warn us of what would happen if we took magic from within Tyeszal. Why wouldn't he?*

To do so would be to reveal a weakness in the castle that could easily be exploited by an enemy.

So it had to be kept secret. Why did the king agree to us trying this within the spire, then?

As Ysser said, it was the strongest magical area in Sseltee. He also said it was worth the risk.

Tyen sighed. With magic at the spire moving north, drawn away by overuse in the Empire, the idea that Leratians might provide the solution as well as the problem would have appealed. And not only solve it, but make Tyeszal the place where magic came from. With control of a commodity in short supply the Sselts would have grown rich and powerful.

Surely the reasons weren't purely about money and power? Ysser and the king didn't seem the type. I think they took the risk for the benefit of their people. But they had learned from Vella that Kilraker had betrayed Tyen. *Why did they trust him to obey their rules about the magic in the spire?*

Because you did.

The words were like a blow to his chest. *So it is my fault?*

No. You did not know what Kilraker planned. You did not take the magic in the spire. If it is anyone's fault it is Kilraker's for ignoring their conditions and taking magic from within the spire.

Tyen thought of the rope Kilraker had been so determined to keep hold of and shook his head. *What was he trying to do?*

Remain in control of you, perhaps. Or be propelled along in your wake.

Why wasn't he brought through with me?

While inanimate objects will travel with you, animate ones must be consciously taken. What little distance he did manage on his own he achieved by using the magic he took from within the spire.

So stupid. A memory of the dark cloud of dust and the stump of the spire flashed into his mind. His stomach clenched. So many people dead. *At least Ysser and Mig got away, along with the other gliding aircart owners and those who got across the bridges. Why did people live there if it was so vulnerable?*

People grow used to a constant but not obvious threat. They put it out of their minds. That's how they can live near volcanoes or other natural threats without fearing the inevitable disasters.

Someone must have made the castle that way. Perhaps they hadn't realised their mistake until it was too late. For the king to abandon a home of such obvious symbolic power would have made him appear weak in the eyes of his people, too.

After all the hundreds of years it had stood there, my visit led to its failure. I should go back. They will need help. There must be a way I can help them. I could help them rebuild. And treat the injured.

But he was no doctor. Not even a trainee one. Would there even be injured to treat? Those who had fallen with the spire would surely all be dead. The rest would be angry. They would blame the Empire, and the Leratian visitors who had caused the spire to fall. Ysser would tell them it wasn't Tyen's fault, of course. But what if they didn't believe him? What if they blamed Ysser? They might be more likely to, if Tyen returned and joined the sorcerer. And then there was the problem of arriving where the palace had once been, high above the fallen spire. *Is it possible to control where you arrive in a world?*

Yes, but it will take time to teach you. And more magic. Better to learn the method in plentiful worlds than weak ones.

Was this a strong world? He concentrated on sensing magic. It was there, but he could see no movement in it. Reaching out a little way, he drew some to himself then used it to create a flame.

A flash of brightness and heat seared his eyes. He covered his face and jerked away, then diminished the flow of magic to the lightest trickle. Even then, the flame was unbearably bright. He extinguished it, then had to wait for his eyes to recover before he could see Vella's page again.

I gather that means we're in a magically rich world.

Yes. Your world was once this strong.

Could it be so again if I take magic back there from here?

Not solely by that method.

How else . . . ah. The usual way. People generating magic through creativity. Which they would go back to, once the magic was all gone and the machines didn't work. His world was not doomed to magical exhaustion for ever.

Yes. I see you believe me now.

Tyen smiled. *Yes, I think I do. I . . .*

A movement caught his eye. Peering down into the forest, he saw dark shapes moving among the tree trunks, coming towards him. He instantly recognised them as human, and a tingle of apprehension ran through him.

What should I do? Go back between worlds?

You could. Or you could see what they want. You are a powerful sorcerer. Even as inexperienced and untrained as you are, you should have no trouble defending yourself against most other people – even sorcerers.

He took in some magic and held it. Something made him pause, to wait before pushing out of this world. He watched the people coming closer, stopping to look up at him apprehensively as they approached, and realised he was feeling curiosity. He remembered what Vella's reply had been, when he'd asked the best way to improve his skills and knowledge.

"The best way would be for you to leave this world and its limitations, and seek out the best teachers of the worlds."

If there were sorcerers in a world this rich in magic, they must know a lot about magic. Perhaps they could teach him. Perhaps they would know how to restore Vella to human form.

He considered the reasons to return to his world. He could help the Sselts. *Who will probably blame me for what happened.* To restore the magic. *Which the Empire will gobble up as fast as I bring it anyway.* To see his family and friends again. *I cannot visit Father. Neel was never really a friend and Miko betrayed me. Sezee doesn't want to be around me. Ysser has enough to worry about without me adding to his troubles.*

He drew in a deep breath and let it out again. It formed a cloud of mist in front of him.

I will go back, he decided. *But not straight away. There is so much I could do outside my world. Perhaps discover things I could bring back to my world, one day.*

The strangers were a hundred strides away now. Their clothing was black with pale trim, and as he made out more details he realised it was animal skin, the fur turned to the inside. Yet it was not made up of irregular shapes, but fitted and stitched in coloured thread with intricate patterns. There were both men and women, but all were carrying weapons. Though only spears, bows and short swords, they were dangerous enough. Taking a little magic, Tyen stilled the air around him to form a shield. He tucked Vella into his shirt again.

The men spread out in a line twenty paces away. One spoke, unrecognisable words mixed in with clicks.

Though Tyen had no idea if the gesture meant anything to these people, he bowed.

"Good day," he said. "Could you tell me where I am?"

The other men looked bemused, but their leader's face remained impassive. Looking closer, Tyen felt something vibrating at the edge of his senses. He focused on it.

Then, as the leader spoke again, Tyen understood that the man was afraid, yet determined to protect his people from this stranger who had somehow entered their land undetected. He was demanding to know Tyen's name and business.

Stunned, Tyen stared at the man in amazement.

Somehow he was reading his mind.

RIELLE

The port city of Llura was as wet as Fyre was dry. Sa-Mica claimed it was no hotter, but she found it hard to believe. Here she sweated constantly and there was little breeze to dry and cool her. Everything was damp. Mould grew everywhere – on buildings, clothing and even on the people – and pools of stagnant water bred stinging insects that swarmed at night and forced them to sleep under stifling tents of cheap, loosely woven cloth.

Rielle could never have imagined how different the world was on the other side of the mountains. At first she'd been fascinated by how *alive* the jungle was. Plants crowded on all sides and towered above. The colours dazzled her, but the heat and constant noise had soon grown overwhelming. After two quarterdays of walking they had reached a tiny village of people with skin so dark that she and Sa-Mica stood out among them like Greya had in Fyre, but who were much more friendly towards outsiders than Fyrians. They continued their journey huddled in the prow of a riverboat, but without trees to shelter them they burned under a relentless sun. Four quarterdays later – a full halfseason – they arrived in Llura. Rielle had been eager to reach the city and coast, sure that it would be drier and quieter. She was sorely disappointed.

Though Sa-Mica had set about finding a ship straight away,

it had taken a quarterday to find one heading in the direction they wanted to go. Now, five quarterdays since she'd met the Angel, she was finally about to take her first sea voyage.

They were waiting for permission to board under the broad awning of a shop selling the local delicacy, known as "sea fruit". The ball-shaped creatures were steamed in their shells and tasted surprisingly sweet, though with a slightly disconcerting flavour of mud. The locals dusted them with spices that Rielle found too strong, but Sa-Mica enjoyed the heat, though it made him sweat even more.

The sea had been both a revelation and a disappointment. The enormity of it both awed and frightened her. Now that she was about to take to a ship all the stories she'd heard of ships sinking or crashing against rocks were lurking at the edges of her mind, adding to the anxiety of starting a new life where she wouldn't know anybody or even speak the language. At the same time she longed to be moving — anywhere so long as it was away from this place.

She sighed and wiped her brow. "The sooner we are gone the better. I don't think I can stand another moment of this heat."

Sa-Mica grunted his agreement. "You may miss it where we are going. Have you ever seen snow?"

"No."

"It is charming at first, but the cold is unpleasant. It can be dangerous, too. Heed what the locals tell you."

Rielle thought of the foreign travellers her brother had once found, dead from thirst a few hundred paces from a well. They hadn't noticed the insects swooping down to drink the water. Every place had its hidden dangers, he'd told her. It was always wise to listen to the locals, even when their advice sounded strange or silly.

She turned to tell Sa-Mica the story. As her escort his manner had been different – more considerate – but his habit of silence remained. He was used to travelling alone or with only the tainted he took to the Mountain Temple as companions. She had grown bored and coaxed him into conversation by asking him about the journey and her destination. But sometimes she could not rouse him from his thoughts, and the frown he was wearing now was a familiar one.

Thinking back, she recalled a conversation from a day when he was in a more receptive mood.

"Do all artists have magical ability as a counterbalance to their talent?" she had asked him.

"No."

"Then why do I have this ability?"

"I don't know. Valhan once told me that this world will not be so depleted of magic for ever. One day, many generations from now, mortals will be free to use it again."

But not until long after she was dead. And probably her descendants, too, if she ever had any. Her bleed had begun during the riverboat ride, confirming that it had been poor diet and exertion that had interrupted her cycle. Though relieved that she didn't have the huge complication of a child to worry about when trying to settle in a new land, a part of her ached with sadness for the future she'd lost. For Izare and Narmah, who would never know she had met an Angel, and that her mistakes and bad choices had been forgiven.

One day, if I repay my debt, I will meet them in the Angels' realm and tell them tales they'll hardly be able to believe.

"Rielle," Sa-Mica said, rising to his feet. "Stay here." He took a step towards the shopfronts, then stopped and, without taking his eyes off whatever had caught his attention, said: "If I don't return, take my pack and get on board. Don't worry if the ship leaves. I will get new supplies at the temple here."

If he doesn't return . . . ? Heart racing, she watched him stalk away. Nearing an alley, he slowed and peered around the corner, then disappeared down it. She sat stiffly, unable to relax. He'd been a constant, reassuring presence for so long that the prospect of being alone was frightening. Especially in a foreign place.

"Are you done?" a voice said from behind her shoulder.

She jumped then looked up. The surly woman who had served them stood behind her, eyeing the empty sea fruit shells.

"Yes."

"Customers are waiting."

Looking around, Rielle saw that all the other tables were occupied and a small group of men was scowling at her. She looked back at the alley entrance. Sa-Mica was nowhere to be seen.

The woman made an impatient huffing noise.

Sighing, Rielle picked up her pack and Sa-Mica's and moved away. That put her outside the awning's shade, however, so she moved down the shopfronts towards the alley. Another awning shaded the shop next to the alley, she noted. Was whatever had drawn Sa-Mica's attention dangerous? His manner had suggested so. But it had probably led him further away by now. Her skin was burning. She walked over to the shade and set down their packs.

". . . was me," a woman's voice said, from somewhere not far down the alley.

"*You* sent the message to me at Breca's?" Sa-Mica replied.

Rielle froze. The priest hadn't continued down the alley. He was just around the corner.

"Yes. Have you received confirmation?"

Realising she was eavesdropping, Rielle bent to pick up the packs . . .

"That the corrupter in Fyre is Yerge?"

. . . and froze again.

548

"Yes." The woman said. "You have, haven't you?"

"I knew it already. One of her victims drew a picture of her. Not all tainted make good use of their second chance at life, Mia. Yerge is not the only one to become a corrupter. And you—"

"Valhan sent her there, Dav. He *asked* her to do it."

"How can you know that?" Sa-Mica's tone was disbelieving.

"Because she told me."

Sa-Mica did not respond. Rielle straightened slowly. If she lifted the packs and walked away, would they hear?

"You don't believe me," the woman said.

"No. Why would he do that?"

"You know my suspicions."

"That he wants to raise an army of sorcerers and take over the world?" Sa-Mica's voice was full of derision. He'd clearly heard this suggestion before.

"That is one possibility. I'm sure you can think of more."

"I think he is merely giving the tainted a second chance."

"Or increasing the strength and numbers of priests, since that's what the tainted become."

"Except for women," Sa-Mica pointed out. "Why do the corrupters target women as well as men?"

"Maybe he dares not target one sex for fear it will draw notice. Yerge thought he was looking for someone with exceptional abilities."

"So is it one person or an army he's after?" Sa-Mica sounded amused.

"Mock me all you like, Dav. Even if you don't believe there is more to this, you know he is not infallible. If you are right he has let tainted go who immediately set out to corrupt others."

Sa-Mica sighed. "A second chance is no more than that. He may know what is in a person's mind when he meets them, but he cannot control their future or their choices."

"So even Angels have limitations?"

"Maybe. Maybe only he has. He is flesh and bone and blood. I believe he took human form in order to deal with the evil at the Mountain Temple."

"And it has forced limitations on him? Well, that would explain why he hides. When he arrived I hoped he'd fix more than just the Mountain Temple." The woman sounded bitter.

"Why do you need more, Mia? He freed you from that place."

"I *always* expect more. It is never enough for me to be safe when others aren't, whether by your actions or his or anyone else's. Didn't that scar I gave you teach you that?" Sa-Mica didn't reply. "So where are you off to now? The south, from the looks of it. Why is he sending you there?"

"He . . . isn't. I am returning to the Mountain Temple."

"And the girl? A Fyrian from the look of her. The south is a long way to go for a second life.

"She wants to get as far from here as possible. I'm sure you can understand that."

"I do. Would you intro—"

"No, Mia."

"I only want to talk to her."

"And corrupt her mind with your ideas of reform and rebellion? I don't think even you would be that cruel. Let her go and find the peace she craves."

"Very well. It is good to see you, Dav. We should meet more often."

The sound of fading footsteps followed. Rielle let out a sigh of relief and grabbed the packs. Sa-Mica hurried out of the alley, then started as he saw her.

"How long were you there?" he asked.

"Since the server insisted I leave." She shrugged in the direction of the shop. "So. The woman who taught me had been released by Valhan."

He scowled and took his pack from her. "Yes. She is not the only one to betray him." He looked away, avoiding her eyes. "I am glad he's sending you to the south."

"I would never teach anyone magic."

He turned back. "No, I believe you wouldn't. But that is not what I fear." He glanced back at the alley.

"You fear her?"

"I fear her cause. She and other women want him to give them the children they birthed. I sympathise, but I also understand why he has not granted them this. It would mean revealing what happened on the mountain, which would cause such chaos and perhaps endanger other lives."

"So she doubts his motives. Maybe it's not so hard, then, to believe he's recruiting corrupters so he can raise an army."

He nodded.

"It's not true, of course."

"No." There was doubt in his voice.

She frowned. "But it doesn't make sense. Who does he need to fight? The Angels have no enemies. Even if they did, they are all powerful. And . . . wouldn't fighting use up magic?"

Sa-Mica smiled. "All good, sensible questions Ais Lazuli. This idea that he is looking for someone with exceptional magical ability makes no sense either. I have never seen anyone who could draw magic from such a distance as you did. Yet he sent you away."

"Unless I'm not exceptional enough."

He frowned, and she could tell he was considering her words. She placed a hand on his arm.

"That's not a serious suggestion," she said. "What is more likely? That an Angel has turned corrupter and is recruiting tainted for a war against an unknown enemy or that people will always draw fabulous and unlikely conclusions when they don't understand something?"

He sighed and nodded. "You are right. I don't understand everything, but I know more than they do and I see nothing other than one Angel dealing with one evil and its consequences. And . . ." he frowned and fell silent.

"See?" She squeezed his arm and let him go. "It's not a corrupt Angel we have to worry about, it's whether others believe what this woman is saying and . . ." She paused as she spotted a man walking towards them. "Is he from the ship?"

Sa-Mica didn't turn to look. He was staring into the distance, eyes wide but unseeing. Then he cursed and swung around to face the seaman.

"Boarding," the man said, then turned on his heel and began walking away.

Sa-Mica dropped to one knee and opened his pack. His movements were quick as he dug through the contents and drew out a flat leather envelope.

"Take this. It contains money and the names and addresses of people who will help you." He pressed it into her hands.

"What? Why are you giving me this?"

He took her arm and pulled her into motion, hurrying towards the ship. "I'm not going with you."

"But I thought . . . I thought you lied to her."

"I did, but I see now that I need to return to Valhan as quickly as possible."

"I can't travel alone!"

They reached the ramp that led up to the level of the ship's deck. He turned and grasped her shoulders, bending to look into her eyes.

"I'm sorry, Rielle. I wish I could escort you, but I can't. You have money and common sense. Use them. And remember, he said you are allowed to use magic in your own defence."

"But . . . why?"

"Because my first loyalty is to him. You are more than

capable of finding your way. Go. Find yourself somewhere quiet and live a good life." He squeezed her arms and smiled. "I wish you all the best, Rielle Lazuli. Goodbye."

Letting her go, he hoisted his pack and strode away. She watched him quickly negotiate the obstacles of the dock. He did not once look back. All too soon he was gone. *Returning to the Angel.*

"Goodbye, Sa-Mica," she whispered.

Then, shivering from shock and trepidation, she obeyed his last instruction and climbed the ramp to the deck of the ship, and the start of her new life.

End of Book One.

The story continues in book two
of The Millennium's Rule

Angel of Storms

ACKNOWLEDGEMENTS

Many thanks to the Orbit team and all the foreign language publishing staff, who never fail to transform my stories into wonderful books and are such a pleasure to work with.

Much admiration and gratitude to someone who inspires as well as supports me, my agent, Fran. Thanks, also, to her lovely assistants, and to all the other agents around the world, with an extra one to Kate and Arabella, and Lora.

Much gratitude to my feedback readers, Paul, Fran, Liz, Kerri, Donna and Ellen. A nod and wave must also go to the friends who read and discussed the ideas in the early version of *Angel of Storms*, written waaay back in the nineties, from which this series evolved. I don't know if they'd recognise the story now, but I'll always remember their enthusiasm with gratitude.

Finally, but always, thanks to the readers and fans, new and old. I hope you enjoy this new universe I've made for you to explore . . . from the safety of the other side of the page.

extras

orbit

meet the author

Photo credit: Paul Ewins

TRUDI CANAVAN published her first story in 1999, and it received an Aurealis Award for Best Fantasy Short Story. Her debut series, The Black Magician Trilogy, made her an international success and her last five novels have been *Sunday Times* bestsellers in the UK. Trudi Canavan lives with her partner in Melbourne, Australia, and spends her time knitting, painting and writing. You can visit her website at www.trudicanavan.com.

introducing

If you enjoyed
THIEF'S MAGIC,
look out for

THE AMBASSADOR'S MISSION

Book One of the Traitor Spy trilogy

by Trudi Canavan

In the remote village of Mandryn, Tessia serves as assistant to her father, the village Healer—much to the frustration of her mother, who would rather she found a husband. Despite knowing that women aren't readily accepted by the Guild of Healers, Tessia is determined to follow in her father's footsteps. But her life is about to take a very unexpected turn.

When treating a patient at the residence of the local magician, Lord Dakon, Tessia is forced to fight off the advances of a visiting Sachakan mage—and instinctively uses magic. She now finds herself facing an entirely different future as Lord Dakon's apprentice.

Although there are long hours of study and self-discipline, Tessia's new life also offers more opportunities than she had ever hoped for, and an exciting new world opens up to her. There are fine clothes and servants—and, she is delighted to learn—regular trips to the great city of Imardin.

But along with the excitement and privilege, Tessia is about to discover that her magical gifts bring with them a great deal of responsibility. Events are brewing that will lead nations into war, rival magicians into conflict, and spark an act of sorcery so brutal that its effects will be felt for centuries...

CHAPTER 1

THE OLD AND THE NEW

The most successful and quoted piece by the poet Rewin, greatest of the rabble to come out of the New City, was called *Citysong*. It captured what was heard at night in Imardin, if you took the time to stop and listen: an unending muffled and distant combination of sounds. Voices. Singing. A laugh. A groan. A gasp. A scream.

In the darkness of Imardin's new Quarter a man remembered the poem. He stopped to listen, but instead of absorbing the city's song he concentrated on one discordant echo. A sound that didn't belong. A sound that didn't repeat. He snorted quietly and continued on.

A few steps later a figure emerged from the shadows before him. The figure was male and loomed over him menacingly. Light caught the edge of a blade.

"Yer money," a rough voice said, hard with determination.

The man said nothing and remained still. He might have appeared frozen in terror. He might have appeared deep in thought.

When he did move, it was with uncanny speed. A click, a snap of sleeve, and the robber gasped and sank to his knees. A knife clattered on the ground. The man patted him on the shoulder.

"Sorry. Wrong night, wrong target, and I don't have time to explain why."

As the robber fell, face-down, on the pavement, the man stepped over him and walked on. Then he paused and looked over his shoulder, to the other side of the street.

"Hai! Gol. You're supposed to be my bodyguard."

From the shadows another large figure emerged and hurried to the man's side.

"Reckon you don't have much need for one, Cery. I'm getting slow in my old age. I should be payin' *you* to protect *me*."

Cery scowled. "Your eyes and ears are still sharp, aren't they?"

Gol winced. "As sharp as yours," he retorted sullenly.

"Too true." Cery sighed. "I should retire. But Thieves don't get to retire."

"Except by not being Thieves any more."

"Except by becoming corpses," Cery corrected.

"But you're no ordinary Thief. I reckon there's different rules for you. You didn't start the usual way, so why would you finish the usual way?"

"Wish everyone else agreed with you."

"So do I. City'd be a better place."

"With everyone agreeing with *you*? Ha!"

"Better for me, anyway."

Cery chuckled and resumed the journey. Gol followed a short distance behind. *He hides his fear well*, Cery thought. *Always has. But he must be thinking that we both might not make it through this night. Too many of the others have died.*

Over half the Thieves—the leaders of underworld criminal groups in Imardin—had perished these last few years. Each in different ways and most from unnatural causes. Stabbed, poisoned, pushed from a tall building, burned in a fire, drowned or crushed in a collapsed tunnel. Some said a single person was responsible, a vigilante they called the Thief Hunter. Others believed it was the Thieves themselves, settling old disputes.

Gol said it wasn't *who* would go next that punters were betting on, but *how*.

Of course, younger Thieves had taken the place of the old, sometimes peacefully, sometimes after a quick, bloody struggle.

That was to be expected. But even these bold newcomers weren't immune to murder. They were as likely to become the next victim as an older Thief.

There were no obvious connections between the killings. While there were plenty of grudges between Thieves, none provided a reason for so many murders. And while attempts on Thieves' lives weren't that unusual, that they were successful was. That, and the fact that the killer or killers had neither bragged about it, nor been seen in the act.

In the past we would have held a meeting. Discussed strategies. Worked together. But it's been such a long time since the Thieves cooperated with each other I don't think we'd know how to, now.

He'd seen the change coming in the days after the Ichani invaders were defeated, but hadn't guessed how quickly it would happen. Once the Purge—the yearly forced exodus of the homeless from the city into the slums—ended, the slums were declared part of the city, rendering old boundaries obsolete. Alliances between Thieves faltered and new rivalries began. Thieves who had worked together to save the city during the invasion turned on each other in order to hold onto their territory, make up for what they'd lost to others and take advantage of new opportunities.

Cery passed four young men lounging against a wall where the alley met a wider street. They eyed him and their gaze fell to the small medallion pinned to Cery's coat that marked him as a Thief's man. As one they nodded respectfully. Cery nodded back once, then paused at the alley entrance, waiting for Gol to pass the men and join him. The bodyguard had decided years ago that he was better able to spot potential threats if he wasn't walking right beside Cery—and Cery could handle most close encounters himself.

As Cery waited, he looked down at a red line painted across the alley entrance, and smiled with amusement. Having declared the slums a part of the city, the king had tried to take control of it with varying success. Improvements to some areas led to raised rents which, along with the demolition of unsafe houses, forced the poor into smaller and smaller areas of the city. They dug in and made these places their own and, like cornered animals, defended them with savage determination, giving their neighbourhoods names like Blackstreets and Dwellfort. There were now boundary lines, some painted, some known only by reputation, over which no city guard dared step unless he was in the company of several colleagues— and even then they must expect a fight. Only the presence of a magician ensured their safety.

As his bodyguard joined him, Cery turned away and they started to cross the wider street together. A carriage passed, lit by two swinging lanterns. The ever-present guards strolled in groups of two— never out of sight of the next or last group—carrying lanterns.

This was a new thoroughfare, cutting through the bad part of the city known as Wildways. Cery had wondered, at first, why the king had bothered. Anyone travelling along it was at risk of being robbed by the denizens on either side, and probably stuck with a knife in the process. But the road was wide, giving little cover for muggers, and the tunnels beneath, once part of the underground network known as the Thieves' Road, had been filled in during its construction. Many of the old, overcrowded buildings on either side had been demolished and replaced by large, secure ones owned by merchants.

Split in two, vital connections within Wildways had been broken. Though Cery was sure efforts were underway to dig new tunnels, half the local population had been forced into other bad neighbourhoods, while the rest were split by the main road. Wildways, where visitors had once come seeking a gambling house or cheap whore, undeterred by the risk of robbery and murder, was doomed.

Cery, as always, felt uncomfortable in the open. The encounter with the mugger had left him uneasy.

"Do you think he was sent to test me?" he asked Gol.

Gol did not answer straightaway, his long silence telling Cery he was considering the question carefully.

"Doubt it. More likely he had a fatal bout of bad luck."

Cery nodded. *I agree. But times have changed. The city has changed. It's like living in a foreign country, sometimes. Or what I'd imagine living in some other city would be like, since I've never left Imardin. Unfamiliar. Different rules. Dangers where you don't expect them. Can't be too paranoid. And I am, after all, about to meet the most feared Thief in Imardin.*

"You there!" a voice called. Two guards strode toward them, one holding up his lantern. Cery considered the distance to the other side of the road, then sighed and stopped.

"Me?" he asked, turning to face the guards. Gol said nothing.

The taller of the guards stopped a step closer than his stocky companion. He did not answer, but after looking from Gol to Cery and back again a few times he settled on staring at Cery.

"State your address and name," he ordered.

"Cery of River Road, Northside," Cery replied.

"Both of you?"

"Yes. Gol is my servant. And bodyguard."

The guard nodded, barely glancing at Gol. "Your destination?"

"A meeting with the king."

The quieter guard's indrawn breath earned a glance from his superior. Cery watched the men, amused to find them both trying—and failing—to hide their dismay and fear. He'd been told to give them this information, and though it was a ridiculous claim the guard appeared to believe him. Or, more likely, understood that it was a coded message.

The taller guard straightened. "On your way then. And...safe journey."

Cery turned away and, with Gol following a step behind, continued across the street. He wondered if the message had told them exactly who Cery was meeting, or if it only told the guard that whoever spoke the phrase wasn't to be detained or delayed.

Either way, he doubted he and Gol had chanced upon the only corrupted guard on the street. There had always been guards willing to work with the Thieves, but now the layers of corruption were stronger and more pervasive than ever. There were honest, ethical men in the Guard who strove to expose and punish offenders in their ranks, but it was a battle they had been losing for some time now.

Everyone is caught up in infighting of one form or another. The Guard is fighting corruption, the Houses are feuding, the rich and poor novices and magicians in the Guild bicker constantly, the Allied Lands can't agree on what to do about Sachaka, and the Thieves are at war with each other. Faren would have found it all very entertaining.

But Faren was dead. Unlike the rest of the Thieves, he had died of a perfectly normal lung infection during winter five years ago. Cery hadn't spoken to him for years before that. The man Faren had been grooming to replace him had taken the reins of his criminal empire with no contest or bloodshed. The man known as Skellin.

The man Cery was meeting tonight.

As Cery made his way through the smaller, lingering portion of the split Wildways neighbourhood, ignoring the calls of whores and betting boys, he considered what he knew of Skellin. Faren had taken in his successor's mother when Skellin was only a child, but whether the woman had been Faren's lover or wife, or had worked for him, was unknown. The old Thief had kept them close and secret, as most Thieves had to do with loved ones. Skellin had proven himself a talented man. He had taken over many under-world enterprises, and started more than a few of his own, with few failures. He had a reputation for being clever and uncompromising. Cery did not think Faren would have approved of Skellin's utter ruthlessness. Yet the stories most likely had been embellished during retellings, so there was no guessing how deserved the man's reputation was.

There was no animal Cery knew of called a "Skellin". Faren's successor had been the first new Thief to break with the tradition of using animal names. It didn't necessarily mean "Skellin" was his real name, of course. Those who believed it was thought him brave for revealing it. Those who didn't, didn't care.

A turn into another street brought them out into a cleaner part of the area. Cleaner only in appearance, however. Behind the doors of these solid, well-maintained houses lived more affluent whores, fences, smugglers and assassins. The Thieves had learned that the Guard—stretched too thin—didn't look much deeper if outward appearances were respectable. And the Guard, like certain wealthy men and women from the Houses with dubious business connections, had also learned to distract the city's do-gooders from their failure to deal with the problem with donations to their pet charity projects.

Which included the hospices run by Sonea, still a hero to the poor even if the rich only spoke of Akkarin's efforts and sacrifices in the Ichani Invasion. Cery often wondered if she guessed how much of the money donated to her cause came from corrupt sources. And if she did, did she care?

He and Gol slowed as they reached the intersection of streets named in the directions Cery had been sent. At the corner was a strange sight.

A patch of green sprinkled with bright colour filled the space where a house had once been. Plants of all sizes grew among the old foundations and broken walls. All were illuminated by hundreds of hanging lamps. Cery chuckled quietly as he finally remembered where he'd heard the name "Sunny House" before. The house had been destroyed during the Ichani Invasion, and the owner could not afford to rebuild it. He'd bunkered down in the basement of the ruin, and spent his days encouraging his beloved garden to take over—and the local people to enter and enjoy it.

It was a strange place for Thieves to be meeting, but Cery could see advantages. It was relatively open—nobody could approach or listen in without being noticed—and yet public enough that any fight or attack would be witnessed, which would hopefully discourage treachery and violence.

The instructions had said to wait beside the statue. As Cery and Gol entered the garden, they saw a stone figure on a plinth in the middle of the ruins. The statue was carved of black stone veined with grey and white. It was of a cloaked man, facing east but looking north. Drawing near, Cery realised there was something familiar about it.

It's supposed to be Akkarin, he recognised with a shock. *Facing the Guild but looking toward Sachaka.* Moving closer he examined the face. *Not a good likeness, though.*

Gol made a low noise of warning and Cery's attention immediately snapped back to his surroundings. A man was walking toward them, and another was trailing behind.

Is this Skellin? He is definitely foreign. But this man was not from any race that Cery had encountered. The stranger's face was long and slim, his cheek bones and chin narrowing to a point. This made his surprisingly curvaceous mouth appear to be too large for his face. But his eyes and angular brows were in proportion—almost beautiful. His skin was darker than the typical Elyne or Sachakan colouring, but rather than the blue-black of a typical Lonmar it had a reddish tinge. His hair was a far darker shade of red than the vibrant tones common among the Elynes.

He looks like he's fallen into a pot of dye, and it hasn't quite washed out yet, Cery mused. *I'd say he is about twenty-five.*

"Welcome to my home, Cery of Northside," the man said, with no trace of a foreign accent. "I am Skellin. Skellin the Thief or Skellin the Dirty Foreigner depending on who you talk to and how intoxicated they are."

Cery wasn't sure how to respond to that. "Which would you rather I call you?"

Skellin's smile broadened. "Skellin will do. I am not fond of fancy titles." His gaze shifted to Gol.

"My bodyguard," Cery explained.

Skellin nodded once at Gol in acknowledgement, then turned back to Cery. "May we talk privately?"

"Of course," Cery replied. He nodded at Gol, who retreated out of earshot. Skellin's companion also retreated.

The other Thief moved to one of the low walls of the ruin and sat down. "It is a shame the Thieves of this city don't meet and work together any more," he said. "Like in the old days." He looked at Cery. "You knew the old traditions and followed the old rules once. Do you miss them?"

Cery shrugged. "Change goes on all the time. You lose something and you gain something else."

One of Skellin's elegant eyebrows rose. "Do the gains outweigh the losses?"

"More for some than others. I've not had much profit from the split, but I still have a few understandings with other Thieves."

"That is good to hear. Do you think there is a chance we might come to an understanding?"

"There's always a chance." Cery smiled. "It depends on what you're suggesting we understand."

Skellin nodded. "Of course." He paused and his expression grew serious. "There are two offers I'd like to make to you. The first is one I've made to several other Thieves, and they have all agreed to it."

Cery felt a thrill of interest. *All of them? But then, he doesn't say how many "several" is.*

"You have heard of the Thief Hunter?" Skellin asked.

"Who hasn't?"

"I believe he is real."

"One person killed all those Thieves?" Cery raised his eyebrows, not bothering to conceal his disbelief.

"Yes," Skellin said firmly, holding Cery's gaze. "If you ask around—ask the people who saw something—there are similarities in the murders."

I'll have to have Gol look into it again, Cery mused. Then a possibility occurred to him. *I hope Skellin doesn't think that my helping High Lord Akkarin to find the Sachakan spies back before the Ichani Invasion means I can find this Thief Hunter for him. They were easy to spot, once you knew what to look for. The Thief Hunter is something else.*

"So... what do you want to do about him?"

"I'd like your agreement that if you hear anything about the Thief Hunter you will tell me. I understand that many Thieves aren't talking to each other, so I offer myself as a recipient of information about the Thief Hunter instead. Perhaps, with everyone's cooperation, I'll get rid of him for you all. Or, at the least, be able to warn anyone if they are going to be attacked."

Cery smiled. "That last bit is a touch optimistic."

Skellin shrugged. "Yes, there is always the chance a Thief won't pass on a warning if he knows the Thief Hunter is going to kill a rival. But remember that every Thief removed is one less source of information that could lead to us getting rid of the Hunter and ensuring our own safety."

"They'd be replaced quick enough."

Skellin frowned. "By someone who might not know as much as their predecessor."

"Don't worry." Cery shook his head. "There's nobody I hate enough to do that to, right now."

The other man smiled. "So are we in agreement?"

Cery considered. Though he did not like the sort of trade Skellin was in, it would be silly to turn down this offer. The only information the man wanted related to the Thief Hunter, nothing more. And he was not asking for a pact or promise—if Cery was unable to pass on information because it would compromise his safety or business, nobody could say he'd broken his word.

"Yes," he replied. "I can do that."

"We have an understanding," Skellin said, his smile broadening. "Now let me see if I can make that two." He rubbed his hands together. "I'm sure you know the main product that I import and sell."

Not bothering to hide his distaste, Cery nodded. "Roet. Or 'rot', as some call it. Not something I'm interested in. And I hear you have it well in hand."

Skellin nodded. "I do. When Faren died he left me a shrinking territory. I needed a way to establish myself and strengthen my control. I tried different trades. Roet supply was new and untested. I was amazed at how quickly Kyralians took to it. It has proven to be very profitable, and not just for me. The Houses are making a nice little income from the rent on the brazier houses." Skellin paused. "You could be gaining from this little industry, too, Cery of Northside."

"Just call me Cery." Cery let his expression grow serious. "I am flattered, but Northside is home to people mostly too poor to pay for roet. It's a habit for the rich."

"But Northside is growing more prosperous, thanks to your efforts, and roet is getting cheaper as more becomes available."

Cery resisted a cynical smile at the flattery.

"Not quite enough yet. It would stop growing if roet was brought in too soon and too fast." *And if I could manage it, we'd have no rot at all.* He'd seen what it did to men and women caught up in the pleasure of it—forgetting to eat or drink, or to feed their children except to dose them with the drug to stop their complaints of hunger. *But I'm not foolish enough to think I can keep it away forever. If I don't provide it, someone else will. I will have to find a way to do so without causing too much damage.* "There will be a right time to bring roet to Northside," Cery said. "And when that time comes I'll know who to come to."

"Don't leave it too long, Cery," Skellin warned. "Roet is popular because it is new and fashionable, but eventually it will be like bol—just another vice of the city, grown and prepared by anybody. I'm hoping that by then I'll have established new trades to support myself with." He paused and looked away. "One of the old, honourable Thief trades. Or perhaps even something legitimate."

He turned back and smiled, but there was a hint of sadness and dissatisfaction in his expression. *Perhaps there's an honest man in there,* Cery thought. *If he didn't expect roet to spread so fast, maybe he didn't expect it to cause so much damage... but that isn't going to convince me to get into the trade myself.*

Skellin's smile faded and was replaced by an earnest frown. "There are people out there who would like to take your place, Cery. Roet may be your best defence against them, as it was for me."

"There are always people out there who want me gone," Cery said. "I'll go when I'm ready."

The other Thief looked amused. "You truly believe you'll get to choose the time and place?"

"Yes."

"And your successor?"

"Yes."

Skellin chuckled. "I like your confidence. Faren was as sure of himself, too. He was half right: he got to choose his successor."

"He was a clever man."

"He told me much about you." Skellin's gaze became curious. "How you didn't become a Thief by the usual ways. That the infamous High Lord Akkarin arranged it."

Cery resisted the urge to look at the statue. "All Thieves gain power through favours with powerful people. I happened to exchange favours with a very powerful one."

Skellin's eyebrows rose. "Did he ever teach you magic?"

A laugh escaped Cery. "If only!"

"But you grew up with Black Magician Sonea and gained your position with help from the former High Lord. Surely you would have picked up something."

"Magic isn't like that," Cery explained. *But surely he knows that.* "You have to have the talent, and be taught to control and use it. You can't pick it up by watching someone."

Skellin put a finger to his chin and regarded Cery thoughtfully. "You do still have connections in the Guild, though, don't you?"

Cery shook his head. "I haven't seen Sonea in years."

"How disappointing, after all you did—all the Thieves did—to help them." Skellin smiled crookedly. "I'm afraid your reputation as a friend of magicians is nowhere near as exciting as the reality, Cery."

"That's the way with reputations. Usually."

Skellin nodded. "So it is. Well, I have enjoyed our chat and made my offers. We have come to one understanding, at least. I hope we will come to another in time." He stood up. "Thank you for meeting with me, Cery of Northside."

"Thank you for the invitation. Good luck in catching the Thief Hunter."

Skellin smiled, nodded politely, then turned and strolled back the way he had come. Cery watched him for a moment, then gave the statue another quick glance. It really wasn't a good likeness.

"How did it go?" Gol murmured as Cery joined him.

"As I expected," Cery replied. "Except..."

"Except?" Gol repeated when Cery didn't finish.

"We agreed to share information on the Thief Hunter."

"He's real then?"

"So Skellin believes." Cery shrugged. They crossed the road and began striding back toward Wildways. "That wasn't the oddest thing, though."

"Oh?"

"He asked if Akkarin taught me magic."

Gol paused. "That isn't *that* odd, though. Faren did hide Sonea before he handed her over to the Guild, in the hopes she would do magic for him. Skellin must have heard all about it."

"Do you think he'd like to have his own pet magician?"

"Sure. Though he obviously wouldn't want to hire you, seeing as you're a Thief. Perhaps he thinks he can ask favours of the Guild through you."

"I told him I hadn't seen Sonea in years." Cery chuckled. "Next time I see her, I might ask if she'll help out one of my Thief friends, just to see the look on her face."

A figure appeared in the alley ahead, hurrying toward them. Cery noted the possible exits and hiding places around them.

"You should tell her Skellin was making enquiries," Gol advised. "He might try to recruit someone else. And it might work. Not all magicians are as incorruptible as Sonea." Gol slowed. "That's... That's Neg."

Relief that it wasn't another attacker was followed by concern. Neg had been guarding Cery's main hideout. He preferred it to roaming the streets, as open spaces made him jittery.

The guard had seen them. Neg was panting as he reached them. Something on his face caught the light, and Cery felt his heart drop somewhere far below the level of the street. A bandage.

"What is it?" Cery asked, in a voice he barely recognised as his.

"S...sorry," Neg panted. "Bad news." He drew in a deep breath, then let it out explosively and shook his head. "Don't know how to tell you."

"Say it," Cery ordered.

"They're dead. All of them. Selia. The boys. Never saw who. Got past everything. Don't know how. No lock broken. When I came to..." As Neg babbled on, apologising and explaining, words running over themselves, a rushing sound filled Cery's ears. His mind tried to find some other explanation for a moment. *He must be mistaken. He's hit his head and is delusional. He dreamed it.*

But he made himself face the likely truth. What he had dreaded— had nightmares over—for years had happened.

Someone had made it past all the locks and guards and protections, and murdered his family.

introducing

**If you enjoyed
THIEF'S MAGIC,
look out for**

COLD MAGIC

by Kate Elliott

*The Wild Hunt is stirring—and the dragons are finally
waking from their long sleep...*

*Cat Barahal was the only survivor of the flood that took her
parents. Raised by her extended family, she and her cousin, Bee,
are unaware of the dangers that threaten them both. Though they
are in beginning of the Industrial Age, magic—and the power of the
Cold Mages—still holds sway.*

*Now, betrayed by her family and forced to marry a powerful
Cold Mage, Cat will be drawn into a labyrinth of politics.
There she will learn the full ruthlessness of the rule of the Cold Mages.
What do the Cold Mages want from her? And who will help Cat in
her struggle against them?*

CHAPTER 1

The history of the world begins in ice, and it will end in ice.

Or at least, that's how the dawn chill felt in the bedchamber as I shrugged out from beneath the cozy feather comforter under which my cousin and I slept. I winced as I set my feet on the brutally cold wood floor. Any warmth from last evening's fire was long gone. At this early hour, Cook would just be getting the kitchen's stove going again, two floors below. But last night I had slipped a book out of my uncle's parlor and brought it to read in my bedchamber by candlelight, even though we were expressly forbidden from doing so. He had even made us sign a little contract stating that we had permission to read my father's journals and the other books in the parlor as long as we stayed in the parlor and did not waste expensive candlelight to do so. I had to put the book back before he noticed it was gone, or the cold would be the least of my troubles.

After all the years sharing a bed with my cousin Beatrice, I knew Bee was such a heavy sleeper that I could have jumped up and down on the bed without waking her. I had tried it more than once. So I left her behind and picked out suitable clothing from the wardrobe: fresh drawers, two layers of stockings, and a knee-length chemise over which I bound a fitted wool bodice. I fumblingly laced on two petticoats and a cutaway overskirt, blowing on my fingers to warm them, and over it buttoned a tight-fitting, hip-length jacket cut in last year's fashionable style.

With my walking boots and the purloined book in hand, I cracked the door and ventured out onto the second-floor landing to listen. No noise came from my aunt and uncle's chamber, and the little girls, in the nursery on the third floor above, were almost certainly still asleep. But the governess who slept upstairs with them would be rousing soon, and my uncle and his factotum were usually up before dawn. They were the ones I absolutely had to avoid.

I crept down to the first-floor landing and paused there, peering over the railing to survey the empty foyer on the ground floor below. Next to me, a rack of swords, the badge of the Hassi Barahal family tradition, lined the wall. Alongside the rack stood our house mirror, in whose reflection I could see both myself and the threads of magic knit through the house. Uncle and Aunt were important people in their own way. As local representatives of the far-flung Hassi Barahal clan, they discreetly bought and sold information, and in return might receive such luxuries as a cawl—a protective spell bound over the house by a drua—or door and window locks sealed by a blacksmith to keep out unwanted visitors.

I closed my eyes and listened down those threads of magic to trace the stirring of activity in the house: our man-of-all-work, Pompey, priming the pump in the garden; Cook and Aunt Tilly in the kitchen cracking eggs and wielding spoons as they began the day's baking. A whiff of smoke tickled my nose. The tread of feet marked the approach of the maidservant, Callie, from the back. By the front door, she began sweeping the foyer. I stood perfectly still, as if I were part of the railing, and she did not look up as she swept back the way she had come until she was out of my sight.

Abruptly, my uncle coughed behind me.

I whirled, but there was no one there, just the empty passage and the stairs leading up to the bedchambers and attic beyond. Two closed doors led off the first-floor landing: one to the parlor and one to my uncle's private office, where we girls were never allowed to set foot. I pressed my ear against the office door to make sure he was in his office and not in the parlor. My hand was beginning to ache from clutching my boots and the book so tightly.

"You have no appointment," he said in his gruff voice, pitched low because of the early hour. "My factotum says he did not let you in by the back door."

"I came in through the window, maester." The voice was husky, as if scraped raw from illness. "My apologies for the intrusion, but my business is a delicate one. I am come from overseas. Indeed, I just arrived, on the airship from Expedition."

"The airship! From Expedition!"

"You find it incredible, I'm sure. Ours is only the second successful transoceanic flight."

"Incredible," murmured Uncle.

Incredible? I thought. *It was astounding.* I shifted so as to hear better as Uncle went on.

"But you'll find a mixed reception for such innovations here in Adurnam."

"We know the risks. But that is not my personal business. I was given your name before I left Expedition. I was told we have a mutual interest in certain Iberian merchandise."

Uncle's voice got sharper without getting louder. "The war is over."

"The war is never over."

"Are you behind the current restlessness infecting the city's populace? Poets declaim radical ideas on the street, and the prince dares not silence them. The common folk are like maddened wasps, buzzing, eager to sting."

"I've nothing to do with any of that," insisted the mysterious visitor. *Too bad!* I thought. "I was told you would be able to help me write a letter, in code."

My heart raced, and I held my breath so as not to miss a word. Was I about to tumble onto a family secret that Bee and I were not yet old enough to be trusted with? But Uncle's voice was clipped and disapproving, and his answer sadly prosaic.

"I do not write letters in code. Your sources are out of date. Also, I am legally obligated to stay well away from any Iberian merchandise of the kind you may wish to discuss."

"Will you close your eyes when the rising light marks the dawn of a new world?"

Uncle's exasperation was as sharp as a fire being extinguished by a blast of damp wind, but my curiosity was aflame. "Aren't those the words being said by the radicals' poet, the one who declaims every evening on Northgate Road? I say, we should fear the end of the orderly world we know. We should fear being swallowed by storm and flood until we are drowned in a watery abyss of our own making."

"Spoken like a Phoenician," said the visitor with a low laugh that made me pinch my lips together in anger.

"We are called Kena'ani, not Phoenician," retorted my uncle stiffly.

"I will call you whatever you wish, if you will only aid me with what I need, as I was assured you could do."

"I cannot. That is the end of it."

The visitor sighed. "If you will not aid our cause out of loyalty, perhaps I can offer you money. I observe your threadbare furnishings and the lack of a fire in your hearth on this bitter-cold dawn. A man of your importance ought to be using fine beeswax rather than cheap tallow candles. Better yet, he ought to have a better design of oil lamp or even the new indoor gaslight to burn away the shadows of night. I have gold. I suspect you could use it to sweeten the trials of your daily life, in exchange for the information I need."

I expected Uncle to lose his temper—he so often did—but he did not raise his voice. "I and my kin are bound by hands stronger than my own, by an unbreakable contract. *I cannot help you.* Please go, before you bring trouble to this house, where it is not wanted."

"So be it. I'll take my leave."

The latch scraped on the back window that overlooked the narrow garden behind our house. Hinges creaked, for this time of year the window was never oiled or opened. An agile person could climb from the window out onto a stout limb to the wall; Bee and I had done it often enough. I heard the window thump closed.

Uncle said, "We'll need those locks looked at by a blacksmith. I can't imagine how anyone could have gotten that window open when we were promised no one but a cold mage could break the seal. Ei! Another expense, when we have little enough money for heat and light with winter blowing in. He spoke truly enough."

I had not heard Factotum Evved until he spoke from the office, somewhere near Uncle. "Do you regret not being able to aid him, Jonatan?"

"What use are regrets? We do what we must."

"So we do," agreed Evved. "Best if I go make sure he actually leaves and doesn't lurk around to break in and steal something later."

His tread approached the door on which I had forgotten I was leaning. I bolted to the parlor door, opened it, and slipped inside, shutting the door quietly just as I heard the other door being opened. He walked on. He hadn't heard or seen me.

It was one of my chief pleasures to contemplate the mysterious visitors who came and went and make up stories about them. Uncle's business was the business of the Hassi Barahal clan. Still being underage, Bee and I were not privy to their secrets, although all adult Hassi Barahals who possessed a sound mind and body owed the family their service. All people are bound by ties and obligations, and the most binding ties of all are those between kin. That was why I kept stealing books out of the parlor and returning them. For the only books I ever took were my father's journals. Didn't I have some right to them, being that they, and I, were all that remained of him?

Feeling my way by touch, I set my boots by a chair and placed the journal on the big table. Then I crept to the bow window to haul aside the heavy winter curtains so I would have light. All eight mending baskets were set neatly in a row on the narrow side table, for the women of the house—Aunt Tilly, me, Beatrice, her little sisters, our governess, Cook, and Callie—would sit in the parlor in the evening and sew while Uncle or Evved read aloud from a book and Pompey trimmed the candle wicks. But it was the bound book of slate tablets resting beneath my mending basket that drew my horrified gaze. How had I forgotten that? I had an essay due today for my academy college seminar on history, and I hadn't yet finished it.

Last night, I had tucked fingerless writing gloves and a slate pencil on top of my mending basket. I drew on the gloves and pulled the bound tablets out from under the basket. With a sigh, I sat down at the big table with the slate pencil in my left hand. But as I began reading back through the words to find my place, my mind leaped back to the conversation I had just overheard. *The rising light marks the dawn of a new world*, the visitor had said; *or the end of the orderly world we know*, my uncle had retorted.

I shivered in the cold room. *The war is never over.* That had sounded ominous, but such words did not surprise me: Europa had fractured into multiple principalities, territories, lordships, and city-states after the collapse of the Roman Empire in the year 1000 and had stayed that way for the last eight hundred years and more; there was always a little war or border incident *somewhere*. But worlds do not begin and end in the steady mud of daily life, even if that mud involves too many petty wars, cattle raids, duels, feuds, legal suits, and shaky alliances for even a scholar to remember. I could not help but think the two men were speaking in a deeper code, wreathed in secrets. I was sure that somewhere out there lay hidden the story of what we are not meant to know.

The history of the world begins in ice, and it will end in ice. So sing the Celtic bards and Mande djeliw of the north whose songs tell us where we came from and what ties and obligations bind us. The Roman historians, on the other hand, claimed that fire erupting from beneath the bones of the earth formed us and will consume us in the end, but who can trust what the Romans say? Everything they said was used to justify their desire to make war and conquer other people who were doing nothing but minding their own business. The scribes of my own Kena'ani people, named Phoenicians by the lying Romans, wrote that in the beginning existed water without limit, boundless and still. When currents stirred the waters, they birthed conflict and out of conflict the world was created. What will come at the end, the ancient sages added, cannot be known even by the gods.

The rising light marks the dawn of a new world. I'd heard those words before. The Northgate Poet used the phrase as part of his nightly declamation when he railed against princes and lords and rich men who misused their rank and wealth for selfish purposes. But I had recently read a similar phrase in my father's journals.

Not the one I'd taken out last night. I'd sneaked that one upstairs because I had wanted to reread an amusing story he'd told about encountering a saber-toothed cat in a hat shop. Somewhere in his journals, my father had recounted a story about the world's beginning, or about something that had happened "at the dawn of the world." And there was light. Or was it lightning?

I rose and went to the bookshelves that filled one wall of the parlor: my uncle's precious collection. My father's journals held pride of place at the center. I drew my fingers along the numbered volumes until I reached the one I wanted. The big bow window had a window seat furnished with a long plush seat cushion, and I settled there with my back padded by the thick winter curtain I'd opened. No fire crackled in the circulating stove set into the hearth, as it did after supper when we sewed. The chill air breathed through the paned windows. I pulled the curtains around my body for warmth and angled the book so the page caught what there was of cloud-shrouded light on an October morning promising yet another freezing day.

In the end I always came back to my father's journals. Except for the locket I wore around my neck, they were all I had left of him and my mother. When I read the words he had written long ago, it was as if he were speaking to me, in his cheerful voice that was now only a faint memory from my earliest years.

Here, little cat, I've found a story for you, he would say as I snuggled into his lap, squirming with anticipation. *Keep your lips sealed. Keep your ears open. Sit very, very still so no one will see you. It will be like you're not here but in another place, a place very far away that's a secret between you and me and your mama. Here we go!*

CHAPTER 2

Once upon a time, a young woman hurried along a rocky coastal path through a fading afternoon. She had been sent by her mother to bring a pail of goat's milk to her ailing aunt. But winter's tide approached. The end of day would usher in Hallows Night, and everyone knew the worst thing in the world was to walk abroad after sunset on Hallows Night, when the souls of those doomed to die in the coming year would be gathered in for the harvest.

But when she scaled the headland of Passage Point, the sun's long glimmer across the ice sea stopped her in her tracks. The precise angle of that beacon's cold fire turned the surface of the northern waters into glass, and she saw an uncanny sight. A drowned land stretched beneath the waves: a forest of trees; a road paved of fitted stone; and a round enclosure, its walls built of white stone shimmering within the deep and pierced by four massive gates hewn of ivory, pearl, jade, and bone. The curling ribbons rippling along its contours were not currents of tidal water but banners sewn of silver and gold.

So does the spirit world enchant the unwary and lead them onto its perilous paths.

Too late for her, the land of the ancestors came alive as the sun died beyond the western plain, a scythe of light that flashed and vanished. Night fell.

As a full moon swelled above the horizon, a horn's cry filled the air with a roll like thunder. She looked back: Shadows fled across the land, shapes scrambling and falling and rising and plunging forward in desperate haste. In their wake, driving them, rode three horsemen, cloaks billowing like smoke.

The masters of the hunt were three, their heads concealed beneath voluminous hoods. The first held a bow made of human bone, the second held a spear whose blade was blue ice, and the third held a sword whose steel was so bright and sharp that to look upon it hurt her eyes. Although the shadows fleeing before them tried to dodge back, to return the way they had come, none could escape the hunt, just as no one can escape death.

The first of the shadows reached the headland and spilled over the cliff, running across the air as on solid earth down into the drowned land. Yet one shadow, in the form of a lass, broke away from the others and sank down beside her.

"Lady, show mercy to me. Let me drink of your milk."

The lass was thin and trembling, more shade than substance, and it was impossible to refuse her pathetic cry. She held out the pail of milk. The girl dipped in a hand and greedily slurped white milk out of a cupped palm.

And she changed.

She became firm and whole and hale, and she wept and whispered thanks, and then she turned and ran back into the dark land, and either the horsemen did not see her or they let her pass. More came, struggling against the tide of shadows: a laughing child, an old man, a stout young fellow, a swollen-bellied toddler on scrawny legs. Those who reached her drank, and they did not pass into the bright land of the ancestors. They returned to the night that shrouded the land of the living.

Yet, even though she stood fast against the howl of the wind of foreordained death, few of the hunted reached her. Fear lashed the shadows, and as the horsemen neared, the stream of hunted thickened into a boiling rush that deafened her before it abruptly gave way to a terrible silence. A woman wearing the face her aunt might have possessed many years ago crawled up last of all and clung to the rim of the pail, too weak to rise.

"Lady," she whispered, and could not speak more.

"Drink." She tipped the pail to spill its last drops between the shade's parted lips.

The woman with the face of her aunt turned up her head and lifted her hands, and then it seemed she simply sank into the rock and vanished. A sharp, hot presence clattered up. The spearman and the bowman rode on past the young woman, down into the drowned land, but the rider with the glittering sword reined in his horse and dismounted before she could think to run.

The blade shone so cold and deadly that she understood it could sever the spirit from the body with the merest cut. He stopped in front of her and threw back the hood of his cloak. His face was black and his eyes were black, and his black hair hung past his shoulders and was twisted into many small braids like the many cords of fate that bind the thread of human lives.

She braced herself. She had defied the hunt, and so, certainly, she would now die beneath his blade.

"Do you not recognize me?" he asked in surprise.

His words astonished her into speech. "I have never before met you."

"But you did," he said, "at the world's beginning, when our spirit was cleaved from one whole into two halves. Maybe this will remind you."

His kiss was lightning, a storm that engulfed her.

Then he released her.

What she had thought was a cloak woven of wool now appeared in her sight as a mantle of translucent power whose aura was chased with the glint of ice. He was beautiful, and she was young and not immune to the power of beauty.

"Who are you?" she asked boldly.

And he slowly smiled, and he said—

"Cat!"

My cousin Beatrice exploded into the parlor in a storm of coats, caps, and umbrellas, one of which escaped her grip and plummeted to the floor, from whence she kicked it impatiently toward me.

"Get your nose out of that book! We've got to run right now or you'll be late!"

I ripped my besotted gaze from the neat cursive and looked up with my most potent glower.

"Cat! You're blushing! What on earth are you reading?" She dumped the gear on the table, right on top of the slate tablets.

"Ah! That's my essay!"

With a fencer's grace and speed, Bee snatched the journal out of my hands. Her gaze scanned the writing, a fair hand whose consistent and careful shape made it easy to read from any angle.

She intoned, in impassioned accents, " 'His kiss was lightning, a storm that engulfed her'! If I'd known there was romance in Uncle Daniel's journals, I would have read them."

"If you could read!"

"A weak rejoinder! Not up to your usual standard. I fear reading such scorching melodrama has melted your cerebellum."

"It's not melodrama. It's an old traditional tale—"

"Listen to this!" She slapped a palm against her ample bosom and drawled out the words lugubriously. " 'And he slowly smiled, and...he...said—' "

"Give me that!" I lunged up, grabbing for the journal.

She skipped back, holding it out of my reach. "No time for kisses! Get your coat on. Anyway, I thought your essay was..." She excavated the tablets, flipped them closed, and squinted her eyes to consider the handsomely written title. "Blessed Tanit, protect us!" she muttered as her brows drew down. She made a face and spoke the words as if she could not believe she was reading them. " 'Concerning the Mande Peoples of Western Africa Who Were Forced by Cold Necessity to Abandon Their Homeland and Settle in Europa Just South of the Ice Shelf.' Could you have made that title longer, perhaps? Anyway, what do kisses have to do with the West African diaspora?"

"Nothing. Obviously!" I sat on a chair and began to lace up my boots. "I was thinking of something else. The beginning and ending of the world, if you must know."

She wrinkled her nose, as at a bad smell. "The end of the world sounds so dreary. And so final."

"And I remembered that my father mentioned the beginning of the world in one of his journals. But this was the wrong story, even though it does mention 'the world's beginning.'"

"Even I could tell that." She glanced at the page. "'When our spirit was cleaved from one whole into two halves.' That sounds painful!"

"Bee! The entire house can hear you. We're not supposed to be in here."

"I'm not that loud! Anyway, of course I spied out the land first. Mother and Shiffa are up in the nursery where Astraea is having a tantrum. Hanan is on the landing, keeping watch. Father and Evved went all the way out into the back. So we're safe, as long as you *hurry*!"

I plucked the journal from her hand and set it on the table. "You go on ahead to the academy. I just need to write a conclusion. It's the seminar the headmaster teaches, and I hate to disappoint him. He never says anything. He just *looks* at me." I excavated my slate tablet and pencil from beneath the coats and caps.

Bee shoved my coat onto one of the chairs, searching for her cap. After tying it tight under her chin and pulling on her coat, she swung her much-patched cloak over all. "Don't be late or Father will forbid us the trip to the Rail Yard."

"Which handsome pupil do you intend to flirt with there?"

She launched a glare like musket shot in my direction and strode imperiously from the parlor, not bothering to answer. I wrote my conclusion. Her little sister Hanan clattered down the stairs with her to bid her farewell by the front door. Up in the nursery, Astraea had launched into one of her mulish fits of "no no no no no," and our governess, Shiffa, had reverted to her most coaxing voice to appease her. Aunt Tilly's light footsteps passed down the steps to the ground floor and thence back to the kitchen, no doubt to consult with Cook about finding something sweet to break the little brat's concentration. I wrote hurriedly, not in my best script and not with my most nuanced understanding.

That is how those druas with secret power among the local Celtic tribes, and the Mande refugees with their gold and their hidden knowledge, came together and formed the mage Houses. The power of the Houses allowed them to challenge princely rule while—

I heard footsteps coming up the stairs, and a key turned in the office door. I paused, hand poised above the slate. Men entered the office; the door was shut.

Uncle spoke in a low voice no one but me could have heard through the wall. "You were supposed to come at midnight."

A male voice answered. "I was delayed. Is everything here I paid for?"

"Here are the papers."

"Where is the book?"

"Melqart's Curse! Evved, didn't you get the book?"

"It must still be in the parlor. Just a moment."

I wiped the "while" from the slate and pressed a hasty, smeared period to the sentence. It would have to do. I scooped up the slate tablet and my schoolbag, bolted for the door, and got out just as the door between the study and the parlor was unlocked.

I halted on the landing to listen. Aunt Tilly was back upstairs, speaking with Shiffa about the girls' lessons for the day while Astraea whined, "But I wanted yam pudding, not this!" Meanwhile, Hanan had gone back to the kitchen and was chattering with Cook and Callie in her high, sweet voice as the three began to peel turnips. Pompey, with his distinctive uneven tread, was in the basement. I fled down the main stairs and out the front door, and it was not until I was out of sight of the house that I realized I had forgotten my coat, cap, and umbrella. I dared not return to fetch them.

Yet what is cold, after all, but the temperature to which we are most accustomed? It is cold for half the year here in the north. However pleasant the summer may seem, the ice never truly rests; it only dozes through the long days of Maius, Junius, Julius, and Augustus with its eyes half closed. I stuffed the tablet in my schoolbag between a new schoolbook and my scholar's robe, and kept going. To keep warm, I ran instead of walking, all the way through our modest neighborhood and then up the long hill into the old temple district where the new academy had been built twenty years ago. Fortunately, the latest fashionable styles allowed plenty of freedom for my legs and lungs.

As I crossed under the gates into the main courtyard, a fine carriage pulled up to disgorge a brother and two sisters swathed in fur-lined cloaks. Though late like me, they were so rich and well connected that they could walk right in the front through the grand entry hall without fearing censure, while I fumbled with frozen hands at the servants' entrance next to the latrines. The cursed latch was stuck.

"Salve, Maestressa Barahal. May I help you with that?"

I swallowed a yelp of surprise and looked up into the handsome face of Maester Amadou Barry, who had evidently followed me to the side door. His sisters were nowhere in sight.

"Salve, maester," I said prettily. "I saw you and your sisters arrive."

"You're not dressed for the weather," he remarked, pushing on the latch until it made a clunk and opened.

"My things are inside," I lied. "I can't be late, for the proctor locks the balcony door when the lecture starts."

"My apologies. I was just wondering if your cousin Beatrice…" His pause was so awkward that I smiled. I was certain he was blushing. "And you, of course, and your family, intend to visit the Rail Yard when it is open for viewing next week."

"My uncle and aunt intend to take Beatrice and me, yes," I replied, biting down another smile. "If you'll excuse me, maester."

"My apologies, for I did not mean to keep you," he said, backing away, for a young man of his rank would certainly enter through the front doors no matter how late he was.

Inside, as I raced along a back corridor, all lay quiet except for a buzz of conversation from the lecture hall. I had a chance to get to my seat before it was too late. In icy darkness, I hurried up the narrow steps that led to the balcony of the lecture hall. The proctor had already turned off the single gaslight that lit the stairwell and had gone in, but I knew these steps well. With the strap of my schoolbag gripped between my teeth, I tugged my scholar's robe on over my jacket and petticoats. I shrugged the satin robe up over both shoulders and smoothed it down just as I felt the change of temperature, from bone cold to merely flesh-achingly chilly, that meant the door loomed ahead.

Had the proctor locked it already?

Blessed Tanit! Watch over your faithful daughter. Let me not be late and get into trouble. Again.

CHAPTER 3

My hand tightened on the iron latch, the metal so cold it burned through the palm of my writing gloves. I applied pressure, and the latch clicked blessedly free. Catching my breath, I listened as female voices gossiped and giggled, schoolbook pages turned, and pencil leads scratched on paper. A heavy tread approached, accompanied by the jangle of a ring of keys. Straightening, I opened the door and crossed the threshold into the proctor's basilisk glare.

She lowered the key she had been about to insert into the lock and attempted to wither me with a sarcastic smile. "Maestressa Catherine Hassi Barahal. How gracious of you to attend today's required lecture."

I opened my mouth to offer a clever reply, but I had forgotten the schoolbag gripped between my teeth and had to grab for it as it fell. The neat catch allowed me to sweep into a courtesy. "Maestra Madrahat. Forgive me. I was discommoded."

Some things you could not fault a respectable young woman for in public, even if you wondered if she was telling the truth. She favored me with a raised eyebrow eloquent of doubt but stepped aside so I could squeeze past her along the back aisle toward my assigned bench. "Button your robe, maestressa," she added, her parting shot.

As I hastened along the aisle, shaking from relief and shivering from the cold, I heard her key turn in the lock. Once again, I had landed—just barely—on my feet.

A few of the other pupils glanced my way, but I wasn't important enough to be worth more than a titter, an elbow nudge, or a yawn. At the back of the balcony's curve, I slipped onto the bench beside Beatrice. Her schoolbook was open to a page half filled in with an intricate drawing, and she was shaking a broken lead out of her pencil as I sat down.

"There you are!" she whispered without looking at me, intent on her pencil lead. "I knew you would make it here in time."

"Your confidence heartens me."

"I dreamed it last night." She slanted a sidelong look at me. "You know I always believe my dreams."

Below, on the dais at the front of the lecture hall, two servants rolled out a chalkboard and hung a net filled with sticks of chalk from its lower rim.

I bent closer. "I thought you dreamed only about certain male students—"

She kicked me in the ankle.

"Ouch!"

The headmaster limped out onto the dais and we fell silent, as did every other pupil, males below on the main floor and females above on the balcony. The old scholar was not one to drag out an introduction: a name, a list of spectacular experiments accomplished and revolutionary papers published, and the title of the lecture we were privileged to hear today: *Aerostatics, the principles of gases in equilibrium and of the equilibrium of balloons and dirigible balloons in changing atmospheric conditions.* Then he was finished, although a surprised murmur swept the hall as the students realized the lecturer was a woman.

"So, did you complete the essay?" Bee demanded, the words barely voiced but her expression emphatic. "I know how you love the headmaster's seminar. It would be awful if you couldn't go."

Under cover of the measured entrance of the dignitary in a head-wrap and crisply starched and voluminous orange boubou, I made a business of extricating my schoolbook from my bag and arranging it neatly open before me on the pitted old table with my new silver pencil set diagonally across the blank page. Meanwhile, I spoke fast in a low voice as Bee fiddled with her broken lead.

"I finished but not quite how I wanted it. It was the strangest thing. Some man had come in through the window and was waiting in the study."

"How did he manage that?"

"I don't know. Uncle wondered the same thing. That's why they'd gone out to the garden when you came down. Then another man came after that. Uncle had to get a book from the parlor for him—I had to run so Evved wouldn't see me. Blessed Tanit! I left the journal I was reading on the table. He'll wonder why it was there!"

"He's been very absentminded and more snappish than usual these days. I think he's anxious about something. Something he and Mama aren't telling us. So perhaps he won't notice or will forget to ask."

"I hope so. What else could I do? I grabbed my schoolbag and my essay, and I ran all the way to the academy, only I forgot my coat, so I was very, very cold." I was still cold, because a third of the long underceiling windows were propped open with sticks to move air through the otherwise stuffy confines of the cramped balcony tiers. "One exciting thing did happen, however," I added coyly. "As I ran into the courtyard, a very fine carriage rolled up and who should step out but Maester Amadou and his twin sisters."

Bee's hands stilled. Her rosy lips pressed tight. She did not rise to the bait. Not yet, but she would. Instead, she said in the most casual voice imaginable, "I saw the twins come in." She gestured to a pair of girls seated in the front row by the balcony railing, resplendent in gold-and-blue robes cut to emphasize their tall figures, their hair wrapped in waxed cotton scarves whose sheen might have given off more light than the poor gas illumination. They recorded dutiful notes, writing in unison, as the esteemed professor sketched the lines of an airship on the chalkboard. "How did they get up here faster than you did?"

I smiled, luring her closer. "Maester Amadou stopped me. To ask a question."

"Oh. A question." She sighed wearily, as if his questions were the most uninteresting thing in the world to her.

"He asked about *you*."

Sprung! I gloated expectantly, but she turned her back on me, her attention flying away to fix on a spill of movement in the hall below us. Certain male pupils were coming in fashionably late and now settled into their assigned places. It seemed likely she would stare at Maester Amadou's attractive form and excellent clothes for the next century just to thwart me of the chance to annoy her, or perhaps she would stare at him because she had been doing so from the first day he and his sisters had arrived as pupils at the academy college, right after the Beltane festival day almost six months ago at the beginning of the month of Maius.

Two could move pieces in that chess game.

I rearranged my skirts, careful to fold back the front cut of the outer skirt so as to reveal the inner layers of petticoats, and tugged on my jacket to make sure it fit properly down around my hips. Then I buttoned the academic robe to conceal it all and folded my hands in my lap.

I tried to listen as the distinguished guest lecturer abandoned the introductory remarks to begin devouring the meat of the talk—the principles of aerostatic aircraft popularly known as airships and balloons. An interesting topic, especially in a time when the new technological innovations were very controversial. It was particularly interesting because the scholar was female and from the south, from the famous Academy of Natural Science and History in Massilia, on the Mediterranean, where female students were, so it was rumored, allowed to sit on the same benches as male students.

Because I had run from our house to the academy, a significant distance and much of it uphill, and because of my late essay, I hadn't had time to eat my morning porridge. So now, despite the unpadded bench pressing uncomfortably into my backside and the chilly draft wrapping my shoulders, I began to doze off.

A body immersed in a fluid is buoyed up by a force equal to the weight of the displaced fluid. Likewise, by this same principle, a craft that is lighter than air will be buoyant . . . gases expand in volume with a rise in temperature . . . by creating a cavity filled with flammable air . . . if pigs could fly, where would they go? . . . Will there be yam pudding for luncheon? . . .

extras

I am sailing across a blinding expanse of ice in a schooner that skates the surface of a massive ice sheet, and a personage stands beside me who I know is my father even though, as happens in dreams, he looks nothing like the man whose portrait I wear in a locket at my neck—

A jab to my ribs brought me to my senses. I jerked awake, grabbing for my pencil, but it wasn't lying on my open schoolbook where I had left it. Bee's right hand gripped my right wrist and pinned my hand to the table we shared. Idly, I noted the smeared gray of pencil lead on the tips of her thin white wool gloves.

"What did he ask about me?" she whispered. Under the gloomy hiss of the gaslights—we female pupils stuck up here in the balcony got only half the light afforded the male pupils in the main hall below—I could see her flutter her eyelashes in that obnoxious way she had, the one that never failed to demolish the objections and reproaches of any adult caught in the beat of those dark wings. "Cat," she added, her voice warming, "you have to tell me."

I yawned to annoy her. "I'm bound by a contract not to tell."

She released my wrist and punched me on the shoulder.

"Ouch!"

Heads turned. Though she might look like a dainty little thing, Bee was a bruiser, really pitiless when she got roused. I glanced toward the curtained entrance where the proctor stood at guard as stiff as a statue and as grim as winter, staring straight ahead. The industrious pupils returned their attention to the lecture, and the bored slumped back to their naps.

"You earned it!" Bee knew precisely how to pitch her voice so only I could hear her. "I've been in love with him forever."

"Three weeks!" I rubbed my shoulder.

"Three months! Ever since I had that dream of him standing, sword drawn, on earthen ramparts while fending off soldiers wearing the livery of a mage House." She pressed a hand to her chest, which was heaving under a high-collared dress appropriate for the academy college's proper halls. "I have kept the truth of my desperate feelings to myself for fear—"

"For fear we'd wonder why you so suddenly left off being in love with and destined to wed Maester Lewis of the lovely red-gold hair and turned your tenacious heart to the beauty of Maester Amadou with his piercing black eyes."

"Which you yourself admit are handsome."

She bent forward to look over the rows of benches and the female pupils seated in pairs at study tables. Given that we were seated in the cramped back row of benches with the other female scholarship students, we could see only the front third of the spacious main hall below us. Maester Amadou lounged in the second row in a chair placed at a polished table close to the podium. His fashionably clothed back was to us, but I could see that he was rolling dice with his tablemate, the equally well-connected Maester Lewis, a youth of high rank who had been fostered out to the court of the ruling prince of Tarrant whose territory included our city of Adurnam. The young men were both so strikingly good-looking that I wondered if they sat together the better to display their contrasting appearances, one milk white and gold haired and the other coffee dark and black haired. On the dais, pacing back and forth in front of the chalkboard and waving a hand in enthusiastic measure, the esteemed natural philosopher launched into an explosive digression on the natural laws pertaining to the behavior of gases, words scattering everywhere.

"Yes, he's almost as pretty as you are," I retorted, "and well aware that his family's wealth allows him to walk in late *and* then to game in the front of the hall, all without repercussion. He's the vainest young man I ever met."

"How can you say so? The story of how he and his three sisters and aunt escaped from the assault on Eko by murderous, plague-ridden ghouls—forced to call their good-byes to their parents and cousins left behind on the shore as the monsters advanced. It's a heartbreaking tale!"

"If it's true. The settlement and fort were specifically established at Eko because it is an island, and ghouls can't cross water. So how

600

could ghouls have reached them? Anyone can say what they like when there are no witnesses."

"You just have no heart, Cat. You're heartless." Her scowl was meant to pierce me to the heart, if I'd had one. With an indignant flounce of the shoulders, she turned away to furiously sketch on a blank page of her book, using *my* good silver pencil with its fresh lead.